Betting It All

Clint nodded to Delilah. "Ladies first."

She drew a three of hearts and sighed with relief. This was one game she would be happy to lose. She had been a fool to taunt the hometown favorite into betting the clothes on his back.

The room grew deathly silent when Clint flipped over a deuce. The crowd groaned.

But Delilah's whisper-thin voice echoed over the noise. "You may send the clothes to the boat in the morning, Mr. Daniels."

Her face burned and she could not bear to look at any of the people surrounding her, least of all Clinton Daniels. Suddenly her attention was pulled back to the table by a soft thump.

Clint's hat dropped onto the pile of cash in the center of the table. Next came his coat, his waistcoat, and a handful of shirt studs. An alarmed Delilah looked at his face with something akin to terror. "My god, Daniels, send the clothes tomorrow...or don't send them at all—I was just making a bad joke."

Clint shrugged off his shirt, revealing a muscular chest flecked with gold hair narrowing to his waistband. Smiling, he said, "I don't think so, ma'am. Remember? You never leave a table without collecting your winnin's... no markers."

CRITICS PRAISE SHIRL HENKE!

"Sensational Shirl Henke is one of the top ten authors of American romance."

—*Affaire de Coeur*

"A true shining star of the genre. Shirl Henke mesmerizes readers with the most powerful, sensual and memorable historical romances yet!"

—*Romantic Times BOOKreviews*

"Henke incorporates witty dialogue and plenty of sexual tension into a suspenseful plot."

—*Romantic Times BOOKreviews* on *Texas Viscount*

"Another sensual treat for readers who like their romances liberally laced with both danger and desire."

—*Booklist* on *Rebel Baron*

"An explosive and passionate love story. . . . Henke cleverly takes the May-December romance to new heights in a wonderful tale."

—*Romantic Times BOOKreviews* on *Rebel Baron*

"The lively dialogue, biting repartee and sizzling sensuality crackle through the pages of this delicious and fast-paced read. Henke captures you from page one. . . . A quick charmer of a read!"

—*Romantic Times BOOKreviews* on *Yankee Earl*

"Readers will need oxygen to keep up . . . Shirl Henke knows how to spin a heated tale that never slows until the final safe kiss."

—*Midwest Book Review* on *Wanton Angel*

Shirl Henke creates "passionate love scenes, engaging characters and a well-researched, fast-paced plot."

—*Publishers Weekly* on *Bride of Fortune*

BESTSELLING AUTHORS PRAISE AWARD-WINNER SHIRL HENKE!

"Shirl Henke is one of the brightest stars in romance. Her engaging characters and talent for storytelling grip readers from first page to last!"

—Katherine Sutcliffe

"A riveting story about a fascinating period. I highly recommend *Paradise & More*."

—Karen Robards

"A grand and glorious novel. . . . I couldn't stop reading."

—Bertrice Small on *Paradise & More*

"*Return to Paradise* swept me away!"

—Virginia Henley

"A romantic romp of a Western. I loved it!"

—Georgina Gentry on *Terms of Surrender*

"*White Apache's Woman* is a fascinating book . . . an absolute must read for anyone who loves American history."

—Heather Graham

"Fast paced, sizzling, adventurous . . . with a hot-blooded hero who will set your heart on fire."

—Rosanne Bittner on *A Fire in the Blood*

"A fascinating slice of history . . . with equally fascinating characters. Enjoy *Love a Rebel . . . Love a Rogue!*"

—Catherine Coulter

SHIRL HENKE

in collaboration with

Jim Henke

The RIVER NYMPH

LEISURE BOOKS   B   NEW YORK CITY

A LEISURE BOOK®

February 2008

Published by

Dorchester Publishing Co., Inc.
200 Madison Avenue
New York, NY 10016

ISBN 10: 0-8439-6011-6
ISBN 13: 978-0-8439-6011-2

The name "Leisure Books" and the stylized "L" with design are trademarks of Dorchester Publishing Co., Inc.

Printed in the United States of America.

10 9 8 7 6 5 4 3 2 1

Visit us on the web at www.dorchesterpub.com.

In memory of
Daniel Anthony Reynard,
Beloved nephew,
And one of the best poker players ever.

First Author's Note

This is the first time my husband Jim and I have collaborated on a book. We sincerely hope it will be the beginning of many more. Not that it was always fun. We had many disagreements over plot twists, dialogue, even the motivations of the major characters, but we managed not to kill each other (as several of my author friends were sure would happen) before completing the manuscript!

Jim first came to me with the idea for *The River Nymph* well over three years ago. I was under contract for two political thrillers using a pseudonym and had no time to write it. Considering that he had not only done a complete plot outline, but roughed out the first scene, I urged him to try his hand as a fiction writer. The opening was outrageously funny, original and had great potential. In his other life as a university professor, Jim has published three scholarly books and dozens of articles. In fact, he's even written numerous humorous pieces about me and my books for *Romantic Times* and other magazines in our genre.

Grudgingly, he agreed to give writing his story a shot. He completed three chapters and gave them to me for editing. I really thought they were good, but fiction is far different from non-fiction...So, when I finished marking up the pages and handed them back to him, he glanced at a few and said, "You wrote more on these than I did." I reminded him of how much editors had written on my early "masterpieces," but he put the chapters in a drawer and we both forgot about them.

Then, about a year ago, Alicia Condon and I discussed returning to my western historical roots. She urged me to send her several proposals. That's when I recalled Clint, Delilah and how she won not only his riverboat but quite literally, the shirt off his back. I included *The River Nymph* and two other proposals, mentioning that it would be a collaboration with Jim. She read the opening and loved it, as well as the idea of promoting us as a husband-wife writing team.

The rest, as is said, is history....

Shirl

Second Author's Note

Once again, Shirl has exercised her selective memory: "disagreements over plot twists, dialogue" etc.? That never happened. I learned long ago that disagreeing with a red-headed German is like debating with a mule. The mule might understand what you want, but it's going to go ahead and do what it wants anyway. I do admit to trying to strangle her when she butchered one of my carefully wrought scenes, but that was useless as well. She bit my wrist and hit me with a skillet.

Oh yes, one other thing: when she was gathering proposals to send to Alicia, the material for the *Nymph* was not among them. When I objected, she said, "Oh, Alicia wouldn't care for that." You will soon be reading the proof of her error. Still, she wouldn't relent, until I threatened to boil one of our new kittens, that black devil that climbs on my shoulder and bites me on the ear. You owe this book to that little ear-chewing monster. If you don't like the work, blame Inky. If you like it, thank me.

Now, that is the real story...you can trust *me*.

Jim

The
River
Nymph

Chapter One

*I*t wasn't every night a crowd on the St. Louis levee got to see a female riverboat gambler. It for sure wasn't every night they got to see Clint Daniels lose his shirt, as he sat across from her in the made-over salon aboard his stern-wheeler, *The River Nymph*.

The boat's long, narrow card room overflowed with goggle-eyed spectators of every stripe, from wizened wharf rats and hard-eyed harlots to staid tradesmen and even a few elegantly dressed bankers and other swells. The lower classes lined the bar at the far end of the room while the rich men sat around tables in the shadowy corners.

Bright lights from the St. Louis waterfront flickered through the windows, but every eye in the place was fixed intently on the center table. A large globe lamp overhead illuminated the players seated around its green baize surface—Clint Daniels, Ike Bauer, Teddy Porter . . . and the female.

Although no lady would ever set foot in a gambling establishment, she certainly looked like one, dressed in a pale green linen suit with dark green piping. The frilly lace collar of her white blouse peeped tantalizingly above the jacket's high neckline, caressing her slender throat. Rich chestnut curls were piled atop her head, where a tiny hat with a dark green feather perched. She had an arresting face with a slender nose, high brow and full pink lips. But the deep-set jade eyes were her best feature. If she knew every man in the place desired her, she gave not the slightest indication.

This was a very high-stakes game, five-card stud St. Louis style: first card down, next three up, last card down. Ike Bauer, who was the dealer, folded after the second round of cards, pushed the remaining few dollars left of his original ten-thousand-dollar table stake into the pot and declared himself out when he finished this deal.

Now, after the fourth round and final up card, Clint bet a thousand. The woman examined his cards and counted out a stack of bills from the obscenely large mound of cash in front of her. "Your thousand and two thousand more." Mrs. Delilah Mathers Raymond possessed a rich whiskey voice, even though she never touched a drop.

Teddy Porter stared at the globe lamp above him as if seeking a miracle to keep him in the game. The freight company owner was an obese man whose tiny mustache could not stem the flow of perspiration dribbling down his upper lip. Pulling a red handkerchief from his pocket, he mopped his down-turned lips. "Damnation! I ain't got that much in my stack." Porter pushed his cards into the middle of the table and started to pocket his remaining few hundred dollars.

"You know better, Teddy. What's left of your table stake remains for the winner." Clint deliberately did not look at the fat man, but every spectator knew that Teddy Porter was within a hair's breadth of being turned into fertilizer.

Porter tossed the money into the pot, then pried himself out of his chair. "Now I know why men oughta keep women barefoot and pregnant." There were snickers of agreement from the bar.

Ignoring them, Mrs. Raymond fixed Porter with a calm stare, then said in that throaty voice, "A woman might find it difficult to deal a hand while nursing a child, sir. But I'm certain even a barefooted woman with a babe at each breast could separate a player of your . . . *skill* from his money." The room filled with laughter. Porter's sweaty red face glowed like the globe lamp overhead when she added, "As for handling cards with a bloated stomach, you could perhaps enlighten us regarding the difficulty?"

The laughter became raucous, drowning out the freighter's snorted obscenity. When he placed his meaty fists on the table and leaned across it, the woman's chaperone, a tall, cadaverously gaunt man of indeterminate age, slid his hand inside the jacket of his frock coat.

"Teddy," Clint Daniels said in a deceptively soft Southern drawl, "you started the mouthin' and you got bested. Hell, you know a man can't beat a woman in a barkin' contest. Take your whipping like a sport and leave . . . while you're still upright." Porter hesitated for a moment, looking from Daniels to the thin man in the high starched collar. Unclenching his fists, he backed off and waddled out of the room.

Mrs. Raymond ignored his retreat. "I repeat, Mr. Daniels, two thousand to you . . . or should I say 'woof'?"

Clint threw back his head and laughed. " 'Woof' would definitely be the wrong language for a lady with cat's eyes." Her deep green eyes did not blink. "You have three spades up, same as me." The odds were getting better. "I'll just call your two thousand."

Bauer dealt the last down cards. Clint watched as she looked at hers. *Damn, she's good.* Absolutely no expression. After playing against her all evening, he expected she would give away nothing. He looked at his last card, his face revealing no more than hers.

"Well, since I'm still high, I'll bet . . ." Clint counted his remaining cash. "Seventeen hundred dollars."

"Call and raise five thousand." Her gaze was cold as ice.

Clint smiled. *Well, that's what you get for playing poker with a beautiful woman.* Mrs. Raymond was a professional, and she was doing what any professional would do. Hell, what he would do in her place. Having cleaned him out of his ten-thousand-dollar table stake, she raised. Since he had no money left to call that raise, he would have to forfeit the game.

"I'd love to play this hand, but at the moment I'm sufferin' from an obvious financial embarrassment." He shrugged carelessly and smiled at her.

Delilah Mathers Raymond tapped her delicate chin with one slender finger as she examined the tall gambler lounging so carelessly in his chair. She did not return the smile. His eyes were palest blue, almost gray, fathomless. Thick, coarse hair the color of straw fell across his forehead. His jaw was firm and his chin possessed a slight cleft. The smiling lips could be either cruel or sensual, or both. Regardless of which, the arrogant clod probably had women, from both sides of the tracks, swooning over him.

Delilah was maliciously pleased to detect a few minor imperfections. A small scar in one eyebrow and another thin white slash that ran from the corner of his right eye an inch down his cheek. His patrician nose was slightly off center, too, probably broken in a fight over a woman. She had seen his type from Boston to New Orleans. Mrs. Raymond smiled inwardly. The way her luck was running tonight, perhaps someone might knock out a couple of those white, beautifully even front teeth!

Damn but she detested Southern cavaliers! She had spent almost a decade holding her own against what they had done. Far easier to handle a bloated pig like Porter. At least he showed his bruised male ego rather than hide behind a facade of polite, supercilious courtesy. She was determined to wipe that superior smile from Clinton Daniels's face.

"For shame, Mr. Daniels. Capitulate so easily? I have a proposition for you."

Clint's smile broadened into a full-blown grin. "A proposition? From a lady? This must be my lucky night."

"Not that I have detected so far." She stared pointedly at the empty expanse of table in front of him. "But that could change." *Lady!* Delilah knew no woman who played cards for a living was ever considered a lady, least of all by a Southern gentleman, even if he was a gambler. "Since you and I are the only players remaining in this game, I propose an alteration to the rules. I'll waive the ten-thousand table stake restriction so you may call my bet . . . if you so desire."

Though his face betrayed nothing, Clint felt a little rush of triumph. *So, Gorgeous, you filled that flush.* "All right, ma'am, I can arrange to have the cash. . . ."

"No cash," she interrupted calmly. "I understand that you

own this boat. I will allow you to call my raise with the deed to *The River Nymph*."

The room could have been a mausoleum. No one moved. The silence was absolute. Even old Timmy Grimes, the waterfront drunk, paused his whiskey glass halfway to his mouth.

Daniels tipped his flat-crowned Stetson even farther back on his head. The corners of his mouth lifted slightly. "Mrs. Raymond, your raise—in fact, all the money in the pot—isn't equal to the value of the *Nymph*."

Delilah counted out a stack of bills and handed them to her gaunt protector. Then she pushed the rest of her winnings into the pot, arching one brow in a dare. Her smile was contemptuous.

"All right, ma'am, we'll say that's close enough. Consider yourself called."

Delilah shook her head. "Oh, I think not, sir. I don't accept markers."

A collective murmur rustled through the card room. Clinton Daniels had been a fixture on the St. Louis waterfront for seven years. His reputation for fair play was legendary. As was his skill with cards and, when needed, a gun.

And this female had just insulted him.

Clint tipped back his chair and stared at the woman as if she were some curiosity in a freak show. He shrugged and motioned to a man behind the bar. "Banjo, please fetch Mrs. Raymond the deed." Banjo Banks, whose nickname was derived from the unfortunate bulk of his posterior relative to that of his upper body, scurried out of the salon.

In the silence that once again settled over the room, Clint decided that it was his turn to catalogue Mrs. Delilah Mathers Raymond as she had so thoroughly done to him earlier. As soon as their eyes met in the thickening silence, she averted her gaze. Calmly, she studied the flickering lights along the St. Louis levee revealed through the door Banjo had left open.

Clint was certain that she was not the most beautiful woman he had ever seen. But he was damned if he could recall when or where he had seen one better. Her hair was a dark, rich brown—except when she turned so the lamplight streaked it with sparkling bursts of dark flame. Her face was that of a mature woman, perhaps in her late twenties. There was none of the pouty softness of a schoolroom miss. High cheekbones, stubborn chin and delicate nose—but it was the dark green eyes, the lush shade of river moss, that held his fancy most. That and her slightly plump lips. Positively wicked, they begged to be kissed.

Clint nodded to Delilah's hand resting on the table. "I take it that you are a widow, Mrs. Raymond?" he said in a soft drawl.

Delilah twisted the simple wedding band. "Yes. I lost my husband during the war. 'Sixty-four."

"You must have been very young. My condolences, ma'am."

"I don't want your condolences, sir, just your boat." The tone of her voice was underlaid with a snappishness at odds with her earlier cool professionalism.

Daniels noticed. "I take it from your Eastern accent that your husband fought for the North."

"And quite obviously, judging from your accent—if you fought at all—you fought for the Rebels." Delilah struggled to control a spurt of dangerous anger.

"You just might be surprised," Clint murmured.

Banjo came barging into the room and hurried to the table. He handed his boss a sheet of heavy vellum. After glancing at it, he gave it to Delilah. She quickly scanned the document and then pushed it back for his signature. Clint shook his head. "Only if you win, Mrs. Raymond. And another thing," he added, his lips thinning, "Since you're such a stickler for details, I still don't reckon that the pot equals the value of my boat, so I consider this deed as calling your bet and a raise equal to the amount of the money you just passed to . . . ?" He looked at the black-clad man towering protectively behind her.

"My uncle, Horace Mathers." She paused and moistened her lips. "Mr. Daniels, there is over thirty thousand in that pot—"

"And a prime shallow-draft stern-wheeler like the *Nymph*'ll go for over forty. Do you call my raise, lady?"

Delilah looked at Daniels's three up cards, all spades. She nodded to Horace, who tossed the stack of bills into the pot. The brunette looked her opponent squarely in the eyes. "Now *you* can consider yourself called."

Clint flipped over his two down cards, both spades, one the king. "King-high flush, ma'am." The tension broken, the spectators expelled a collective sigh.

Delilah turned over her two down cards, both spades, one the ace. "Ace-high flush, sir. I believe I hold the winning hand."

From the moment that Horace had tossed in the money to cover Clint's raise, neither Clint nor the woman had bothered looking at the table. They had locked eyes and had never broken contact. His eyes were empty, even when he smiled. She almost shivered. But when the crowd broke into astonished cries of disbelief, Delilah deliberately allowed a fleeting spark of triumph to flash across her face.

Daniels registered no response. In fact, his eyes, intently studying her, remained devoid of any emotion; certainly they did not reveal the anger or sense of defeat she had hoped to glimpse. After a moment, he merely smiled that smile that did not reach his eyes, pulled the deed across the table and signed it with a flourish, then tossed it cavalierly on the pile of currency.

"Well, ma'am, you wouldn't accept my condolences, but I do trust you'll accept my congratulations." He rose, touching the brim of his hat, and turned to leave.

Delilah was furious. The bastard was patronizing her. Refuse to admit defeat, would he! She waited until he almost reached the bar. Then her husky voice stopped him. "Mr. Daniels, please don't leave just yet. I pride myself on being a magnanimous victor."

Her uncle Horace bent down and put his hand on her arm, whispering something, but she shook her head.

"I always like to leave my less fortunate opponents with something. How about one last bet, sir, a chance to win back a stake for another game? I'll bet a thousand dollars against the clothes you're wearing that I can beat you cutting for high card." The crowd was stunned into silence. No one up or down the river had ever heard such an outrageous proposition.

Clint cocked his head, studying the beautiful woman.

Delilah had expected shock or anger, but not curiosity . . . or was it disappointment? At least his eyes were now alive. She flushed, suddenly uncertain of her triumph.

Clint finally replied, "I'll accept your wager, ma'am, if you'll allow me to exclude my weapons and cigar case from the bet."

Delilah nodded woodenly. She had done what no professional ever did. What Uncle Horace had warned her not ever to do—let her emotions interfere with business.

Clint moved back to the table but did not take a seat. Delilah had not realized he was quite so tall. He picked up the deck and riffled it contemplatively. Then he handed it to Ike Bauer, who was watching from the sidelines. "Would you shuffle the cards?" When Bauer nodded, he looked over at Mrs. Raymond's protector. "If that's all right with you?" he inquired.

With a disgusted look at his niece, Horace agreed, eager to terminate the distasteful business. Bauer shuffled, then laid the deck on the table and stepped back. Clint nodded to Delilah. "Ladies first."

She drew a three of hearts and sighed with relief. This was one game she would be happy to lose. She had been a fool to taunt the hometown favorite into making the bet.

The room grew deathly silent when Clint flipped over a deuce. The crowd groaned.

But Delilah's whisper-thin voice echoed over the noise. "You may send the clothes to the boat in the morning, Mr. Daniels."

Her face burned and she could not bear to look at any of the people surrounding her, least of all Clinton Daniels. Delilah knew she had humiliated him. He represented the life she hated, but the man had nothing to do with her past. A hard lump formed at the back of her throat. She turned away, staring out one of the side windows, recently installed to turn the open hurricane deck into an enclosed salon. The winking lights from the city above the levee seemed to mock her.

Suddenly her attention was pulled back to the table by a soft thump.

Clint's hat dropped onto the pile of cash in the center of the table. Next came his coat, his waistcoat and a handful of shirt studs. An alarmed Delilah looked at his face with something akin to terror. "My God, Daniels, send the clothes tomorrow . . . or don't send them at all—I was just making a bad joke."

Clint shrugged off his shirt, revealing a muscular chest flecked with gold hair narrowing to his waistband. Smiling, he said, "I don't think so, ma'am. Remember? You never leave a table without collecting your winnin's . . . no markers."

The stillness remained palpable as he continued to undress. But everyone's hostile eyes fixed on her.

Delilah could not seem to stop staring at the cunning pattern of his chest hair until he bent down and yanked off his hand-tooled leather boots and socks. When he straightened up and reached for the top button of his fly, her face was flame red. She bit her lip to keep from gasping aloud. But she could not force her gaze away from his hand as he deftly unfastened his trousers and shucked them down his long legs. Calm as could be, he peeled off the last item, silk unmentionables which almost floated onto the pile of clothing littering the money-covered table.

Finally, he was newborn-naked, the most striking specimen of masculine beauty Delilah could ever have imagined. *Like a Greek statue.* Sinking her teeth into her lip with renewed vigor, she forced herself to look away from his coolly detached gaze. He was completely unconcerned about his nudity in a room full of people—in front of her. And why not? The rotter knew how humiliated she felt. He knew, too, that she had been fascinated looking at his body.

He casually slipped into the shoulder sling of his .38-caliber Smith & Wesson, picked up the small Colt Derringer that had been tucked in his waistcoat, then held up a cigar. "Do you mind?" he asked.

She shook her head in a daze. He fired up the stogie, then picked up his wallet, knife and cigar case. Clinton Daniels strolled out the door in an easy, long-legged gait, completely at his leisure, leaving pandemonium in his wake as the room exploded with furious whispers and muffled curses.

"Unnatural bitch!"

"I never seen anything so goddamned vicious in my life."

"Poor bastard was lucky to get outta here with a full set of balls."

"Damn, not even Red Riley would do something this nasty!"

"Bullshit! That wasn't our deal."

Big Red Riley wasted little time meeting with Delilah and Horace to conclude the arrangement he had made with them the week before. The morning after the card game, he was seated at the large poker table in the salon of *The River Nymph*, glaring at his co-conspirators. *Hell, I built this damned gambling hall!*

As his face turned puce with rage, Delilah thought that it clashed horribly with his bright red hair. The nickname "Big" was either a sop to the man's inflated ego or an allusion to his undeniable power on the St. Louis riverfront. It certainly had not the remotest connection to his size. The scrawny little creature was at least two inches shorter than her own five feet seven. Adding to the "charm" of his weasely, narrow face was a boil on his oversized nose, an ugly thing that looked ready to erupt. She fervently hoped it would not do so before he could be removed from the premises.

"Please, Mr. Riley, be rational," Delilah cajoled softly, pushing the large stack of currency across the table. "You must admit—"

"I ain't admitting nothin'. Look, after losing this boat to that goddamned card hawk Daniels, I don't intend to lose it a second time, least of all ta a female!" He punctuated the declaration with a thump of his fist on the oak table in front of him. "I looked high 'n low for somebody like you ta lure that bastard into a game. Get the *Nymph* back. My sources said you was top shelf. Never been this far west before. Nobody'd recognize you. I paid to bring you here, and by God, I offered you the sweetest deal any ringer could ask for—"

"Mr. Riley—"

"Mr. Riley, my ass! I put up the ten thousand dollars for your stake. Alls you had ta do was sucker Daniels into putting up the *Nymph*, win the game and give me back my stake money and the boat deed. You got lots of cash winnings for yourself."

Delilah's impatience with the little man's pigheadedness was reflected in her voice. "As of this moment we have a new arrangement. The sum in front of you is exactly thirty-five thousand dollars, your ten-thousand-dollar stake, plus a twenty-five-thousand-dollar profit. Take it!"

"You double-dealing bitch!" Riley had not even seen the old man move, but he was keenly aware of the muzzle of Horace's .45-caliber Colt pocket revolver jammed into his right nostril.

The old man's voice was surprisingly deep and strong. "Sir, you have a mouth as filthy as the floor of a stockyard. I grow tired of subjecting my niece to it. An English friend of mine is of the opinion that shooting an Irishman in the head is as feckless as shooting an elephant in the rump. While the target is large, the area of vulnerability is so minuscule that it is difficult to injure the beast. Would you care to put his theory to the test?"

Riley very cautiously shook his head, no mean feat with a gun barrel stuffed up one sinus cavity.

"Then," continued Horace, "I can count on your exercising a modicum of civility?" Although the king of the St. Louis levee was as uncertain of the meaning of *modicum* as he had been of *minuscule,* it seemed wise to agree.

"Now," Horace continued, "before you pocket your money, you will sign this note indicating that your loan of ten thousand dollars has been returned, along with twenty-five thousand dollars interest. All dealings between you and Mrs. Raymond are concluded."

Red looked at the paper, unable to swallow his rage. "I didn't ask you to sign nothin'," he said petulantly.

"No," Horace agreed, "but then, you are intellectually deficient. Be a good fellow and sign, Mr. Riley."

"Yeah, I'll sign, but this don't change shit, old man. I converted the *Nymph* into the classiest floating gamblin' hell and cathouse on the levee and I'm gonna get her back."

Delilah climbed to the wheelhouse, watching her uncle escort Riley down the gangplank and off *The River Nymph*, then turned her attention south along the cobblestone levee. As far as she could see there were steamboats, scores of them, so many that their tall black smokestacks formed what appeared to be a forest of denuded tree trunks. Not a particularly appealing vista. Although it was almost noon on a weekday, the levee was not especially busy.

She drew her cloak more tightly about herself. It was only February. She knew that in another few weeks the last traces of ice would be gone. The levee would start to swarm with freight wagons and hand carts, furiously loading the boats for their summer runs on the Mississippi and the Missouri. Then the scene would compare with a large litter of greedy piglets vying for their mama's teats.

"St. Louis, the Sow of the West!" Delilah laughed. She was still young, and now she was finally free. She and Uncle Horace were the owners of a fine steamboat and had, counting their own savings, a bit over twenty-five thousand dollars in capital. As of this morning they were in the freight business—no more corpse-eyed cardsharps, no more smirking simpletons intent on her breasts rather than her hands.

She took a deep breath, and even in the chill air she could smell that peculiar blend of decay and fecundity that was the river. That was life. She slapped the *Nymph*'s wheel. "Damn all of them to hell, I *will* keep you."

* * *

Clint Daniels pushed his half-eaten breakfast away and poured another cup of coffee. He opened the humidor on his desk and absently selected a cigar, clipped the tip, lit up and leaned back in the big leather chair. He rolled the smoke around in his mouth, then blew a large blue-white cloud toward the ceiling, watching cat-green eyes and burnished hair materialize in the haze. Suddenly it registered on him that he was smoking, something he made it a rule never to do until after supper.

"Damn." He put the cigar in the large brass ashtray and slid it across the desk next to his empty breakfast plate.

There was a soft knock at the door, but before he could respond, Banjo came bursting in. Clint sighed. Banjo could not seem to grasp the concept that knocking on a door did not automatically confer upon the knocker the right to enter. Daniels had tried to explain the idea of waiting for a response, but to no avail. A man might as well try to convince a loyal hound not to drag home dead things.

"Well, you pegged it, boss. Big Red had hisself a visit with the widda this mornin'." Banjo grinned, revealing several missing teeth.

"On the *Nymph*?" Clint asked his pear-shaped informant.

"Yup, but get this: that feller with the widda tossed his ass off the boat. Old Red's face was redder 'n his hair. Rat Turner was waitin' at the end of the gangplank fer his boss. He started to reach fer his gun, but the old guy—just as cool as ya please—shook his head and grinned like a skull. Pointin' a gun at Red. Shit, the old feller looked like one of them stiffs up at Hackameyer's funeral parlor. 'Nough ta give ya the creeps. Hell, Rat turned into a statue. Bet he was drizzlin' down his laig."

"From what the boys picked up this morning, I figured she was some sort of ringer Riley had imported, but if you're right, the lady may have reshaped the deal." Daniels grinned.

"Sharp, shrewd, vicious, bottom-dealing, beautiful little bitch," Clint murmured to himself. "Red wanted to get back the boat, but it would appear the widow, with an assist from her dear uncle Horace, has decided to keep it. Why, I wonder? And just what will his majesty, the king of the St. Louis levee, do to avenge himself on our delectable double-crosser? This should prove very interesting." A smile spread across his face.

Banjo grunted, "That little bastard's mean 'nough to burn the *Nymph* to the waterline outa spite. I'll put the boys to watchin' real careful. I know you want her."

"Make no mistake about that, Banjo. I want her . . . and I intend to have her."

Chapter Two

That afternoon Delilah and Horace moved their belongings from their hotel rooms to cabins on the *Nymph*. Not only would they save money, but they would be able to keep some sort of watch over their new property in spite of their business excursions along the waterfront. When they returned in the early evening, they were greeted by the young bartender who took the first shift until Banjo arrived. But all of them knew that Daniels's friend would not be in to spell Todd Spearman. Nor was there any reason for either employee to be there. Customers who usually trickled in by this time had yet to arrive.

As Horace was stowing their trunks and bags in two of the cabins behind the salon, Delilah spoke with the young man. "I'm afraid that your services as bartender will no longer be required. We'll be tearing out the card room and bar, making it into a hurricane deck again, to carry extra cargo. My uncle and I are going into the upriver freighting business."

Young Todd Spearman's usually smiling face fell. "But, ma'am, it's off season now, and jobs ain't easy to come by. Won't you at least need somebody to fetch and carry fer you and your uncle? He don't look too sturdy . . ." Just then the feeble one, having unloaded his and his niece's trunks, entered the salon. Todd flushed and tried to stammer out an apology. "I didn't mean anythin', sir."

Horace held up his hand. "You are quite right, young man. While there may remain a week or two of breath in these decaying lungs, I'm not 'too sturdy.' And we do require a stout lad to keep the fire going, quite literally, and to keep the interior of this vessel clean. We are also in need of someone to man the galley. I assume that cooking is not one of your many skills?"

"Naw, sir. My aunt, she says that if the meat warn't dead, it'd get up and run from me. But I can read and do figures, and I bet I can get my aunt to come cook fer you. She's cookin' in a fancy house now and don't much care fer it."

Horace smiled at Delilah. "So, young man, you are literate and possessed of math skills and an aunt who can cook. You have just earned a berth on *The River Nymph.*"

The next morning Todd's aunt, Luellen Colter, arrived to take command of the kitchen, her nephew and, for that matter, the boat itself. Each day, she rousted her sleepy nephew to fire up her stove. She made coffee and took it in small pots to the cabins of her employers—"the Lady" and "the Gentleman." That was how she had come to think of them, no matter that they had been gamblers. They were quality and a more decent pair Luellen had never met.

Each morning after breakfast, Delilah and Horace headed off on their rounds of the waterfront emporiums and mercantiles, attempting to learn the intricacies of the Missouri River freighting business. There was so much to find out and so little time. Fortunately, it took only a few days for them to locate the man whom everyone on the riverfront considered to be the most informative instructor and honest businessman in the city, Mr. Joseph Krammer, owner of Krammer Mercantile and Provisioning, located on Broadway.

After they had introduced themselves to the short, stocky man with the round face and smiling blue eyes, Horace departed on another mission, leaving his niece to begin shopping for trade goods. While Herr Krammer went to measure out a length of cotton cloth for an elderly woman, Delilah began wandering through the farm supply section.

Finishing with his sale, Mr. Krammer approached her, shaking his head. "*Nein,* Frau Raymond, these stuffs are not the thing for the Fort Benton trade. Farmers, they are few

there. Miners many. Custer and his troopers are making safe
for them the far western lands. Picks, shovels, wheelbarrows,
some light mining machinery and the dynamite, ya, those are
what you want the most to buy. And strong tents, warm coats
and pants and boots you will need. Miners must eat too. Take
basic foodstuffs. And they work up a great thirst digging in the
ground, so whiskey you will sell them. Only a small amount
of farm implements to sell on the way will you need."

He gave a great booming laugh. "Ya, miners' greed for
gold will bring you gold. Please, good lady, come this way and
I will show you your cargo."

In a few days, Delilah and Horace fashioned a deal with
Krammer. Their poker winnings would supply them with a
handsome freight load for the Benton trade, but they also required a warehouse in which to store the goods. If they had
that, they could free up space in his mercantile, and in return
he would give them a 5 percent rebate. That would help with
the expense of renting the storage area for their cargo until
spring. But the cost of storage and the teamsters to haul the
goods was more than Delilah had to spare.

Herr Krammer came up with a solution. He had faith in
their venture and would advance them credit for the bulk of
the goods, so they would have cash for their other expenses.
He even knew of a sound, relatively inexpensive warehouse
on Biddle Street. Compared to others closer to the levee, it
was a bargain.

Nonetheless, Delilah had misgivings that she shared with
Herr Krammer. If they spent their entire nest egg this way, in
spite of his generous terms, they would have little left to hire
a crew or see to their own basic living expenses until the
spring thaw. She asked the German if it would be possible to
obtain a bank loan.

The beefy man chewed on one corner of his thick gray
mustache and stroked his ruddy jowls. "Such a thing is difficult, Frau Raymond, but impossible *nein*."

Encouraged, Delilah laid out her plan. "I could use the
Nymph as collateral for a substantial loan."

Krammer shook his head. "Perhaps. But since the great levee fire of 'forty-nine that destroyed so many boats, steamboats are not so good collateral at most banks. Local banks have long memories and short pursestrings. Also they will tell you that, since you will carry the cargo up the dangerous Missouri, good surety any steamboat is not."

Chewing meditatively on his mustache as if it were a cud, the merchant continued. "And if you could get a loan, never must you do it here in St. Louis. *Nein*. Many here there are that will sell your note to a third party even before it is due. That I know." He shook his head. "To St. Charles you and your uncle must go. Take the train. With the Consolidated Planters Bank you might do business. Hard bargainers they are, and you will not get as big a loan as here perhaps. But you can make them sign an agreement not to sell your note before it is due."

Big Red Riley was not scheduled for a long life. From a tin of Miner's Delight he took a large pinch of snuff and packed it against his lower gum on the left side of his mouth. Then, he shook a tailor-made cigarette from a pack of Elegant Gents, fired it up and inhaled like a hog sucking slop. Next came a deep gulp from his glass of Who Shot John whiskey, as he surveyed his domain. He leaned back in his oversized chair behind an oversized desk and looked about his office. Its garishness expressed his idea of opulent luxury and refined taste.

When the expected knock came, Riley barked, "Drag it in."

The door opened, and Leo "the Leopard" Lewinsky slipped into the office, his head bobbing like a rooster hunting for grasshoppers. "How do, Mr. Riley, sir."

Red stared at Leo with what he meant to be lordly gravity. Lewinsky was one of his brigade of wharf rats who slunk and scurried through the alleys and side streets of the waterfront gathering information useful to him. Indeed, the Leopard was one of his favorites. He was very ugly. The little man's neck and lower face were mottled by a pattern of purplish liver spots.

Lewinsky possessed yet another quality that Big Red

prized in his employees. He was short, some two inches less than Red's own five foot, five inches. Riley was not aware of a contemptuous axiom along the riverfront: Any man had a chance at landing a spot on Red's payroll if he was willing to saw off his legs and go on stumps. It also was said that a dwarf was a shoo-in for a high-paying job, and a midget could expect to be appointed second-in-command of Red's entire operation.

Riley was not well-liked.

"Well?" Red asked impatiently.

"The woman and her uncle took the morning train to St. Charles. Yesterday, they looked at the old Hauser warehouse up on Biddle." Leo shifted his weight and rubbed his spotted face.

Riley took another drag on his Elegant Gent. "All right. They have to be going to Consolidated Planters for a loan, which means they wrapped up all their cash in cargo and warehouse space. Son of a bitch! Using my boat for collateral!" The little Irishman pounded his desk in a rage. He took another drag on the Gent. "Where'd they get the freight goods?"

"Looks like Krammer gave 'em credit fer most of it." Leo shifted his weight again, thankful that he wasn't old Joe Krammer.

Big Red stubbed out his cigarette and let loose a string of obscenities that was neither imaginative nor colorful. "Well, that Kraut's business career is just about at an end. He'd better get his tin bill ready, 'cause he's gonna be pickin' shit with the chickens. And Leopard, pass the word. Any steamboat men that take a berth on the *Nymph* will never work the levee again. That smart-assed heifer and her bag-o-bones uncle might have a boat and a cargo, but they ain't goin' to have a crew to move 'em. Not while Red Riley is king of the St. Louis levee."

When Delilah and Horace alighted from the train the following evening, she felt frustrated and angry. "Talking with those bankers was like being back in Pittsburgh."

Horace nodded, remembering the crooked game in that city, one of the few times his brilliant young player had lost at cards. "Consolidated Planters certainly gave us a smaller loan than we'd hoped."

"*Smaller* is an understatement," she said as he hailed a hack and they climbed in for the ride back to the levee. "Only ten thousand dollars on a boat that the banker admitted was worth between forty-two thousand and forty-five."

"Even that wouldn't have been too bad if not for his insistence that half the loan be used as a surety bond payable to the bank should the *Nymph* be destroyed on the trip. He certainly made a point of explaining the risk of using steamboats as collateral, even when they're moored up at the levee."

"Yes," Delilah replied stiffly. "Not only the disastrous fire of eighteen forty-nine that Herr Krammer told us about, but the eighteen fifty-six ice flow down the Mississippi that crushed over twenty boats. Was he making that up, do you think?" she asked, chewing her lip.

After spitting a wad of tobacco from the side of his perch, their driver turned around and interjected, "Warn't no tall tale, ma'am. I seed the big crash up in 'fifty-six. Boats smashed like kindlin' wood, yessir."

"I thank you for that verification, good sir," Horace said. Then, patting his niece's hand, he averred, "The jovial, pink-faced little banker indeed ran a perfectly legal shell game on us."

"And smiled when he shook our hands, as if he was doing us a favor!" she added indignantly. By the time they reached the levee and alighted from the hack, she decided that riffling cards was perhaps not as despicable a trade as banking.

The next morning she and Horace did considerable damage to Lou's breakfast of fried ham, biscuits and cream gravy before heading up the levee to Eagle Boat Stores. The mercantile doubled as the meeting place for the steamboat elite— captains, pilots, engineers and mates. Here they would begin their search for a crew.

Passing by a wooden rendition of a mermaid located on

the sidewalk, Horace and Delilah entered the large, shabby emporium. "Are you certain you wouldn't prefer that I handle this?" her uncle asked her.

In spite of a sudden wave of trepidation that swept over her, Delilah shook her head. "No. If I'm going upriver with these men, I can't be afraid of them."

They waited for a moment as their eyes adjusted to the dim light. Just inside to the right, they could see a short counter, and across from it three empty tables. The rear of the building was filled with stacks of boat tackle and hardware. Horace seated his niece and then walked to the counter and rang the bell on it.

A clerk in a leather apron appeared from behind a pile of oak spars. At the same time, two men whose faces bore the mark of wind and water emerged from the backroom, eyeing Horace and Delilah with open hostility.

"Good day, sir," Horace said to the clerk. "My niece and I are interested in hiring experienced men to take our boat up the Missouri."

Before he could say more, one of the steamboat men interrupted. "Your boat the *Nymph*?"

Horace replied, "Indeed, it is."

His companion gave the older man a long look but did not say a word. Then he headed for Delilah's table, with Horace right behind. He did not look friendly. The clerk and the first steamboat man grinned nastily, watching their friend give Delilah a hostile perusal.

Refusing to be cowed, she in turn studied him. He was tall, thin and balding, but his beard was thick and well trimmed. He wore a black, rumpled suit and a wrinkled blue shirt with no collar. When he pulled out a chair and sat without waiting for an invitation, she nodded to Horace, who understood that he was to back off . . . for now.

"You be thet gamblin' female whut cleaned out Clint Daniels?"

"I won a poker game, fair and square," she stated calmly. "*The River Nymph* came as part of the pot."

"Wall, missy, ye'll be gettin' no crew on this waterfront. Red Riley's got the word out on ye. There be them thet'll heed the little fart. Then, there be them thet be Mr. Daniels's friends. We don't give a skinny rat's arse fer what Riley says, but Clint be a decent man. Helped out many a down-and-outer on this levee. None a' us goin' to work fer a female thet made 'im strip buck-arsed nekked 'cause he lost a hand a' cards. Ye take Tucker's word fer it. Thet boat of yers ain't leavin' this levee unless ye gets yerself a crew of gypshun galley slaves. Good day t'ye." The river man got up and stomped back to the counter.

Delilah felt her stomach churn during Tucker's diatribe. Once he was out of earshot, she stood up and asked her uncle, "Any idea what we should do now?"

"First, we depart these hostile environs," he replied, taking her arm. Backs ramrod straight, they walked out into the bright morning sunlight. Once on the sidewalk they headed briskly down the levee toward the *Nymph*.

Later that afternoon, Delilah sat drinking coffee in the riverboat's salon. She awaited her uncle's return. He had insisted that she stay aboard while he checked around to ascertain whether Mr. Tucker had indeed expressed the prevailing sentiment on the levee. The moment he stepped in the door, the grim expression on his face indicated that "gypshun galley slaves" might be their only option. Damn Clint Daniels and Red Riley both!

On the verge of rage, Delilah pounded the table. "This all started because that arrogant exhibitionist wanted to humiliate me!"

"Ah, Delilah, your interpretation of events is quite at odds with the general perception. Mr. Daniels disrobed in response to a bet that *you,* dear child, proposed. And he humiliated *you?* Don't blame the local population if they consider you the humiliator."

She bit her lip, a small part of her admitting some degree of culpability in the fiasco. "He stands for everything I detest," she said stubbornly, as if trying to convince herself she'd done no wrong.

Horace wisely refrained from comment on that remark. He'd already opened old wounds with his admonishment and did not look forward to laying out the limited options they had left. "I fear we have only two choices: We can seek to cut a deal with Mr. Riley . . . or with Mr. Daniels. Since we can safely assume that Riley would rather cut our throats than cut a deal, that leaves . . ." He paused.

"That leaves Daniels. But if we go to him, it would be like crawling!"

The old man lifted an eyebrow. "My darling, I think we will find it much easier crawling to Mr. Daniels than rowing up the Missouri."

The next afternoon, Delilah and Horace climbed into a dilapidated hack drawn by an even more dilapidated horse that clopped its way up Walnut Street. They left the waterfront and headed toward one of the city's more notorious sporting districts. Clinton Daniels resided at the Blasted Bud Café.

"Leave it to a man such as your Mr. Daniels to reside in the midst of a host of bordellos. The Blasted Bud indeed," she huffed as they lurched up Walnut on their way to unthinkable humiliation.

"It is rather, er, colorful," Horace replied, suppressing a chuckle beneath a cough.

Delilah tried to keep her mind off the impending meeting by observing her surroundings. She had never been this far uptown before and was surprised to find that it was much cleaner than the levee area. They passed rows of small shops and mercantiles. The buildings here were mostly of brick, probably courtesy of the great fire of '49 that had destroyed not only steamboats but also wiped out over fifteen blocks of the city itself.

When they began to hear the tinny tinkle of barroom pianos and occasional bursts of loud, raucous laughter, she muttered aloud, "It's bad enough to be forced to seek out the man's help without having to barter for it in a whorehouse."

"You were the one who insisted on coming along. I would've approached Mr. Daniels alone," her uncle reminded her.

"And give him the satisfaction of thinking I was afraid to face him? Never." Suddenly, she laughed as a new thought struck her. This meeting would not be a humiliation for her. After all, this time it would be the man forced to sell himself. *If he's so destitute as to live in a brothel, I should be able to offer him more than enough to work for me.* Delilah chuckled again, her mood improving.

Horace didn't like the sound of her laughter but held his peace.

The Blasted Bud was housed in a rather large and relatively new two-story brick building. Inside, a long flight of stairs to the top story divided the bottom floor into two large rooms. To the left was obviously a ballroom. At the far end was a slightly raised platform upon which sat an upright piano, chairs and music stands to accommodate a small orchestra. A gaslight chandelier hung over the center of a highly polished dance floor. Tastefully appointed settees and lounges, together with low glass-topped tables, were positioned around the dance area.

To the right was a second room sporting a long, highly polished bar. A mirror ran the length of the wall behind it. The floor was covered by a plush blue carpet, and paintings of hunting scenes hung on the walls. The area contained several card tables and one billiard table in the far corner. The overall effect was not unlike a select gentlemen's club, the antithesis of Red Riley's makeover of *The River Nymph.*

Hidden in the shadows at the top of the stairs, Clint Daniels observed the old man and his niece as they entered the Bud, pausing to take in their surroundings. He had wondered how long it would take her to realize that he was the only game in town. Again he tried to assure himself that she wasn't the most beautiful woman he had ever seen.

But he wouldn't bet on it . . . no matter how good the odds.

Today, she was dressed in a slender skirt, red with thin vertical gold striping. As she had on the boat, she wore a snug-fitting waist-length jacket of solid red, fastened all the way to her throat with small frog clasps. Her hair was piled up on top of her head again and crowned with another foolish little hat that he wanted to pluck off that mass of curls and stuff down a crapper. He smiled. That hat was the only frippery about the woman. She wore no bustle and, in spite of her tiny waist, he would bet that she wore no corset.

As Eva would say, "Show time!"

Daniels descended the stairs and strolled over to the couple standing barely inside the doors of the Bud. "Mrs. Raymond, Mr. Mathers, I'm surprised to see you here."

Horace arched a brow. "Ah, Mr. Daniels, why do I doubt that?"

"A long association with mendacious people?" Clint laughed.

Delilah smiled, smugly certain of her advantage. "And you would not be familiar with mendacity, would you, sir?" Without waiting for an answer, she continued, "Do you have a place where we might talk privately? I wish to make you a proposition."

Clint began to strip off his perfectly tailored pearl gray jacket. Delilah's composure slipped. "I told you, sir, that the last was an ill-considered jest! This is a serious business proposal."

Daniels slipped his jacket back on. "Thank God, or pretty soon I'll be wearing loincloths." He flashed what he felt certain Delilah would think a particularly hateful smile. "Let me offer you a seat so we can discuss your . . . proposal. Oh, yes, and do note that there is not a single nude painting on the walls."

He led the way to one of the corner card tables, pulled out a chair for her, gestured toward another for Horace and then seated himself with his back to the wall. "May I offer you some refreshment—some tea, a cup of coffee, a shot of rotgut?"

Delilah shook her head. "We're fine."

The gambler nodded. "Yes, you are. Now, how may I help you?"

Sensing the way the gambler brought out the worst in his niece, Horace spoke up before she could begin. "My niece and I would like to hire . . . or rather commission you to assist us in assembling a crew to man *The River Nymph,* Mr. Daniels. We have a cargo of freight that we wish to take upriver to Fort Benton. It has come to our attention that you have . . . ah . . . numerous connections among the local community of riverboat men . . ."

Delilah broke in. "We would be willing to pay you generously to recruit a crew for the voyage."

The gambler picked up a deck of cards sitting on the table and began to riffle them absentmindedly. The seconds dragged by, and just when Delilah thought she would scream at him to say something, he asked, as if mildly surprised, "You are offering me a job?"

Delilah responded sharply, "I do believe that is our intent."

Silence again. This time the void was disturbed by the click of high-heeled slippers on the stairs. Then a slender silver-blond woman made her way across the carpeted floor to stand behind Daniels. Through his straw-colored lashes, he watched Mrs. Raymond examine the blonde, who placed her hand possessively on his shoulder. Delilah's green eyes narrowed and her lips thinned.

"Mrs. Raymond, Mr. Mathers, meet Eva St. Clair, an old and dear friend," he said with a perfectly straight face. Eva's long fingernails dug into his jacket, but she didn't say anything.

Horace rose from his seat, took the blonde's hand and kissed it with a courtly flourish. Delilah nodded, just barely. The woman was undeniably a beauty, and the brunette had to admit that her Scandinavian fairness was certainly genuine. She wore a revealing silk wrapper that displayed a number of her other charms, which were also obviously genuine.

"Business, Clint, honey?" Eva virtually purred, never taking her eyes from Delilah's.

"So it would seem, Eva. My guests are offering me a job."

Eva threw back her head and laughed. The sound was beautiful, and Delilah's green eyes became greener and harder. *She probably practices . . . probably can do it even on her back . . . especially on her back!*

"Don't be rude, Eva. You see, Mrs. Raymond, the reason your offer amuses my friend is that I am the majority owner of this establishment. Mr. Brummell—" he nodded over his shoulder to a thin black man who had begun to play the piano in the other room—"is one of my partners. He gets 20 percent for hiring musicians and managing musical entertainment. Eva, here, gets 20 percent for recruiting . . . er, other performers and managing the . . . ah, upstairs entertainment. I own the rest of this rather profitable business."

He let that fact sink in before continuing. "While I thank you for your interest, I'm not in need of a job. I'll have the bartender hail a hack for you." His pale blue eyes went flat gray. "Good day."

Delilah Mathers Raymond sat stunned.

Chapter Three

*H*orace was the first to recover. "Mr. Daniels, let us not be too hasty. Perhaps we could revise our proposition from one of employment, which you obviously do not need, to a business venture that might be of some interest."

Clint, who had already risen, heading toward the stairs, turned and cocked his head. "A business venture? Hmm." He stroked his jaw, allowing his eyes to flick briefly to Delilah, then ignore her and return to her uncle. "What do you have in mind?"

Bristling at his curt dismissal, she cut in. "What *I* have in mind is—"

"Er, would you pardon us for a brief conference?" Horace asked, now interrupting his niece. He didn't like the look in her eyes. "Could we use one of the tables at the other end of the room?"

Clint nodded, and the old man practically dragged her across the floor. Daniels could see the fury radiating from every delectable inch of her body. *Quit thinking with your nether parts, old boy, or that female will land you in deep water.* Ah, but what a wonderful way to drown! Then Eva glided up to him, and he realized that it might be wise for more than one reason to put on a show of indifference to the beauteous widow. Mrs. Raymond knew how to handle a deck of cards, but he doubted she'd fare very well in a catfight with Eva. Then again . . . the gambling lady might just surprise him.

Dismissing the visions of a naked Delilah draped across his big bed upstairs, he resumed his seat at the table. Daniels again riffled through his deck of cards, although he watched his guests from the corner of his eye. While Horace leaned across the table talking intently, Delilah shook her head stubbornly. Her chestnut curls bounced and those cat eyes glinted dangerously whenever she turned to glance in his direction.

Clint waited with an air of supreme indifference as Eva lightly stroked his back . . . more possessively than he liked. He enjoyed her company and respected her business acumen, but no female would ever again own his heart. That had only happened once and it remained a raw, aching wound. Besides, he thought, diverting his attention to the woman standing beside him, it never paid to mix business and romance. A man always ended up with a losing hand both ways.

Finally, Delilah and Horace returned to their seats across from Clint. Delilah was flushed and began to speak, "First of all—"

"Perhaps it might be wise if I do the talking, my dear." Horace's voice was rife with caution.

When Daniels's whore laughed softly, Delilah could feel her cheeks burning. *Slut, I'd love to give you a real belly laugh by jamming an ostrich feather right up* . . . Forcing herself to take a deep, calming breath, Delilah ignored the blonde and fixed her gaze firmly on Clinton Daniels. Her nemesis . . . her business associate. Damn him! "I believe Mr. Daniels and I can come to an . . . accommodation."

"As you wish, my dear," Horace said in a resigned voice.

"I'll speak frankly, sir. We are prepared to make you a very generous offer. Ten percent interest in the *Nymph* and, of course, in our present venture, for your good offices in obtaining a crew."

Clint looked from her to her uncle, then back to her, riffling the deck in front of him with one hand, drawing out the time before he replied, watching her delectable derriere perched on the edge of the chair. Then he drawled softly, "By all means, Mrs. Raymond, let us do be frank. Without my help, you'll never get the *Nymph* up the Missouri. Unless, of course, you can find a crew of Egyptian galley slaves."

Eva's beautiful laugh splashed over Delilah like a bucket of lye water, but this time she did not allow her face to betray her fury. *Think of this like a poker game.* She focused on Daniels's long tanned fingers expertly massaging the deck of cards. No, not a good idea. *Think of the boat.* That aided her concentration, until his next words jarred her.

"Everybody on the levee knows that Riley's blackballed you. No one else will work for you because . . ." Clint paused and smiled at Delilah. It was not a nice smile. "Let's just say they have the bizarre notion they might end up working mother naked."

"You . . ." Delilah choked on her rage.

"You . . . 'bastard'?" Daniels offered helpfully.

"Yes," Delilah snapped.

"You chamberpot with ears? Son of a bitch?" Clint added.

She was furious and didn't give a damn if he knew it. "Yes, all of the above, and any more filth the cesspool of your mind can dredge up!"

"Ah," Clint said pleasantly. "We're making progress. I'll take two-thirds of the boat."

Delilah gripped the edge of the table with both gloved hands to keep from pounding on it. "Never!"

"Everybody on the levee knows everybody else's business," Clint said relentlessly. "You have a serious cash problem. Even if you can afford to buy what you want from Krammer, you'll need to move your goods to storage. Then to have them loaded on the boat in spring, you'll need teamsters. While the goods are in a warehouse, you're going to need guards. A good upriver captain, or pilot, costs a thousand a month, his second six hundred to seven hundred dollars, not to mention a chief engineer and assistant, a first and maybe a second mate, even a meat hunter. Oh yeah, and a crew. They'll all expect a month's salary in advance before you pull out of your berth."

Delilah pursed her lips. "My uncle's research indicates that your figures are inflated, especially the captain's pay."

"Mr. Mathers, where did you get your information, sir?"

Horace cleared his throat nervously. "From what I was

given to understand was an impeccable source of river lore, a Mr. Claude Beloit."

Daniels cursed, disgusted. "What did he tell you was the going wage for a captain?"

"Six hundred to seven hundred dollars."

"Did you tell him that you intended to take a boat up the Missouri?" Clint asked, already knowing the answer.

Horace felt like a schoolboy who had botched his homework. "I don't believe so, no."

"The Mississippi and the Missouri aren't the same beast. Claude figured you were askin' him about downriver runs from here to New Orleans. That's all he does. He couldn't get a canoe past Kansas City without ripping the bottom out of it. Upper Missouri men are a different breed, and they're damned expensive."

Clint turned his attention from Horace back to Delilah. Her fierce anger had faded, the poker professional's control gone. Her expression now was an open book. He read desperation, despair and denial. There was far more to the widow than he'd ever imagined. Why would she want to leave what was obviously a comfortable life to brave the hardships and take the financial risks of going into the Fort Benton trade?

She started to speak, but he raised his hand. Holding her eyes with his, he asked the woman behind him, "Eva, didn't I see Ronnie Bates come in a while ago?"

"Yeah, he came in just before these two."

"Darlin', send Walter upstairs and ask Bates, if he's not busy, to come down here for a minute."

Eva snickered, "Clint, honey, Ronnie's so quick on the trigger he should've been one of those Texas gunmen instead of a river man. I'll guarantee that his *busy* has been over for at least five minutes by now." She sauntered to the bar, hips swaying, mules clicking. The bartender hurried around the bar and headed upstairs.

Clint leaned back in his chair and spread his hands on the

table in front of him. "Ronnie Bates has been a mate on Missouri River boats for over twenty years. You can double-check your information on crew salaries with him." God-damned greenhorns! He refused to admit that he couldn't bear to see the expression on Delilah Raymond's face.

Delilah felt nauseous. Every night since she had won the *Nymph* she had gone to bed with fear gnawing at her. It had seemed too good to be true, given the hard knocks life had dealt her in the past decade. The riverboat was to be their transport back to respectability, yet each night in the silence of her cabin a bone-deep foreboding seized her. Things were going too smoothly, moving too fast.

Under her lashes she studied Daniels, who oddly for once did not boldly return her perusal. His straw-colored hair fell across his forehead, but he made no effort to shake it back. The indolence of his lanky body belied an underlying tension that she could not identify. But one thing she did feel for certain—he was not gloating. In fact, he appeared to be hold-ing back anger. Why?

Ronnie Bates bounded down the stairs. Delilah thought that for a man with over twenty years of river experience, the slender, smiling fellow seemed exuberantly youthful.

"Didn't see ya when I come in, Clint. What can I do ya fer?"

Daniels made introductions and said, "Just answer some questions for my guests. I'll be over at the bar. What if I send you a bottle of sour mash to oil your brain? On the house, of course."

Ronnie grinned. "Hell, man, for that I'll give 'em the wis-dom of the ages. Or at least tell 'em where half the bodies on the levee's buried."

Clint rose and headed for the bar. Walt quickly appeared with a bottle and a glass. Horace and Delilah commenced their interrogation. Half an hour and half a bottle later, the question-and-answer session ended. Bates wobbled to his feet and started to the bar, the remainder of his whiskey in hand.

Eva, who had been lounging at the bar with Daniels, waved the man up the stairs. "Keep the bottle, Ronnie, and tell Stella that you're a guest of the house . . . but not for too long." She laughed, and once again fey music filled the room.

Clint returned to the table and took his seat. With a proprietary air, Eva returned to stand beside him. He said, "Other river men will give you the same information. Hell, go ask Beloit. See if he doesn't agree with Bates."

Horace held up his hand. "Mr. Daniels, I appreciate your, ah, straightforward dealing. My niece and I are satisfied that Mr. Bates knows whereof he speaks. And it would seem that you, yourself, have somewhat understated the case. Apparently Captain Grant Marsh commands fifteen hundred dollars a month."

Daniels shrugged, "Maybe so, but Marsh and his *Far West* are now Custer's 'navy' in the war against the hostiles. The army is making the land safe for *civilized people.*"

The way he stressed the last words and the harsh cast of his features indicated great bitterness. Delilah could sense his hatred of the blue-coated soldiers, even a decade after the war had ended. Well, he wasn't the only one who'd suffered . . . Her uncle's response brought her back to the matter at hand. The *Nymph* was her ticket to freedom, well worth the price of dealing with the Yankee-hating Mr. Clinton Daniels.

"Mr. Bates left a list of top-notch men, all of whom demand at least a thousand dollars a month," Horace said. "You have made your point, sir. We sorely underestimated start-up expenses . . . and we need your good offices to obtain a crew. Now, shall we craft a deal?"

Daniels smiled. "I'll have to contribute several thousand dollars to the venture. And you won't obtain a crew without me. Does my request for majority control still strike you as unreasonable?"

Horace started to reply, but Delilah placed her hand on his arm. "Please, Uncle, allow me."

When she turned to face Clint, he was surprised to see a devastatingly beautiful smile. *Damn, those lips . . . those eyes.*

"It would appear, Mr. Daniels, that while distasteful to us, a business arrangement with you would be mutually beneficial.

You'll obtain a crew and contribute a few thousand dollars for the start-up. None of which requires much financial risk on your part." She paused. "So you can see why we're fiscally compelled to reject your request for a two-thirds share of the venture."

Clint slouched farther back in his chair. "Go on."

"We'll give you 20 percent. Quite lucrative for a one-hundred-percent return on your investment, don't you agree?" Her husky voice was genial; her entire presence radiated friendliness now.

Daniels felt as levelheaded as a drunken teamster when he looked at her plump pink lips, but he forced himself to focus and return her smile. "On reconsideration, I agree a two-thirds share was perhaps a touch greedy. An unfortunate failin' of mine." Now it was his turn to pause. "But since the venture's doomed without me, let me revise my offer. Sixty percent."

Her smile never wavered. She was hitting her stride now. Clint had to hand it to her. He watched with admiration that he skillfully hid. The woman wanted the boat and this business venture so bad she could taste it. But she was up against a stacked deck, forced to salvage what she could. He'd bet the sweat was rolling down her back or between those breasts that needed no corset to push them high and taut.

Mind on the game, Daniels. He waited her out.

"All right, Mr. Daniels," Delilah replied congenially, "we both know you have us over a barrel. I'll make my final offer. A forty-nine percent interest in the _Nymph_ and our present venture in return for your assistance in obtaining a crew and for providing us with additional funds."

Clint examined the green tabletop for a moment and then raised his eyes to hold Delilah's. "I must insist upon 60 percent, ma'am."

Her smile faded now. "I don't believe you understand. Before I give up controlling interest in the _Nymph,_ I'll sell her to another interested buyer, anyone except you. Or . . . I'll torch her to the waterline."

"Now, Delilah—" Horace remonstrated.

But Delilah was on a roll, unable to stop. "I'll get a refund from the warehouse owner. One way or another, my uncle and I will leave town with substantially more money than we brought here. But take this as gospel: If I do not destroy the boat, I will keep majority control of it."

Delilah stared across the table at that handsome face, so totally devoid of expression, and hated its owner. The very absence of male superiority in his eyes fanned her rage because she knew it had to be there, hidden. This Southern lothario had the power to destroy her dreams. He'd do it with casual indifference. The thought drove her almost beyond control. Almost. She waited him out.

Across the table Clint was anything but indifferent. He studied her eyes, measuring the suppressed anger that turned them deepest green. They flashed a barely leashed wildness. The woman was magnificent. Velvet over steel. He would have to be very careful. *Daniels, you're a fool.* "Forty-nine percent for me. And—"

"I give the orders."

Clint shrugged. "Why, certainly, ma'am. As senior partner, that would be your prerogative," he drawled. *Until you get yourself in so deep you'll be begging me to pull you out of Missouri mud.*

Delilah stared at him intently. There was no hint of smirking condescension in his face or in his voice. She rose and extended her hand. "Then we have a deal, Mr. Daniels."

He rose and shook her hand, and then Horace's. "Let's hope it proves profitable." He looked at Eva and smiled. "If Bill Holland is still in with Marie, could you ask him to come down, please? My partners and I need his services."

"Who is Mr. Holland?" Delilah asked more sharply than she intended.

Eva paused, waiting for Clint's response.

"Bill's a bank officer and a notary. He'll draft a business agreement for us and then notarize it."

Delilah froze. "Are you insinuating that my word cannot be trusted?" Her words were like icicles.

Clint lost his hard-won patience. "I'm not insinuatin' your word can't be trusted. I'm *saying* your word can't be trusted. You, madam, are as slippery as cow slobber on a flat rock. God, you think the twist you turned on Riley isn't common knowledge on the levee? The stupid ass never thought of a signed agreement."

He walked around the table and stopped within inches of her. "I'm not Riley. And you, for certain, aren't a poor, helpless widow. You, ma'am, howl with the wolves." He smiled enigmatically. "My people upriver have always respected the wolves . . . but we sure as hell don't trust them."

Horace interposed himself between the two and glanced over to the silver blonde. "Miss Eva, would you be so kind as to see if Mr. Holland is available and willing to provide us his services?"

Loving the way Clint had put the gambling hussy down, the blonde smiled at Horace with his courtly manners. "Why not?" She headed upstairs.

"Please sit down, my dear," Horace said soothingly to Delilah, then asked Clint, "While we wait for Mr. Holland, would you perchance have brandy for a toast to seal our bargain?"

"Why, certainly," Daniels replied with a grin.

Oh so civilized. A Southern gentleman who lived in a bordello! Gritting her teeth, Delilah silently watched him select a bottle from behind the bar. His private stock, no doubt. She was certain it would be swill.

Clint poured a snifter and handed it to her, deliberately allowing their fingers to brush. She didn't flinch. Neither did he. But both of them felt the sizzle like a lightning strike.

What the hell have you dealt yourself into? Delilah's and Clint's feelings, for once, were in perfect accord.

She took one sip of the brandy. Damn the man; it was excellent. Trying to ignore him, she studied the ornately framed mirrors and paintings, the heavy masculine furniture. Anything but look at her new business partner. A partner who had outsmarted her at every turn . . . so far. And a man who made her feel things she had never imagined before. And would not allow herself to imagine ever again!

Eva swished back down the stairs and resumed her position beside Daniels. "Bill'll be down in a couple, Clint." One smooth, pale hand rested on his shoulder, her long, lacquered nails kneading into the expensive wool of his jacket like a contented cat. Looking at Delilah, she said, "Well, honey, since we're both doin' business with Clint, I guess we're sorta partners-in-law." She paused for a moment and then sank the harpoon. "Sorta sisters under the skin."

Delilah blanched. "Only like Cain and Abel were brothers, *madam*." Her voice thickened with anger to a low, throaty rasp. "In addition to the more obvious dissimilarities in our *positions* . . ." She watched Eva draw back at the barb, then continued, "I'm the majority owner in my venture with our mutual partner, while—as I understand it—you own only 20 percent."

Eva studied the seething brunette. Uppity woman thought she was better just because she talked fancy and dressed oh so ladylike, but she made her living gambling. Not any more respectable than Eva's chosen career. "The way I figure it, my 20 percent is worth a lot more than your 51 percent."

Delilah arched her brow condescendingly. "Indeed?"

"Deed? That's right, honey!" Her eyes remained locked with Delilah's. Before Clint could stop her, she bent over his shoulder and slid her splayed hand down his chest until it disappeared below the tabletop. "See, Mrs. Raymond, with my 20 percent comes the deed to some fertile Southern territory . . . the same one you're interested in."

Delilah snapped back in her seat, too appalled to utter a word. Denial would only give credence to the harlot's absurd accusation.

Removing Eva's hand from the waistband of his pants, he kissed the palm lightly and murmured, "Behave yourself, darlin'. Can't you see you're embarrassing my new partner?"

There was just enough steel beneath the softness of his voice to make Eva subside.

To Delilah, however, his remarks were a red flag. She rose so quickly that her chair tipped over. "You coarse, vulgar little trollop!" Illogically, she attacked Eva rather than the man between them.

Eva emitted a hiss of indignation and jerked her hand free of Clint's grasp, moving around the table. Both Clint and Horace jumped to their feet. Clint seized Eva's arm as Horace murmured in Delilah's ear, "Dear one, unless you wish to dispute ownership of the aforementioned territory with Miss Eva, I suggest that you let me right your chair and that you be seated."

With a most unladylike oath, Eva jerked away from Daniels and stomped to the bar, loudly ordering a double whiskey.

Once satisfied that the foe had been vanquished, Delilah sat back down.

A stone-still Clinton Daniels stood pondering the distinct possibility that God had created female rage as a male purgative. Then Attorney Holland clamored down the stairs, interrupting Clint's ruminations.

"I understand you need some legal work done. Hell of a time, Clint."

"There are paper and pens in my office. You know where to find whatever you need," Daniels replied, ignoring the lawyer's ire. He gave the man too much business for it to last.

In a quarter hour Bill Holland returned with two copies of a contract between Clinton Daniels and Delilah Mathers Raymond. After the copies had been signed and notarized, the attorney returned to unfinished business upstairs.

Horace raised his glass in a perfunctory toast. Warily, his niece and Clint joined in. The two men arranged a business luncheon for the following afternoon. The older man wanted to get Delilah out of the immediate vicinity of the beauteous Miss Eva, who had spent a quarter hour at the bar slugging back shots before retiring upstairs, the remains of the bottle in hand. She was well on her way to inebriation, and he had always observed that women and alcohol were a most combustible commodity.

As he and his niece were departing the Blasted Bud, Delilah murmured, "Don't worry, Uncle Horace. I'll strip him of his share of the *Nymph* just as easily as I stripped him of his clothes."

Horace whispered vehemently, "My dear, you must stop underestimating this man. You didn't win that cut by chance. He cheated. As he was examining the cards, I saw him palm one. Well done, too. I almost didn't catch it. I thought he had palmed an ace. I said nothing because I thought he would take his thousand and save you from acquiring the unfortunate reputation to which, alas, you now have fallen victim."

Delilah halted abruptly on the walk outside of the Bud. "You mean he deliberately palmed the deuce so he'd lose?"

"Do you believe a man that skilled would filch a deuce instead of an ace by accident?" The moment he asked the rhetorical question, Horace realized he'd just made a major tactical blunder.

Before he could stop her, Delilah spun on her heel and slammed through the door. Clint was still standing at the table, brandy glass in one hand, contract in the other. He looked up in surprise as his new partner made straight for him with purposeful strides. "Back so soon, Mrs. Raymond? What can I do—"

She swung her reticule by its drawstring. It connected with the side of his face, making a satisfying *thunk*. "You sneaky, conniving . . . deceitful wretch!"

The attack was so sudden that Clint could not even get out a curse. He simply stumbled backward, got his feet tangled with the chair legs, and landed flat on his back. Delilah stood motionless in front of her prostrate tormentor as he struggled to a sitting position, shaking his head to clear the ringing in his ears. "What the hell's—"

"I'll give you hell, right enough!" She drew back one foot and tried to kick him in that hateful face. Unfortunately, the toe of her slipper caught in her petticoat and snapped the rear hem of her narrow skirt against the heel of her other foot, sending both feet flying upward. She landed in a sitting position in front of Clint. Her spine felt like a compressed accordion.

"Merciful God, woman, what's in that bag? A hunk of brick?"

In spite of her pain, Delilah noted with satisfaction that the upper left side of his face was beginning to swell. "A .41-caliber double-barreled Remington Derringer!"

"A must for any lady of fashion." Daniels touched his throbbing face, muttering, "I'm gratified you used it as a bludgeon rather than shooting me with it."

"Don't tempt me, you . . . you . . ."

"My brain's too rattled for me to provide you with cuss words at the moment," he muttered.

"You deliberately lost that cut! You did it so I wouldn't be able to get a crew."

He shrugged, then winced. "I had no idea you were going to haul freight. I thought you intended to keep the *Nymph* as a floating gambling palace, same as Riley. I don't need competition from a lady gambler. I let you win to protect my business here at the Bud. No man would sit down at the table with a woman who humiliates other players. If I'd known you were going into the upriver trade . . ." He shrugged, then grinned. "Hell, I'd 'a probably done it anyway."

Delilah stared at the grinning oaf. In just two meetings, he had succeeded in stripping her of a lifetime of refinement, not to mention the hard-earned self-discipline she had acquired over the last decade. Now here she sat spraddle-legged on the floor of a bawdy house. What was happening to her? His congenial expression was intolerable. He'd succeeded in making her lose her temper, her self-control, everything she prided herself on. She needed to make him pay, but how? Then, noting the way he looked at her, an idea occurred . . .

Clint watched the confused expression on her beautiful face. A minute ago she had been all self-righteous anger, enraged sufficiently to try to kick out his teeth. Now she looked like a lost child. He came up on one knee and leaned forward with deliberate slowness. She seemed so very fragile and vulnerable that he held his breath, afraid to frighten her, but she didn't move.

A part of his brain sounded warning bells. He dismissed them as the aftermath of her blow to his head. With exquisite care, he placed the lightest kiss on Delilah's luscious mouth. Gentle, oh so gentle. She closed her eyes. He leaned away, watching as they opened and she smiled tentatively. God, she was precious. God, he was crazy!

She rose to her knees in a seductively fluid movement and reached out one hand to his cheek, then slipped it to the back of his head. Grasping a fistful of straw-colored hair, she drew him to her. His lips parted as he prepared to kiss her again with much more vigor.

She sunk her teeth into his lower lip. And held on.

"Auugh! Godda eh! Leggo! Awww! Daa!" He couldn't get his mouth to form the curses while she held him in the agonizing liplock.

Abruptly, Delilah released his lip and he snapped his head back. Still a bit groggy from the blow to his skull, Clint lost his balance and toppled onto his rump again. Blood streamed down his chin, staining his jacket and shirtfront. He pulled a handkerchief from his breast pocket and pressed it to his lacerated lip.

From the top of the stairs, Eva's beautiful laughter filled the room. "Clint, honey, let that be a lesson. If you don't wanna lose that valuable Southern bottom land, you better keep your fly buttoned when that bitch is around!"

Chapter Four

*T*he only thing you need to button, Mr. Daniels, is your lip," Delilah snapped as she seized the back of the nearest chair and used it for leverage to get back to her feet. She smirked down at Clint, who remained on the floor with his long legs spread wide, dabbing at his bleeding mouth. His fancy shirt was ruined. Good. Served him right for his clumsy attempts to win her over with his charm. Women such as the harlot standing at the top of the stairs might find him irresistible, but she certainly did not.

Horace looked like a man asked to choose between death by hanging from a long rope or garroting with piano wire. His horrified eyes took in their new business partner sitting bloodied on the floor and Delilah struggling to stand upright in her fashionable skirt. Having been raised a gentleman, he took her arm just as she righted herself. It was also a precaution. Considering the reaction Mr. Daniels elicited from his niece, she might just take the chair and brain him with it if not restrained.

But he could see the gloating satisfaction on her face and thought that she would be content to allow a truce . . . for now. Their new associate climbed to his feet while wincing at his swollen and bloody face. Not good. "Mr. Daniels, please accept my niece's sincere regrets for this most unfortunate, er, altercation."

"No, Mr. Daniels, please do not," she snapped, shaking her uncle's hand from her arm as she glared at Clint. Then she swiveled her head around and glared at Horace. "He accosted me. He's the one who should apologize."

Having seen the whole episode explode so quickly that he could not prevent it, Horace knew that Delilah had played her biblical role. She'd deliberately lured the man into that fleeting kiss. But he was not fool enough to say it in front of witnesses. The past week had been arduous enough without adding further humiliation to her lot. Instead he equivocated, "Nevertheless, I fear that your blow to his head incited the matter."

"As if a blow to his head could hurt a skull as thick as his." How dare her beloved uncle take the ruffian's side!

"Judging by the look of his face, I believe you underestimate your strength . . . or overestimate the thickness of his aforementioned skull," Horace said dryly, then turned to Clint. "Please accept *my* apologies, if you will, sir."

"No need. There's an old saying down where I come from: Once a yellowjacket stings a fellow, he'd be a fool to stick his face near the hive a second time." His words were muffled by the white linen handkerchief he held over his mouth to staunch the bleeding.

Horace took hold of Delilah's arm again, then looked over at Daniels. "The two of us may, I hope, still discuss our business affairs amicably tomorrow over luncheon?"

"I'll pass on lunch. Your niece has loosened all the teeth on the left side of my mouth and I doubt I'll be able to open my swollen lips wide enough to bite into anything. Let's just meet for coffee here at the Bud, say around ten?"

As the old man nodded and turned Delilah around to depart, Clint could swear he heard her chuckle softly. *What the hell was I thinking?* Then he watched her lush little derriere disappear out the door and knew blasted well exactly what he had been thinking . . . and what part of his anatomy had done the thinking.

It was not his brain.

"Ooh, honey, that looks bad. Here, let me make it well," Eva said, holding up a bag of ice she had fetched from the kitchen. She gave him a kiss on his uninjured cheek.

"Thanks, darlin'." Clint accepted the ice bag and headed

for the stairs, but when she followed him and took his arm, tugging him toward her room, he stopped and gently disengaged. "Sorry, I'm not in the mood right now. Think I'll just try to get some sleep."

"But I could take your mind off that bloodthirsty little bitch," she cajoled, feathering kisses along his neck.

"Who says I'm thinking about Mrs. Raymond?" he asked irritably. Could every female on the river suddenly read his mind?

"Clint, I watched her sucker you. You usta have more sense 'n that. She's poison."

"More like a cross between a cannibal and a gator. But I made a deal—a very profitable deal—with her and I aim to collect every last dollar of it when the *Nymph* steams back downriver this fall."

"Yeah, 'n all you gotta do is keep her from drowning you somewheres along the way," Eva said and flounced away in a snit. Clint didn't usually turn down offers to share her bed. She knew the female gambler with her fancy airs was the cause of it . . . even if he didn't. All men were idiots.

When Horace Mathers arrived at the Blasted Bud the following morning he was uncertain what his reception would be. Although a bit worse for wear, Clint attempted a smile through his swollen lip and shook hands cordially, ushering him to the office at the rear of the spacious building. It was furnished with expensive leather chairs and an oak desk covered with papers.

"Please have a seat while I ring for coffee. Have you had breakfast? Our cook whips up a mean omelet with hash browns and bacon on the side."

Considering that all his host had probably been able to manage was oatmeal, Horace declined with thanks. "Coffee will be fine. I broke my fast before leaving the boat."

"Heard you hired Luellen Colter. She's a fine cook. Tried hiring her for the Bud, but she didn't much cotton to Eva," Clint said, using a small silver bell to summon one of Miss Eva's girls from the kitchen.

"I would expect Miss Eva is an attraction sufficient to render the need for fine cuisine irrelevant," Horace said dryly.

As soon as the coffee was poured and the server dismissed, Clint leaned forward across his desk and said, "Shall we get down to business?"

Horace replaced his cup in its saucer on the small table beside his chair. He noted that the set was fine bone china, reminding him of all he and his niece had lost. "Before we begin, there is something I believe it best to explain . . . er, regarding my niece and myself."

Clint leaned back in his chair and took a sip of the hot coffee, careful not to let it touch the place where Delilah had bitten him. "That she's hell on wheels when you aren't around to rein her in?" he offered, curious in spite of himself. His new partners were really an enigma—well educated, obviously from the upper class, yet making their way in life by the turn of a card.

"The Matherses were wealthy businessmen in Gettysburg before General Lee swooped over the Mason-Dixon. My brother's daughter, Delilah, had just married a young cavalry officer in the Union army. She was only seventeen. Her groom of one week, Lawrence Raymond, was a lad of nineteen from a prominent family in Maryland. Both he and my brother perished in the battle. All my brother's property was laid waste by Confederate forces and the Raymond family refused succor to Delilah because they disapproved of the marriage.

"I was abroad at the time but rushed home immediately upon learning of the tragedy. Ever since she was a small child, we shared a special bond." He paused to smile wistfully. "She was always bright and ever so curious. I must confess to teaching her the finer points of card games whenever I chanced to visit. Another sin to lay at my door, in my brother's opinion.

"I won't bore you with the reasons why I had earlier been sent away by our father. Suffice it to say, he had just cause. But after Delilah's widowhood, I employed my skills to keep a roof over our heads and food on the table. Not the best life for a gently reared young lady, but considering the circumstances, the only option either of us had . . . until . . ."

Horace held out his left hand. For the first time, Clint noticed that the fingers were slightly curled. "Besides being the black sheep of the Mathers family, I also had the grave misfortune of having my hand broken by a gentleman who took umbrage after losing a considerable sum in a game of whist some years back."

"So you taught your niece to do what you couldn't do any longer—handle cards," Clint supplied, nodding. A lot of things about Delilah Mathers Raymond now made sense.

"If there had been any other way . . ." Horace placed his hands on the arms of the chair and seemed to shrink against its back. "All I could do was act as her chaperone and protector. Another of my skills is shooting. I rarely miss."

"You kill a fellow in a duel? That's what got you banished from the family?" Clint asked.

"Among other sins, that was the petard that hoisted me, to clumsily paraphrase the Bard." He looked pensive for a moment, then sat up and reached for his cup. "Now that you understand Delilah's antipathy for men with Southern drawls, I hope you will be tolerant of her behavior. I will endeavor to keep her from inflicting any further injury to your person."

"I'd take it right kindly if you'd do that. It's a long way up the Missouri to Fort Benton and back, long enough for her to gnaw me to death." Then recalling Eva's prediction about Delilah drowning him, his tone became almost pleading. "Please tell me you didn't also teach her to shoot a gun?"

Horace sighed. "I fear I did. She is almost as proficient with shortarms as am I."

Clint said in a resigned voice, "Lovely. I guess there's nothing left to discuss now but business . . . except maybe my funeral arrangements."

It was midafternoon by the time Horace returned from his morning coffee meeting with Clint Daniels. Delilah watched him walk up the gangplank, eager to learn what Daniels had done about getting them a crew. All around the *Nymph* she could see activity increasing as the days grew longer and warmer and the river rose with spring rains. Within weeks the steamboats would head up the deadly, swift-flowing Missouri, laden with cargoes for the gold-camp trade deep in Montana Territory.

"Well, what has he done? Do we have a pilot and crew?" she asked, breathless after her dash down the stairs from the hurricane deck.

Horace smiled at her. "You're expecting miracles, my dear. Mr. Daniels has scarcely had time to make contact with his friends along the river. His face is really quite a fright and speech is difficult because his lip is so swollen." There was a hint of admonishment in his tone. "But he will persevere, nonetheless. In fact, tonight several candidates for the captain's position are coming to his business establishment to discuss terms. He is an engaging and adroit man of business."

"Oh, I've seen firsthand what his business is. How can you trust him?"

She knew her uncle well. He had said little yesterday after the debacle at Daniels's bordello, yet she could sense his disapproval of her behavior. Delilah rarely lost her temper. She had spent the past decade schooling herself to control it just as she learned, with Horace's coaching, how to keep her face utterly neutral when she picked up a hand of cards.

At the green baize tables, she was always in command. Until the fateful night she met Clint Daniels. The man infuriated her in a way that was utterly irrational, and she knew it. That was what frightened her. And now he appeared to be winning over her only ally in life, her beloved mentor and uncle, all the family she had left in the world.

Horace could read her like the Latin texts he'd studied in his days at Princeton. "I can trust Mr. Daniels because it would be foolish for him to risk 49 percent of the considerable profit he will make at journey's end. And so must you not only trust him but treat him with all due civility, my dear."

"He does make it difficult. But I'll try," she replied grudgingly.

Delilah was put to the test three days later en route to Anderson's Mercantile, where she wanted to purchase some goods that Mr. Krammer did not stock. Horace had reminded her that any further major purchases would require funding from their partner. Daniels had to be consulted. He had come to the levee to pick the two of them up in his fancy rig, complete with driver.

"Mr. Anderson's inventory is well stocked with luxury goods that rich men in the camps will want for their wives," she said as she sat across from Clint in the open carriage.

She was irritated when he made no comment, then apprehensive. What did the slick devil have up his sleeve now?

The day had dawned bright and sunny with a cool breeze coming off the rapidly rising river, where chunks of ice still floated here and there. To Delilah, Clint seemed to take up more than his share of the rig. The man was tall, lean and rangy, dressed in a black suit and starched white shirt that contrasted with his darkly tanned face. When he slid one long leg irritatingly near the hem of her pale gold skirt, she planted her closed parasol's sharp tip close to one custom-made boot. He grinned at her, understanding the tacit threat.

Horace suddenly found the crowded brick warehouses lining Walnut Street fascinating, staring intently at them while the two young people postured.

Delilah watched Clint's windblown hair gleam a dull gold in the sunlight. He held one of his fancy flat-crowned hats on his lap, letting the warm morning sun caress his face. As he combed his fingers through the thick, straight thatch and pushed it from his forehead, she noted that his bruises were turning greenish and his lip was still quite swollen. She sighed to herself philosophically. It would be best if he continued to heal, considering that any merchandise not from Krammer's would have to be paid for with his capital.

In moments the driver reined in the carriage in front of

Anderson's and they alighted. The mercantile looked quite different from Mr. Krammer's establishment. This one was devoted only to cloth. Bolts of every hue and texture imaginable were stacked on long tables floor to ceiling. Delilah greeted Kurt Anderson, a tall, pale man with thinning white hair, then introduced him to her uncle and their partner.

His taciturn face instantly lit up as he shook hands with the gambler. "So good to see you again, Mr. Daniels. I understand you're going into the upriver trade."

Was there no one in St. Louis the lout didn't know? Delilah forced a smile as Clint replied, "Looks that way. We'll need some bolts of trade cloth. Mrs. Raymond tells me you have some items Krammer's doesn't carry."

"I have the widest selection in the city," Anderson replied with a flourish of one long arm toward the tables.

Delilah wandered over to the more expensive fabrics and fingered a length of bronze brocade. "This would be perfect, don't you agree?"

Clint shoved back his hat. The perverse man carried it when outdoors and wore it inside. When he shook his head, she put on her best poker face, revealing none of the vexation she felt. "Whyever not?"

"Oh, it'd be perfect . . . for a ball gown for you," he allowed. "Go right nice with the reddish highlights in your hair." His eyes swept from her chestnut curls down the curves of her bodice and slim skirt.

"You don't think other ladies would favor the color?" she asked sweetly, ignoring his perusal of her body.

Butter wouldn't melt in her mouth. Clint shrugged. "Doesn't matter whether or not any females along our route would like it—they can't afford it."

"But the men in Montana are making fortunes in the gold fields," she said impatiently.

Clint looked from her to Anderson, then replied, "And when they come home with their strike money, they'll buy frippery—here, where their wives and lady friends can wear it. Isn't that true, Kurt?"

Anderson reluctantly nodded agreement. He had been trying to unload the overbought inventory since last winter. It was mostly too pricy even for men flush from the gold fields. He'd sold what he could to the city's wealthy matrons and the excess was taking up valuable space.

"What the pioneering womenfolk along the way upriver will want is sturdy, practical goods, calico and denim. If you're going upriver with us," Clint drawled, "that's what you should wear, too. No fine worsteds or brocades."

Delilah smiled, but the smile did not reach her flashing green eyes. "Surely there are 'ladies' such as Miss Eva in the gold camps, are there not? I did note she has a fondness for silk."

Horace suddenly found a bolt of blue wool fascinating, while Anderson stared at the high, open rafters above him, shifting from foot to foot.

"Oh, Eva likes silk, looks good in it, too. I guess you noticed," Clint replied, cocking his head and grinning. "But you'd never get her within a thousand miles of a gold camp. She's a city girl, born and bred. Women in the camps aren't too picky about what they wear . . . or don't wear. Besides, there aren't enough of them to make us a profit. This is a volume business. Perishable stuff like this isn't worth the risk."

"I thought you were a gambler, Mr. Daniels, a natural-born risk taker," she replied, using a low, husky tone to disguise her irritation that he had not taken the bait and gone to the defense of his harlot. Delilah moved closer to him, daring him. Her uncle did not intercede as she had expected. Now he sided with Daniels, which added to her carefully leashed anger. "Surely losing the *Nymph* and . . . a few other things didn't cause you to lose your nerve as well?"

"My nerves are just fine, although I do regret losing 51 percent of my boat. As to the rest . . ." He looked down at his body, then grinned rakishly. "I thought you were the one who lost her nerve . . . or maybe it was your temper."

"That's because I expected a modicum of civilized behavior from you." The retort was lame and she knew it, but still she was unable to stop herself from moving closer.

Clint shrugged. "You were the one who offered the wager. Isn't a gentleman supposed to do anything to oblige a lady?" He was unable to stop himself from pushing her, if only to see what would happen. Just as long as it didn't include the side of his face connecting with that loaded reticule a second time, he reminded himself when she began to swing the small velvet bag by its drawstrings.

"A gentleman doesn't strip to the altogether in the presence of a lady," she snapped.

"A lady doesn't spend her time playing cards with the likes of Teddy Porter either," he drawled easily. His arms casually crossed, he leaned against a support post and studied her face in the soft light filtering in from the front windows of the mercantile.

Horace started to clear his throat in warning to Clint but reconsidered. Delilah had a set down coming. Instead, he walked quietly over to Kurt Anderson and asked if he would be interested in having a cigar out in the back alley.

Happy to escape the contretemps between Mrs. Raymond and Clint, Anderson eagerly agreed. A cigar sounded like a great idea. He did not even smoke.

"Teddy Porter is a scholar as well as a gentleman compared to the likes of you, sir." she said, mimicking Clint's drawl.

"Ah, Delilah, how are we goin' to make it twenty-six hundred miles up the Missouri and back feuding this way?"

"Who says both of us will return?" she asked in a dulcet tone. "Accidents are bound to happen. I hear the river is very dangerous."

"Can you swim?" he countered, straightening away from the post. His greater height forced her to lift that stubborn little chin several notches to look him in the eye.

"Quite well." Her sweet tone vanished. Both syllables were crisp and sharp.

"Too bad. I would've loved to teach you." He reached out with his left hand and barely touched her cheek. When she didn't pull away or raise her reticule, he let his fingers glide down the side of her throat, where her pulse beat furiously, giving the lie to her veneer of calm. His own heartbeat had begun to accelerate dangerously, but that didn't prevent him from saying, "All that creamy white skin, glistening wet in the moonlight. You ever take a midnight skinny-dip, ma'am?"

Delilah stepped away from his disturbing nearness. "If I ever do, it certainly won't be with you!"

"Nothin's certain on the Missouri, Deelie."

"My Christian name is Delilah, but I've not given you leave to call me by it."

"Deelie suits you, so that's what I'll call you. . . . You already said I'm no gentleman, so I reckon I'll do what I want."

"We'll see, Mr. Daniels." She spun on her heel and walked with carefully measured steps toward the open rear door where Horace and Kurt Anderson were standing.

Clint's soft chuckle echoed over the click of her heels on the hardwood planks.

"Clint has secured Captain Jacques Dubois, one of the best upriver pilots between St. Louis and Fort Benton. Captain Dubois will bring with him a full complement of crew—a second pilot, two engineers, a mate and roustabouts. Now, what did Clint call them? Ah, yes, *roosters* was the quaint phrase, I believe," Horace said with relish as he strode into the sitting room that he and Delilah shared aboard the *Nymph*.

She looked up, annoyed in spite of the good news about the pilot and crew. Clint now, was it? Her uncle and that odious gambler had become practically inseparable in the past week. "Jacques Dubois. Sounds French," she murmured absently as she skimmed an inventory of last-minute trade items from Mr. Krammer's mercantile.

Horace chuckled. "The gentleman was born in New Orleans. A French Creole, descended from a long line of Free Men of Color. One can imagine if he's accepted up and down the Missouri in spite of his mixed race how good he must be."

Delilah's head snapped up, the columns of figures in front

of her forgotten. "A Colored man who'd agree to work for a Johnny Reb like Clinton Daniels?" she asked suspiciously.

Horace shook his head, well aware of the continued animosity his niece bore their partner. "As a matter of fact, Captain Dubois is a long-time friend of Clint's. Just because the man may have fought for the South doesn't mean he believes other races are inferior. Considering that his business partner, Mr. Brummell, also has African antecedents, I fail to understand why you would accuse him of such base prejudice."

But Horace understood that Delilah was not rational when it came to Clinton Daniels, a man he had come to consider a friend . . . a man he might even consider worthy of marrying his niece. Only a fool would not understand the sparks that flew every time the two of them came within fifty yards of each other.

A pity the sparks always seemed to lead to a conflagration sufficient to burn down the entire St. Louis levee! Horace sighed and poured himself a healthy tot of whiskey.

"If we have a crew lined up, how soon can we head upriver?" she asked, changing the subject.

"Why don't you ask Clint when we join him for dinner tonight at his establishment? He is presently discussing terms with the teamsters who will haul the freight from Mr. Krammer's mercantile to the warehouse and, ultimately, to the steamer."

"You made a dinner engagement with Mr. Daniels without consulting me?" she asked more sharply than she'd intended, then immediately backtracked. "Well, I suppose it will be bearable—as long as that dreadful Eva isn't cooking. She'd poison both of us, given the opportunity."

Horace wisely declined to comment on the beauteous Miss Eva.

While her uncle was taking his afternoon nap, Delilah continued to pore over invoices and ledgers, then compare the amounts of goods with the cargo space aboard the boat. Finally, she rubbed her eyes, weary from the past weeks' arduous preparations . . . and Clinton Daniels's hovering presence. Every time she turned around, the man seemed to be looming over her shoulder. Calling her Deelie. She hated the schoolgirl name. Besides, it sounded Southern!

A sharp rap sounded on the cabin door. Todd Spearman stood outside holding a note awkwardly, shuffling from foot to foot.

"Please, come in, Todd," she said, arising.

He handed her the folded piece of paper, which had Clint's name scrawled on the outside in a broad, looping script. "Er, a messenger just delivered this. Said to give it to Mr. Daniels. I tried to tell him he didn't live here no more, but the feller said it was 'bout your upriver business. If'n you want, I'll take it up to the Bud." Knowing the circumstances under which Clint had lost the *Nymph* to his new employer, Todd was not comfortable giving her the missive but had no idea what to do without first asking permission.

Delilah shook her head. "It's all right, Todd. I'll see that he receives it tonight."

When Todd departed, Delilah held the note, which seemed to burn her fingers. She could smell cheap perfume emanating from it. Placing it on her desk, she rubbed her hands on her skirt, loath to have the odious smell on her skin. She paced for a moment, fighting the curiosity that ate at her. Who was Clint seeing now? Some new whore must have displaced Eva. Surely he didn't intend to take such a female upriver with them . . . did he?

Finally she could stand it no longer. After all, it was not sealed, only folded. She walked over to the desk and snatched the piece of stationery. When she opened it and scanned the message inside, a very unladylike oath passed her lips before she clamped them closed.

"Clinton Daniels, I'll kill you for this!"

Chapter Five

Delilah alighted from the rig she had rented at the levee and surveyed the brick warehouse where all their trade goods were going to be stored tomorrow—if Daniels's arrangements with the teamsters were settled. "Of course, he may not be alive tomorrow," she muttered to herself as she paid the driver and told him to wait for her. "I'll only be a few moments."

The greasy-looking little man in the battered bowler hat grunted, then spit an ugly glob of chaw on the cobbled street as he pulled his shabby rig around the corner into the shade. Once assured that her transportation from the warehouse district was secured, she drew the key to the front door from her reticule. They had rented space on the first floor, but she had not been with Horace and Clint when they inspected it.

Fortunately, her uncle had given her his key and a floor diagram after they signed the lease, and she had put both in the safe aboard the boat. All she wanted was to see if Eva's fancy house furnishings and personal belongings had been moved into part of the space allocated for the *Nymph*'s cargo. That was what the note said, but she had to be certain before she created another scene and further alienated her uncle. Perhaps Eva only hoped Daniels would allow her to turn their respectable steamer into a floating bawdy house!

Not that Delilah would put it past the rotter.

The heavy door opened with a creak, groaning on rusty hinges as she pushed it wider. Delilah peered inside. The warehouse smelled musty and the only light was what little filtered inside from a few dirty windows high on the walls.

Bales, crates and boxes were stacked everywhere, leaving only narrow aisles between them. An involuntary shiver ran down her spine in spite of the warm afternoon. The only sound she could hear was the scurrying of rats.

Ugh. Best to discover the truth and get out of this dreadful area as quickly as possible. She dropped the key inside her reticule and extracted the diagram, holding it outside the door to see better so she would know where to look. "I could probably follow the stink of her cheap perfume instead," she muttered, squinting at the sloppy pencil markings scrawled on the page.

Suddenly a large callused hand smothered her mouth and she was lifted off her feet as her attacker wrapped his arm around her and yanked her inside the warehouse. Delilah kicked and tried to scream, but his grip never faltered. A second, smaller man emerged from the shadows and quickly closed the door.

"We got 'er now, jest like Red said!" The little weasel rubbed his hands.

Delilah recognized the driver who had conveniently pulled up near the *Nymph*'s berth when she came down the gangplank in search of a hack.

"Quit yer jabberin' 'n git to work."

"Seems kindy a shame to waste sech a purty 'un. Couldn't we—"

"Boss said to be quick about this. No time," the big man barked at his companion as he effortlessly carried Delilah deep inside the warehouse.

Delilah forced her racing heart to slow and tried to think. These were Red Riley's men. That note had been a trap, whether it was from Eva or not. And she'd fallen for it like a fool. Her reticule's drawstring was still wrapped around her wrist with the Derringer inside, but a mere blow to this brute's head wouldn't deter him as it had Clint.

Think!

She went utterly limp, feigning unconsciousness. Dead weight. The big man almost dropped her. He snarled a curse and continued down the narrow aisle. When he reached a large open space, he tossed her like a rag doll onto the hard, filthy floor. The landing was rough but nothing appeared to be broken. Delilah watched through slitted eyes as he turned around and yelled at his accomplice.

"Fetch the coal oil. We got us a fire to set. Pronto."

The moment his gaze left her, she plunged her hand inside the reticule and withdrew the small gun. He caught the movement from the corner of his eye and laughed.

"Wall, now, ain'tcha th' brave 'un. His grin revealed crooked yellow teeth surrounded by a filthy, untrimmed black beard.

She fired directly at him. If he hadn't seen her raise the pistol, she would've hit him dead in the heart, but he dodged surprisingly fast for such a big brute. The .45-caliber slug only grazed his left side, eliciting a string of curses as he grabbed his ribs and brought back bloody fingers.

"Ya shot me, ya bitch!" he cried, amazement tingeing his hoarse cursing.

She didn't wait for him to reach her, but rolled to her feet and dashed to the nearest aisle, then darted around the corner behind a stack of flour sacks. If someone heard the shot, they might investigate, but she knew that was unlikely. She couldn't afford to waste a second bullet since the weapon only fired twice before she would have to reload, and her extra shells were in her reticule back where she'd dropped it. The place was huge. If she could outsmart her captors and reach the front door, she might stand a chance—at least be able to pick off the first man who emerged from it.

Clint sat in his office at the Blasted Bud, looking down at the contract he'd just negotiated with the Hessler brothers. Tomorrow, their wagons would transport to the warehouse all the cargo they'd purchased on credit from Krammer's Mercantile and a few other merchants. He reached for the bell to summon Cora and ask her to clean up the mess of coffee cups and whiskey glasses the teamsters had dirtied while the deal was struck, but before he could ring it, the door flew open and Banjo Banks burst inside. No attempt at his perfunctory knock this time: a bad omen.

"Banjo, what the hell—" Banks was sweat-drenched and panting so hard he doubled over. Alarmed, Clint rounded the desk and helped the man into a chair, then yelled for Cora to bring water. He had dispatched Banks and several other of his most trusted riverfront intelligence men to check on the route from Krammer's to the warehouse, just in case Riley's thugs were hanging around, waiting to make trouble when the cargo was moved. "What's happened to our cargo?"

"Not th' g-goods," he wheezed. "Th' gal. G-grabbed 'er when she walked . . . inside . . ."

"Delilah! Inside where?" His heart started to pound. Surely Riley wouldn't try to harm Delilah at a place as busy as Krammer's.

"Warehouse." Banjo struggled to get his breathing under control as he continued. "Ole Wally Behrman wuz watchin' the warehouse. He near run hisself to death tryin' ta reach me. Lucky I left Krammer's 'n headed down to check on him. Said them fellers—Riley's men—dragged her inside 'n didn't come out. I sent him back ta keep watchin' whilst I run fer you."

"Good work, Banjo." Clint grabbed a holster from his desk drawer and strapped an Army Colt .45 to his side, then took his Spencer carbine from its cabinet on the opposite wall. He was inside the stable behind the Bud in a moment's time, swinging bareback up on his fastest horse and kicking it into a hard gallop toward the warehouse district ten blocks away.

Delilah could hear the big man yelling orders to the little one. "Git ta th' front door, Earl. Shoot 'er if'n she tries to git past ya!"

Delilah's heart lurched when Earl trotted by her hiding place to the front door, gun drawn. In high-heeled slippers, she could never outrun the big lummox even if she shot the little weasel. There had to be another way.

Then she spotted a huge pyramid of what appeared to be whiskey barrels. The load didn't look too carefully positioned. She crept to it, keeping alert for the creaking floorboards that gave away her pursuer's position. Now she needed something to use as a pry bar. She looked frantically around, then saw the smashed crate in the next aisle. Barely daring to breathe, she tiptoed toward it. Her lighter weight enabled her to move without making noise, unlike the wounded man.

She picked up a loose board, feeling the bite of splinters through her gloved hands. Ignoring the sting, she moved into position and slowly forced the wood between two of the bottom barrels like a fulcrum. Once enough pressure was exerted, the front barrel would slip free and the whole load would tumble down in an avalanche, burying her tormentor. At least that was the plan.

When she was satisfied the board was in place, she slid off her jacket and covered the board with it. She hoped in the dim light the big man wouldn't see what the jacket was hiding until it was too late. She could push the board forward to destabilize the load, then leap back. The maneuver had to be timed just right and he had to approach her from the front. She listened to the sound of creaking floorboards. Maybe the blood loss would eventually make him pass out, but she doubted it. A graze on the ribs would more likely only infuriate him.

As if to prove her right, he finally yelled, "Come on out, ya bitch! Damn unnatural gamblin' female! It'll go a lot easier on yew if'n we do this quick like."

He was getting closer but approaching from the wrong direction. She had to lure him around the square of crates to her left so he'd approach the way she needed. Delilah left her jacked hanging over the board and cut down the next aisle, allowing him to see her and give chase around the corner, then the next corner. Now he approached from the right direction. He was less than a dozen yards from her and coming fast when she dashed around the fulcrum and pushed with all her might.

It didn't give. She shoved again and was rewarded by the groan of wood grating against wood until the barrel popped free and the others cascaded down, bouncing in every direction. One hit the big man squarely in the chest, but somehow he managed to stay on his feet long enough to leap through the smashing chaos of wood and whiskey. He emerged, bruised, bloodied and soaked with alcohol, but still on his feet.

"Pardee, yew git 'er?" Earl called out. Then, upon hearing the big man's scream of rage, he asked, "Yew hurt?"

Delilah could hear him trotting up the aisle as she backed away from the staggering Pardee. Two bloody paws reached out for her, but she was swift to spin out of his grasp, clutching the Remington in her hand as she dashed for the door, weaving in and out between bales and boxes. At least she'd slowed him down with the barrels. She was making noise now, and Earl heard her.

"Pardee, she's over this'a ways," the little man yelled.

He suddenly jumped directly in front of her, trapping her between himself and the enraged brute chasing her. Delilah didn't hesitate. She fired from two feet away, and Earl catapulted backward with an amazed expression on his face. He had barely raised his own weapon before it clattered to the floor. Just as she started to jump across his body, Pardee caught up with them and grabbed a fistful of her hair, pulling the pins from it as he yanked her back to him.

The overpowering reek of unwashed flesh and cheap whiskey made her gag. With one big hand he squeezed her throat. This time she might not have to feign passing out. Every bone in her body ached, her scalp stung and her breathing was effectively cut off, but still she struggled, flailing wildly.

Suddenly she felt his grip miraculously loosen and air rushed into her lungs as he dropped her. Then she heard Clint's voice.

"Let's see how you do against someone more your size, Pardee." Daniels punched the thug in the temple, spinning him around, then landed a vicious blow to his gut.

With an oath, Pardee stumbled backward, tripping over Earl's body and falling to the floor. He rolled over several yards in front of Delilah, then rose on his hands and knees.

"Clint, he's got a gun!" she cried as Pardee turned and squeezed the trigger at Daniels.

The shot grazed Clint's right shoulder as he crouched, splintering a crate behind him. He drew his Colt with amazing speed and fired before Pardee could get off another shot. He did not miss. The big thug teetered on his knees for a moment, then fell face forward, landing in a tangled, bloody heap with Earl's body. Clint walked quickly to the pair and knelt to examine them. Looking up at Delilah, he asked, "Are there any more?"

She shook her head.

"These two are dead. You kill the little one with that toy?"

"Yes, and considering that I also wounded the big one, I would scarcely call it a toy."

She looked pale, but her poker-player's face remained calm, expressionless. Too expressionless. Clint had seen people in shock before, and she was skirting damn close to it. He stood up and walked over to her, gently tipping her chin up with one finger. "Point taken. Horace said you were almost as good as he with a gun."

She stared into his glowing eyes, so pale in the dim light that their color was indeterminate. The intensity wasn't.

He nodded solemnly, letting his other hand touch the soft chestnut curls that fell around her shoulders in wild tangles. "You could've been killed." Her green eyes were dark and he felt himself drowning in them. Without conscious thought, he dropped one arm around her slender body, drawing her warmth to him while the other hand dug into her thick, silky hair and caressed her scalp. His mouth lowered to hers.

Delilah knew he was going to kiss her again, but this time no thoughts of ambush entered her mind. Nothing did. Just the heat and hardness of his long body, surrounding her with a sense of protection she'd never felt before in her life. *Cherished*. The word passed fleetingly through her thoughts as their lips met.

The soft kiss very quickly grew in intensity as her arms wrapped around him and she pressed herself closer, closer to the warmth, the safety that he embodied. When his tongue teased the soft seam of her lips, she opened them in invitation. Her heart was pounding more swiftly than it had when Pardee had been threatening her life. And it was Clinton Daniels, drawling Southerner, reckless gambler, bordello whoremaster, who drew this rough passion from her—who incited the madness she couldn't stop . . . didn't want to stop. When his fingers found a breast through the sheer silk of her blouse, the nipple hardened abruptly. She gasped with pleasure and dug her nails into the sinewy muscles of his shoulders, then slanted her mouth against his with wilder abandon.

Clint suddenly withdrew from the kiss, holding her at arm's length, his breathing ragged—and his lip bleeding once more. Her hand came up to her mouth as horror and embarrassment flooded over her. "I didn't mean—"

"I know," he replied with a smile that turned into a grimace when his lip split further. "You can sure kiss a man into submission, Deelie. That's a more deadly weapon than your pea shooter, believe me."

The drawling words ignited her temper, not the least of which was directed at her own wanton behavior as well as at his grin. After all, he'd been the one to stop things before they spun even more wildly out of control—and she was supposed to be the one with willpower. She started to slap him, then saw the blood already staining her fingers. It could not be from his lip. "You've been shot," she accused.

"I didn't do it on purpose," he said, trying to shrug. But it turned into a wince when he raised his right shoulder.

Then she saw the ragged tear in his jacket and the blood seeping through the white linen shirt beneath. "Pardee hit you before he went down."

"'Pears so," he said nonchalantly. "Ruined another good suit. Deelie, you are purely hard on a man's wardrobe."

"And you are purely hard on a woman's temper. I've told you not to call me by that odious nickname," she added.

When he pulled a white handkerchief from his vest pocket and reached up to her face with it, she ducked backward. "What do you think you're doing?"

He grinned. "Tendin' to you before you tend to me," he replied, wiping his blood from her mouth, then using the same handkerchief to blot his own mouth.

Delilah wanted to drop through the hard plank floor. Instead she scrubbed her hand over her lips and tasted the salt of his blood. Her white glove was stained with it. "Don't be ridiculous. You'll need to see a doctor. That gash will probably require stitches," she said.

"You sound as if you'd enjoy watchin'," he drawled.

"I'd enjoy hearing you yell while I'm in the outer office," she countered. The tiniest hint of a smile tugged at her lips but she fought it down.

"Watch out, you just might break down and grin like a Cheshire cat . . . Deelie."

"My name is Delilah. And I suppose, since you've saved my life, I'll allow you the liberty of addressing me by my proper Christian name."

"Anything you say . . . Deelie."

Before she could do more than huff in exasperation, Wally Behrman yelled from the front of the warehouse, "Clint, you 'n the lady all right? Thought I heerd shootin' a couply blocks back but my laigs ain't so good. Like to nigh busted a lung runnin' to fetch Banjo. He tole me to come back here. He run to get you."

"We're fine, Wally," Clint called out. "Can't rightly say the same for Riley's men, though."

Delilah heard the rough breathing and clumping gait of someone drawing near. Then a little wizened man with a shiny bald head and humped back made his way up the side aisle to where they stood. She quickly scrubbed at her mouth again, relieved to see it come away without any telltale traces of Daniels's blood on it. The elderly man tipped his small head toward her politely, then looked up at Clint.

"You don't look too good, Boss."

"Better than those two," Clint replied, motioning to the bodies lying in an ever-widening puddle of whiskey. The floorboards were stained pink from blood mingling with the amber liquid.

"Clem Pardee 'n that leetle weasel Earl Barker. Yep, them 'er Red's rat droppin's, all right. You want me ta fetch the police, Boss?" The old man looked about ready to join them on the floor, he was so breathless and pale.

"I'll—"

His reply was interrupted by Banjo Banks, who burst through the front door. "I'm here, Boss. Got me one of yer shotguns," he added in the meanest voice he could manage.

Within minutes, Clint gave everyone his orders. Banjo was to wait with the bodies. Wally was to ride Pardee's horse, hidden behind the warehouse, and summon the authorities. Clint would escort Mrs. Raymond back to the *Nymph*. "She'll bandage me up," he added with a dare in his eyes for her.

Happy to get out of the warehouse and back into fresh air and sunlight, Delilah didn't bother to argue the point in front of two strangers.

When they reached the street, Clint walked over to a magnificent black horse standing nearby and picked up his trailing reins. Patting the big gelding's head, he said, "Knew you'd show up."

"Is that your horse?" she asked. Surely he hadn't ridden bareback . . . had he?

"Samson, meet Delilah," he said with a grin.

"That can't possibly be his name!"

"Samson," Clint said, stepping back and releasing the hackamore. The horse raised his head and nickered, then stepped toward his master. Clint looked at her as if to say, *told you so.* "If you ever want to ride . . ."

His tone was altogether too rife with suggestion for her liking. "We'll be heading upriver in a couple of weeks. I won't have time for recreation." *Bad word choice, you ninny!*

The grin widened. "Don't know what you're missing."

After the kiss they'd just shared, she had some idea but

would die before she dealt him that ace—or admitted to herself how much she had enjoyed it. When she started to climb
into Earl's rig, he gallantly assisted her. Then he walked over
and tied Samson's hackamore to the rear of the carriage before he climbed into the driver's seat, taking the reins. She
stood up and reached over, placing her blood-stained glove on
his hands. "Are you certain you're capable of driving? Perhaps it would be best if I—"

"I've been hurt lots worse and had to ride bareback for
hours. This is only a scratch."

Delilah suddenly imagined his big, lean body, naked and
muscular, tanned skin scarred from knife and bullet wounds.
To erase the disturbing images, she glanced back at the horse
and asked, "You rode him bareback?"

"When Banjo told me you'd been kidnapped, I knew it was
Red Riley's men. No time to waste with a saddle." He slapped
the reins, and the nag harnessed to the rig trotted from the alley.

She squirmed in her seat for a moment, and then a lifetime
of manners bred into generations of Mathers women asserted
itself, forcing her to say, "I have not thanked you for risking
your life to save me."

"Oh, I think you already did." He chuckled.

Delilah glared daggers at his back. Then he interrupted her
angry, jumbled thoughts with a question whose answer
would further add to her humiliation.

"What in tarnation made you come to the warehouse before our cargo was even delivered? Alone in this rough neigh-
borhood, to boot? Why didn't you bring your uncle for
protection?"

Horace! She would have to explain this debacle to him!
Delilah started to raise her hands to her cheeks, then quickly
stopped. She'd clenched her hands together and now both
gloves were bloody. Her hair was a tangled fright, her skirt
filthy and torn and she wore only her sheer white silk blouse.
Her jacket remained at the warehouse, soaked with whiskey,
pierced with splinters, ruined. Horace would have a heart attack when he saw her!

"It's goin' to come out sooner or later, Deelie, so maybe I can help you explain to your uncle," he coaxed.

Was the man one of those circus mind readers? "I'll manage to explain to my uncle without your help," she replied. He turned and gave her an expectant look. She knew before they reached the levee he would force some story out of her. Sighing, she said, "I received a note from Mr. Riley, deceiving me into coming to check on our warehouse space. After all, I am assuming the duties of clerk since our payroll is already too high."

Clint shook his head without turning to look at the prevaricating female sitting behind him. "Our cargo is still mostly at Krammer's Mercantile and a few other places until tomorrow—and you know it. Besides, you're too smart to listen to anything Riley would say."

Her mouth felt like a box filled with fruit flies that sucked every drop of moisture from her tongue. It cleaved to her palate. She swallowed desperately. *Calm. Control. You outsmarted two men with guns. You can handle this one, too.* "A messenger delivered a note to me indicating that you'd already placed some additional cargo in the warehouse. I went to see what it was."

"Now, whose signature would make you believe a note like that, hmmm?" He reined in the nag and let a teamster carrying a wagon of beer kegs pass, then turned to face her again. "Time to tell the truth, Mrs. Raymond."

His no-nonsense tone made her realize the jig was up. "It was from Eva," she admitted. "Saying she was having her private belongings and furniture placed in our storage space at the warehouse. I couldn't believe you intended to turn the *Nymph* into a whorehouse, so I went to check for myself . . . to make certain before I accused you falsely."

"I'm touched by your faith in me, Deelie, I truly am," he said solemnly.

When he turned around and slapped the reins again, she sat back in the seat and breathed a sigh of relief.

★　★　★

As they reached the boat, Horace Mathers strode from his cabin and walked the length of the boiler deck, heading toward the stairs. The moment he caught sight of her and Clint, he climbed down to the main deck with surprising agility for his cadaverous frame. He was at the gangplank when they stepped aboard, scanning their bloody and disheveled appearance.

"Thank God you're all right! When I awakened and found you gone, my dear, I feared Red Riley had kidnapped you. Then Todd told me about the messenger. As soon as I read the note to Clint, I knew where you had gone."

"The note was addressed to me?" Daniels asked innocently.

Delilah looked down at the swirling, muddy Mississippi, for once in her life mute.

Clint threw back his head and laughed out loud. *She's probably considering throwing herself overboard to drown.*

That was when she pushed him.

Chapter Six

Clint tumbled from the plank into the river with a loud splash. For a moment he vanished beneath the debris-filled water. Horace cried, "Man overboard!"

Todd and two deckhands who had seen what happened came running, about to leap to Clint's rescue, when his head broke the surface and he swam toward the shallows with strong, sure strokes.

Horace stared aghast at his niece. "Delilah, what on earth have you done, child? You could have killed the man. And I would judge from the bloodied appearance of both of you that he has just risked his life to save you from your own jealous folly."

"It was folly, but I was *not* jealous," she replied stubbornly. "I could hardly let him turn our boat into a floating bordello—but I did give him the benefit of the doubt and went to verify what that . . . that harlot said."

"But the note was not addressed to you. I read Mr. Daniels's name, written quite legibly on the outside," he said patiently, watching from the corner of his eye as Clint stood at the foot of the gangplank. He removed his dripping jacket and tossed it to one of the deckhands, then shook his head and began squishing up the narrow wooden planks.

"I could smell her perfume. I just knew she meant trouble. *He* means trouble. We never should have gone into partnership with him, the insufferable . . . loutish . . . brute." She struggled to find words adequate to describe what she should feel toward the man now striding up the plank toward them. But Delilah knew her feelings for Clint Daniels were far more complicated than she wanted to admit, even to her beloved uncle.

Horace coughed discreetly to suppress a smile as Clint drew near. Then he saw the bloody gash on Daniels's shoulder and noted traces of dried blood on his lip. His eyes swept from the man to his niece, looking for traces of his blood on her mouth. Yes, there was a faint smudge. Now he was the one who wanted to throw back his head and laugh. A line from *The Tempest* flitted through his mind: "It goes on, I see, as my soul prompts it." However, his willful niece and Clint were hardly youthful innocents, and he most certainly was no Prospero.

Still, this time she had well and truly kissed him. It was a very long voyage to Fort Benton. There would be plenty of time for the two stubborn imbeciles to realize they were made for each other. He clasped Clint's hand and ushered him safely away from the gangplank. "Are you further injured by that untimely fall, Clint?"

"I've had better days," Daniels replied, looking at the fuming, red-cheeked Delilah. "But then again . . . maybe this one will end up better than it started."

Delilah felt his eyes on her face and knew she was blushing with humiliation. When Horace ushered the dripping Daniels toward their quarters, she had no choice but to follow. Her uncle's expression grew very stern. He had always been endlessly patient with her. She knew he was deeply disturbed by her behavior.

If only that rotten scoundrel hadn't laughed at me.

If only you weren't jealous of Eva, none of this would have happened, a small voice taunted in return.

She ignored the inner turmoil and walked past Horace, trying not to look at Clint Daniels as he stood dripping cold, muddy water on the rug. She waited for her uncle to speak. And speak he did. "First, Delilah, you shall apologize to Mr. Daniels," he intoned gravely. "Then, after he has bathed, you shall tend his injuries."

She opened her mouth to protest, but he held up his hand

and gave her a withering look. She subsided as he continued, "I can see that he received a bullet gash from Riley's ruffians when he rescued you. As if that were not sufficient, you have now subjected Mr. Daniels to heaven knows what diseases the flotsam and jetsam of the Mississippi may yield."

Delilah could see the grin spreading across Daniels's face and wanted to sink through the floor to the main deck below. Even landing on her derrière with feet flying in the air in front of the whole crew would be preferable to this. But, surprising her, Clint did not say a word. Neither did she when her uncle added, "I shall have Todd prepare a hot bath for you in my quarters, Clint. You can scarcely return home in this condition." He turned to Delilah. "In the meanwhile, my dear, why don't you work on that apology, hmmm?"

With that pronouncement, he left the room. Neither of them heard him begin to whistle softly as he walked down the stairs in search of Todd. Clint stood casually in the center of the small room, dripping water as if nothing were amiss. Smiling wickedly at Delilah, he crossed his arms and waited.

Her mouth was dry. It was not only from nervous resentment at being forced to apologize. His shirt—what there was left of it—was plastered to his body, revealing the muscles of his chest, shoulders and arms through the wet, translucent fabric. She could see the pattern of gold hair veeing downward toward his breeches, although she did not dare to drop her eyes lower. The biceps on his arms were hard and sinuous and his shoulders were impossibly broad. The bloody gash only added to the raw, masculine magnetism emanating from him. He seemed to fill the whole room, but Delilah Mathers Raymond had never been a woman to back down from any man.

Clenching her hands into fists, she stepped forward, standing directly in front of him, and forced herself not to grit her teeth when she said, "My uncle is quite correct, Mr. Daniels. I owe you an apology for my rash actions of a few moments ago. It was ill repayment for risking your life on my behalf."

His left eyebrow lifted, the one with the scar, giving his amused face an almost satanic look. "Handsomely done, Mrs.

Raymond. I accept." He sketched a bow, then added, "Now, if you'll excuse me, I think I could use that bath."

Just as he reached the door, he paused without turning around and said, "I'll expect you in your uncle's quarters with medical supplies in, say, an hour . . . Deelie." He strolled out the door with the same arrogant nonchalance he'd exhibited the night he left the *Nymph* buck naked.

The moment he was out the door, Delilah uttered a string of oaths she'd picked up in gambling establishments over the past decade, then kicked the heavy ottoman in front of her uncle's reading chair in furious frustration. Instantly a pain shot up from her soft, kid-slippered foot all the way to her hip. She was too angry to feel it.

"Deelie, my dying arse!" She seized a pillow from the chair and started to throw it, then forced herself to stop. She had to calm down. He was besting her in their war of wills. That would never do. Then a slow smile curved her lips . . .

Clint climbed into the big, round tub that Todd had just filled with clean, warm water. He gazed absently around Horace's bedroom. Like most cabins on a stern-wheeler, it was small and Spartan with one window, the curtain discreetly drawn. A neatly made-up narrow bed lay against one wall. A kerosene lantern glowed softly on a small table beside it. On the opposite side of the room, a steamer trunk stood, containing all of Horace Mathers's worldly goods. Again, Clint wondered what had made the erudite man the black sheep of his family. A complex enigma, but not nearly as fascinating as his niece.

Passionate one moment, killingly angry the next. Was he the only man who brought out such conflicting emotions in Mrs. Raymond? The thought held appeal until he quashed it. She was his business partner and the kind of woman whose favors meant permanent commitment. That was something he would never give again. It cost too dearly.

He leaned back and sank into the water. Heavenly. But not nearly as heavenly as the chestnut-haired witch in the sitting room next door. He had heard a loud thunk followed by some muffled words, probably cussing after she stubbed a pretty little toe on some object kicked in place of him. Clint reached for the sponge lying on the floor next to the tub and felt the pull of torn skin from the bullet gash. He began carefully cleansing the dried blood away. As he winced at the sting of soapy water, he wondered why Horace had insisted his niece tend the wound.

Naturally, the old man had been upset because she'd almost been killed, grateful that he had saved her, even appalled by her dumping him into the river. But why further penance after the apology? Ah, well, might as well enjoy seeing her squirm, he thought, scrubbing the muddy Mississippi from his body. She did owe him—and Clint, like Mrs. Raymond, always collected on his markers, even if he was more patient than she when it came to terms of payment. Once he'd finished washing, he settled back in the tub and waited for his nurse.

While Clint bathed, Delilah went through the basket of medicinal supplies she always carried. Over the years, she had tended her uncle's injuries, an occupational hazard for a man playing bodyguard to a female gambler. She checked a roll of snowy bandaging, then considered whether or not she'd need to stitch the gash. Recalling that it had bled freely and appeared shallow, she regretfully concluded that would not be necessary. The idea of repeatedly stabbing Clinton Daniels with a dull needle held considerable appeal.

She examined an array of liquids used to kill germs. Carbolic and bourbon solution, which stung painfully, would do nicely. After all, a woman had to have some enjoyment in life. Her foot ached like the dickens from its impact with the ottoman. But then her better nature reminded her that he had received his injury saving her from Pardee. She dug out a jar of soothing aloe salve.

Best to get the irksome task over and done. Delilah refused to acknowledge the butterflies that fluttered deep inside her stomach whenever she touched him. He made her behave in ways she did not like. Say things she did not like. As if she were a woman such as Eva. Ridiculous! She set the basket down and walked over to the small mirror on the wall to inspect her appearance. She had changed clothes and refashioned her hair into a prim bun at her nape. The dress she'd chosen was one of her least flattering, deep violet from the latter stages of mourning for her dead husband. It was painfully plain, with a high neckline and long sleeves without a trace of trim.

If she ruined it with bloodstains, that would be no loss. The wool was scratchy and hot on the rather brisk sunny day. Soon the river would be clear of ice flow and they would begin their journey. With that comforting thought, she strode from her cabin, chin held high, shoulders straight. Nurse was a role she had played often before, she reminded herself . . . only never for one of the enemy.

She knocked on the cabin door, calling out, "Mr. Daniels, are you properly attired?"

"I'm decent," he replied.

"I doubt it." The man had never seen a decent day in his depraved life! Delilah opened the door and stepped into the dim interior, blinking to adjust her eyes after the bright sunlight outside. When the room came into focus, she almost dropped the basket. Clint Daniels sat on the edge of the bed with a large white towel wrapped loosely around his narrow hips. From the top of his straw-colored hair to the soles of his feet, it was his only piece of attire.

"You are not dressed," she said, realizing how idiotic that sounded. As if the rascal didn't know it! "I'll come back when you have donned the fresh clothing my uncle furnished," she said.

But Delilah did not move. She stood rooted, unable to tear her eyes from his darkly tanned, naked chest. She had thought seeing his upper body wet through his shirt revealed everything. How mistaken she'd been!

Now each vein wending sinuously over his muscles was clear. Pale gold chest hair led her trespassing eyes down the hard, flat surface of his belly, where its narrowing pattern vanished beneath the towel. She'd been right about his having more scars than those on his face. There was one long slash across his side, another small puckering mark just above his heart and yet a third scar that started near his navel and stretched below the towel's concealment.

She clutched the basket and stared at the rug, gathering her composure.

"You goin' to tend my wound—" Clint stretched out his long, bare legs and crossed his feet at the ankles—"or inspect me like I was a prime piece of beef?"

His mocking words hit her like a splash of icy river water. "I'll tend to your injury, Mr. Daniels. There's no need for crudity. But I must insist that you first don some clothing."

He shrugged, then winced from the pain in his shoulder. " 'Fraid I can't fit into your uncle's britches."

"Too big for your britches?" she asked with an oversweet smile.

"But they aren't my britches. They're your uncle's, and he's a mite thinner than me . . . which you may have noticed." He gave her a sharkish grin and watched her glower. "I sent Todd to the Bud to fetch me fresh clothes. Even if Horace's shirt fit, what sense in putting it on before you dress my shoulder?" He paused and scratched his jaw, considering her with glowing eyes. "I guess you never had to patch up a man before. Leave the basket and I'll tend to myself."

Delilah stiffened her spine. "I spent years volunteering in military hospitals during the war, nursing wounded soldiers in the most dire of conditions . . . Union soldiers."

"Ah, and that makes them different from me. What if I told you I once wore a blue uniform?"

"I wouldn't believe you."

"I figured as much. Now, how about fixing me up . . . if you have the nerve."

She stalked across the small cabin and plunked her basket on the table beside the bed, then adjusted the wick on the kerosene lamp, which had been turned down low. Now she could see him far more clearly. Even his legs were tanned.

Did the man run naked like a savage? Not that she would ever ask. Delilah could just imagine the pitfalls in that conversation. The lout would probably give her a demonstration!

All business, she laid out the roll of bandages and removed the cork from the bottle of carbolic and bourbon. "This may sting a bit," she said, soaking a small square of gauze with the disinfectant, then steeling herself to touch him. Already she could feel his body heat, remember how his skin had felt when they'd kissed back in the warehouse.

She pressed the wet cloth into the top of the long, ugly gash and started cleaning it assiduously.

"Ouch! You have all the gentle touch of a wood hawk dumpin' logs on a boiler deck. What's that stuff you're scrubbin' on my shoulder? Greek Fire?" Clint's wound felt as if it had been cauterized by glowing coals.

"Simply a mixture of carbolic acid and whiskey," she informed him with mock solicitude.

"Oh, my God! Woman, they use carbolic acid to clean cutting-room floors in hospitals. You ever hear of iodine? My arm's on fire!"

"Now, now, don't be such a crybaby," she said, crooning. "There, that should do it. I don't think stitches are required after all."

"Thank the Almighty for that," he said adamantly.

"I'm doing my best. As my uncle reminded me, I was the one responsible for dunking you in that filthy river. I wouldn't want to be guilty of letting you die of infection."

He took her chin in his hand and lifted it so their eyes met. "But you'd like to see me dead, hmmm?"

She dropped the cloth in the basket, breaking the contact, but she could feel those fathomless eyes watching her. "You are my business associate and we have an upriver run to make. After that, you can indeed go to the devil for all I care."

Clint threw back his head and began to laugh, then stopped when his lip split again. "Lady, you will be the death of me, one way or another."

Delilah sighed. "Let me clean that lip. Considering the language so often proceeding from your mouth, the real danger of infection is more probably there than in your shoulder."

"Either way, you're responsible, and you don't want that on your conscience, do you?"

"Certainly not." She set to work with a fresh napkin and this time only cool water. "If you attempt to keep your mouth closed for a few days, the injury will heal more quickly."

He did not flinch, just studied her face as she worked on his lip. She was chewing on her own, a trait he found disconcertingly endearing.

"You'll probably have another scar."

He chuckled. "So, you noticed."

"I meant on your face," she snapped. "But it does appear you've led the life of a banditti."

His expression darkened. "Somethin' like that."

For the next several weeks Delilah tried to avoid Clinton Daniels whenever he came aboard to discuss business or socialize with Horace. She tended to the bookkeeping and inspected all the cargo, making certain that Daniels was occupied elsewhere before she had Todd drive her to the warehouse. To further complicate matters, her uncle seemed determined to throw the two of them together at every opportunity.

Tonight the odious man would be their guest for dinner, ostensibly so he could describe the voyage upriver. He'd just finalized the arrangements for a complete crew with Captain Dubois and had quite a bit of information to share. Since all three of them, particularly she and Horace, were novices at running an upriver trade boat, they had a great deal to discuss.

Delilah looked out the window of her cabin and watched the waterfront hum with activity, even though it was nearly dusk. Teamsters goaded mules and oxen with whips as the beasts pulled heavily laden wagons across the levee. Frantic roustabouts, or roosters, balanced incredible loads on their backs, scurrying over the long gangplanks with an ease that still amazed her. Every day another stern-wheeler or two took off, most headed up the Missouri for the lucrative trade in gold country, with stops along the way to sell farm goods.

"We're losing money and return passengers by waiting," she murmured to herself, turning from the disconcerting sight to pace the confines of the small room.

But Clint insisted that they wait. Horace agreed, saying Captain Dubois also concurred. Well, she intended to put the gambler's feet to the fire and find out exactly why, if they now had the crew, they could not load their cargo and embark immediately. She had been put off long enough. If he thought she would stay out of "men's doings," he would be sadly disappointed. Horace had encouraged her to discuss details with Clint several times, but after the debacle at the gangplank and its aftermath, she had wanted some time to sort out her feelings . . . and bring her irrational attraction to Daniels under control.

It would be just like the arrogant man to try to discourage her from going. Well, if he thought tall tales about the rigors of the mighty Missouri would deter her, he did not know the hardships Delilah Mathers Raymond had already survived.

She looked at herself in the mirror one final time. Her uncle had commented with displeasure about her wearing old mourning clothes every time they met with Daniels, but she would go to perdition before she gave him the satisfaction of dressing up so he could rake her with those fathomless blue-gray eyes. The high collar of her black dress snagged the heavy knot of hair at her nape. She lifted the bun free and smoothed the hair back in place. Her fingers played nervously with the long row of jet buttons down the front of the gown.

"I hate this," she said, looking at her crowlike appearance. The weather had turned much warmer in the past few days, too hot for wool. But all the clothes so appropriate in the Eastern winter did not accommodate the humidity of the Mississippi Valley. Still, she looked suitably aloof and asexual to send the Southern lothario fleeing back to his Eva as soon as he made his pitch to frighten her about upriver travel. Determinedly, she set off for the salon, where Luellen would serve dinner.

Clint watched Delilah enter the room and pause at the bar to speak with Mrs. Colter. "She's probably trying to get Luellen to slip some poison in my bowl of soup," he said in a stage whisper to Horace.

The old man chuckled. "Does Mrs. Colter have any reason to take such an outlandish suggestion to heart?"

"Other than my being a gamblin' man . . . well—" he shrugged and conceded—"I do own controlling interest in a fancy house."

With casual disinterest, Horace took a sip of his wine and asked, "How is Miss Eva these days?"

"Fine as ever." That was far from the truth, but Clint would never admit that he and his bordello madam had had a beaut of a fight before he left the Blasted Bud. He wasn't certain whom he sparred with more—Eva or Delilah. Eva had accused him of being smitten with the lady gambler. All because he had been too busy to share her bed for a spell. He refused to consider that the spell had begun just about the time he'd become Mrs. Raymond's business associate.

Women, he thought in disgust, had been placed on this earth to torment men. He inspected Deelie. Her appearance was enough to make him want to . . . no, best not dwell on that idea, especially while sitting across from her protector.

Horace watched the way Clint's eyes followed Delilah. She was doing everything but wear a chastity belt to keep him at bay. But once they were confined on the boat together, the problem would be resolved. Those hot wool dresses would have to go, else she'd pass out from heatstroke!

Both men stood as she neared the table. "Mrs. Colter says she will serve whenever we wish," Delilah said as she gave her uncle a quick buss on the cheek and Daniels a frosty nod.

"Hope she hasn't prepared anything too spicy," Clint said.

"I'd scarcely think a chicken consommé, roasted pork with vegetables and a dried apple pie would challenge your digestion, Mr. Daniels."

"Wasn't me I was worried about, ma'am. You're the one

likely to pass out if the meal generates any more heat than you must already be feeling in that black wool."

Horace smothered a chuckle as he assisted her in taking her seat. Then, he made a sweeping gesture. "To quote the Bard, my dear, 'Fie, doff this habit, shame to your estate, an eyesore to our solemn festival!'"

She glared at both men but made no reply, except to thank her uncle for pulling out her chair.

"Would you care for a glass of sherry, my dear?"

"Yes, please," she gritted out.

"Best put that on ice," Clint offered cheerfully.

As soon as Horace walked out of earshot, she leaned forward. "Must you insist on encouraging him and provoking me?"

"Me? Provoke you?" he asked incredulously.

While Luellen placed steaming bowls of rich broth before them, they sipped wine and discussed various towns along the route to Fort Benton.

"Our first stop will be Hermann, and then Boonville. Not a big profit, but worth the doing until the railroads lower their freight rates. Then we have to make a brief stop at Weston, across from Fort Leavenworth. After Sioux City, there are a whole bunch of forts, but Grant Marsh and his investors have the army contracts pretty well sewn up," Clint said, taking a swallow of the broth. "My compliments to Mrs. Colter. This is right tasty."

Delilah raised her spoon and observed the steam swirling from it. Knowing that Daniels was watching her, she swallowed. By the time she'd slowly eaten half her portion, her whole body felt as if she had stepped into a riverboat boiler. Ignoring her discomfort, she asked Daniels, "I've heard army provisioning and troop transport are very lucrative. Can we compete?"

He shrugged. "Maybe someday. But this is our first trip runnin' mining supplies up and rich miners back down, and it's guaranteed to turn a handsome profit. Jacques and I agreed to wait and see how it goes. We'll have all next winter to woo the army," he said with a grimace.

"I can imagine that a Confederate sympathizer would have difficulty dealing with the Grand Army of the Republic. Perhaps my uncle and I would have more luck?" *And perhaps we'll cut you out of all future voyages once we repay your loans.*

"You just might be right. Head on down to Jefferson Barracks and try your luck." He polished off the last of his consommé and shoved the bowl away just as Luellen arrived with a steaming platter of pork roast and fresh vegetables.

Delilah dabbed at the corner of her mouth with her napkin. "Wooing the army will be a bit difficult if we don't pass the inspection at Fort Leavenworth."

Clint slowly put down his napkin. "And what do you know about the inspection at Fort Leavenworth, Mrs. Raymond?"

"Oh, I listen to the men talk. You know, 'men's business,' that sort of thing. It seems the fort inspects all upriver boats for contraband. And if they find it, the army is authorized to seize the boat. As I understand it, their primary target is whiskey, such as we had in our warehouse."

Horace looked at Clint questioningly, but Daniels kept his eyes on the lady. "You are well-informed, ma'am. Leavenworth does search the boats for whiskey, but the inspections are cursory, or the inspectors can be easily bribed."

"From what I understand, that isn't always true."

"No, not always, but there are ways to beat the inspection, and the risk is well worth it. Fifty hogsheads of rotgut purchased here in St. Louis for around two hundred dollars a barrel can be sold to the merchants at Benton for seven hundred apiece."

"That is a twenty-five-thousand-dollar profit." Horace whistled softly.

"I do not intend to risk my boat for any illegal profit, Mr. Daniels," Delilah said coldly.

Clint's lips thinned. Before he lowered his gaze to the plate in front of him, his eyes changed from blue to gray. His hands tightened into fists on the table and then slowly eased. But the tense silence seemed to drag on forever, until he looked over at Horace. "You think twenty-five thousand is worth a gamble?"

Horace appeared to consider, knowing that this contest of wills was about considerably more than hauling whiskey. His niece was scarcely Temperance. "Perhaps it would be wise to consult with the captain before you make a final decision. Would you not consider that prudent, my dear?" he asked Delilah.

The ball had been lobbed neatly into her court. Delilah hesitated until Clint said to her, "Your 51 percent of the boat entitles you to give that order . . ."

Despite his apparent capitulation, Delilah did not feel as if she'd won the battle. Attempting to moisten her parched lips, she sipped sherry, then replied, "Perhaps I will consult with Captain Dubois."

Delilah swallowed another sip of sherry. Drat, she was so uncomfortable she couldn't think straight. She had left her bowl of consommé more than half full, hoping Daniels would think she was a dainty eater. When Luellen took the bowl away, she raised her glass again. The cool liquid tasted heavenly, but at this rate she'd be inebriated before Luellen served the main course! As the great orange ball set on the western horizon, Delilah watched through the salon window and prayed for nightfall and a brisk breeze off the water.

Luellen, knowing how the Missus usually ate, served up a hearty portion and set it before Delilah. Although the aroma was redolent of fresh dill and the tang of asparagus and sweet new potatoes, her taste buds could not appreciate it. They were sweating too much. The men tucked into their food, giving enthusiastic compliments to the cook. Clint paused with a big slice of pork halfway to his mouth and looked over at her with a smirk.

Defiantly, she sliced a tiny sliver of tender meat, dripping with brown gravy, and ate it. She doggedly forced down bite after bite of pork and vegetables, trying not to think about the rivulets of perspiration soaking through her dress. Thank heavens it was black and the dampness would not show.

To take her mind off her misery, she brought up another issue she'd wanted to discuss all evening. "You've reiterated several times that Captain Dubois wants to wait another week at least before embarking upriver, yet I've seen one stern-wheeler after another pull away from the levee in the weeks past. We're losing money with every day we dally. Why not start loading our cargo immediately?"

Clint set down his fork and replied, "Good question. Same one Horace asked Jacques yesterday." He watched in amusement when she turned to her uncle and gave him a scowl. "Look out the window on the river side. What do you see?" he asked.

Delilah had to stand up and move across the salon to get a clear view to the east. The vast sweep of the Mississippi at the narrows around the bend of the St. Louis levee ran swift and deep as darkness descended. She was grateful for the chilly breeze coming off the water. After looking out at the gathering darkness for as long as she could stall, she returned to the table, where Clint solicitously held out her chair.

"Well?"

"The water is high. That's a good sign, isn't it?"

"Some ways yes, others, no. Winter out west was one of the worst in decades. Lots of snow melt to fill the Missouri's tributaries. But a hard current means a harder pull upriver . . . and, did you notice anythin' floating with the current?"

She made a dismissive gesture. "Some pieces of driftwood, the usual mess that comes downriver."

"Spoken like a true Easterner."

"And a true Yankee?" she asked sweetly, seething at what she considered his condescension.

"That 'usual mess' you mentioned isn't just a few sticks of kindling. Those were barns, cabins and trees. Whole trees, clusters of wood locked together, sweeping downriver. Just one big log can smash a shallow draft stern-wheeler to bits."

"I thought your captain was an expert at avoiding such exigencies," she said, glad for the argument and time for her food to cool. Clint, like Horace, kept shoveling in the hot meal.

After taking one last bite, he replied, "He's one of the very best, but for every captain like Dubois or Marsh, there are

dozens who've beached or smashed their boats to kindling—
or worse yet, blown their boilers sky high, killing every person aboard, in an attempt to beat the competition."

"There appears to be a high enough demand for the goods
we carry that another week or two won't make any difference. We'll make a handsome profit," Horace assured her.

Delilah gave her uncle a sharp look, but before she could
say anything, Luellen approached the table, tsking about the
Missus's half-eaten food as she cleared plates and replaced
them with apple pie still warm from the oven. The crust was
flaky and the dried apples gave off a hint of cinnamon. But
the Missus looked at the piece set before her as if it were a
burning lump of coal.

Both men complimented Mrs. Colter effusively. She withdrew, her already ruddy face beet red from the praise. She
turned an inquisitive eye to Delilah, who nodded woodenly
and took a forkful of pie. In moments the cook returned
with a big graniteware pot of scalding hot coffee and thick
cream. Without asking, because her mistress normally loved
after-dinner coffee, she poured a full cup, allowing scant
room for cream. The Missus always drank hers black.

Enviously, Delilah watched her uncle lace his cup with the
cool, pale liquid, then stir. She felt the steam rising from her
own cup and said, "Pass the cream, please, Uncle."

He looked at her, raising both eyebrows. "You detest
cream," he replied, puzzled.

"Well, I've decided to try it this evening," she said, reaching for the small pitcher and filling her cup until it overflowed into her saucer. "Oh, now I've gone and ruined it."

"I'll ask Mrs. Colter to bring more," Clint said helpfully
and started to rise.

"No! Er, that is, I mean, I really don't want any coffee tonight. I haven't been sleeping well. I imagine I'm just excited
about the prospect of the voyage," she added, feeling a trickle
of perspiration travel down her temple.

Before she could bat his hand away, Clint took his napkin
and reached over to dab at it. "You do look a mite flushed,

Mrs. Raymond. I'd hate it if you fainted before we finished our business meeting."

As if on cue, Horace stood up. "If you'll excuse me, I believe I shall retire for the night. My niece is not the only one missing sleep over this venture, but she is considerably younger and more resilient than am I. You two have a great many other things to discuss, I believe?"

With a bow to his niece and a handshake with Daniels, he left the two of them alone in the empty salon.

"Well, Deelie, what do we talk about now, hmmm?"

Chapter Seven

Delilah scooted her chair back, out of his reach, and started to rise. But instead of getting up, he leaned back and said in that lazy, infuriating drawl, "Runnin' like a scared jackrabbit, Deelie? Thought you had more sand than that."

She stopped and glared down at him. "Mr. Daniels, you have the manners of a man raised by savages."

"All depends on your definition of savages," he replied, standing up now, stepping closer to her, daring her to back away.

His eyes glowed gray in the soft lantern light, and glinted with something she could not read, something savage in itself. For the first time since she'd met him, he actually frightened her. She set her chin and said, "I've read newspaper accounts of scalpings and torture, other things so grisly—"

"Eastern newspapers. Mostly the blathering of damn fools who wouldn't know a Sioux from a Scotsman. The West is filled with all kinds of tribes, men and women as good or as bad as any whites."

"I thought you said you'd never been to the far West, Mr. Daniels," she said, wondering what had made him so angry. There was so much neither she nor her trusting uncle knew about their associate.

"Never said I hadn't been upriver, only that I never traveled on a stern-wheeler."

Well, that certainly cleared matters up! But, somehow, Delilah did not want to press him with more questions. "Perhaps you can explain to my uncle about your time on the upper Missouri tomorrow. As for tonight, sir, I'm going to retire."

Abruptly, the old familiar grin spread across his face. The mercurial mood shift startled her. She merely nodded and started for the door. But when she stepped into the blessedly cool night air, he was right behind her.

"It wouldn't be polite for a gentleman to allow a lady to go unescorted to her cabin. The roustabouts and rivermen aren't the most mannerly sorts." He took her hand and placed it over his coat sleeve.

Oh, so proper now. Was this the same man who had frightened her only a moment ago? "Neither are you, but I imagine your charms work quite well in the sporting district."

He chuckled. As they strolled down the deck toward her cabin, Delilah cursed her uncle for once again throwing her to the wolves—or wolf, in this case. When they reached the door, she slipped her hand from Clint's arm and started to turn the knob. "Good night, Mr. Daniels."

Clint watched the moonlight gleam on her hair and reflect in her big green cat's eyes. Why couldn't he seem to leave well enough alone? This female was pure poison. But instead, he found himself wrapping one arm around her and pulling her close to him. The faint hint of her floral bath salts teased his nostrils. He stared into her eyes, willing her not to resist as his other hand reached up and loosened the pins from the heavy mass of hair at her nape, letting it tumble down her back in a cascade of curls.

"Your hair is so beautiful. Why have you taken to hiding it lately?"

His voice was a low hum. Delilah could feel the vibration from his chest travel to her breasts. She sucked in a shaky breath as long, clever fingers massaged her scalp. The feeling was mesmerizing. When he planted his lips against the side of her throat, she could hear the possessiveness in his male growl. The whispering magic of his mouth on her skin sent shivers through her overheated body. She let go of her last ounce of sense.

His heat enveloped her. She felt powerless to speak until he began unfastening the buttons at the neck of her gown.

"Stop," she whispered against his shoulder. Her voice held no conviction and she knew it.

"You were glowing from the heat, near choking in your high collar and black wool. I'm only helping you cool off. Feel the river breeze on your neck . . ."

The devil possessed incredible dexterity. He had jet buttons slipped from six loops before she regained the presence of mind to reach up and seize his hand. "I can see how your skill with a deck of cards has other applications, Mr. Daniels. But I am not your Miss Eva and you will stop undressing me this instant, else I'll scream until my uncle shoots you dead."

Her voice was a hiss of indignation. Clint released her and watched her back against the door of her cabin. Those big cat's eyes shot sparks. He could see a narrow vee of creamy skin and just the hint of cleavage from those sumptuous breasts where he'd opened the foolish high-necked dress. Lordy, she was a magnificent piece of woman flesh! *Daniels, stop thinkin' with your gonads.* He grinned and tipped his head. "What, didn't you bring your Derringer to dinner so you could defend yourself?"

As he turned and sauntered toward the stairs to the main deck, he heard her retort. "A mistake I will never again make, I assure you!"

"I must insist on accompanying you, Uncle. If we're to trust our whole future to this captain that Mr. Daniels has hired, I want to meet him . . . and to hear directly from an expert why we must wait another week, not to mention why we should risk carrying whiskey upriver."

Horace noted the way she said Clint's name as if she'd sucked on a lemon. He wondered what had transpired that night after he'd left them alone in the salon. It had been nearly two weeks and she had avoided Clint as if he had typhoid. "Very well, but I need not remind you that a lady visiting a man of color at his dwelling will cause gossip."

"Being a female gambler has already taken me off the social registry," she replied dryly. "Come, let's go meet Captain Dubois."

On the carriage ride into the countryside north of the city, Horace ruminated about what might have been while making small talk with Delilah.

He knew she'd hated the way she'd been forced to survive after her young husband died. The Raymonds did not approve of the Matherses, who were not among the landed gentry of Maryland. Instead Delilah's great-grandfather had made the family fortune as a Pennsylvania shoe manufacturer, then branched out into other businesses.

Delilah had been cosseted by her family since birth. Being Arthur's only child and losing her mother so early had contributed to her being indulged. But the war had changed everything. Survival had at first only entailed following her uncle from city to city as he plied the cards. Although she had no friends, at least she had not been forced to associate with the unsavory elements in gaming establishments—until his injury.

"Do you ever resent what I've taught you, child?" he asked.

Delilah knew what he meant. She took his gnarled left hand and placed both of hers around the crippled fingers. "Never. You've cared for me as if I were your own daughter. I shall always be in your debt—" She raised her hand when he started to protest.

"No, it's true." She paused thoughtfully for a moment as the narrow city streets with brick-lined buildings gave way to rolling hills. "You know, I've now and then imagined what might have happened if Lawrence had lived. After the communications I exchanged with his parents, I know they would've disinherited him. He was equipped to do nothing else but live the life of a gentleman farmer. His only option after the war would have been to eke out a meager existence as an army officer. I've read enough about life on military posts out West to know it would have placed a dreadful hardship on our marriage."

Horace had often considered the same dire outcome. "At least your life as an officer's wife would have been respectable," he said with a wistful smile.

"Horsefeathers. Can you imagine me pouring tea for senior officers' wives? Being stuck in the middle of the wilderness? The highlight of my year, a trip to some frontier cow town to purchase calico." A pensive expression crossed her face. "I fear we married too young. I can't even remember what he looked like. And as the years have passed, I've scarcely taken out his photograph to remind me. . . ."

Horace patted her arm. "As you said, you were both too young. There's no shame in that."

"This sounds terrible, but I'm not certain now that I was ever in love with Lawrence . . . at least, well . . . I don't know . . ."

Her voice faded away and she turned her head and watched the countryside. *She's thinking of Clint and how he differs from her husband.* Horace had hoped she would come in time to realize that mourning for poor Lawrence was a waste of her vibrant young life. She craved independence and a boy from his background would never have accepted that, nor would his family. A man such as Clinton Daniels would appreciate a strong woman.

Now it was his turn to pat her hand. "I believe everything will work out for the best. Only give it time."

With that cryptic remark hanging in the air, the carriage pulled up in front of a small, neat frame cottage shaded by two tall white oaks. It was situated high on the river bluffs overlooking a wide stretch of the Missouri.

Captain Jacques Dubois was a small man, wiry and nattily dressed in a cream linen suit. His complexion was the color of café au lait. Black, curly hair sprinkled with gray receded from a high forehead, the only thing that gave away his age. A younger woman with handsome features and piercing black eyes stood behind him in the doorway, a small boy clinging to her skirt. Her straight black hair was parted in the middle and braided into long, gleaming plaits. Although she wore a linen day dress, her strongly chiseled face and mien suggested she was Indian. She waited impassively while her husband stepped from the veranda and walked down the flagstones to greet his visitors.

"Good day, Captain Dubois. I hope you do not mind my bringing my niece with me," Horace said as he alighted from the carriage. "She is the majority owner of *The River Nymph.*"

If the captain was disconcerted, he did not show it. Smiling, he approached Horace, saying, "I am honored by the lady's presence." The soft cadences of New Orleans mixed with just the hint of a French accent. "You are most welcome to my home. Please, will you partake of some cool lemonade while we discuss business?"

Horace offered his hand, which the captain shook formally. Then Mathers introduced Delilah to him. When she held out her gloved hand, he gave it a courtly salute worthy of any Creole gentleman.

Turning to the woman, who had sent the boy inside before approaching them, he said, "May I present Dawn Woman? She is a member of the Ehanktonwon or Yankton Sioux, and my wife. That little rascal who just returned to his toy boats is our son Etienne. Our daughter Bernadette is away at school."

"A pleasure, madam," Horace said, saluting her hand and introducing his niece.

Delilah had never seen a real, live Indian before and was amazed that she looked quite civilized. She smiled, and Mrs. Dubois returned the smile, saying, "Please come inside and I'll fetch the lemonade that Jacques promised." Her voice was low, well modulated and she was obviously educated.

They entered the front parlor, furnished with beautiful cherry wood chairs upholstered in deep green brocade. The wallpaper was a soft floral in complementing shades of green and russet. A large oval rug covered the center of the polished oak floors and several paintings of river scenes hung on the walls. Delilah imagined they were all depictions of the upper Missouri. Being one of the most highly respected captains to pilot stern-wheelers up the Missouri had earned Dubois a handsome living indeed.

"Your home is lovely," she said to Captain and Mrs. Dubois.

"A bit far from the riverfront, but we find it pleasant to have privacy. It's better for the children, as well," Dubois replied. "When I'm working, my brother Etienne stays with my family. Not everyone in the area finds it acceptable for a man of color and an Indian to own property."

"I can imagine it must be difficult, even dangerous," Horace ventured. He had noted several armed men, all of mixed race, working at various tasks around the house, and suspected that their secondary duty was to act as bodyguards.

Delilah was overcome with curiosity. "How long have you and Mr. Daniels known each other?"

Dubois's face split into a wide smile, revealing small, even teeth. "Clint and I go back quite a way. In fact, he is a kinsman of Dawn's, in a manner of speaking. . . ." The captain paused and cleared his throat as his wife brought in a tray with tall, sweat-beaded glasses of lemonade, then said only, "I think it best if he explains that to you."

"There are a few other matters he has not explained to me."

Dubois cocked his head politely, encouraging Delilah to continue. "Such as?"

"So many boats have already departed the St. Louis levee, and yet we're still waiting, paying warehouse fees while our competitors steam toward Fort Benton. Mr. Daniels insists it is too dangerous. Are you of the same opinion, Captain?"

If Jacques Dubois knew of the friction between Clint and his beautiful female partner, he revealed nothing. Instead, he asked, "You have seen the clusters of driftwood swirling past the levee over the past weeks, yes?" At her reluctant nod, he continued, "They can smash a boat or force it into shallows where it will remain hopelessly grounded for the summer. And the current this year is running particularly hard because of the harsh winter on the high plains."

"How does the weather affect the river?" Horace asked. He had already heard Clint explain but wanted to play devil's advocate for Delilah.

"When the extraordinary snowfall melts, every tributary of the Missouri runs high. As the river flows downstream, it picks up an excess of this water, along with trees and other debris swept into the current. I can gauge the shallows and keep a sharp watch for the sawyers—bobbing, partially hidden trees that have snagged in the river bottom—as well as the drifting wood. But running against a hard current is the greatest danger—the one that can cost every person aboard their lives."

"Boiler explosions," Delilah said, having heard the horror stories about them. When the captain nodded, she countered, "I understood that such explosions occurred because irresponsible captains raced against each other and put impossible strains on the engines."

"That happens all too often, *alors*. But never aboard a boat of which I was captain. I've seen the carnage when steam boilers explode. I do not race against any other boat on the river." The haunted expression in his dark eyes indicated that he had witnessed such senseless destruction . . . and perhaps had been taunted by white captains for not taking their dares. "But pushing against high, swift currents can place a strain on boilers equal to racing. I have never lost a boat. I will never lose one by starting upriver before it is safe to do so." He smiled now. "If we arrive a few weeks later than those more foolhardy, the demand for our wares will be no less. You have my word on it. The mining camps have an insatiable demand for supplies."

"What about the risks involved in carrying whiskey? The army does comandeer boats caught smuggling, does it not?"

Dubois shrugged. "Very rarely, and those occasions are when the whiskey is sold to Indians, which is the real reason for the prohibition."

"I understand the profits are quite high," Horace interjected.

The captain cited the same figures Clint had given them, and Delilah deflated as he continued, "Evading detection during inspections at Levenworth is quite simple. I confess I've done it many times over the years, although more often a small bribe will suffice."

She sat back, keenly disappointed. Daniels had not exaggerated the profits or minimized the risks. They would have to wait longer before departing. There was no help for it. She knew now that she could trust Captain Dubois implicitly. She smiled at him. "I accept your word without question, sir."

Horace smiled to himself. *But you wouldn't accept Clint's.*

"However," she added, noting the gleam in her uncle's eye, "I do not feel comfortable breaking the law by carrying contraband. No matter the profit."

The captain nodded. "I shall be most content to abide by whatever decision you make."

They shared the cool, tart drink and discussed the length of the journey and what other hazards, such as hostile Indians, they might face. "Not all Sioux have been educated in white schools as has my wife. Their entire way of life is being systematically destroyed along with the buffalo," Jacques explained.

"All we've heard in Eastern newspapers are gory tales of savage depredations—journalism at its worst, I suspect," Horace said.

The captain and his wife gave grisly accounts of the atrocities visited upon native populations by whites. "Earlier we spoke of the vile treatment of people of African blood by whites. What is being done to the Red peoples is every bit as monstrous," Jacques said. "Treaties are made only to be broken. Corrupt agents of the federal government steal food and supplies intended for the tribes. Instead, they sell them to the highest white bidders."

"Or make the Indians pay again for what is already supposed to be theirs," his wife added quietly.

"But that's illegal as well as morally reprehensible," Delilah said, setting her glass carefully on a frilly white doily to keep it from staining the cherry-wood table.

"I appreciate your indignation, Mrs. Raymond, but just as the government upheld slavery until the very end of the late war, it is the stated plan of those in power in Washington today to clear the land of all its native inhabitants so that farmers and miners can put it to 'more productive use.'"

Dawn Woman's emphasis on the last words reminded Delilah of something Daniels had said the day they struck their business arrangement . . . something about the army making western lands "safe for civilized people." Had he actually lived as a Sioux in the wilderness? Jacques Dubois knew him from upriver. The captain's further elaboration interrupted her disturbing thoughts.

"General Sheridan, commander of the Missouri Division of the army, has been given the task of herding all the great Sioux Nations onto reservations . . . or annihilating them. So far, disease and starvation have worked even more effectively than military campaigns," Dubois added sadly.

As they talked about the injustice of Indian policy and racial tensions that forced a man as skilled as Captain Dubois to hire guards for his family, Delilah's mind kept returning to thoughts of Clint. A kinsman of this Sioux woman? How could that be? And how could a Southerner like he become friends with Dubois?

All Delilah could be certain of was that she had been a fool to feel drawn to a man she knew nothing about. His past was shrouded in mystery. If even his friend, the captain, felt it prudent not to discuss Daniels's time upriver, that certainly did not bode well. She and her uncle were entrusting their lives and everything they owned to Clinton Daniels. Would they come to regret their devil's bargain?

By mid-April, the massive clumps of debris passing the levee were almost gone. The current slowed. The muddy taint of the Missouri no longer colored the Mississippi quite so brown. At last, Clint and Captain Dubois agreed it was time to load the cargo and head upriver. They would have plenty of time to make the run, sell their wares along the way, book passengers from the gold fields of Montana for the return trip and reach St. Louis before the winter freeze-up began.

Delilah could hardly contain her excitement when she came out onto the hurricane deck. She leaned over the railing to watch the burly, sweating teamsters dump crates of mining machinery, picks, shovels and axes on the levee. Unwieldy stacks of wheelbarrows were lined up alongside barrels and boxes of flour, sugar, salt and tinned foods. A tower of crates containing men's heavy work boots, denim pants and flannel shirts sat beside lesser stacks of seeds, plows and a few other farming implements. Seeing the bolts of calico, she remembered her foolish gaffe at the fabric store. Everything Clint Daniels did seemed calculated to infuriate or embarrass her.

The roosters hoisted barrels and boxes carelessly on their shoulders and nimbly climbed the gangplank to deposit them in the vast open area on the main deck. But one item they handled with utmost care: dynamite. A vital tool of the miners, it would become increasingly unstable as the weather grew hot under cloudless western skies.

Clint watched from the top of the gangplank as the mate directed the loading. Occasionally, when a particularly heavy or unwieldy load was being brought aboard, Daniels would help with the heavy lifting.

Gone were the fancy gambler's duds. Now he wore denims that fit his long legs indecently, in her opinion. His arms were bare, the sweat-soaked white shirt's sleeves rolled up above his elbows. "I wouldn't doubt he'll remove it and work bare-chested," she muttered to herself.

Horace walked up behind her in time to hear her words and smiled. *And wouldn't she enjoy that in spite of herself!* "Ah, child, it is a very warm day. Look at how many of the other men have already divested themselves of shirts. Of course, if it offends you, you should perhaps retire to our sitting room."

She shook her head. "No, Uncle. You know I saw far worse in hospitals during the war."

He knew she wanted to stay and watch Clint, so he suppressed his smile when she turned to him. With a worried frown, he said, "I overheard a rumor this morning that Red Riley's sending teamsters with heavy loaded wagons to fill the levee with the intent of sabotaging our cargo."

"What can we do?"

"I have faith that Clint knows how to handle the matter. That is why he is down there with the mate."

"Must he work like a common laborer, half dressed?" She snapped open the frilly little parasol she'd carried out onto the deck. Suddenly the morning was growing very warm.

Horace made no reply, only stood beside her as she watched every move of Clint's tanned, muscular body. He brushed that straight thatch of straw-colored hair from his forehead, then removed a red workman's handkerchief from his pocket to wipe perspiration from his face. When he turned and looked up at her, Delilah felt as if she had been caught like a peeping Tom peering in a bedroom window.

"Want to lend a hand, Deelie? After all, you *are* majority owner of the cargo," he called up with a chuckle.

Insufferable lout. "I'm scarcely dressed for the occasion." A paltry retort, and she knew it.

His eyes swept over her yellow dimity dress trimmed in frilly white lace. She looked as delectable as a sunflower, only she was shaded from the bright sky by a silly little parasol instead of a leafy tree. Walking over until he stood directly beneath her, he said, "No, you're certainly not dressed for heavy labor, but that pretty outfit is a real treat for the eyes. Once we're on the river, you'll have to wear more practical clothes. Still, I'm happy to see you've decided to dress for life instead of hiding from it."

Somewhere during the time their exchange had begun, Horace disappeared. He'd seemed to do that often these past weeks. That, as well as Daniels's insult, stung. Delilah stiffened, her earlier mood of buoyant optimism ruined. "I see that you've given up pretensions to being a dandy. A dirty red handkerchief instead of monogrammed white linen, denims and a stained shirt instead of fancy lace and black wool tailoring. This suits your true nature better."

"And just what would you know about 'my true nature'?" he asked with a dark undertone in his voice.

Delilah would not back down. "Oh, I cannot be certain . . . bordello owner, imposter posing as a gentleman, womanizer, Southern sympathizer."

"That last one is what you dislike the most, isn't it?" Without waiting for a reply, he added, "I notice you didn't mention gambler, since you're one yourself. Not respectable for a man, but for a woman . . ." He shrugged and walked back to the gangplank, where Mr. Iversen, the first mate, yelled at a teamster whose freight wagon blocked another half-unloaded wagon of cargo.

Delilah watched as he strode down to the levee, where Iversen and the teamster were ready to engage in fisticuffs. From what she could gather, the man worked for Red Riley. He must be one of the ruffians employed to delay loading their cargo. Glad of any excuse to stop their backbreaking labor, the roosters urged their boss to give the intruder a sound thrashing—only not in such genteel terminology.

She had heard language as bad in gaming halls from the Atlantic to the Mississippi. Still stung by Clint's insult, she stepped back from the rail, intending to go in the salon. Then Daniels interposed himself between the two giants, either of whom outweighed him by fifty pounds. Her heart inexplicably leaped into her throat. Was he insane? He could be crushed like a bug!

She could hear him trying to placate the brutish teamster after ordering Iversen to return to work. The mate stepped back, but his foe tried to shove Daniels aside to get at him. That proved unwise. The whole thing happened so quickly that Delilah could scarcely believe it. In a blur, Clint slid his leg in front of the heavier man and tripped him. When the teamster lost his balance, Daniels pushed him forward. He landed hard on the uneven cobblestones.

In an instant Clint knelt with one knee squarely in the center of his back, seized a fistful of the troublemaker's hair and raised his head, smashing it onto the stone surface. The teamster lay unconscious and bleeding, his nose obviously broken, and heaven only knew what else! Delilah watched Clint stand up and look around at the other men on the levee.

He pointed at one man standing at the rear of the gathering crowd, which had now gone quiet, disappointed that the entertainment hadn't lasted any longer. "You pick up this bastard and haul his ass back to Riley. Tell the little son of a bitch to come himself next time he wants a fight."

The man singled out glanced nervously around, as if checking to see who might back him up. Men sprinkled through the crowd nodded ever so slightly. He began to swagger down the cargo-filled levee, passing roustabouts and teamsters hired by the *Nymph*. When he reached his fallen companion, he knelt down to hoist him up, then slung the big thug over one brawny shoulder and turned.

But instead of walking back up the embankment, he spun around toward Clint and swung the considerable weight of his cohort's inert body directly at Daniels. Clint dodged the human club by a hair, then punched the big teamster carrying him hard in his gut. Not expecting such a swift retaliation, the thug doubled over. Daniels chopped the back of his neck with the side of his hand and sent him and his unconscious cohort sprawling.

But unlike the first of Red's men, this one did not stay down. Shaking his head, he stumbled away and rolled back to his feet. On a prearranged signal, the whole levee erupted in a free-for-all. Crewmen leaped from the boat to join their compatriots on the bank. Everything was a blur as men cursed, kicked and punched each other, crashing into the loads of carefully stacked cargo. Delilah lost sight of Clint in the melee.

Then she heard a shot and her mouth went dry.

Chapter Eight

Horace stood at the top of the gangplank, holding a lethal-looking .56-caliber Colt revolving rifle, complete with a telescopic sight. He had fired it in the air to get everyone's attention. It worked. Men stopped in mid-swing, their heads swiveling toward the *Nymph*, where the tall, frightening-looking man with the piercing dark eyes now casually pointed the weapon toward the thick of the fight.

"The next man to throw a punch will be shot. In case you fear my bad aim might hit some innocent bystander—" he paused for the irony to sink in—"I shall demonstrate that I do not bluff, nor do I miss my intended target. The letter *i* on the side of Mr. Slikes's freight wagon."

With one smooth action, he brought the weapon to his shoulder and fired so swiftly that no one saw him take aim. But they could see the result.

"By damn, he plumb erased the *i*!" one of the crewmen said in awe.

"Dead center." A teamster working for their supplier inspected the lemon-sized hole where the letter had been, jamming two big fingers in the perfectly centered target.

"Niver seen sech shootin'," another avowed.

Murmuring swept through the crowd as every man stared up at the cadaverous figure looming over them like some gargoyle from childhood nightmares. The big Colt swept across the assembly, its scope winking in the sunlight like a malevolent eye. Horace Mathers paused each time he came to one of Riley's men, zeroing in, letting them know that he would not hesitate to kill them where they stood. Not a man in the crowd doubted he would do it.

Then Captain Dubois called out from the wheelhouse, "Should any gentleman on the levee fire upon Mr. Mathers, I will personally shoot him." The little Creole rested a Springfield carbine on the windowsill of the wheelhouse. He leveled it downward at the crowd. His skill as a marksman was already well established from St. Louis to the far West.

"Sonofabitch, Riley didn't say shit 'bout takin' a bullet fer 'im." This from a burley teamster who turned and stalked up the levee. He jumped aboard his wagon and backed the team skillfully away from the cargo on the ground, then whipped his horses into a brisk trot up the hill.

The rest of the intruders followed his lead, backing away from the fight. The men driving wagons quickly returned to the reins. Those unlucky enough not to catch a ride ran down the waterfront. One fellow tripped over a shovel and sprawled face down in an offering just deposited by a draft horse that regarded the cursing man with large, impassive eyes.

Delilah found herself scanning the levee for Clint's tall figure. Where had he gone? Was he injured? She had seen that the damage she'd done to his lip was healed, but the gash on his shoulder could not possibly be mended. It might bleed. Then she chastised herself for worrying when she saw him hoist a scrawny little roustabout up on one broad shoulder.

As Captain Dubois issued crisp orders to the crew and the *Nymph*'s teamsters, Clint strode effortlessly up the gangplank. That long, straight lock of hair hung over his forehead and his shirt was filthy and torn half off his body, but she could see no traces of blood on his broad shoulder.

Oh, and what a magnificent set of shoulders he had! *Stop it!* Delilah could see that a number of their crew had been injured. Since coming to St. Louis, she had used her nursing skills more than in the preceding decade since the war's end. She leaned over the deck railing and called out, "Uncle Horace, have the injured sent to the dining room. I'll tend to them there."

Horace listened to her footsteps overhead as she rushed to her cabin to retrieve her medical kit. He saw Clint with the semiconscious boy and nodded to him. "I believe you heard my niece."

"So did everyone else on the levee. She's good at givin' orders."

"She is also a fine nurse, as I know you can attest," the old man said with a smile he did not attempt to conceal.

Clint wasn't certain he liked the guile behind the grin, but there were more important things to consider now. "Captain told Iversen to post armed guards with the cargo while those who aren't hurt start to clean up the mess, but Riley isn't done with us by a long shot."

"An excellent plan, although I agree about Mr. Riley. I shall keep watch from here," Horace replied.

"By the way, that was one hell of a demonstration. If I'd known you could shoot that well, we could've appointed you our meat hunter."

"Alas, no. I do not like to kill things," Horace replied gravely.

Clint gave him a dubious look. "Could've fooled me. Did fool everyone else who watched you drill that target."

"I did not make myself clear. I dislike killing animals. They are innocent creatures of God. Most men, on the other hand, can make no such claim. Suffice it to say, I've had no problems dealing with them as circumstances demanded."

Clint digested that, never doubting the old man would do whatever *circumstances demanded* to protect his niece and anyone he cared for. "You just made it considerably harder for Red to hire cheap thugs. Also made yourself a target. Red Riley's a bad man to cross. Captain Dubois and I, we're already on his list. Now you are, too."

"I shall bear that in mind," Horace replied serenely.

Clint carried the boy—Currie was his name, as he recalled—up the stairs and into the salon. Several other men with everything from bloody noses to broken knuckles and cracked skulls were beginning to assemble. Normally, river men tended to fisticuff injuries themselves, spitting out loose teeth and wrapping bleeding cuts with dirty rags. But that was before a beautiful angel of mercy came onto the scene.

As if reading his mind, Currie asked hopefully, "Will the gambler lady really take care of us?"

"Those who really need care." He sat the boy down on a chair with the admonition, "Don't you move until she's checked your head. It may be hard, but the cobblestones you landed on are harder."

"Yessir," Currie replied with a big smile in spite of the swelling lump on the side of his head.

I wouldn't be surprised if she stitched up that man of Riley's I took down, just to spite me. He watched as she set out bandaging, using rolls of gauze and antiseptic on one of the tables at the end of the room. He noticed that she did not include the wicked carbolic mixture she'd used on him. Clint walked past the men, who had formed a surprisingly orderly line, checking to see that there were no malingerers.

"Bailey, I've seen hangnails look worse than that scrape on your finger. Back to work. You, Masters, wipe your nose clean. The bleedin's already stopped." He singled out several others, aware that Delilah had left her post and was headed directly toward him. He could hear the click of her high heels on the floorboards, then over the noisome odors of the crew, smell her floral fragrance.

"Perhaps it would be better if I judged who is in need of medical attention, Mr. Daniels," she replied in that no-nonsense tone she often used on him.

"I know the difference between a man needin' medical attention and one needin' female attention," he said, looking down at her set, angry expression.

Delilah stifled the impulse to slap the arrogant grin from his face. Touching him in any way always got her into trouble. She never intended to let him near enough for temptation again. But here he stood, half naked, his shirt in tatters, revealing more than it concealed. She could remember how hard his chest was, how crisp the hair, the scars . . . Delilah shook herself mentally, noting with satisfaction that his right eye was beginning to swell. "Do you believe me incapable of determining a man's needs?" she asked.

"Oh, you seem to understand a man's needs all too well." He cocked that scarred eyebrow at her roguishly. "Just tryin' to save time, Deelie. You were the one itchin' to get the cargo loaded and head full steam upriver. Oh, you might want to take a look at Currie first. Kid's got a nasty bump on the noggin." He gestured to where the boy sat, staring in rapt fascination at her.

Delilah watched Clint saunter away. Deelie, indeed! But there was no time to worry about Clinton Daniels and his big ego . . . or broad shoulders. She walked down to where Currie sat and gently probed his thick, unwashed hair to reveal the extent of his injury. "Look in my eyes," she instructed, checking his pupils as she'd seen doctors do with concussion victims during the war.

By the time the dinner bell rang, Delilah had bandaged, stitched, smeared ointment and generally medicated a score of men. Others who were not really in need of help, she sent back to work, hating to admit that Clint had been right about the crew's infatuation with her. Although most were respectful, a few had made her feel as if she worked at the Blasted Bud. No one would dare to insult the majority owner of the boat, but she was acutely attuned to how men perceived a woman gambler.

They judged almost as harshly as *respectable* women. Since she'd been forced to join her uncle's profession, Delilah had not had a single female friend. Those from her childhood turned their backs on her when they learned that she had taken up with her scapegrace uncle, whose reputation in Gettysburg was as tarnished as unpolished silver. But now, for the first time in all those years, she had a friend, Luellen Colter.

The large-boned, plump woman with kind hazel eyes had become almost maternal toward Delilah. "Now, yew set a spell and let me get yew some cool water and a couply slices of my fresh-baked ham," she said when her boss lady came into the kitchen to help her serve the meal for the hungry crew. Todd, who normally performed that task, had both eyes swollen almost closed from the brawl.

"I'm really not hungry, Luellen, thank you."

"Pshaw, you're so thin I swear a good wind on the river'll blow you clean off the boat. Couldn't have yew drownin', so you eat. And don't be giving me that look. I kin handle the kitchen even if that fool nephew of mine's laying down with ice on his face." She harrumphed about men and their fool-ishness as she slapped two big pink slices of ham and a heap-ing serving of sweet potatoes on a plate. Then she added another generous portion of fresh green beans and placed the plate on the table, pointing to a chair. "Set and eat."

Knowing when she was defeated, Delilah complied. The food did taste good—until Luellen started up about Clint Daniels again. At first she'd been disapproving about having a man from a fancy house as her employer, but once Daniels turned on his charm, she had quickly changed her mind.

"That man sure is the soul of Christian kindness. He came in and got a plate fer Todd and one fer thet boy Currie. Takes his responsibilities for the crew real serious, does Mr. D."

Trying to change the subject and save her appetite, Delilah said, "It's criminal that a boy so young has to work alongside hardened men. Currie can't be more than fourteen years old. He should be in school."

"He's lucky to have a job on a boat like this 'un. Lots of street boys, them without families—or families that has too many mouths to feed—end up working for the likes of Red Riley, or signing on with captains what works 'em to death. Goin' upriver ain't easy, but it beats goin' hungry."

"You've been upriver before, haven't you, Luellen?" Delilah asked.

As she continued slicing from the huge hambone, Luellen nodded. "Twice. Wanted ta see what my late husband's great uncle seen in the far West. John never stopped talkin' 'bout the man he was named fer."

"John Colter, the man who went with Lewis and Clark?" Delilah had heard stories about the fabled expedition to the Pacific at the opening of the century but had not considered that her friend might be related to one of its members.

"The same. He saw boiling pots o' colored mud that spewed into the air like ole Satan hisself was stirring 'em up. Bears with paws big 'nough ta split logs and Injuns . . . all kinds o' tribes. We'll be meetin' up with what's left along the way. Some's friendly, some not."

"Captain Dubois and his wife explained about the government's plans to place the Indians on reservations—or kill those who refuse to go. It's monstrous."

"Cain't rightly say I blame the heathen for fightin' back," Luellen agreed. "On my last trip—" Her words were cut short by a commotion down on the levee. "Whut in tarnation now?"

"It isn't Red Riley's men back for more trouble, is it?" Delilah asked, shoving her plate away. This time she'd get in a little target practice herself.

"No. It's Mr. D's rig. He's got a rooster unloadin' luggage. Looks ta me ta be female fixin's." Luellen's voice was puzzled as she peered out the window. "Real expensive stuff."

That was absolutely the last straw! Delilah snapped her napkin as she flung it onto the table. She stood up, letting her chair wobble as she shoved it out of her way. If that whoremaster thought he was going to bring a fancy woman aboard to keep him company—just because she would not succumb to his blandishments—well, he had another think coming.

Luellen watched in startled amazement as the Missus stomped from the kitchen and headed toward the stairs at the opposite end of the boat. "Whut in tarnation got her tailfeathers all ruffled?" Then she smiled. Well, if another female could get the Missus this riled up, maybe she and Mr. D weren't feuding the way everyone thought they were.

Clint, all bathed and dressed in a frilly white shirt and gray linen suit, jumped from the rig and helped the woman alight. "Your eye is better, but you could've been badly hurt,

Lightning Hand. I don't like it that you're crossing Big Red Riley. He's dangerous," his companion said.

"Not as dangerous as the woman headin' our way," Clint replied as he looked over her shoulder to the advancing Deelie. As the young woman turned, he said, "Way she's stompin', she'll bust up the cobblestones."

"This, I take it, is the 'ancient crone,' your partner?" she asked with one black eyebrow raised.

"Evenin', Mrs. Raymond. I want you to meet someone very dear to me." He could see her seething and suppressed a grin in spite of Sky's knowing look at him. He was over his head in river silt. Why was he happy that Deelie was jealous?

Delilah stopped short when the raven-haired woman turned around. Woman? The beautiful creature before her was practically a child. Why, she could be no more than seventeen or eighteen! And she was breathtakingly lovely. Her golden skin and strong, perfectly chiseled features indicated some Indian blood. The contrast with her vivid blue eyes was startling. She wore a traveling suit of deep blue silk that matched those eyes. Masses of shiny black hair were piled atop her head in a smooth heavy coil of braids. From her crown to the dainty blue slippers on her feet, she was a vision of exotic allure.

"Mr. Daniels, this is the final indignity! You, sir, are a monster, a rogue, a charlatan, a man of no principles but those of whoremaster. If you expect for a single instant that I or my uncle will allow you to debauch this lovely child—".

Clint interrupted her tirade by throwing back his head and laughing. Then he held his sides and doubled over, tempting Delilah to use one of those chops to the back of his neck that he had so ably demonstrated that morning. "Don't you dare laugh at me, you cad, you, you cradle-robber, you snake, you pedophile—"

When Clint saw her move closer and raise her hand, he recalled what a fast learner Delilah Raymond could be. He straightened up and put out his hands, palms forward, to hold her at bay before she broke his neck. "You think Sky's my mistress, don't you, Deelie?"

She jerked back her head, glaring at him. "What else am I supposed to think, pray tell?" When one of the roosters started up the gangplank with a trunk, she turned and called out, "Put that down at once!"

The puzzled crewman looked from the irate Mrs. Raymond to the chuckling Mr. Daniels and had no idea whose orders to follow. Daniels was the man, after all, but the female gambler was majority owner, or so the rumor on the riverfront went. He stood still but did not drop the trunk. It might be politic to wait for this to be sorted out before he made a move either way.

Taking Delilah by one arm and motioning for Sky to follow, he walked a ways down the levee for some privacy. "Let's talk without an audience, all right?"

Delilah jerked her hand from his grip, although she was aware that she had just made a perfect spectacle of herself in front of a goggle-eyed crew. Dozens of men aboard the *Nymph* had stopped working and were watching Daniels and "his women." "All right, explain . . . if you can. You did intend to take this child upriver aboard our boat, did you not?" She tapped one toe on the cobblestones.

"Oh, I will take her upriver with us. Mrs. Raymond, meet my sister, Sky Eyes. Her father is a leader among the Ehanktonwon Sioux, or Yanktons, as the whites misnamed them. She's just completed her education here in the city and it's time for her to return home to her father's people."

Delilah was speechless.

Clint was delighted.

Sky Eyes took in the exchange with a tiny smile dancing in her blue eyes. But she was careful to keep her expression impassive, waiting like the roustabout to see how this would play out. *My, my, big brother, you are full of surprises.*

"Your . . . your sister? How do you expect me to believe that?" Delilah blurted out.

"It's not complicated," Clint replied calmly, knowing that his time with the Sioux was very complicated indeed. But he was most certainly not going to share that information with the judgmental Mrs. Raymond. "I told you I lived upriver for some years. The Ehanktonwon are my family. Sky's father adopted me. I'm honored to be a member of their nation."

"But she's part white," Delilah said, knowing at once how obvious and stupid the remark was. But if the Sioux woman took offense, none was apparent.

"So is her father. That's why he wanted his daughter to have an education in the world of whites so she could return and teach his band how to survive. Talks Wise knows it's only a matter of time until all the Indian nations will be forced to adapt to the white man's 'civilization,' whether they want to or not. It's that or die." His mouth was now a grim slash, his eyes gray and fathomless, cold as ice as he stared at Delilah.

Delilah remembered what the captain and Dawn Dubois had explained to her and her uncle and felt ashamed. It was clear that she had made a horrible mistake. Yes, she admitted to herself, a jealous mistake. Swallowing her gorge, she turned to the young woman. "Please accept my sincere apology, miss. I had no right to assume you were anything but what you are—a fine young lady. I hope you will forgive my impertinence."

"Handsomely done." He turned to Sky. "She makes wonderful apologies . . . but then, with that temper of hers, Deelie has lots of cause to practice."

Now Sky did smile openly. She extended her hand to Delilah. "My brother can be a trial. Please forgive *his* impertinence," she said impishly as she clasped the beautiful green-eyed brunette's hand. "I hope we can become friends on the voyage upriver."

"That would be marvelous," Delilah replied with a smile. "Please, let me show you to the cabins. They're somewhat cramped, I fear, but you may have your choice of any you wish. Then we'll see to having your luggage brought aboard."

As the two women approached the gangplank, chatting animatedly, Clint rubbed his chin and watched them nervously, none too happy at the turn of events. "Whenever two females band together against a man, whatever hand he's holdin' isn't worth a pair of deuces."

Horace bowed gracefully over Sky's hand when Delilah made introductions in their sitting room that evening. "Your brother told me his sister was a remarkable young lady, but he did not do you justice, my dear."

"Watch out for this smooth-talking old rascal. Soon he'll have you engaged in a game of five-card draw," Delilah said.

Sky smiled at Horace. "Mr. Mathers, is it true that you taught Delilah such skill that she was able to win this boat from my brother? He has always been incredibly good with cards."

And with women. Delilah fumed, remembering how he'd outsmarted her with the card trick that had cost her 49 percent of the *Nymph.*

Horace was nonplused that Delilah had confessed anything of her background to Clint's foster sister. The bond between the two women was remarkable. Even if it was only for the duration of the voyage, it would be wonderful if Delilah at last had a friend besides Luellen. The kindly older cook was really more of a mother figure than a companion. After Sky left the boat . . . well, mayhap they would visit Clint's Sioux family when Delilah became Mrs. Daniels. "My niece exaggerates my modest instruction. She has a natural mathematical mind."

"What he means is she's a calculatin' woman," Clint said, silhouetted in the sitting room door.

Delilah looked up at him from her perch on the settee. His tall frame filled the doorway. He still wore the expensively tailored linen suit. The ruffled shirt, so common on the riverboats, usually made men appear effeminate. On him, it merely accentuated his masculine magnetism. "If your definition of calculating means that I possess the skill to best you at poker without resorting to palming cards—and that I drive a hard bargain in business—then, yes, I am a calculating woman indeed."

"I do believe you've met your match, Lightning Hand," Sky said gleefully.

Clint tried to think of one good reason he had not stayed in his cabin and drunk himself to sleep. For the life of him, he couldn't think of any. Except the obvious: He had to keep an eye on the two scheming females.

"Lightning Hand?" Delilah repeated, looking curiously at Clint. So much of his past remained shrouded in mystery. "Is that a name given to you by the Sioux?"

Clint tried not to snarl. "I earned it," was the terse reply. His eyes met Sky's with the unspoken command that she should let the rest remain buried with his past. He was relieved when she nodded slightly.

Sensing an undercurrent between Clint and his sister regarding his Indian name and his past, Horace leaped into the awkward silence to prevent Delilah from pressing their associate further about a subject he did not wish to discuss. "Clint told me earlier that your father had white blood. What of your mother, if you do not mind my asking."

Sky smiled. "Many people, red and white, notice my eyes. That's how I received my name. My mother was Swedish, an immigrant to this country, en route to Oregon on a wagon train when the Pawnee attacked. She was rescued by a hunting party led by my father. In time, they fell in love and married. She had golden hair, so took the name Sunrise. As a child I learned Swedish from her and English from my father, even though I considered myself wholly Sioux. When I was twelve, she died in a cholera epidemic. My father still mourns her loss."

"I am so sorry if I raised painful memories, child," Horace said as Delilah patted Sky's hand.

Sky shook her head. "No, I take joy in the years we shared. She was a remarkable woman. If I can be half the blessing to our people that she was, I will be grateful. Few men and women ever share the kind of bond my parents had." As she spoke, Sky glanced from Delilah to Clint, then back to Horace.

"Sky, you'll have your pick of men in Montana Territory, red or white. One will be right for you, just as Talks Wise was right for Sunrise," Clint said, diverting his matchmaking sister from further speculation about him and Delilah. Still, he couldn't resist taking a seat on the chair nearest Deelie. She smoothed her skirt and lifted it away, as if to avoid contamination. The woman had been skittish ever since the incident with the buttons. Damn his nimble fingers for unlooping a virtual Pandora's box that night!

As the conversation moved to other topics, Delilah grew increasingly aware of the man sitting so close to her. She could smell the faint scent of shaving soap, starched linen and male musk. Why did he have to be so infuriatingly attractive? Even the swelling around his eye had almost vanished. How did the devil manage that? Before she could stop herself, the words tumbled out. "Your eye's almost healed, but you had quite a shiner this morning. You should share the remedy with the rest of the crew."

He winked at Sky. "Ehanktonwon magic. The two of you can share medicine-woman information." *Lord help me, I know you'll share enough else to drive me to perdition before this trip's over.*

Chapter Nine

Clint had difficulty falling asleep. It was his first night aboard the *Nymph*. As soon as the last of the cargo was loaded, they would embark. But it was not excitement about the trip that kept him tossing and turning. It was the picture of Deelie and Sky conspiring together in that sitting room earlier. Sky had given her new friend several remedies from her Sioux people for everything from reducing swelling and healing bruises to setting broken bones.

If his little sister had been so inclined, she would have made a wonderful physician. But what their band really needed was someone well versed in the white man's ways. That had been why she had willingly left her home and family to spend the past seven years receiving the finest education his business enterprises enabled him to provide.

After being tutored by professors from Washington University in math, literature, geography and history, Sky had read law for the past two years with one of the finest attorneys in St. Louis. When the time came for the Ehanktonwon people to give up their land—and his foster father knew it would not be long—Sky could negotiate the best possible terms for them. The tribal leaders, for a change, would know what they were signing.

He chuckled, remembering when she'd browbeaten him into taking her to old Gemmer, who now owned Jake Hawken's gun shop. The craftsman had customized a Winchester Yellow Boy for her. And the brat became a crack rifle shot. Now she was a woman of considerable academic and practical knowledge.

His little sister's education was not what was keeping him tossing and turning tonight. It was her acumen at reading people, something her medicine-woman grandmother Little Foot had schooled her well in doing. She seemed to imagine Deelie was the woman he should marry. Even if he ever did marry again—and he had no intentions of taking that risk— he would certainly choose a more pliant wife than Delilah Raymond. Horace had glossed over her relationship with her first husband, only saying they had been young and his family had refused to take her in when she was widowed.

"Maybe they got to know her and decided she was too much of a shrew," he muttered to himself as he swung his long legs off the narrow bed and sat up, cradling his head in his hands. Damn beds were made for midgets. His feet hung over the end. As he started to pull on his breeches, he wondered idly how Horace slept; they were the same height. No use lying there staring at the ceiling. Maybe he should return to the Bud and wake up Eva.

Somehow the idea held little appeal. They had parted coolly this morning. She knew he had to return Sky upriver and had accepted that—until Delilah entered the picture. He'd kept the *Nymph* when he first won it to show off for his little sister. He'd planned to give her a ride home in high style on Red Riley's floating bordello—after redecorating to make it respectable, of course.

He'd never realized the cabins were so cramped, though. He felt claustrophobic in the small space. Perhaps some fresh night air would tire him sufficiently so he could sleep without having nightmares about what deviltry Deelie and Sky were cooking up. Or was it the pull of the past that tugged at him . . . the wild, unfettered life he had left behind when he'd brought Sky downriver for her education? A wave of darkness swept over him whenever he thought of living Sioux and what it had cost him. No. Never again.

Clint slipped on an old shirt and slid his gold cigar case into his pocket. He opened the door to let the cool, pungent air of the Mississippi fill his nostrils. Stepping onto the deck, he walked toward the stern to better see the night sky. He fired up an expensive cigar and took a deep, fragrant draw. Then, as he exhaled, he looked at the heavens. Even the Bud had turned out its lights by now. There was nothing to impede a full view of the myriad of stars filling the inky void.

"Not as many stars as we'll see upriver, but still splendid."

Sky's voice cut into his reverie. He turned and looked at her. She was dressed in a demure cotton wrapper that covered her modestly from throat to slippered feet. She looked the perfect lady . . . just as Deelie did. "You're up late. That pretty little head too busy cooking up schemes for you to sleep?"

A slow smile lit her face. "Why, Lightning Hand, why would you accuse me of such a thing?" Before he could remonstrate, she added, "I will never use your Ehanktonwon name in front of your white friends. . . ."

"Thank you."

"But you will have to explain it some day—to the woman you call Deelie. She hates the nickname, but then you know that. I suppose that's why you use it. To provoke her. Do you ever ask yourself why?"

"Do you ever ask yourself why you feel bound to stick that pretty nose into everyone else's business?" he asked, placing one finger on its tip with a teasing grin.

"I'm just naturally curious, but you haven't answered my question. Why do you antagonize Delilah?"

"Maybe because she's as touchy as a rattler with the piles. Ever think of that?"

Sky laughed, a rich, youthful sound. "What a crude thing to say about a lady, big brother."

"I notice you don't argue about whether or not the description fits her."

"She's antagonistic toward you because she's defending herself from the way you make her feel," Sky replied with the sangfroid of a woman of the world.

"Yeah, like wanting to kill me—that what you mean?"

"No, like wanting to share your bed."

His head snapped around and he choked on a lungful of cigar smoke. Coughing gave him time to gather his thoughts. "You're not supposed to think about things like that until you're older."

She shook her head patiently. "Lightning Hand, you know among our people I would already be married with several children by now. I know about how men and women become attracted to each other."

"Somehow I doubt they teach that in school or law offices."

"You are evading the issue, which is—"

He interrupted gruffly. "You sound like a lawyer."

Sky made a mock curtsey. "Why, thank you, sir. I do believe that was the intent when I came here to study."

"Well, you didn't study matchmaking, so can we discuss something besides Mrs. Raymond?"

Her expression changed from playful to serious. "Are you certain it's wise for you to return?"

He took another long drag on the cigar and considered. "You mean, will I stay and revert to what I was?"

"What you were," she replied gently, placing one hand on his arm and looking into his harshly set face, "was a man driven mad with grief. You've built a good life here. You could send me home with Mr. Mathers and the captain. They'll see me safely there."

"No. I need to do this, Sky." There was finality in his voice.

Sky knew the subject was closed. Giving him a sisterly pat on the back, she smiled. "I didn't expect you would change your mind. At least you'll have Mrs. Raymond to divert your wits . . . and other things."

He snorted and threw his cigar into the water.

Delilah could feel the hum. Below her their mate, Mr. Iversen, directed the last of the cargo loading. Roustabouts brought the crates up the gangplank and lashed them in place on the main deck under his stoic Norwegian gaze. Men swore and sweated in the hot spring sunlight. The stench of a hide and tallow factory wafted from up the hill, blending with the musky aroma of rotted driftwood and other offal disgorged on the levee.

Delilah had never experienced a more beautiful scene.

The river, swift and still deadly, had slowed enough for the *Nymph* to begin its long run. Tomorrow at dawn. She could feel the excitement dancing in the humid air and breathed deeply.

"Happy, child?" Horace asked as he looked down from their vantage point. He casually held the Colt revolving rifle in his right hand. Ever since Riley's men had attempted to sabotage their venture, he had assumed charge of the men hired to guard the cargo.

"I've never been this happy. We're off for Montana Territory to make our fortune, Uncle. We'll be respectable people of business—and think of the adventures we'll have!"

"Be mindful of the dangers we'll encounter. The captain's stories about river pirates, angry Indians, tornadoes and storms were not tales spun for our amusement. They were cautionary."

"I know, but if I could escape Red Riley's men, I can handle anything the Big Muddy throws at me," she replied, undaunted.

"As I seem to recall, for all your nimble actions, without Clint's help you would not have survived Riley's men," he said, dryly. In truth, when he'd heard the full story, he had been sick to think of how it could have ended if not for Daniels and his spy system on the riverfront.

Delilah bit her lip to keep from snapping at him. Between him and Sky she was driven to distraction. The two of them used every opportunity to play matchmaker. *A match made in hell.* "I will not allow thoughts of Red Riley or Clinton Daniels to ruin this wonderful day."

Horace put up his hand in surrender. "As you wish, my dear, but we do have dinner this evening with Captain Dubois . . . and our business partner Clint. We embark in the morning and I assume you will wish to have your say about our itinerary since you insisted on performing the clerking duties."

"I want to tally every piece of merchandise loaded and unloaded at every stop, not trust strangers . . . or Mr. Daniels," she said.

Horace sighed patiently. "Clint's trustworthiness aside, we are operating on a very strict budget with little to spare for extra crew—the fact of which you have reminded both of us. Repeatedly."

"I've merely been frugal. After this voyage I want to make enough profit to pay off our partner and be sole proprietors of the *Nymph*."

Horace made no reply, hoping that an utterly different sort of partnership would be in place between his niece and Clint before the end of the voyage.

The dining hall smelled of fresh lumber and paint. The cabins on the boiler deck had interior doors, allowing owners, officers and passengers indoor access to the dining hall for meals. A table at the far end accommodated the second pilot, Mr. Hagadorn, the mate, Mr. Iversen, and the first and second engineers, Belson and Kline.

At the opposite end of the room, the captain's table held Jacques Dubois, Clint, Sky, Horace and Delilah. While Beth and Sadie, Mrs. Colter's assistants, served the officers, Luellen and Todd placed steaming bowls of fried chicken, mashed potatoes and creamed peas in front of the owners, captain and their lone passenger. Delilah sat directly across from Clint in spite of her uncle and Sky's efforts to place them next to each other.

They had business to discuss and she could not afford the distraction of having him beside her, in his fancy ruffled shirt and dark blue suit. The man had more clothes than Beau Brummell, she thought crossly. He was freshly shaved. The golden stubble had been scraped away and his long, straight hair was still damp from his bath.

In spite of herself, she imagined the scent of soap and man that she'd smelled when he pulled her into his embrace that night. The night she'd almost permitted him to undress her in public, she reminded herself indignantly, returning her attention to the discussion of their stop in Hermann, where they would drop off farm implements and possibly take on passengers bound for the gold fields.

Before he took a sip from his glass of wine, Clint raised it in a silent salute to Delilah. Since the excitement of embarking had seized hold of her, she had forsaken her widow's weeds. Perhaps his answer to the challenge of her being buttoned up like a preacher's wife had convinced her it was a bad idea. He damned himself for the interlude but knew if offered the opportunity again, he would probably do the same thing.

And, oh, was she tempting tonight, in a pale gold silk gown that revealed just the smallest hint of the treasures he had felt the night he'd unlooped those buttons. Her hair, held up by jeweled combs, curled softly around her face. A simple cameo on a deep gold velvet band encircled her slender throat. The lanterns cast a warm glow on her silky skin and he smiled, noting that in spite of her parasols, a faint tracery of freckles dotted her nose. Soon the reflection of sun on the water would bring out more of them. She would look adorable—if a shrew could ever be considered adorable . . .

"We will stop at Pining's place for wood, about midday. Prices are good there and we can take on enough to reach our first night's berth just above St. Charles," the captain said.

"It seems a pity that's as far as we can go in a whole day," Delilah responded.

"We have to make wood stops twice a day and we'll moor up every night," Clint interjected. "Remember, Captain Dubois has never lost a boat. Traveling at boiler-bustin' speeds against fast currents and night runnin' have littered the Missouri with wrecks. No profit in that."

The way he pronounced *Missouri* as Missourah irritated Delilah. But not half so much as the way he continued to taunt her with subtle memories of the night outside her cabin. How could she have been so stupid? As if reading her mind, he paused and took another sip of wine, then raised his glass.

"Here's to a profitable partnership, Mrs. Raymond."

"Here, here," Horace seconded.

Delilah could do nothing but join in the toast with the others, even though she was acutely aware of Clint's mocking gaze directed at her.

"The river is high because of spring rain up north, but on our return, the summer snow melt will ease us down in excellent time," Dubois said. He sensed the undercurrent between his employers. He had been friends with Daniels for many years and had come to like the lady and her uncle. Although Horace Mathers and Clint appeared most cordial, Mrs. Raymond and Clint fenced verbally every time he overheard them.

Several times during dinner Mr. Mathers or Miss Sky jumped in to smooth things over. It was a puzzling development. Considering all the difficulty with Red Riley and gathering a crew, the captain already had enough to worry about. The business partners would have to work out their own accord. He accepted a second helping from the heaping platter of fresh chicken Todd offered. It wasn't New Orleans cuisine, but he was happy for the distraction of such excellent food.

After her uncle had retired for the night, Delilah took the cargo manifest from the writing table in their sitting room and began rechecking the items to be offloaded at their first stop. She'd kept her own tally as everything was loaded but found what appeared to be a discrepancy between her lists and those of Mr. Iversen. "I explicitly told that odious saloon owner we were not to carry whiskey," she said through gritted teeth.

But she would certainly not put it past him to have ordered the mate to load it under cover of darkness, as was the usual practice for hiding illegal cargo on the levee. Furiously, she yanked off her robe and night rail, then donned a simple cotton day dress. She was the majority owner of this boat and its cargo and by damn, she would carry no contraband. The army could confiscate their boat—even throw them in jail!

"I don't care how profitable selling whiskey to the miners is, we will not take that risk." She flung on a cloak and opened her cabin door. In minutes she was tiptoeing down the stairs to the main deck, being careful not to awaken the roustabouts sleeping on the forward part of the open floor. Little worry; they reeked of their last night on the town, drunkenly snoring. Beyond them the dark hulk of cargo was piled everywhere, from floor to ceiling, with only narrow aisles between crates, barrels and boxes. Although the moon was bright, she realized in her haste she had forgotten to bring a lantern to see among the narrow alleys.

Mumbling a curse, she turned to retrace her way along the railing to the stairs at the opposite end of the boat.

"Well, lookee here. Evenin', boss lady," a raspy voice whispered. It sounded like cracking ice.

Delilah saw a mountain of a man who stank of stale tobacco and sour sweat materialize out of the dark piles of cargo, blocking her return path. He was one of the new roustabouts the captain had been forced to hire when several of his regulars ended up with broken bones after a series of brawls. The men claimed they had been attacked deliberately. Dubois had tended to agree and placed the blame on Red Riley. Not only did Riley hate the captain because of his mixed blood, but he also had a score to settle with her.

And she had just played right into his hands, coming onto the deck in the dead of night without her Derringer. This was what her temper over Clint Daniels's trickery had wrought. She cursed them both. This ruffian could strangle her and drop her into the river and no one would ever find a trace of her body as it floated down to the Gulf.

Straightening up, Delilah gave him her most imperious look. "Yes, I am indeed your 'boss lady.' Go back to sleep and we will forget that this impertinence ever happened. Now, be so kind as to let me pass."

The roustabout did not move. Even in the dim moonlight, she could see how his yellow eyes swept over her, undressing her. She fought the urge to pull her cloak protectively around herself.

"I don't b'lieve I will."

"There are men all around this deck. I'll scream and they'll come running," she said in a level voice.

He chuckled malevolently. "Most is drunk, come staggerin' in from the bars and whores up on First Street so's Iversen could check 'em off his list. They's passed out cold. Upstairs, the muckity-mucks won't hear you."

Delilah feared he was right. "Do you work for Riley? If so, I'll double what he's paid you."

He appeared to consider her offer. "Dunno. Pissin' off Big Red's real dangerous. He wants you dead. A hunnert bucks worth. How much yew offerin' ta stay alive?"

That was when she saw the gleam from his belt, the blade of a big, ugly Bowie knife. She knew that no amount she proposed would work. But it might buy her time to bolt into the cargo aisle. Just as she started to jump, a voice came from the darkness behind her and the roustabout's eyes widened.

"Save your money, Deelie."

Clint stepped out of the shadows. He shoved her behind him. She could see he was half dressed, with his shirt hanging open as if he'd just slipped it on to take a late-night walk. He was also barefoot and unarmed. Still, the big man backed up, raising one hand as if in supplication.

"Watch out, Clint. He's got a knife!" Delilah screamed loud enough to crack plaster, but all she could hear in return was the faint snores of a drunk at the opposite end of the big boat. She searched for something to use as a weapon. The two men advanced on each other.

The giant had composed himself once he realized his opponent was unarmed. Now he grinned. "Red, he said ta take keer 'o yew, too. 'Nother hunnert. Didn't figger on luck 'nough ta git yew both at th' same time."

"You a bettin' man, rooster?" Clint asked, circling the brawny outstretched arm that held the knife, looking for an opening. "I make it seven to one you don't live to collect your pay from Riley."

"Seed yew kick Pack Wilson in th' knee thet day on th' levee. Busted him up real good. But yew ain't got no boots now. No gun neither." He made a swift slash with the knife, narrowly missing Clint's belly.

"Get Horace," Clint said to Delilah, never taking his eyes from his foe.

"I'm not leaving him to kill you."

"Should've thought of that before you went for a two A.M. stroll," he gritted out. "Go!"

As he spoke he jumped agilely to one side, maneuvering so she could slip past, using his body for cover. But Delilah continued to scan the deck. Then she saw what she wanted—but it was on the side nearest the roustabout. She dared not allow herself to be grabbed and used as a hostage, but she had to reach the long ax handle protruding from a pile of cargo covered by canvas. She darted into the aisle from which Clint had emerged and tried to figure a way around to the weapon.

Her sudden movement diverted the roustabout's attention for just a second. But that was all Daniels needed to move in and seize hold of the larger man's arm, twisting it upward while applying pressure on the wrist. The giant emitted a hiss of surprised pain. Clint's shoulder came in under the man's arm and he used it as a fulcrum. Daniels threw his foe over his shoulder. The roustabout landed directly at his feet with a loud thud. As he got to his hands and knees, Clint kicked the knife away from his grasp. It clattered toward the side of the boat, then plunked into the water.

Delilah could hear the sounds of the fight as she frantically circled the cargo. Unlike the warehouse, this was not arranged in neat rows but lashed haphazardly to the deck. She tripped in the darkness, clawing onto a splintery crate to keep from falling. *I have to get that ax!*

At last she saw dim moonlight on the opposite side of the deck and ran toward it, then around to where the sounds of the fight continued. She knelt by the ax handle and seized it, tugging with all her might to free it from the lashing. It barely moved, unlike the two men tumbling around on the deck. She saw no sign of the knife, which was good, but the roustabout was huge, dwarfing Clint's tall, lean body by at least three inches and seventy pounds.

Daniels rolled away from his attacker's attempted choke-hold and got to his feet only a second before his opponent. Clint used that time to land a hard right punch to his jaw, followed by a series of left jabs to his eyes and nose, staggering the roustabout backward. Daniels pursued, now landing a powerful blow to his opponent's throat, and followed up with a knee to his groin. The roustabout dropped like a stone into water.

This time he did not get up. He lay curled in a fetal ball, immobilized. Only then did Clint see Delilah, still struggling to pull an ax from the canvas. In spite of the night chill, he shook with red-hot fury. "You could've gotten us both killed, you damned little idiot!" he shouted, yanking her up from the floor.

"What about your seven-to-one odds that you'd whip him?" she asked, hating the crack in her voice. She could feel his hands tremble as he grabbed her by the upper arms and shook her until her teeth rattled.

"Do you have pasteboards between those pretty ears instead of brains? A woman alone and unarmed, walking around in the middle of the night aboard a steamer filled with drunken steamboaters—not to mention the stray assassin or two Riley's managed to plant aboard. Didn't you hear the captain explain how he'd had to hire men he didn't know and couldn't trust to fill our minimum quota?"

Her teeth kept chattering, whether from fear of their brush

with death or from the way he was glaring at her, she did not
know. He continued to shake her until her hair came loose
from its pins and fell around her shoulders. Then, realizing
what he was doing, he stopped . . . and reached up to lift a
gleaming fistful of curls, letting them fall like silken water
through his fingers.

"Clint—"

He muttered an oath and cupped her head, pulling her
against his body with his other arm. His mouth savaged hers.
No subtle, nuanced seduction, this. No, this was raw, primitive, lustful. An affirmation of life . . . and something more.
His hand pressed her jaw, literally prying open her lips for his
invading tongue. He slanted his head, shifting position, pressing her lower body against the straining erection in his
breeches. She could feel the arousal through the thin cloth
separating them and for a moment wondered if he would
throw her to the floor and rape her.

Delilah had never seen him lose control this way. It was . . .
savage. She pushed her hands against his chest, trying to get
free, writhing away from the bulge in his pants that probed
the vee of her legs.

Suddenly, he released her and she stumbled backward. Her
mouth burned from the abrasion of his whiskers. She raised
one hand to touch her lips and found that it was trembling.
All thoughts of the illegal whiskey had fled. She dared not
speak to him while he was in this state.

As he silently strode on bare feet to the unconscious
roustabout and knelt with a length of rope to tie him up, she
fled toward the stairs and the safety of her cabin.

Neither of them noticed the tall, thin form hidden in the
shadows, nor saw him uncock the Colt pocket revolver
gripped in his uninjured hand.

Chapter Ten

The air held the tang of spring and a warm breeze ruffled her hair, allowing it to blow gently around her shoulders. But Delilah did not notice. All she could think about was the man standing at the opposite end of the deck from her, talking with their first mate, Mr. Iversen. Clint Daniels wore a plain cotton shirt with the collar open and the sleeves rolled up, revealing the golden hair on his chest and arms. Heavy black twill breeches clad his long legs. His tall boots were scuffed and creased. Work boots!

The outfit was made for heavy labor, not lounging in a salon. He could have been a mate or engineer instead of part owner of the vessel. But he *was* a gambler. *He's ready to risk my boat for the quick profit from illegal whiskey.*

She had talked with her uncle earlier in the morning about the whiskey, but told him nothing of what had occurred between her and Daniels after Riley's man had been taken from the boat. Horace startled her by revealing that he knew about the contraband. "The intent of the law is to keep whiskey from falling into the hands of warring tribes along the river. The army cares nothing about sales to thirsty gold miners in Montana Territory. The worst that might happen is having to give a modest bribe to the inspector," he assured her.

"Just so long as the bribe money comes out of Mr. Daniels's pocket, not ours," she retorted.

"He has already agreed to that, my dear."

Delilah was not happy about the matter, but Mr. Iversen and the captain had both given her assurances that the profits were well worth the risks. The mate even showed her the ingenious method for hiding the whiskey barrels when inspectors came aboard, dropping them over the stern of the boat in rope nets so they'd be hidden beneath the paddle wheels.

She returned her thoughts to Clint, watching the breeze catch his hair. He shoved it from his forehead, gesturing to the cargo that had been stored on the hurricane deck in the space that had formerly been Riley's gambling salon, the very place where she had won the boat from Daniels. If he noticed her glaring at him, he gave no indication, but turned his attention back to Iversen. Clint didn't appear dangerous in the morning light. But he certainly had the preceding night. She had seen something in those glowing gray eyes that was savage—not the wildness of unbridled lust, but something . . . other. Just what it was, she could not guess, but it troubled her.

She was traveling nearly three thousand miles with a complete stranger. They would be in close proximity, unable to avoid each other unless she hid in her cabin like a mouse. That was something Delilah Mathers Raymond had not done since Lee and his Confederate forces invaded her town and destroyed it. But she had been a green seventeen-year-old girl then. Now she was a battle-hardened survivor . . . just as he was. But still she found her feelings toward him unsettling. What had turned him from her protector to her attacker?

In retrospect, she realized that it had been irresponsible of her to venture to the lower deck unarmed, in the dark of night. She and her uncle had speculated with Captain Dubois and—yes, Mr. Daniels—about the possibility that one or more of the replacement roustabouts he'd recruited might have been Riley's men. But that did not explain Daniels's actions once he had disposed of the man who'd tried to kill her. After fleeing upstairs, she had watched from her cabin window while he and Iversen hauled her attacker down the gangplank and up the levee. She suspected they had taken the man and dumped him on the doorstep of Riley's saloon.

Her troubling thoughts were suddenly interrupted by the noise and vibration of the steam engines being fired up in preparation for departure. The very floorboards beneath her feet seemed ready to jar apart. She stumbled and grabbed the railing to orient herself to the alien sensation. Her only other time on a steamer had been crossing the Gulf to New Orleans several years earlier for a high-stakes poker game. But that had been with placid seas aboard a huge side-wheeler. This felt totally different.

Placing her fear of Daniels and worries about the whiskey aside, she felt the excitement hum through her blood. It was time to cast off! She wanted to be in the wheelhouse with Captain Dubois, who had invited her to join him for a bird's-eye view of the river and levee as they departed. Carefully Delilah made her way to her cabin for a wrap. In spite of the warm day, once they were under full steam in the fast-moving current, the wind would be chilly.

Horace watched her enter her cabin and then shifted his gaze to Daniels. Their partner was not as uninterested in his niece as he had appeared to be a moment ago. After witnessing the scene on the main deck last night, Horace had to reassess whether his initial intuition about Clinton Daniels had been correct. The best way was to speak with the person who had known him the longest, the one dearest to him—his young sister Sky.

He would do just that. But first he wanted to witness their departure with his niece. He joined Delilah on her climb up to the small wheelhouse perched on top of the boiler deck. The small single room had windows on all four sides, allowing the pilot a 360-degree view of the treacherous river. Just as he called out to her, a shrill whistle pierced his eardrums. He watched her climb the steep stairs with cheeks flushed by excitement. For better or worse, they were on their way up-river with Clint. Now he only prayed it had not been a mistake to make the journey.

Delilah stood behind Captain Dubois after exchanging greetings with him, watching in rapt awe as the big paddle-wheel at the rear of the boat began to churn up the water. "The vibration is incredible. Is everything all right?" she asked.

Dubois smiled reassuringly. "This is perfectly normal. Only wait until we're in the main channel, forcing our way against the current. Then the vibrations will grow worse." At her look of dismay, he went on, "You will get used to it. My engineers are very careful not to overtax the boilers. Have no fear that the boat will explode."

Delilah sighed in relief. "If you say it's safe, then I have no fear." At least she had none about the boat. As to other matters . . .

Horace entered the Spartan wheelhouse and made a quick visual inspection as he greeted his niece and the captain. A small cot in one corner and an iron stove for heat in cold weather were the only furnishings. The centerpiece of the cramped quarters was the giant wooden-handled wheel facing the bow of the boat. "Do you sleep on that?" Horace gestured to the cot incredulously.

Jacques Dubois smiled. "I would only do so in extremity, I assure you, M'sieur Mathers. My second pilot is a man I've known for twenty years. With him spelling me, I am able to rest in my cabin. Having two pilots in the wheelhouse is a precaution when captains choose not to berth at night but travel by moonlight."

"I thought the river was too dangerous to do that," Delilah said, her uneasiness returning.

"Tut, I found the cot and ignored it. Neither I nor M'sieur Hagadorn intend to run by night. We will not be on the river in heavy rain either. One must see the serene surface of the Big Muddy to navigate safely."

Delilah looked out at the rushing water and did not see a trace of serenity in its unfathomable depths. And this was the Mississippi, known to be far safer than the Missouri! But she held her peace as gangplanks were pulled aboard, hawsers untied and coiled up. Everything was secured and ready. Captain Dubois tugged on the whistle, signaling the engineers below that the boat was backing away from the levee. As the spoon-shaped bow began its slow turn away from the shallows beneath the captain's skillful steersmanship, she could feel her excitement build again. Danger be damned! Clinton Daniels be damned, too! She was going to be a rich woman of business, independent and owing no man but her beloved uncle.

Horace watched as Dubois centered the boat's bow in the channel, pointed north to the confluence with the Missouri just above the city. When he looked down at Delilah's face, he could see triumph written all over it. If only things worked out as they planned . . . He excused himself and headed in search of Sky.

Sky carefully arranged her blue cotton skirt on the small settee in her cabin's sitting room as she looked over at Horace Mathers. "There is much you need to understand about my brother . . . you and your niece, although I doubt she's willing to confess her interest yet."

Horace suppressed a smile at the young woman's acumen. "No, Delilah can be . . . headstrong, but I've sensed her interest in our new business associate from their first meeting— and his in her. Initially, I believed it would work out well for both of them, but after last night . . ." He had already outlined what occurred after Clint had rescued Delilah from Riley's henchman.

"I am not certain it's my place to tell you everything. It would be best if Delilah heard the whole story from my brother. But I will say this: He is a good man who has endured much suffering. When he caught three soldiers under his command raping me and my older sister Teal, he rescued us. He told our father that he was shamed by the blue coat and would never wear it again. He became one of us and married Teal."

Horace's body moved ever so slightly, giving away his surprise. "He has a wife?"

Sky's expression darkened. "She is dead now . . . killed by a Pawnee raiding party while the men in our village were away hunting. After that, Clint's grief knew no bounds. He avenged her death by killing many of them." She shuddered. "It's for him to explain the rest."

"Is that why he's called Lightning Hand?"

Sky shook her head. "No, that was because he killed the three blue coats before they could fire a shot, although all were armed."

"He does have a reputation as a fast gun on the river," Horace said, turning over in his mind Clint's Southern drawl and trying to reconcile it with a blue uniform. He had a feeling that what Daniels had done to retaliate for his wife's death was better left unknown. Instead, he asked, "Was he a galvanized Yankee, perchance?"

Sky smiled now. "Yes. But that, too, is a story for him to tell," she replied enigmatically. "I have known him since I was eleven years old and, as I said, he is a good man. He brought me here and paid for my education."

"And now he's taking you home to your people."

She nodded. "Yes . . . but . . ." Her hands, clasped together, began to twist nervously. At once, she forced herself to relax and smooth her skirt again.

"But it would be better for him to return here, not remain with them?" he said gently.

Sky's blue eyes were dark and troubled, yet she smiled at Horace. "You, too, are a good man—and a very perceptive one as well, Uncle Horace."

"Thank you, child."

They pulled into a small outpost just below St. Charles to fuel up early that afternoon. The boat's hungry engines demanded huge quantities of wood to keep the boilers pushing steam through the pipes to drive the engine. When they tied up for the night, they would have burned most of the wood on board and would require another load. Delilah knew they were short of roustabouts, already having lost one, but she was surprised to see Clint stride ashore with the mate.

After a brief negotiation with the woodhawk, a tall, emaciated man in ragged leather breeches and a filthy flannel shirt, Daniels paid the fellow. But instead of returning to the deck, he joined the men loading bundles of wood on their backs and toting them up the gangplank to the open deck in front of the boilers. As sweat plastered his thin cotton shirt to his torso, his muscles were outlined, indecently appealing. Of course, all the other men were equally sweat-soaked but none held the slightest attraction for her.

Why him, of all the men on earth?

His straight, dark gold hair hung in lank damp hunks around his sun-darkened face. Now and then he'd stop and wipe the perspiration from his eyes with his forearm. Her mouth went dry just looking at the flexing glisten of his skin. She tried to remember how frightened she'd been of his fierce, brutal kiss last night, but in spite of it, she could not stop looking at him. Then, as if sensing her, he raised his head and locked gazes with her. His face was grim, his mouth an angry slash, as he continued up the gangplank with his burden.

Delilah turned and walked away, considering what his expression meant. Was he sorry for what he'd done? Or still furious with her for being on the main deck late at night? More likely the latter. She doubted if the arrogant lout had ever apologized for anything in his life.

Clint watched her stalk off. The sun caught the red highlights in her dark hair and the yellow dress she wore set off the faint golden glow of her skin. His groin tightened as her hips swayed with every step. Last night he'd nearly done something unforgivable. The woman drove him to distraction. Yet neither she nor he appeared able to control their attraction for each other. He muttered an oath and hurled his load of wood onto the pile in front of the boiler's steaming maw.

Why her, of all the women on earth?

Bathed, shaved and dressed in fresh clothing, Clint sat in the dining room of the *Nymph*, hunched over a table with a glass of Who Shot John in his hand. He looked down at the bourbon, then tossed it back, polishing off the glass. As he reached for the bottle, his sister's voice interrupted.

"Will that give you the courage to apologize to her? I

don't think you'll find it in the bottom of a bottle, Elder Brother."

He set the bottle back on the table and turned to her. "And what's that supposed to mean?"

"Uncle Horace told me what happened between you and Delilah last night. He heard the fight and came down just after you'd dealt with Riley's man."

"Great! Now he'll probably shoot me." Clint reached for the bottle again.

"I think not. He is an exceedingly good judge of character. He'll give you the benefit of the doubt . . . this time. But I wouldn't try his patience any further." She came over and took a seat across the table from Clint. "Put the bottle down and tell me what you're going to say to Delilah."

He did as she asked, then combed his fingers through his hair, muttering, "You're enjoying this, aren't you? Women!"

She placed her hand over his gently. "No, I am not. I can see when you're hurting and I understand why. Which is the reason you must apologize. If you didn't already know that yourself, you wouldn't be sitting here stewing."

He looked up, his expression grim. "She'll gloat. She'll probably throw things, maybe even use that little pea-shooter of hers on me."

"Better that than Uncle Horace's more formidable Colt," Sky said dryly.

"I'm only doing this because we're business partners and can't afford to be at each other's throats for the rest of the trip."

As he stood up and began to put on his jacket, which he'd hung across the back of his chair, Sky hid her smile. "Just so you make a handsome apology," was all she said.

"Yep, I'll use my Southern charm. We both know how much she likes that."

Like a man facing execution, Clint walked to Delilah's cabin and paused before the door. Dinner was in half an hour and he had to get this over with before they were forced to sit at a table together with her glaring daggers at him . . . or, fearfully looking away. No, she was too much woman to do that in spite of his abysmal behavior last night. He'd seen her watching him this afternoon. If she were afraid, she wouldn't have stood out on the deck and stared down at him as he toiled with the roustabouts.

Delilah Mathers Raymond was calm, brave and incredibly self-possessed—when she wasn't displaying the devil's own temper. Then bravery became reckless abandon. Somehow the vision of her with green eyes flashing and a gun in her hand ignited a fire deep in his belly. How in hell could he desire a woman he mostly wanted to strangle? Sighing in resignation, he raised his hand and knocked.

"I have something to say to you, Deelie. Please."

Inside, Delilah had heard his approach and peeked through the window curtains, watching as he stood motionless for several moments before he announced his presence. *I bet he choked on the* please *part.* Deelie, indeed! He was dressed in what she had come to think of as his gambler attire, an expensive dark suit, ruffled white shirt and polished black boots. He looked obscenely handsome. She made him wait for several more moments, then opened the door.

"Yes, Mr. Daniels?" she asked coolly, not inviting him to enter.

She wore one of her best gowns, a deep violet silk with a low neckline and clever cap sleeves. The neckline and skirt hem were trimmed with matching violet lace. She knew the cut of the dress emphasized her cleavage and small waist. As his eyes swept over her, she felt an odd frisson of excitement mixed with perversely pleasurable fear.

Clint glanced away from the incredible enticement of her body, checking up and down the walkway to be certain no one was near. "This is very personal business. It might be better if I spoke my piece in private." He gestured toward the sitting room behind her. "Unless you're afraid to let me in. I'd understand if—"

Delilah yanked open the door and spread her arm to indicate he should enter. "By all means, do come inside to 'speak your piece,' Mr. Daniels. I am *not* afraid of you." To emphasize that, she closed the door, even though she could smell whiskey on his breath. Then she walked purposefully to the settee and plunked herself down. It was that or fall down most ungracefully. Her knees and heart were pounding counter-rhythms as he stood in the center of the room, hat in hand.

He cleared his throat. "Look, what I did last night after the fight, it was abominable. I deeply regret losing my temper and hurting you. Please accept my apology."

"Handsomely done. Apology accepted, Mr. Daniels," she added with a half smile to calm her nerves. When he nodded and turned toward the door, she found herself blurting out, "Tell me, did it take a full bottle of contraband whiskey to work up your courage?"

His pale eyes bored into her when he turned back. For a moment, Delilah was afraid she'd pushed too far. In poker she'd done it. Now she was doing it again. And her aggressiveness always cost her dearly. When would she ever learn? She forced herself to stand up and face him in spite of her pounding heart. But he surprised her with a long, slow grin that spread across his face, adding to the sun creases at the corners of his eyes, revealing the startling whiteness of his teeth in that bronzed face.

"Nope. But it did take half a bottle."

With that, he tipped his hat and walked out the door.

She fought the urge to throw a handy statuette from the side table after him. Instead, she settled for a pillow from the settee. He wouldn't be able to hear it bounce off the door.

They settled into a routine as the steamer struggled mightily against the powerful Missouri currents. Tying up nights, and sometimes during the days when torrential spring rains came sweeping down, they were always forced to stop midday for loads of wood. Several times, when wooding stations were not nearby as the fuel grew low, the cautious Dubois had them pull over and the crew went ashore with axes and saws to chop dead falls for the voracious boilers. Clint always went with the men and returned as sweaty and disheveled as any of them.

Sky told Delilah after his first chopping foray that she'd had to treat his hands with herbal ointment because of blisters. His once-calloused palms had grown soft dealing cards in St. Louis. Clint's sister, along with Horace, had become intermediaries between the two, who spoke politely at dinner but avoided each other the rest of the time.

The *Nymph* dropped off cargo in Hermann, a small, bustling German settlement around a hundred miles upriver. The picturesque river town was situated on the bluffs in a heavily forested area that the industrious farmers were quickly taming to the plow. Vineyards stretched their long, twining branches in rows following the contours of the rolling hills. For the first time, Delilah left the steamer after finishing her tally of the goods unloaded and money collected for plows and other farm implements.

It felt good to plant her feet on solid ground, and the town was charming in an old-world way. Horace accompanied her and Sky on an excursion to the merchants on the main street. A dressmaker's shop caught her eye when Sky pointed out a gown in the window.

"It would be perfect for you, Delilah! Look at the color. Why, it matches your eyes exactly," she said, tugging her friend across the street.

"I already have several green dresses, Sky. I don't need any more, and besides, we can't afford—"

"Tut, my dear. If you want the dress, we can afford it," Horace said, taking her other arm.

Standing in the door of a beer hall down the street, Clint watched them coax Deelie into the dressmaker's place. He found himself wandering casually, too casually, nearer to that shop window. Before the proprietress removed the mannequin with the gown, he saw why they wanted her to buy it. The deep green velvet rippled with light, changing from almost black to vivid grass green.

Green as cat's eyes. He banished the thought, or tried to, then waited in the shadows across the street, watching to see what would happen. Soon Deelie emerged from a fitting-room door wearing the green velvet. At Sky's urging, she turned in a circle. There was some exchange between the seamstress and the potential customers. In a few moments, the trio left the shop sans dress.

Clint waited until they were out of sight down the busy street, then entered the shop, all the while cursing himself for a damned fool. A thick-set, gray-haired woman with wire-rimmed spectacles squinted as she smiled at him.

"What can I do for you, sir?" she inquired in a heavy German accent.

"That dress—" he gestured to the green velvet folded over the counter behind her—"why didn't the lady buy it?"

"Ach, first it cost too much, she said. Then the alterations I could not do before their boat leaves. Too many excuses to me it seemed for such a dress. Made just for her it was and her uncle, to buy it he offered, but no, no, said she." The old woman threw up her hands in disgust.

Obviously the gown must cost a pretty penny, but he'd seen the way Deelie had touched the fabric, the way it matched her eyes and set off the fire in her chestnut hair. "Tell you what, we leave in three hours, give or take, when the cargo's unloaded and passengers come aboard. Will you have time to take in the waist about so?" he asked, holding his hands in a small circle to indicate the size of Delilah's waist. "And let out the bodice about so?" Again, a gesture. "Length looked all right."

The German woman nodded. "Ya, and it is a good eye you have for the lady's measurements," she said with a mischievous grin. "Is she your *schatz?*"

"My fiancée? Lordy, no! Er, that is, well, let's just say I owe her one and am trying to make peace."

Her shrewd blue eyes now measured him as her grin widened. "And you are willing to pay how much extra for this peace, hmmm? I will have to close my shop and work without stopping."

Clint threw down a wad of bills on the counter beside the glistening velvet. "If you need more, just send the bill along with the dress to *The River Nymph* by three this afternoon."

"This I can do," she said, scooping up the money.

Clint ambled out of the shop, cursing himself for ten kinds of a fool. Deelie'd probably throw the damn gown into the Big Muddy before she'd give him the satisfaction of wearing it . . . unless he convinced Horace to lie and say he'd bought it for her.

He smiled grimly. Clinton Daniels was as good at manipulating people as he was cards . . . except for one contrary female.

Chapter Eleven

The days grew longer and the temperatures rose higher as they reached the twisty stretch of the river bordering Kansas. In spite of her antipathy toward Clint and her anger over the whiskey, Delilah greatly enjoyed Sky's company. Since her widowhood and the tragedy that followed, she had not had a woman friend. Although Sky was eight years her junior, she had seen much of life. Being of mixed blood, she had experienced prejudice just as Delilah had as a woman in her profession.

"It must have been terrible when your husband fell in battle," Sky said after her friend had mentioned Lawrence Raymond in passing conversation as they strolled along the hurricane deck one sunny afternoon.

Delilah appeared to consider for a moment. "It all seems so long ago . . . a lifetime, really. This will sound terrible, but there are times when I find it difficult to remember his face."

"That's only natural, considering everything you've been through. Among my father's people, men have always prepared to face death as part of our culture. Long before the whites came, nation warred against nation, even groups within a tribe raided and killed each other."

"I hope your education will help your people survive in a world where whites rule. It must have been very difficult, being alone in a big city all these years," Delilah said.

Sky smiled. "Oh, but I was never alone. Clint brought me here and paid for my schooling. He visited me often when I was at the ladies' academy, hired tutors for me and then arranged for me to read law." She paused, as if considering whether she should continue, then said, "Our lives have been rather analogous in a way—you with your uncle and I with my brother. Horace has been your protector and Clint has been mine."

Somehow the idea of Clint Daniels as a protector of female virtue seemed hard for Delilah to grasp. "You have remained in the respectable world while I have been forced far outside its pale, I fear—although certainly through no fault of Uncle Horace," she quickly added.

Her reply was an evasion and Sky knew it. "You believed the worst of my brother from the first time you met him, didn't you?"

Delilah could feel her cheeks heat. "I take it you heard the story about the poker game and its . . . er, aftermath."

With a mischievous smile, Sky replied, "All of St. Louis heard, although please don't tell Clint that I know he stripped naked in front of a lady."

"I scarcely qualify as a lady, but it was a clever maneuver on his part, the wily devil," Delilah said grudgingly. "After that debacle, I couldn't get a crew or do anything to operate the *Nymph* without his help."

"He can be trying at times, but as I told Uncle Horace, he is a good man." Sky was not certain how much of their conversation Horace had shared with his niece. "Did your uncle explain how he rescued me and my sister from the soldiers?"

Puzzled, Delilah shook her head. "No, only that your sister was his wife and she died. I'm so sorry for your loss."

A faraway expression washed over Sky's face. "My sister and I were raped by three blue coats under Clint's command. He was out on reconnaissance. When he returned and caught them, he killed all of them before they could fire a shot in return."

Delilah processed this startling information as she reached out and took Sky's hand in hers. "Oh, my dear friend, you've suffered far more than I ever did. Is . . . is that incident how he earned the name you first called him by—Lightning Hand?"

"He does not like to remember it, or any of the rest . . . after Teal died. He was a good husband to her. And I think he needs a wife now, even if he does not yet know it."

Wishing to divert Sky from that line of conversation, Delilah quickly asked, "He was in the Union army? But I thought he was a Confederate, or at least a sympathizer."

"Have you ever heard the term *Galvanized Yankee*?" Sky asked. When Delilah nodded, she went on, "Clint agreed to serve the Union out West in exchange for the repatriation of two men under his command who'd contracted tuberculosis as prisoners of war."

"That was a noble thing to do." Delilah hoped her doubt did not reveal itself in her tone.

"Yes, it was. There are many noble sides to my brother's personality that you don't know . . . yet." The gleam returned to Sky's eyes when she added, "But you will one day soon."

Fort Leavenworth's imposing stockade perched one hundred and fifty feet above the river on a high bluff, like a sentinel guarding the mighty Missouri from trespass. In spite of its martial purpose, the outpost was situated against a scenic backdrop. Stately elms covered the hilltop, promising shade from summer's heat, even though their spring buds had only now begun to open.

After Captain Dubois pulled the boat close to the shore, a hand-picked group of roosters quickly lowered the barrels of contraband whiskey over the starboard side in specially designed nets that would hide them under the now still paddle wheels at the stern.

Clint oversaw the process while the captain watched from the wheelhouse, keeping lookout for the army inspector coming down from the fort. Delilah paced nervously in her cabin, terrified that all their plans and dreams might be swept away in one brief moment.

"You're going to wear out that lovely hand-braided rug, child," Horace chided from the settee where he reclined. "Perhaps a tot of that whiskey might soothe your nerves."

She looked at the twinkle in his eyes and smiled in spite of herself. "You know I never drink anything stronger than sherry, and that only when I'm not working."

"These days, you appear to be working without respite," he replied, gesturing toward the neatly stacked piles of inventory listings on the small desk in the corner. "The captain tells me there is a lovely spot a few days upriver where we can stop for a picnic, providing that we continue making such excellent progress. The wildflowers are in bloom, and their color should create quite a scenic panorama from the bluffs above the Missouri."

Delilah gave an indelicate snort. "Providing we still have a boat in which to travel and aren't in federal custody, awaiting trial. Do you think the inspector will ask to see my cargo manifest?"

"I'm given to understand the inspections are fairly cursory, so I doubt it. But if they insist on seeing the manifest, I will deliver it to them without the page listing the whiskey barrels. You will not be involved, my dear."

"And what? Allow the army to carry you off in chains because Mr. Daniels insisted we carry contraband? No, if anyone is going to lie to the inspectors, let it be Clinton Daniels."

Horace watched her expression change as she chewed on her lip, turning over the situation in her mind. "Now, Delilah, what are you thinking?" he asked uneasily, knowing that look on her face often meant she was planning some deviltry.

"Perhaps it would be best if neither of you spoke with the inspector. I'll do it."

"Now, my dear—" Before Horace could remonstrate, he knew he was defeated. When Delilah made up her mind, nothing could change it.

"I'm the principal stockholder, and when need be you know I can charm birds from trees. Let us hope the inspector can fly."

Just then a hail sounded from the shore and they could hear men's voices below, welcoming aboard visitors. With one quick glance at the wall mirror to inspect her appearance, Delilah opened the door and stepped into the bright morning sunlight with Horace behind her.

Clint knew the minute he saw the little runt that they were in for trouble. The army inspector, a shave-tail lieutenant from West Point, walked up the gangplank as if he owned the boat. There was a scent about men who came from old money that Daniels could always smell. Usually it worked to his advantage—when he sat across from them at card tables. But this was not a game of chance. He remembered Delilah's fear and fury about the illegal whiskey. Judging from the look of self-righteous priggishness on Lieutenant Grayham Astor's face, Clint would've known bribery was not an option even if Captain Dubois had not recognized the young man from his last trip upriver.

"Good morning, Lieutenant," Clint said to the bandy-legged little man, being careful to conceal any trace of Southern accent, something he had trained himself to turn off and on at will, depending on circumstances. The little fellow wore a heavy mustache whose bright red color ill matched his auburn hair. *Probably thinks it makes him look like a grown-up.* "Welcome to *The River Nymph.* Can I offer you—"

"I'm here to inspect your cargo, sir, not socialize," Astor replied curtly. He was flanked by two well-armed soldiers who knew what they were supposed to do. They snapped to attention, then swarmed over the densely packed stacks of cargo like angry ants.

Delilah could sense the short, homely little man's imperious dislike of the tall, handsome gambler. She was glad she'd worn flat-heeled slippers, else the lieutenant would have had to look up to her, too. Never a good idea when appealing to male vanity. "I do declare, Mr. Daniels, where are your manners?" she asked, brushing past Clint to beam at the officer. "You must forgive my business associate, sir. My uncle and I are principal owners of this boat, and as such I should be the one to make you feel welcome. I am Mrs. Raymond."

Clint stepped back, admiring the way she worked on the

inspector's ego, batting her lashes flirtatiously as Astor saluted the back of her gloved hand and introduced himself. She wore a simple yellow dimity gown sprigged with tiny white flowers. Its low neckline revealed the golden, sun-kissed glow of her skin. She had tied back her hair with a yellow ribbon. Clint found himself imagining burying his hands in the thick cascade of chestnut-red curls falling down her back. Squelching the disturbing image, he listened as she spoke.

"This is our very first voyage up the Missouri, Lieutenant Astor. It is so frightening, the wide openness of all this land. And we've heard about terrible wild Indians and ghastly storms. You are so brave to serve your country out here."

Astor cleared his throat, bobbing his oversized head in agreement. "It is a difficult task, but one that duty compels me to perform. Meeting a beautiful lady such as you certainly lightens my burden, however."

Delilah tipped her head and smiled. "Ooh, you are the charming one. And so dashing in your uniform. Please allow me to offer you some tea. Our cook has just baked an apple pie this morning. She really is a jewel. I'm certain you'll enjoy it. Perhaps your men could have a piece, too . . . once they have completed their inspection."

"You do understand that we must search every boat for contraband," Astor said almost apologetically.

"Most certainly! Unthinkable for vile spirits ever to find their way to savages."

She looks about to have a case of the vapors. Clint hid his grin as she steered the enthralled officer to the bow of the *Nymph*. As they climbed the stairs to the hurricane deck and strolled toward the dining room, the indomitable Luellen would see that the aroma of apples and cinnamon quickly diverted the men below from their search. Clint would bet neither of them had tasted a piece of home-baked pie since they'd enlisted. The inspection would be cursory, indeed, thanks to his partner's cleverness.

In a few minutes, Luellen Colter was mothering the two soldiers, urging them to have seconds of the warm pie while

Delilah sipped tea with their peerless leader upstairs. Horace strolled toward the stern of the boat, where Clint stood with his arms casually crossed over his chest.

"By the time those two females are through, we'll be steaming safely upriver, cargo intact. Lord help a man faced with beauty and good cooking," Clint said.

Horace nodded. "I must confess that Mrs. Colter gave my niece the idea of diverting them with the pies she'd just taken from the oven. After filling their bellies, they dare not let the lieutenant know they wasted so much time that they could not complete their assignment with the thoroughness he doubtless expects."

"He doesn't strike me as the understanding sort," Clint said dryly.

An hour later Delilah and the smitten young Astor emerged from the dining room. Sure enough, his men reported that the cargo was all legal and everything shipshape. Luellen Colter, empty pie plate in hand, had already returned to her kitchen. Clint and Horace watched the lieutenant click his heels and kiss Delilah's hand again before strutting down the gangplank.

As she waved farewell to Astor, Clint walked over to her and said quietly, "If we run into any river pirates, you be sure to invite them in for tea. You'd have ole Bluebeard himself eatin' right out of your hand."

"My, now your accent has returned. You are a chameleon, Mr. Daniels, as changeable as Missouri weather."

"And you, Mrs. Raymond, are *more* changeable than Missourah weather, from cold-as-ice gamblin' lady to vaporing belle. Ever consider a career on the stage?"

"All the world's a stage, Mr. Daniels. I do what I must to survive. You would do well to remember that."

"You didn't finish the quote." Clint appeared to consider a moment, then recited, " 'All the world's a stage, and all the men and women merely players.' *As You Like It,* Act Two. Jacques goes on to say, 'One man in his time plays many parts.' You'd do well to remember that."

Puzzled and surprised, Delilah looked up into his pale blue eyes. "Quoting Shakespeare as well as my uncle. Since you possess such erudition, I assume your family was wealthy before the war."

Clint laughed without humor. "Hardly. My mother died when I was just a tadpole and my father was the town drunk. We weren't rich slaveholders."

"Then why did you fight for the secessionists?"

"When we first met, you were certain I never fought for any cause," he said, evading her question. "Have I risen in your esteem, Deelie?"

"Not esteem. I'm simply curious about a man of mystery," she replied, recalling Sky's words about his *noble* virtues.

He leaned closer to her, inhaling the fragrance of her hair as he placed both hands on the railing, trapping her between his arms. "Beware curiosity, Cat Eyes." Then before either of them could say more, the whistle sounded from the wheelhouse and the engines thrummed to life.

The sudden vibration caused Delilah to lose her balance and pitch against the hard wall of his chest. She felt his heartbeat and knew her own matched it when he smiled down at her, then chivalrously steadied her with his hands before stepping back. He sketched a slight bow and ambled away.

Delilah stifled the urge to stamp her foot, then realized that he'd never detect it over the vibration of the steam engine. *No, I'll not allow him to make me lose my temper . . . ever again.* Even as her mind formed the words, she knew she was lying to herself. Clint Daniels could make St. Peter swear.

The monotony of upriver travel continued as Nebraska and Iowa yielded mostly flat, desolate prairie and occasional homesteads interspersed with rolling hills and steep bluffs. In Nebraska City, Omaha and Council Bluffs they dropped off cargo and took on passengers bound for the gold fields. The current was swift, causing them to burn wood at a furious pace, but in spite of it, the captain guided the *Nymph* skillfully past clumps of driftwood and treacherous sawyers, huge tree trunks with one end tangled on the river bottom while the other bobbed up and down in the water as if waiting to rip the bottom out of an unwary boat.

About a day's journey below Sioux City, they made a wood stop in the area Horace had told Delilah about, where wild-flowers grew in rolling meadows surrounded by birch and oak trees. "I understand there's a perfect spot for a picnic be-yond that stand of timber," he said to his niece as the roosters headed ashore to load fuel from the woodhawk with whom Mr. Iversen had already struck a deal.

"We don't have time to waste picnicking," she replied, looking up from the constantly changing inventory lists.

When she rubbed her head and returned doggedly to the columns of figures, he remonstrated, "You need a bit of recreation. Those numbers will add up more easily—not to mention more accurately—when you're rested."

"I can rest in my bed tonight," she said stubbornly, scratch-ing out a figure with her pen and starting over again.

"Captain Dubois has already given the crew several hours off after the wood is loaded. It seems the engineers have to make some minor repairs to one of the boilers. We've made excellent time thus far, my dear. In fact, I've already taken the liberty of having Mrs. Colter prepare a repast for us."

"I suppose Mr. Daniels will be joining us," she said, know-ing he would, if for no other reason than to annoy her.

"So will your delightful companion, Miss Sky, and the cap-tain and his officers, once their duties are fulfilled. Mrs. Colter will serve as your chaperone," he added with a twin-kle in his eyes.

Tossing down her pen, she capitulated. Soon the jolly cook, Sky and Delilah were climbing the gentle rise from the river, walking in fields of flowers. Sky was like a child, eager to tell Delilah the names of every variety. "I've not seen a spring like this in seven years! Look, that's purple bull thistle. And the bright red is Cardinal flower! Over there—yellow sweet clover."

"What are the ones with gold-tipped petals and bright rust-colored centers?" Delilah asked.

"Blanket flowers," Sky answered. She turned in a circle, arms open wide, a look of radiant joy on her face.

"I must admit, short of horticultural conservatories back East, I've never seen such brilliant and varied flowers—and to think they just grow wild here." She could see that even Todd and second pilot Zeke Hagadorn, who carried the heavy picnic baskets for the women, were awed by the display.

The day was unusually warm for early May in Nebraska and the young women had both dressed accordingly in light colors of cotton, although Luellen held to a sensible gray blouse and black skirt. Sky looked radiant in bright yellow, and Delilah had chosen a pale lavender that turned her eyes a lighter shade of green.

"You gals match the wildflowers," Luellen said as Sky bent to snip a bunch of lavender chicory for the bouquet she planned to set on their picnic blanket.

"Mmm, that baked ham smells heavenly. Do we have to share with the men?" Sky asked as Delilah laughed.

"Uncle Horace, for all his thinness, can eat his weight. Best not to deprive him. I imagine your brother will want his share as well." Delilah paused to wipe a thin sheen of perspiration from her forehead with a lacy square of white linen.

"All the menfolk've worked right hard. That's why we can take time for this here party," Luellen said. "Why, my Todd's a skinny 'un, too, but, lordy, can that boy eat!"

"I don't see how you can keep up with all the cooking for such a large, hungry group of men with only Beth and Sadie to help you," Sky said as she inspected her bright array of flowers. "And the kitchen fires are almost as hot as the boiler room."

Luellen shrugged her plump shoulders. "Heat never bothered me. Where are them girls? I tole 'em to git up here pronto 'n help me set out the food."

The two sturdy young women appeared as if summoned,

dashing through the wildflower meadow, giggling like children. Todd called to Sadie, "Lookee up yonder. On the crest
'o the hill. A level place in the shade 'o thet oak." Then remembering that it was his aunt who was in charge, not the
pretty little Irish cook's helper, he turned to Luellen. "It's
perfect fer a picnic, ain't it?" She trundled toward him, leaving Delilah and Sky to their flower-gathering.

"Coming from Pennsylvania, I'm afraid this river humidity
bothers me," Delilah confessed as she dabbed at her neck and
forehead again.

"I remember this place. On our journey to St. Louis we
camped here," Sky said. "Behind that stand of birch trees,
there's a hidden pool of spring-fed water." She pointed to a
hill in the distance. "We camped there for a couple of nights
while my brother hunted antelope to resupply our larder. I
remember swimming in cool, clear water. Wouldn't that be
fun? Oh, I still forget after all my years in school—ladies
don't learn to swim, do they?"

"I'm no lady, remember?" Delilah said, this time light-
heartedly. Suddenly life seemed filled with possibilities as
limitless as the vast blue sky overhead. "I did learn to swim,
and a dip in a clear, cool pool sounds heavenly! Baths using
muddy river water have not been exactly satisfactory. Oh, but
we'll need someone to serve as lookout while we're in the
water. There'll be men all around, and we wouldn't want
them spying on us."

Sky nodded, the nibble of an idea beginning to form in
her mind. "I think Luellen would be happy to oblige. And
what man would dare to cross her? After all, she could
threaten to feed them fried rocks."

"A real threat, considering how excellent a cook she is,"
Delilah replied. Then an unsettling thought occurred to her.
"Do you think your brother remembers the pool?" She
would not put it past the lout to spy on her in the privacy of
her bathtub, much less out in the open. He was slippery
enough to find a way past Luellen, too. After all, he'd lived

with the Indians for years. Maybe the swim was not such a good idea after all.

"I doubt he'd remember. He was too busy hunting. Anyway, he would never spy on me—or you either," she quickly added. Delilah could not see her fingers crossed behind her back as she uttered the words.

Under Luellen's watchful eye, Todd and Zeke laid out the blankets, and then Beth and Sadie unpacked the feast of baked ham, sweet and sour potato salad, bread fresh from the oven with butter and peach preserves, home-cured dill pickles and an array of layer cakes, including chocolate and spice, all slathered with rich creamy icing.

Delilah sat beside her uncle and cut a slice of fork-tender ham, trying not to watch Clint as he stood talking to Captain Dubois about the next leg of their journey and the dangers they might encounter along the way. Daniels towered over the diminutive pilot and looked utterly at ease as he leaned against the trunk of the big oak tree, a plate in one hand, a fork in the other. He threw back his head and laughed at some bon mot from Dubois, allowing a shock of straight, straw-colored hair to fall across his forehead.

The other men had Todd barber their hair, but it seemed the farther upriver they went, the more Daniels let go of the trappings of civilization. His hair was growing longer with the passing of every week, now reaching his broad shoulders. He wore buckskin breeches with fringe down the side seams. His open shirt of coarse blue cotton had the sleeves rolled up. Most of his chest was visible, and she remembered the feel of that crisp gold hair against her hands and bosom. *Don't think about that!*

She lowered her lashes and took another bite of the meat, but her appetite had fled, damn the man. To complete his savage ensemble, Delilah could see he'd given up his scuffed work boots in favor of moccasins. *So much better to sneak up on you, my dear.* In spite of the irritating thought, she could barely tear her gaze away from the soft tan leather molded to his long legs. All he needed was some war paint and earrings and he'd be Lightning Hand, Ehanktonwon warrior, again.

"He looks different, I must confess," Horace said, as if intuiting her thoughts. "But the clothing is practical, since he's taken on the responsibility of hunting wild game for our table. The venison we had last evening was quite tasty, if I do say so myself."

"This from a man who's vowed never to shoot an animal in his life," Delilah replied, trying for a light tone in spite of her irritation.

"I have never turned my hand against a pig or cow, yet I've always had passing fondness for pork and beef," he replied. "The idea of wild meat never appealed . . . until now, do you not agree?"

Delilah almost dropped her plate. Of course her erudite and genteel uncle would never use bawdy double entendres in her presence! What was she thinking? What was that man across the way making *her* think? It was all his fault, not her dear uncle's.

Somehow Delilah managed to eat most of what was on her plate, although she declined the rich cake that everyone else exclaimed over. Even sitting in the shade, she was burning up as the midday temperature climbed. Dare she and Sky go to that pool? It was insanely risky. Why, some wild Indians could come along and kidnap them! No, all the natives this far downriver had already been killed or herded onto reservations far to the north and west. It was perfectly safe as long as they had someone trustworthy to stand watch while they bathed.

After everyone was finished with the repast, the captain and his officers excused themselves to return to the *Nymph*. The boiler repair was important if they were to continue safely on their way upriver and not lose a significant amount of time rebuilding the troublesome machinery. Horace decided to return to his cabin for an afternoon nap. When Clint said he wanted to discuss something with the first mate back at the boat, that left only the women and Todd.

"Now we can go for that swim," Sky whispered to Delilah.

Before she could reply, Luellen gave some instructions to her nephew and the girls about packing up the baskets, then walked over to where Delilah and Sky were sitting. "I reckon it would be right fun to set a spell more, but we got us a whole passel 'o work for tonight's dinner, makin' a venison stew. Yew young 'uns stay and talk some girl talk. Cap'n says it's safe 'nough hereabouts."

Delilah sighed as she herded Todd and the maids down the hill. "So much for our chaperone and lookout."

"We don't need anyone to watch over us. She's right—no one's around for miles except for the men on the boat, and they're all going to be busy. Besides, who'll know if we slip away and cool off in the water?"

"You should've been named Lilith instead of Sky Eyes," Delilah said with a grin. "All right, let's do it!"

They waited until everyone was out of sight. Then Sky led the way through the birch trees and around a blackberry thicket. "A pity it's too early for the berries," she said as they passed by and neared the pool. "I'd love a big hunk of blackberry pie right now."

"How do you stay so slender and eat the way you do? You had two pieces of cake."

"And you didn't have any," Sky replied as she kicked off her soft slippers, peeled down her hose and started to unfasten the buttons on her dress. "Last one in has to sit next to my brother tonight for dinner!" she dared Delilah.

Her friend quickly began stripping off her clothing. Did everyone aboard the boat know how she tried to avoid Clint Daniels? She stopped shedding garments when she reached her chemise and pantalets. Sky was stripping completely, innocent as a baby in her nakedness.

"No fair! You have to take everything off," she cried as Delilah beat her to the water by a second, then jerked her foot back when it touched the icy cold.

"Just plunge in and it'll feel much better. That's the way

my people do it. See, over there is the deep end. You can dive from that rock. I did and the water wasn't as high as it is now. I dare you!"

"Just because I'm an Easterner doesn't mean I'm afraid of catching a chill!" Delilah let out a shriek of laughter, feeling like a twelve-year-old girl again as she dashed to the rock and leaped. The cold took her breath away for an instant, but then she shook her head and began to swim across the pool. The warm sunlight filtering through the trees combined with vigorous exercise made her forget the chill. "This is fabulous. I wish I'd brought soap to wash my hair. I could probably lose a pound of river mud."

"Too bad we didn't think of it," Sky said as she jumped after Delilah. They bathed, splashing and swimming like a pair of sleek young otters. Then suddenly, Sky cried out and swam quickly to the shallows, where she sat down.

"What's wrong?" Delilah asked.

"Just a cramp. I ate too much cake. This always happens. I should've known better, but Luellen's cakes are hard to resist."

"We should go back—"

"No! That is, I'll be fine. This has happened to me ever since I was a little girl. All I need to do is walk for a bit and it'll go away. You stay and finish your swim. I'll take my time, then return to the boat."

Delilah climbed out of the water, her undergarments dripping water. "I insist on seeing you safely back."

"You should've done as I did and taken off everything. If you try to put on your dress now, it'll be soaked. Everyone will know you were swimming. Stay and dry off in the sun." Sky quickly wrung out her heavy mane of straight black hair and skillfully plaited it into a long braid, then slipped into her clothing. "By the time I get to the boat, no one will know I was ever wet."

With her naturally curly hair untamable while wet, Delilah knew Sky was right. "Are you certain you'll be safe to walk that far?"

"A lot safer than strolling some of the streets in St. Louis," she replied, and started off at a slow pace. As soon as she was out of Delilah's sight, she picked up her skirt and began to dash down the hill.

Chapter Twelve

Clint was playing an idle hand of cards with Sam Belson, the first engineer, when Sky reached the boat. She sauntered casually by the table with a sly expression on her face. "You should be ashamed of yourself, taking honest men's money." She turned her attention to the engineer. "Do you know, Mr. Belson, that he's a professional gambler who owns a saloon back in St. Louis?"

She was certain Belson, who hailed from St. Genevieve, had never heard of the Blasted Bud or its owner before he signed on with Captain Dubois the preceding year. He gave a snort and pulled a ragged red handkerchief from his back pocket to blow his nose.

"Can't rightly say I did, but since't I been beatin' him, I reckon he better find a new line 'o work."

"He's just letting you win at first to learn your tells," she said to the older man, whose seamed red face bore witness to how he earned his livelihood.

Clint tossed down his cards and glared at Sky. "We weren't playing for money, just matchsticks. A man's gotta stay in practice, after all. When I get back to St. Louis, I'll have to go to work again."

"Speakin' of work, capt'n'll be wantin' me ta check the boilers. Have to fire 'em up in a couple 'a hours." He grinned at Clint. "I could tell you was a gamblin' man, but like you say, a feller's gotta practice."

After tipping his battered cap at Sky, he walked over to the giant maw of a boiler and yelled to the unfortunate crewman assigned to shovel out the accumulation of river mud left behind when the water was turned into steam. After a brief consultation, he shrugged and told Clint, "Be a while. Got a lot of muck to go yet."

"Captain Dubois won't like the delay," Clint said almost to himself, then noticed that Sky had returned to the boat alone. "Say, where's Deelie?"

"Oh, she must've sneaked by you and returned to her cabin. You know she's avoiding you, Clint."

"As if I had typhoid fever," he replied glumly. "What were you doing all this time?"

"I stayed behind and went for a swim," she said, running a hand over her sleek, still-damp hair.

He looked at her slightly rumpled clothing and noticed that her hair was now down in a plait instead of up in the elaborate chignon she'd worn earlier. "You look cool and content."

"That's because I am. Remember the spring-fed pool we found on our way to St. Louis? I recognized the landmarks when we pulled over for the picnic. It was a perfect day for a swim." She eyed the trickles of sweat running down his face and neck. *Let this work!*

"Yeah, I do remember it." He looked over to where the two engineers were conferring about cleaning out the boilers and knew there was plenty of time. "Maybe I'll go for a dip myself." He paused and gave her a stern look. "And next time, keep your pretty little nose out of my card games. I'd never take advantage of an employee."

"I'm sorry, Clint. I should've known that," she said with false contrition. As soon as he walked toward the gangplank, whistling to himself, a big smile spread across her face.

Clint's long legs ate up the climb through the meadow. He quickly reached the woods and made his way on moccasined feet through the spring greenery. That was when he heard the sound of a woman humming and froze. Instantly, he recognized Delilah's low, whiskey voice. *Sky, I'm gonna yank every last strand of lovely black hair off your scalp!* She'd set a trap and he'd almost fallen into it. She and Deelie must have been swimming together and she'd come back to the boat to lure him here. He'd bet the Blasted Bud itself that Mrs. Raymond had no idea how close she'd come to having him see her in the all-together.

He started to turn around and backtrack before she spotted him through the leafy cover of trees and brush. That was when he caught sight of her backside. Lordy, she was perched like a mermaid on a rock, finger combing her long hair, spreading it like a fan in an attempt to dry it. Her hair was still damp, but his mouth had suddenly gone very dry indeed. Vivid reddish highlights danced in the silky chestnut strands as dappled sunlight shone through the trees.

Her lavender gown and undergarments were carefully spread on the ground by the side of the pool, the dress and petticoats dry but the translucent silky unmentionables still wet. He grinned. He'd bet Sky had swum mother naked, but the proper Mrs. Raymond's modesty wouldn't allow that. Clint stroked his jaw, wondering if any man—including her bridegroom—had seen her bare skin.

I bet they spent their honeymoon under the covers, both of them in nightclothes. Not the way he would ever do it. How could any man resist the creamy smooth skin he saw through the curtain of her hair? The curve of her spine was supple, her waist tiny and buttocks lush. If only she'd turn so he could see those glorious breasts he'd lain awake fantasizing about for weeks. His eyes strayed again to the clothes set out so neatly on the grass. Nope, no corset. But he could envision the sheer silk of that chemise clinging translucently to her skin.

Just then, she swept her hair over one shoulder and twisted her body around to let it hang free. One pert, high breast came into profile, the pink nipple standing at attention as her still-damp hair brushed over it. He stifled a groan and felt himself hardening to the point of bursting. A good thing he'd worn buckskin breeches, cloth would never have withstood the pressure. Sweat beaded his forehead, this time having little to do with the outside temperature. He felt as hot as one of the *Nymph's* boilers at full steam!

Clint knew this was wrong. He was watching her like some peeping Tom. It was depraved and despicable and most ungentlemanly to spy on a lady. Then he remembered how often she'd reminded him that he was no gentleman and she was no lady. *Maybe depraved and despicable aren't all that bad.* Still, if she caught him, she'd be furious—and who knew? She just might have that little gun hidden somewhere in her clothing. Glancing down, he could see that he was certainly providing her with a large enough target to shoot at.

Time to turn around and backtrack out of here. Clint actually took a couple of steps away before the sound of her screech froze him. When he turned around, he could see her jump up and leap into the water. What the hell was wrong? He drew his Colt and scanned the surrounding woods to be certain no intruder—animal or human—was threatening her. Nothing. Then he saw it. A very startled raccoon crouched in terror beside her clothing.

Before he could stop it, the laughter burst out of him. He doubled over as tension-purging guffaws overcame him. "It's . . . a coon . . . Deelie. They're . . . just naturally curious," he finally managed to get out.

Even though she couldn't see the bounder, Delilah recognized his voice as soon as he uttered the first word. She slipped into the water, up to her neck, hair floating around her like a halo. So much for drying it before returning to the boat! "How dare you spy on me like a common voyeur, you wretched pervert, you evil emissary of Satan! You . . . you chamberpot with ears!" she finally sputtered as he emerged from the brush holding his lethal-looking sidearm.

"Do you intend to shoot me or that—that wild creature?" she asked through gritted teeth.

He slid the Colt back into its holster and crossed his arms. "The coon's harmless. You scared him more than he scared you," he replied as the masked bandit made off with her lavender hair ribbon in his teeth.

"That ribbon matches my dress and I looked all over Boston to find it." She took a step toward the shallows before realizing she was naked and Clint Daniels was standing alarmingly close to the water. Delilah could feel his eyes burning her skin—her bare, naked skin. Immediately she sank back into the deeper water. "Go away. Shoo just like that . . . that coon creature you frightened off."

Instead, his gaze locked with hers, pale blue and jade green. Without another word, he unfastened the buckle of his gun belt and dropped it on the grass, then tugged his shirt over his head in one swipe. The muscles in his arms and chest rippled as he tossed it on top of the weapon.

"What do you think you're doing?" she demanded in the calmest voice she could muster, proud that it did not wobble . . . too much.

"Protectin' you, darlin' . . . from snapping turtles. Once one of those big suckers clamps onto something, they never let go."

Delilah looked frantically around the pool. "Turtles? Snapping?"

Clint laughed again. "It was only a joke, Deelie. I just came to take a swim on a hot day, same as you."

"B-but you can't," she protested. The wobble was back, worse than ever, as he began to unfasten the fly of his leather breeches. He'd already kicked off the moccasins. "You sneaked up to spy on me—deliberately! Not to swim."

"Nope. My dear little sister reminded me about this pool and suggested a swim would be a good idea. Said you were in your cabin," he replied matter-of-factly.

"I don't believe she'd do something so . . . so . . ." Her voice faded away as she recalled the way Sky had arranged everything. It was true.

"You don't know her like I do. She may be all grown-up now, but some day her husband's gonna have to give her a good paddlin'." As he spoke, he struggled to remove his breeches, which had become extremely uncomfortable. "Only thing that'll cool me off now is being drenched in ice water. We both better hope it's cold enough to do the job," he said as the pants finally slid free.

Delilah could not tear her eyes from him. Or the size of the erect male member that sprang free when the pants dropped. His body was bronze; the hair on his chest and forearms, bleached pale gold by the sun, contrasted with the darker gold nest surrounding that magnificent specimen of masculinity. Had Lawrence been that big? They'd only consummated their marriage twice, both times in darkness, with him in a long nightshirt. Delilah doubted it, even though it had been damnably uncomfortable and awkward.

She gave herself a mental shake and started to backpedal away from Clint as he walked unconcernedly to the diving rock. How dreadfully disloyal of her to make such comparisons between her lawful husband and this rapscallion! Life in gambling salons had made her as crude as Eva St. Clair, even if she had never slept with any man she met there.

"I'll get out if you get in," she said, immediately realizing how that sounded.

His grin indicated he understood the double entendre. "Oh, I'll plunge in, but I doubt you'll want me to get out after I do."

With that arrogant remark, he dived into the water and began swimming around the large pool, seemingly ignoring her. Standing still, she began to shiver, but it was not from the cold water. Deep in her belly she could feel tingling warmth. And something else, that elusive, magnetic attraction to this man, unsuitable, indeed detestable as she found him on every possible level . . . except one.

But that was utterly unexplainable, because she'd never enjoyed making love with Lawrence, had not honestly even participated in the act. Or been tempted to repeat it with any other man—until now. Still, the insidious heat built inside her body and brain. Maybe she was coming down with a summer ague.

Clint felt the icy water close over his head, broke the surface and started to swim furiously, as if a whole horde of snapping turtles were chasing him through the water. But he could not rid himself of the ache in his groin. All he could think of was the woman standing in the water, arms wrapped around her lush body, hair floating like russet silk on the water, wide green eyes following his every move. Damn her! Damn Sky! Damn Red Riley for starting this whole mess in the first place by importing a female card shark to steal his boat!

"Last chance to get away, Cat Eyes," he found himself saying as he cut through the water. It was either let her go or take her, and soon. His body was near to bursting with desire.

"How can I leave with you watching me?" she asked, trying to sound reasonable. That was difficult because she couldn't take her eyes away from his powerful shoulders as his arms cut cleanly through the water and his thick hair fell in an unruly shock over his forehead. On their second encounter she had sunk her hands into that hair and bitten him. Now she wanted to seize fistfuls of it and kiss him. Kiss him and never stop.

"I won't watch. Word of honor," he called out, but he had rounded the opposite side of the pool and was heading in her direction now.

"As if I place any credence in the honor of a gambler."

"Takes another one to know, doesn't it?"

Suddenly he was directly in front of her, standing up in what was barely chest-deep water a few feet away from her. Droplets trickled over his pectoral muscles and became trapped in the golden hair. Delilah could think of nothing more to say. Perhaps this had been inevitable ever since the first night she'd met him aboard the *Nymph*. She had detested his drawling charm so much that she'd allowed emotion to cloud her judgment at the table, something that had never occurred before.

Clint watched various emotions fleetingly pass through those cat's eyes and wished to hell he knew what they meant. "I won't do anything you don't want me to do, Deelie," he said hoarsely, not certain if he could keep his word with her standing so close, so naked and enticing it was driving him insane with want.

Each of them was surprised when the other took a step

forward. But neither retreated. "Come ahead, Clint," she said with what sounded almost as if it were resignation. She raised her hands and reached out to him.

"This wouldn't be a replay of what happened at the Bud, would it?"

"No tricks . . . except for the one Sky played on both of us," she whispered as he extended one large, warm hand and grasped her slender wrist, gently pulling her to him.

She went into his arms, raising her own around his broad shoulders. He pressed her body against his and cupped her soft buttocks in his hands, lifting her in the water while he bent his head down to kiss her. Delilah dug her fingers into the hardness of his muscles, tiptoeing to reach his mouth. The warmth built in her when she felt that hard staff press against the vee of her legs. It seemed the most natural thing on earth to roll her pelvis . . . and feel his big, powerful body tremble. That was only fair since she was trembling, too.

Delilah anticipated the kiss, remembering the other ones they had shared. The one in the warehouse had been fierce but life-affirming. Outside her cabin she had been too appalled by her own passion to allow his seduction. After he'd saved her from Riley's killer, he had taken her lips roughly, frightening her with savage anger. How would this time be? Oddly, she was beyond caring, ready for anything, yet relieved when he brushed her mouth softly. Then he traced the seam between her lips with the tip of his tongue, as if asking permission to enter. She opened for him and he tasted her. She returned the delicious invasion, and their tongues dueled in a delightful dance that only increased their hunger for more.

Clint slanted his mouth across hers, changing the angle, cupping the back of her head in one hand as the other roamed up and down her spine, tracing the delicate vertebrae, lingering at the deep indentation before her derrière flared. He played her like a Stradivarius. Music sang through her body while she writhed against him, drawing him closer, feeling the delicious abrasion of crisp chest hair against her pebbled nipples. There was something more . . . more, and Delilah knew she must have it—have Clinton Daniels—in a way she could never have imagined before he strode into her life.

Her small, low moans and little gasps of surprised pleasure nearly drove him mad. Again, some subliminal part of his mind wondered just how much experience—or how little— she had had during her brief marriage. Instinct told him to go slow. His mouth moved from hers, trailing soft, wet kisses down the arch of her throat while he lifted her higher so he could reach those tantalizing breasts that teased and enticed him. The breasts of his imagining. He had never forgotten them since she had first taken a seat across the poker table from him.

No wonder I lost almost every hand. All I could think about was this!

When Clint took one hardened pink nipple in his mouth and suckled it, Delilah felt the jolt shoot all the way to her toes. She buried her fingers in his long, thick hair and arched closer, wrapping her legs around his narrow hips. His erection jutted beneath her, rubbing a newly sensitized area of her body, a place she could never have imagined would welcome a man.

Feeling her squirm against him, Clint could barely restrain himself, but this was not the time to rush. He moved his attention from one breast to the other, murmuring, "I knew they'd be beautiful."

Clint walked slowly toward the edge of the water, carrying her to the soft grass beneath the trees. Very slowly, he let her slide down his body, still pressing her close to him. He looked down into her eyes and read confusion—and hunger. Unasked, she answered his question. "Yes, Clint," was all she said.

That was all he needed to hear. He knelt and laid her on warm spring grass, then followed her down, taking her into his arms. She came eagerly, rubbing her face against his chest, clutching his shoulders, her nails digging into his skin. He took her chin in one hand and tipped it up for another long, slow kiss that had them both moaning, then moved his attention to her breasts again, loving the way her body unconsciously arched each time he lowered his head to lave and suck a nipple. She was learning an ancient rhythm, one she had not known before.

He moved over her, holding his weight on his elbows, whispering, "Open your legs, Deelie," as he gently probed with his aching staff. But he would be its master and would not simply plunder her warmth and beauty. It would take extreme care and concentration. But he had done that once before . . . with Teal. No! He would not think of her now. The memory was too painful, and Delilah deserved better than a comparison to his dead wife.

Delilah complied with his command. In truth, her legs seemed to open of their own volition, welcoming his invasion. If the price of all the pleasure she had just experienced was pain at the end, it would still be worth it. She wanted him inside her body, no matter the cost. She wanted this joining, unsanctioned by wedlock though it was. Perhaps she had been destined for it since the loss of her comfortable existence in the wealthy Mathers family. Mrs. Raymond was a gambler . . . and this was the greatest risk of her career.

Clint teased the wet opening to her feminine core, waiting for her response before he moved further. Her body tensed, but when he did not immediately plunge in, he could feel her lift her hips in unconscious supplication. He kissed her again, softly, tenderly, while the tip of his rigid staff circled and teased the sensitive opening it craved. When he could stand not another instant of waiting and knew she was ready, he began a slow, careful penetration. She was slick and hot, incredibly tight. Yet he could not rush this.

Delilah felt his hardness teasing her, awakening a fierce hunger, one she had never imagined she would experience. She could also sense he was holding back, waiting for her to prepare for the final onslaught. Better to have done. She released a warm hiss of breath and kissed him fiercely, lifting her hips and wrapping her legs around his waist. With a gasp of pleasure he sank deeper, stretching flesh so long untried.

She expected it to hurt, but in spite of the pressure, it did not. She wriggled her lower body, giving him leave to move deeper, deeper yet, until he was buried totally inside her.

"Aaahh, Deelie," he murmured into her mouth, not even aware of how his body trembled. She was so virginally tight, it took his breath away. He held still for a moment and forced himself to let her body adjust. Then, very slowly, he started to move.

She could feel him begin to withdraw and wanted to cry out, "Stop!" but before she could utter a sound, he filled her slowly once more . . . and she was lost to the slow, languid movement, in and out, stretching her, making her feel cherished, fulfilled. And it all seemed so effortless. Delilah closed her eyes and held him fast, unaware of how her knees clamped on his hips, how her own hips rose and fell with each thrust, urging him on. She floated for several moments, although she was never aware of time, only the joining.

But gradually sensations never before experienced made her reach for more. Her fingers dug into his back, feeling his muscles ripple with each thrust. She felt her hips rising and falling faster, demanding an ascending pace that would take her . . . where? She did not know but craved the learning of it. Knew deep within the core of her woman's body that it would be beautiful and necessary, oh yes, very necessary.

Clint could sense her response and gladly obliged, following the subtle, unconscious cues she gave. He buried his face in her sweet, silky hair, kissing her throat, leading her higher and higher. When he heard her sudden gasp of wonder and felt her flesh convulse around his, he slowed again, holding off his own fulfillment to make this first experience for her as long and wonderful as he could.

But her determination to seize this new pleasure was wild and uncontrolled. His Deelie was a woman who knew what she wanted—and right now she wanted this, wanted him. How like her, always determined to have her way . . . and in this case, he wanted to give it to her! With a great release of breath, he let go, spilling himself deep inside her in a final burst of white-hot climax, unlike any other he had ever felt. Spent and sweating, he collapsed on top of her, then rolled them over so she lay on his chest with her hair curtaining them in the warm sun.

Delilah loved the weight of his body on hers, the shuddering power of his release, so long held back. She was faintly disappointed when he reversed their positions. She was no fragile doll, yet it felt wonderful to lie molded over his long frame. She nestled her head in the crook of his arm and closed her eyes, feeling his hands lightly stroke her back, fingers playing with her hair.

Delilah felt suddenly awkward. What did one say after making love in broad daylight, without a stitch of clothing, outdoors in a wild place? How did one disentangle? Her husband had simply rolled away and gone to sleep in the dark. She had pulled down her night rail and done the same. This was utterly beyond her experience, and she did not know what to do. Delilah Mathers Raymond greatly disliked not knowing what to do. Now that the intense pleasure was fading, she began to wonder if she had just made a monumental mistake.

"Maybe I won't drown Sky after all," he said at length.

She could feel the slight rumble of a chuckle deep in his chest. "She arranged this very cleverly," she replied carefully, not moving.

He stroked her cheek. "Ah, Deelie, regrets so soon?"

"I don't know," she surprised herself by confessing. "That is . . . I've never . . ."

He tipped up her chin and gazed into her eyes. "I know," he said simply. "Your uncle and my sister seem determined to get us together—"

"Uncle Horace would never countenance making love without marriage," she interrupted indignantly, trying to extricate herself.

He let her go, helping her to kneel as he did the same, but when she reached frantically for her clothing, he placed his arm around her shoulders and turned her back to face him, brushing bits of grass and twigs from her tangled hair. "Why, Deelie, are you proposing marriage?" he asked, trying for a teasing tone. The feelings he had for this woman were enough to make the Thebans at Thermopylae turn tail and run. He honestly didn't know what he'd do if some misguided sense of propriety made her say yes.

"Certainly not!" she snapped. "I'm only concerned with how I can preserve my reputation, such as it is, not to mention keeping my uncle from shooting you. Perhaps *I'll* drown Sky," she added grimly.

"I'll admit my sister's people have less subtle ways of matchmaking than whites," he replied with relief, "but I'm touched that you're concerned with saving my miserable hide."

When he plucked another twig from her hair, she pulled back and scrambled toward the pool. "I have to bathe before I can dress," she said as she quickly sank into the water and began scrubbing and finger-combing her hair.

He followed her into the water and took her hands gently in his. "We need to talk, not turn tail, Deelie." Although he was damned if he knew what to say, and he surely wanted to see more of the tail she was preparing to turn. "I really did intend to slip away without letting you know I was here until you let out that shriek over the coon. You are a city girl, no doubt there."

"Are you sorry my outcry caused you so much amusement that you . . . we . . . well, we did what we did? I'll lay claim to my share of blame. You certainly didn't force me," she admitted, as much to herself as to him. "You're the epitome of everything I despise, yet I've found you . . . distracting, disturbing . . ."

"Attractive?" he suggested hopefully. Without giving her a chance to reply, he made an admission of his own. "We've been strikin' enough sparks to burn down half of St. Louis ever since we first met. You made it pretty clear how you felt about Southern men. I know your husband was a Yankee—"

Her brief hiccup of laughter stopped him. "Actually, although he fought with the Federals, Lawrence's family was

Southern. Very old, landed money. They just happened to be Unionists."

"The Matherses were wealthy but not aristocracy," he guessed.

"Hardly. My grandfather emigrated from Scotland and became a cobbler in Gettysburg. Within a decade he owned a shoe factory. By the time my father took it over and enlarged his business holdings, we were quite comfortable. But not good enough for my husband's father."

"Why did that make you dislike me on sight?" he asked, wanting to understand her antipathy toward him. He continued picking bits of grass and twigs from her hair, waiting patiently for her to explain.

"I've sat across from men like you at gaming tables for the past seven years, wealthy, condescending, judging me a fallen woman. The Southerners were always the worst because they'd mask it with charm."

"Just like I did?" A lot of pieces of the puzzle of Delilah Raymond were falling into place now. "Or you thought I did. I wasn't condemnin' you, although I do confess to a little distraction because you're so damned beautiful I couldn't concentrate. I reckon you've used that to your advantage in more than a few games."

"I used whatever was necessary to survive—I'll never be dependent on a man again. Except for my uncle. I owe him my life, and I'll take care of him when he can't use his guns to protect me."

"A big responsibility," Clint said. "I know how it is to struggle, wonderin' how you're gonna survive from day to day. I told you I don't come from money. Everything I ever owned I worked for, including my book learning."

"By playing cards?"

"Among other things," he admitted, then shifted the conversation back to her. "You really hated being a gambler, didn't you?"

Her eyes took on a hard, cold gleam. "Can you imagine what it's like for a woman surrounded by men who only play against her to prove they're superior—or to lure her into their beds? And don't insult my intelligence by saying that thought never entered your mind."

Clint raised his hands. "I'd have to be a gelding if *that thought* never entered my mind, but you beat me fair and square, Deelie. You're that good."

"Not exactly a skill women of quality are supposed to possess."

"Neither is running an upriver freightin' business, but you want to compete in a cutthroat man's game."

"It's a respectable business, even if it is dangerous. I'll take my chances."

He looked at her, seeing the steely determination in her eyes. "Always the gambler, even if you have quit the cards." He grinned at her. "Let's make a whole pile of money this summer, Deelie."

She turned away from his admiring gaze, knowing she'd revealed far more than was wise to this enigmatic man. "Don't call me Deelie." She wanted him to leave her alone so she could think, but then found herself saying aloud, "What will everyone say when I return to the boat looking like a drowned rat? We're due to take off any time."

"I'll stall the captain while you fix yourself up." He splashed to the shore where his clothing lay and fished through the pockets of his shirt, holding up a small comb. "Not much for all that hair, but it should work. You untangle that lovely mane and I'll slip aboard while no one's lookin' and send Sky back to help you dress. She got you into this— she can help get you out of it." He tossed her the comb.

She caught it deftly, then started to work furiously, detangling her hair. All the while she tried not to watch as he slipped into his clothing. He was bronzed as a savage everywhere except—no, she vowed never to think of that part of his anatomy again. He was the one who ought to worry about snapping turtles! Delilah was unable to keep her eyes from straying toward him as he slid into those indecent buckskins and slipped on his moccasins. He started toward the river, then stopped suddenly and turned around to face her with a serious expression on his face.

"We'll talk some more, Deelie. After we've both had time to think about it."

Was that a threat . . . or a promise? Delilah was not certain at all. But she would have the last word.

"Don't call me Deelie!"

Chapter Thirteen

Sky and Delilah returned to the boat before the captain blew the deafening whistle signaling their departure. All the wood had been gathered and stored for the voracious boilers. Within a quarter hour of their arrival, the boat was once again fighting the upriver current. No one appeared to notice that Clint had returned not long before the two women. Sky and Delilah had obviously been bathing, but no one else knew about the private pool. A dip in a secluded brushy area of the river on a hot day was perfectly reasonable for the two friends. Delilah's reputation was intact.

But her peace of mind was not. "You're angry with me, aren't you?" Sky asked Delilah as the two women stood on the upper deck watching the muddy water churned up by the big paddlewheel.

Delilah's eyes remained on the wildflower-strewn hill receding in the distance, remembering the taste and feel of Clint's body. "More with myself, I guess," she equivocated.

"Did you not enjoy it—oh, I know ladies aren't supposed to admit such things, not even talk about them, but the Ehanktonwon view has always made more sense to me when it comes to making love."

Delilah could feel the heat in her face but kept it turned steadfastly toward the cooling river breeze. "Yes, I enjoyed it, just as you were certain I would," she admitted grudgingly. "Altogether too much."

Sky's face lit with a big smile. "I knew you were destined to be together. Anyone with eyes, including your uncle, agrees with me. One has only to watch the way you look at each other to know." Then she sobered. "Don't feel as if you've betrayed your husband. Surely he would wish you happiness after all these years."

"I have no idea what Lawrence would've wished. We were two children, fumbling in the dark. Oh, that sounds terrible . . . but it's the truth."

"And there has been no other man since," Sky said with certainty. "You have a right to be happy, my friend . . . and so does my brother. He, too, has suffered much."

"Does he still mourn his dead wife?"

Sky's expression grew troubled. "He mourns . . . other things, I fear. His spirit has been wounded. But you can heal it," she quickly added.

"I'm not certain of that. I don't understand him . . . and I'm not sure I want to."

To that, Sky made no reply. Horace hailed them from across the deck. If Delilah noticed her friend's sudden hesitation defending Clint, she said nothing.

Delilah dreaded the evening meal, having to face Clint across the table and act as if nothing had happened that afternoon. She felt certain every intimate detail would be etched clearly on her face for the entire assembly to read. And his parting words promising further talk did nothing to reassure her. What was there to say? Did he regret it? Did she? In the midst of passion, she had loved it, but now, as she sat before her mirror, untangling the makeshift hairdo Sky had created, she grew increasingly wary. What was he going to say to her? Would he smirk or tease . . . or even blackmail her over the management of the boat? She knew from experience that he had not been above such things before.

When she and her uncle had been forced to support themselves by gambling, she'd been cast outside the social pale. No offers of marriage would ever be forthcoming from respectable men. Yet those same respectable men felt no qualms at all offering her very disrespectable propositions at every opportunity. *I might as well be a member of the demi monde.*

As the years passed, it had been she and Horace against the world. All she wanted was financial freedom and to be quit of smoke-filled card rooms and leering gamblers. But when she finally felt the first stirrings of attraction for a man since Lawrence, who did that man turn out to be? Another gambler, a rogue who represented everything she had come to detest. As if that were not bad enough, he brought a violent and troubled past with him. Clint was a man she knew little about—and every bit she did know should have warned her off instead of stirring her desire.

There, she had finally admitted it. Delilah put down her hairbrush and stared disconsolately into the mirror. She did desire him, but she would never give up her hard-won freedom by marrying him. She didn't even trust him as a business partner! But the idea of marriage was ridiculous anyway. She was certain a man who owned a brothel would never be interested—or if he were, he would not be faithful to his vows.

No, he only wanted to talk about continuing their liaison for the duration of the voyage. That would be convenient. He could enjoy her—and indeed he had seemed to enjoy her very much—yet have no strings attached to lure him into matrimony. After all, the beauteous Eva St. Clair awaited him back in St. Louis . . . and that was if he did not decide to remain with Sky's people.

How should she respond to such an offer? Passion for a few months, then a mutually agreed upon parting. Delilah stared into the mirror as if looking for an answer. But there was none. Somehow she had to get through dinner, and then they would have their *talk*. Best to get the matter settled one way or the other, even if she had not the slightest idea what that would be.

She finished her toilette and stood just as Horace knocked on her cabin door from the adjoining sitting room. "Are you ready for dinner, my dear?"

She stepped outside. "Yes, although I ate so much this afternoon, I doubt I'll have much appetite."

"Odd you should say that. Clint, too, was eager to forgo the evening repast. It seems our first mate Mr. Iversen has come down with an infected tooth. Clint volunteered to take his place supervising the roustabouts and passengers on the lower deck. Mrs. Colter is fussing because he wanted no evening meal sent down."

Delilah breathed a sigh of relief. At least she'd be spared a confrontation across the dinner table before matters were settled between them . . . however that would go.

Below them on the main deck, Clint checked the list of men who had boarded along the way, en route to the gold fields. The cost of passage depended on how long the *Nymph* carried their weight and fed them. They slept with the roustabouts around the cargo, wherever they could find space. It was the equivalent of steerage passage from the Old World to the New, a difficult voyage, but lucrative for the boat owners.

Taking over the first mate's assignment was a welcome respite from thinking about what had happened this afternoon and what it would mean for his business arrangement with the delicious Delilah. His first impulse had been to blame Sky for the whole fiasco, but upon reflection he knew that was wrong. Sooner or later the inevitable would have happened, whether or not his meddlesome little sister arranged it. She and Horace had both sensed the attraction between himself and Delilah. Hell, a deaf and blind man could probably have done that!

The only problem was that his little sister and Deelie's uncle expected their mutual attraction to end in marriage. Clint had vowed on Teal's bier that he would never again give hostages to fate. He would bury no more wives or children. The cost was simply too high. He had yet to come to terms with his actions after tragedy had first touched his life. There was a darkness buried deep inside him that he wanted no one in civilization to see. Nor did he wish to examine it himself. Sky knew part of it, but she had been raised in both worlds and could understand. A woman from the East, raised in privilege such as Delilah Raymond had been, would never understand . . . and he would never tell her.

But they had months before this voyage was complete. Working together in such close quarters created a situation as combustible as dry pine branches stoking a boiler fire. He'd never be able to leave her alone now that he'd tasted the delights of her body. And, having taught her the pleasures of making love, he doubted that she would be able to resist temptation any better than he. But if Horace caught them together, it would mean a marriage—or a murder. Continuing as lovers was playing with dynamite.

His mind spun in circles until he threw the passenger manifest against a barrel of dried fruit and sat down beside it, combing his fingers through his hair. Before he spoke with her again, he needed to gather his thoughts. Iversen's toothache had furnished the perfect excuse to avoid her until he decided what to do. That was, if he had the slightest idea what he *should* do.

The night sky was starless and dark, with a brisk wind that promised, and then around midnight delivered, a soaking storm. The boat rocked from the onslaught even in the shallow inlet the captain had chosen to protect them from the elements. All the better cover for a meeting with Clint, Delilah thought. If he knocked on her cabin door, her uncle, always a sound sleeper, would hear nothing above the pelting rain. No one would be out on such a night to see him enter.

"Please come and let's put this behind us," she murmured to herself as she paced on silent, bare feet.

Finally, at one in the morning, Delilah gave up. She quickly and angrily undressed, yanking off her garments and tossing them in a messy pile on the cabin's lone chair. She donned her lawn night rail, all the while cursing the perfidy of the male of the species. He was doing this deliberately to torture her. He'd never had any intention of talking to her. When the opportunity presented itself, he would simply appear and expect her to fall into his embrace. "Well, you're in for a big surprise, Mr. Clinton Daniels," she muttered through gritted teeth as she doused the lantern and turned back the covers on her bed.

She lay down and stared at the ceiling in the darkness, hearing the pounding rain lash the boat. The storm was fierce. Perhaps Clint had been forced to remain below with the crew since Mr. Iversen was ill. The thought offered small consolation. Sleep eluded her as the night wore on. Bright slashes of lightning ripped jagged patterns across the sky. Spring weather back East had never been this fierce. It was as if the elements mirrored her own inner turmoil. Delilah tossed off the covers around three in the morning and lit a lantern, turning the wick low.

Waiting out the storm was her only choice. Perhaps by dawn it would end and they could resume their journey. But she had heard Captain Dubois and his crew talking about storms that ripped violently across the open plains, destroying everything in their path. What if the boat was smashed against the trees lining the inlet? Or the cargo washed overboard? They could lose everything, even their lives.

Suddenly the rain slowed to a drizzle and the wind died down. She breathed a sigh of relief. It was over! The preternatural calm continued until she could see the faintest yellow light heralding dawn through the curtain on her cabin window. That was when she heard the roar. It sounded like a great freight train bearing down on the Nymph. But there were no railroads within hundreds of miles. What on earth could it be?

Seizing her wrapper, she slipped it on and cinched it tightly, then found her slippers. When she opened the door, a dark figure stood silhouetted against the pale light. Delilah gasped even though she instantly recognized Clint. His hair and clothing were plastered to his head and body. He was soaked to the skin, dripping a puddle of water on the door sill. "What—"

"No time. Tornado's coming. Everyone off the boat," he said in low, urgent tones, speaking rapidly without a trace of lazy drawl in his voice.

"Uncle Horace—Sky—"

"I've roused him. Already sent her below. She knows what to do in a tornado. Promised Horace I'd fetch you. Come on." He seized her arm and pulled her out of the cabin.

"I'm not going anywhere without my uncle," she said, heading toward his cabin door.

But Clint had other ideas. "He's depending on me to get you to safety, dammit!" he said, scooping her up and tossing her over his shoulder as his long legs quickly moved to the stairs at the front of the boat.

She started to squirm and hit him until she raised her head and saw Horace emerge from his cabin in carpet slippers and a robe, following close behind them. His face was grim and she knew it had nothing to do with the impropriety of seeing Clint carry her off in her nightclothes. "Let me down. I can walk."

"No time," he said, sprinting down the steps.

Two crewmen had pulled down the gangplank, and passengers dashed recklessly to shore. Sky stood in the dim light, shoving panicked men this way and that until Clint yelled for her to get away from the boat. She waved and disappeared into the darkness. Many of the roustabouts simply leaped overboard into the muddy water.

Clint grabbed a lantern, then carried Delilah down the plank and ran toward a low thicket of willows where a small stream fed into the river. Its banks were about three feet high, offering some protection from the onrushing wind.

She tried desperately to see where Sky and her uncle had gone but she could not discern either of them in the melee of running, shouting men. Over the cacophony, she heard the faint sound of Captain Dubois's calm voice ordering everyone to abandon ship. Clint splashed down the side of the creek bed until he found a deeply eroded gouge in the earth.

"Lie down," he commanded, sliding her from his shoulder as he knelt on the mossy ground. It was soaking wet and chilly, but he gave her no choice. His big body quickly covered hers, burrowing them inside the shelter of muddy ground and wild honeysuckle vines.

The noise grew even louder, closer, like some great mythological beast come to devour everything around it. Delilah could hear the roaring as it passed overhead. Then the lantern went out and all was blackness. She closed her eyes and prayed for her uncle and her friend. *Please let them be safe!* Almost as quickly as it had come, the deafening noise abated and the rain resumed.

Several minutes passed before Clint rolled away from her. Their makeshift little cave hollowed from the side of the creek bed offered some protection from the rain, but the false dawn had faded into blackness once more. It was as if the tornado had swallowed up the very sunrise itself.

"It's over. I didn't hear the sound of timber splitting. Reckon the *Nymph* made it. Good thing, because Dubois stayed aboard."

"Oh, my God! Why?"

"He's the captain," Clint replied simply. "He's never lost a boat. Doesn't figure to start now. I saw your uncle with Hagadorn. Sky got them down the creek a ways. Should be fine," he added, knowing that would be her next question. "We'll have to stay here until daylight."

She could not see him in the pitch blackness even though his voice gave away his position barely a few feet from her. "I pray everyone is all right," she said with a shiver.

"We were lucky. Dubois knows all the best hidey-holes along the river, places where it's safest to ride out storms or twisters. Long as you have time to get off the boat and onto land and lay low, chances are good you'll make it."

The silence between them thickened. The only sounds now were faint voices in the distance. Apparently most, if not all, had survived the tornado. Finally, Delilah could not abide lying beside Clint, feeling the tension crackling between them. "How long until dawn?" she asked.

"An hour, maybe less. You want to escape, don't you, Deelie?"

She swallowed for courage. "No, but I do want to thank you for saving my life. I've never heard anything like that noise. The destruction must be horrible."

"Yes, it can be . . . but you don't really want to talk about the weather now, do you? By the way, thanks accepted." He waited, but she uttered not a sound. He combed his wet hair from his forehead and sat up, hugging one bent knee with his arms. "Guess I don't want to talk about yesterday either, but we need to."

"I waited for you until one this morning," she replied crossly. "We can't avoid each other for the rest of the voyage, Mr. Daniels, but that doesn't mean we have to continue . . . well, doing what we did."

He threw back his head and laughed aloud. "Now I'm Mr. Daniels again. You really are upset that I didn't come knocking at your cabin door, aren't you, Deelie?"

"I am *not* upset for that reason. I merely think you're a coward—or worse yet, you have made the erroneous assumption that I'll fall into your arms any time you touch me. Well, I won't."

"You seemed willin' enough yesterday. Enjoyed every minute, too, unless I'm badly mistaken."

"You arrogant lout, if you're fishing for compliments, I'll grant that you possessed considerable skill," she admitted forthrightly.

He shrugged in the dark. "Practice makes perfect, whether you're makin' love or playin' cards."

"A man like you *would* equate one with the other," she replied with a sneer in her voice.

"Not really. Playin' cards is a lot more important," some inner devil made him say, knowing the remark would provoke her.

"If I could see your face, I'd claw that smirk right off it. But I suppose I should be grateful you've revealed your true nature. I'm certain you've had as much *practice* with your harlot Eva as with a deck of cards. When we return to St. Louis, you can go back to shuffling her."

Since he hadn't shared Eva's bed after meeting Delilah, that struck a nerve. "Eva is my business associate at the Bud. She has nothing to do with us. But I am afraid we won't be able to resist temptation while we're cooped up on the *Nymph.*"

"What do you mean, *we?*" she asked sweetly. "I won't become your temporary paramour, a—a convenience."

"Sounds as if you want a more permanent arrangement . . . like a weddin'," he drawled. Intuition told him she did not mean that, but who knew with a woman like her?

"You are the last man alive I'd marry—if I ever intended to tie myself to a man again—which I do not." Her voice was as calm as she could make it. All the snappishness and something else she refused to recognize, she kept hidden.

"Ah, Deelie, what are we gonna do? I certainly desire you. And, considerin' yesterday, we both know you desire me. Now, before you get your feathers all ruffled, be honest."

She let out a long whispery sigh of capitulation. "Just because I enjoyed what we did doesn't mean I have to repeat it."

"You think your uncle and my little sister will give up?"

"We'll just have to be wary of their schemes from here on. Forewarned, you do possess the intelligence for that, don't you?"

Clint suddenly realized this was not the answer he had hoped she would give. "I'll try, Mrs. Raymond," he replied. "All either of us can do is try."

The River Nymph miraculously received little damage from the night twister. A few canvas covers had been ripped from the cargo on the open main deck, but that was quickly repaired. Nothing had been swept overboard and no crew or passengers had been seriously injured in the mad rush to shore. One roustabout sprained his ankle when he jumped into the shallows and a burly farmer bound for the gold fields broke a tooth when he fell over a tree root in the dark.

Sky had found Horace amid the confusion and kept him safe, much to Delilah's relief. Everything returned to normal when they pushed off upriver the next day . . . or almost everything. Clint and Delilah acted as if nothing had changed between them, but Horace and Sky sensed a strange truce. No more of his teasing or her snappish replies. They worked smoothly, crossing paths as little as possible.

She checked inventory lists when cargo was unloaded and passengers were added to the growing roster. He assisted the first mate, overseeing the roustabouts as they hauled goods to shore. Clint collected the money due them and Delilah tallied their profits. They were civil to each other at the dinner table, but Clint often ate with the roustabouts on the lower deck, saying he had too much work to dine formally. Mr. Iversen's infected tooth made him violently ill. When they reached a doctor in Sioux City, he was told he was too sick to continue the trip. After they paid him what he was owed, Clint assumed his duties.

Within days they reached Dakota Territory, and the landscape evolved gradually, growing more stark and wild. The river became shallower. No more high bluffs but wide, treacherous shoals lay hidden, waiting like the Sioux, Cheyenne and Arapaho who had the past winter refused an army ultimatum to go meekly to reservations or face the wrath of the Great White Father in Washington. But it was not the government or even the ruthless little general, Phil Sheridan, who would attack the tribes. Commander of the Missouri Sheridan issued orders to a lieutenant colonel who had advanced his career by massacring high plains horse Indians.

They called him Long Hair.

Aboard the *Nymph,* Captain Dubois and Clint knew little about the army's battle plans for that spring but were aware of the long-standing antipathy of the tribes toward the fire canoes that brought soldiers and supplies for the invading hordes of whites. The steamers also brought disease, the inadvertent and fatal accompaniment of government-issued trade goods. In return for buffalo hides the natives often received blankets contaminated with smallpox or whooping cough, a certain death sentence for people with no natural immunity to white illnesses.

Although the Ehanktonwons, or Yanktons, as the whites misnamed them, had been pacified and placed on reservations, most of the Sioux tribes and their allies still roamed free and often attacked steamers. Every time they rounded a bend in the river or slowed for shallow water for fear of running aground, Clint, Horace and crewmen who were proficient with firearms watched the shoreline apprehensively, anticipating ambush. The same was true when they had to pull over to refuel or tie up for the night. Guards patrolled the decks and kept watch from the wheelhouse for any signs of hostiles.

At a wood stop near the mouth of the White River, Delilah was finishing a count of men who had paid for passage to the Montana gold fields when a loud commotion drew her away from her work. She heard the captain's voice from above call out a warning. It was quickly followed by the sounds of guttural cries in a foreign language. Dropping her pen, she dashed out onto the deck. Clint strode slowly down the gangplank after ordering the crew back toward the boat.

The men backed up as a large party of Indians followed them, some mounted, most dismounted. The hostiles shouted what she knew must be insults, even though she couldn't understand a word. "They're spoiling for a fight," she said to Sky, who looked worried when Clint, armed to the teeth, stood on the bank while the crew returned to the boat.

"Let Clint handle them, my dear. He's familiar with their ways," Horace said, although he carried his Colt rifle. "Perhaps it might be wise for you ladies to remain indoors."

"They're Teton Sioux. Renegades, and they're demanding whiskey," Sky said, showing Horace and Delilah the customized Winchester Yellow Boy she had partially concealed in the folds of her skirt. "I'm a very good shot, Uncle Horace."

"As am I," Delilah said, turning swiftly back to her cabin for the Hopkins & Allen .32-caliber revolver that she seldom carried on her person because of its long barrel.

Sighing, Horace said, "Let us hope your brother can defuse the situation before it escalates."

"We should never have brought that whiskey," Delilah said as she returned with her weapon ready to fire if necessary.

"I doubt they know whether or not we have contraband aboard," Horace replied dryly.

"He's right," Sky said. "They look for any excuse to fight. Nothing would make them happier than to burn a fire canoe to the waterline."

"There is some justification for their anger," Horace replied with a reflective expression on his face.

"Not *my* fire canoe," Delilah said, her eyes never leaving Clint, who made a broad gesture with one hand. "What's he saying to them?" she asked Sky.

"He is introducing himself as Lightning Hand, an Ehanktonwon. He calls them cousins."

"We hear of you, great Pawnee killer," the leader of the Tetons said in a loud voice in English. He crossed his arms over his chest and gave a proud smirk. "I see your squaws with weapons. They must not trust you to fight for them. And they are very pretty. Two fine ponies for the one with fire in her hair," he said, pointing at Delilah. "I want her for my blankets."

"I will give two ponies for the other," the man standing next to him said in their own language.

Sky's eyes narrowed dangerously. "They've insulted us. A healthy young woman is worth at least a dozen ponies."

Delilah gasped, giddy with fear, uncertain whether to laugh or be as angry as her friend.

Clint answered the chief. "White men—even those who have lived as Ehanktonwon—do not sell their women. You know this. We have no firewater to trade either. Go in peace."

"No! We will have whiskey first. Then we leave," the leader reiterated. The men around him began to murmur restively. Farther back, those on horses scattered across the riverbank, waiting to see what would happen. One of the roustabouts reappeared with several sticks of dynamite and matches.

"What on earth . . ." Horace said in a low voice as the man handed the volatile materials to Clint, who had obviously asked him to fetch them.

"As I said, my canoe does not carry firewater, but we do carry fire sticks, and these I will share with you." Clint struck a match, then touched the flame to the wick on one stick of dynamite. He appeared to admire it calmly for what seemed an eternity to Delilah and the others.

"What on earth is he doing? Is he insane?" she asked of no one in particular.

Then Clint said to the young chief, "Look you."

With that, he threw the lighted explosive between two of the mounted warriors some distance up the bank. Their horses shied when the dynamite exploded, gouging a big hole in the soft earth, sending dirt and rocks flying all around them. A small crater remained where the stick had landed. A collective gasp and murmurs of astonishment echoed through the assembly of Tetons.

Very calmly, Clint lit a second stick with a slightly longer fuse. "Let us smoke this fire stick as cousins. Very strong medicine." He stuck it in his mouth as if it were a cigar, rolled it around, then extended it to the leader. "Now you puff."

The chief's eyes grew round and his dark skin paled noticeably. He stepped back, as if Daniels had offered him a live rattler. "The Grandfather Spirit has touched this one. Let us leave him in peace as he has said!" he commanded his followers in their own language.

From above, Delilah, Sky and Horace watched the stampede that ensued when Clint tossed the second fire stick. The Tetons raced up the bank, some chasing horses that had already run off in terror, others leaping on their mounts to gallop away. Clint followed on foot, laughing as if he were indeed touched.

"What did their leader say?" Delilah asked Sky.

"He said my brother has been touched by God. It's their way of saying . . . saying he's crazy. Most tribes honor those who are insane—and yet avoid them as bad medicine," Sky replied reluctantly.

"Come back, Cousins!" Clint lit another stick and again tossed it where no warriors were too close. "See, there are fire sticks for everyone!"

A third explosion rent the muddy ground, scattering horses and Indians. One rider was thrown from the back of his terrified pony and quickly jumped up to pursue the fleeing animal. Across the prairie braves were trying to control bucking horses or simply running away from the boat as fast as humanly possible. Several tripped and fell, only to bound up and continue the mad dash.

"He looks as if he's actually enjoying this," Delilah said incredulously. "He could be blown to bits!" She watched in horrified fascination while Clint threw back his head and laughed wildly, shouting in a mixture of English and Sioux as he continued to lob the dynamite. "Do not flee, Cousins. Come back and smoke with Lightning Hand!"

Sky looked down at the deck, a worried frown creasing her brow. Horace said in a low voice, "I begin to understand why you feel it would be judicious for your brother to return to St. Louis."

"Why, Sky? Why is he acting this way?" Delilah asked, stricken.

Lightning Hand, the Pawnee Killer, was still laughing.

Chapter Fourteen

ome. I will try to explain," Sky said to her friend.

The two women walked into Sky's cabin and sat down side by side. After gathering her thoughts for a moment, Sky began. "You know Clint saved me and my sister Teal from the blue coats, that he joined our people and married my sister. He lived as an Ehanktonwon. And he was happy for a while, I think. . . ."

Delilah intuited that she was about to hear something awful, cruel and frightening. She was going to hear about the side of Clint Daniels she had seen that night when he kissed her so roughly after disposing of Riley's henchman. She rose and walked over to the secretary. After opening a small compartment at the top, she pulled out a bottle of brandy. "My uncle's tonic," she explained as she poured a little of it into two tea cups and handed one to Sky.

They each took a sip. Sky made a slight grimace, then set it down, and Delilah followed suit. "When I was ten, I was sent by my parents to the school the Episcopalians ran for my people, just as my sister had been sent before me. I was not in our village when it happened. A raiding party of Pawnee ventured far to the north, marauding as they went. They had worked for the blue coats as scouts, but even the army could not abide their drunken insubordination. They were dismissed without pay. They turned against anyone in their path, red or white.

"Teal was expecting her first child. When I visited a month earlier, she was just beginning to show the roundness that makes women everywhere joyous." She stopped and took a second sip of brandy. "That was the last time I saw my sister alive. When the Pawnee reached our small village, all of our young men were out hunting. Lightning Hand was with them. I have only heard accounts of what the raiders did and I regret the knowledge. It is too horrible to describe."

When she shuddered, Delilah placed her arm around her friend's shaking shoulders and held her as both women felt tears slipping down their cheeks silently. Now she feared that she understood what the Teton chief had meant, calling Clint the famous Pawnee Killer.

"My brother was the first to return to what was left . . . to find his dead wife. He would not listen to the pleas of the survivors to wait for the other warriors to return. There were a dozen Pawnee and he was but a single man. Yet he rode after the murderers in a rage of unbearable pain. Our cousin Blind Owl caught up to him just before he found the Pawnee camp that night. Lightning Hand gave Blind Owl his Spencer repeating carbine and told him to guard his back. Then . . . then he just walked into their camp and began killing everything that moved, shooting with both hands. When his pistols were empty, he used his knife. He killed them all."

"But they outnumbered him twelve to one. How could he have survived?" Delilah asked hoarsely.

"When a man does not care whether he lives or dies, our mythology says it makes him invincible. I don't know if it's true, but I do know this: My brother did not wish to live after what he did to those raiders. . . ."

Delilah's arms dropped to her sides. She gripped the edge of the settee until her nails bit into the brocade. "The darkness inside him . . . when his eyes turn from blue to gray . . . he's remembering, isn't he? He doesn't care if he dies."

Sky nodded as tears continued to stream down her face.

"He scalped them?" Delilah asked, the gorge rising in her throat.

"No one among our band wishes to remember that tragedy, but they do laud his bravery. He brought back the trophies to our village. When word of the raid reached the mission school, they sent me home. I saw long rows of scalps hanging outside his lodge on poles and knew the savagery of his vengeance would remain a blight on his soul.

"He tried repeatedly to raise war parties against the Pawnee and other raiding tribes. Some of the young hot-heads agreed, but our father, Talks Wise, said this was not the way to teach red people to stand together and learn to co-exist with the whites. Clint drank whiskey and rode off alone many times. And . . . and he always returned with hair . . . Pawnee hair."

"He was trying to get himself killed," Delilah said, reaching out to hold Sky's clenched hands in her own.

"He would've succeeded if my father had not intervened. He decided Lightning Hand should once more become Clinton Daniels and my guardian. He asked Clint to escort me to school back East and see that I received an education so I could help our people."

"How did your father convince him to do it?"

Sky smiled. "At first Clint fought the idea, but a guilty man will do many things to atone. Teal and their child were gone, but I was his little sister, and he knew our father was right about the good that might come from my education. Before we left the reservation, he broke the scalp poles and buried his trophies. Then he sat and stared at the raw earth over them for several days. After that, he stopped drinking."

"You gave him a new reason to live," Delilah said warmly. "And to think I accused him of being your despoiler."

"You were jealous, else you'd have seen that was not true."

Wanting to discuss anything but her tense relationship with Clint, Delilah shifted the subject back to Sky's story. "How could he afford to educate you? And why so far away in St. Louis?"

"St. Louis was the closest large city with fine universities, and he'd grown up in Missouri. That part of his life he has never spoken about. Someday, he will tell you. To make money for our journey, he went to the fort near our village and won enough for a stake. We traveled by horseback to the

city. He worked as a dealer at the Bud before the owner lost
it to him in an all-night poker game. After that he made
enough to enroll me in a female academy."

"He supported you the same way my uncle did me,"
Delilah said. There was an ironic parallel between their lives.
In spite of all he had done, Clinton Daniels possessed true
nobility.

"Yes, but I was not always grateful," Sky confessed. "I
quickly grew bored with learning how to pour tea and paint
watercolors. I was rebellious, impatient to learn something
useful."

Delilah smiled wistfully. "Yes, I felt the same way in finishing school. Perhaps that's why I jumped at Lawrence's proposal." She shook her head, remembering those days of
childhood innocence. "You have obviously had a superior
education. Not an easy accomplishment for a woman."

"Clint hired tutors from Washington University to teach
me literature, mathematics and science. Then, in exchange for
his forgiving a rather large gambling debt Attorney Burrows
had run up at the Blasted Bud, Clint struck a bargain with the
old curmudgeon. I read law with him for the past two years."

"You will do remarkably well for the Ehanktonwon, I'm
certain."

"And when you and my brother return to St. Louis, what
then, my friend?"

Delilah met her gaze. "Are you certain he'll agree to return?"

"If he has you, he will," Sky replied.

Clint's disquieting confrontation with the Teton renegades
continued to worry Delilah, but she kept busy with her work
as they made their way northward through Dakota Territory.
Clint, too, worked diligently at being first mate, spending
more time on the main deck than he did above it. So far, in
spite of Sky and Horace's attempts to throw them together,
they managed to avoid each other most of the time.

When they reached the bustling town of Bismarck, Captain Dubois announced that they would have to lay over a day

while the engineers made more boiler repairs. Since the arrival of the railroad in 1870, the city had prospered from both river and rail trade. It was named after the German chancellor in hopes of enticing German American investors. Although that ploy had come to nothing, the brick and stone buildings on the bank of the Missouri indicated that it had become a city of some influence.

"Hardly Chicago, but it does have a decent hotel and even an opera house," Clint said as Delilah looked at the bleak, treeless hillsides and muddy streets.

"We'll have time enough for recreation after we return to St. Louis with our money," she replied.

"You mean to tell me you don't want to spend a night sleeping in a spacious hotel bed that doesn't sway with the current? Take a hot bath in clean water?" he added.

"All right, that's an enticement I can't resist. I haven't been able to wash my hair in clean water since . . ." She stopped and looked up at his grin. "Keep up the smugness and I'll push you overboard again, Mr. Daniels," she said, stalking away.

"You're going to like the town," he called after her.

The Prairie Grand was a solid brick building, two stories of large, square, unimaginative architecture. But Clint had been right about the size of the beds and the baths. She and Sky could even have heated water delivered to their rooms. "I can't wait to get out of these muddy clothes and have a good, long soak," Delilah said to Sky as they inspected the sitting room they shared between their bedrooms. The wallpaper was a garish red and the gas lamps were tarnished. "Your brother was certainly right. It isn't Chicago, but it seems like being back in civilization after so long on the river."

"Just wait until sundown. Bismarck isn't called the hardest town in the West without reason. It's a good thing the saloons are on the other side of the railhead."

Delilah chewed on her lip. "Yes, I didn't like the looks we received from some of the rougher elements when we disembarked. Adding alcohol to the mix won't help their manners."

"Their hard looks were for me, not you," Sky said. "They

hate to see a woman of mixed blood pretending to be white. I've experienced that since I came to live in *civilized* society."

"Well, no one had better say one word around me or I'll show him just how uncivilized a woman of *un*mixed blood can be," Delilah replied adamantly. She had noted the hotel clerk's sour expression when they had signed in and requested baths. But her uncle and Clint were with them, so the nasty little pipsqueak had not dared to say anything. "Was that why Captain Dubois didn't come to town?" The thought had not occurred to Delilah until Sky's explanation reminded her that he, like Clint's sister, had mixed blood.

"No, his reputation is legendary up the Missouri. They'd allow him a room, but he never leaves his command until a voyage is complete."

"That's a pity. I would love for him to accompany us to the opera house tonight," Delilah replied. In truth, she wanted him to act as a buffer, inhibiting Sky and Horace's schemes. Her uncle had already hinted that Clint would escort her to the theatre and he would squire Miss Sky. She knew the two devious matchmakers would contrive to vanish and leave her alone with Clint.

"Well, he won't be there, but we will enjoy it. They're performing *Hamlet*. Oh, what are you going to wear?" Sky asked casually as she opened the door to her bedroom.

"It's a bit chilly. I brought one of my old half-mourning gowns. I instructed the maid to hang it so the wrinkles will fall out a bit. I'll probably have to pay to have it pressed," she said.

Sky placed her hand across her mouth to hide a grin. "Perhaps."

"What do you mean?" Delilah's mind went on alert. Sky was up to something.

When she turned to Delilah, her face was utterly innocent. "Oh, nothing, only that I hope your dress has survived the voyage. I'll see you after we both soak in bliss."

With that, she closed the door behind her, leaving Delilah perplexed. Shortly after, two men carrying huge tin buckets of hot water filled the large tub, then left. Delilah locked the

door behind them and then took the extra precaution of sliding the bolt on the door adjoining the sitting room. She
wanted no surprise visit from Clint while she was relaxing in
the water.

After slipping from her clothing, she placed her toes in the
steaming water and quickly withdrew them. Very hot! But
the evening promised a chill now that they had traveled so far
north. Late May in eastern Pennsylvania would be almost
summery. The West was a strange and hostile place, hot as
blazes one day, cold as winter the next. She padded across the
room and picked up a bar of scented soap from the wash
table. The essence of roses teased her nostrils. Lovely.

She looked in the wavy mirror that hung over the table
and inspected her body. Heavens, she was as golden brown as
Sky! And there were freckles on her nose. Every part of her
skin that was not covered—and that included her arms, face,
neck and even the upper portion of her chest—had been
tanned. Thoughts of Clint's bronzed, naked body flashed
through her mind. How did he manage to stay that way after
spending so many years in civilization?

"Why am I even thinking about it?" she scolded her image
and turned back to the tub. "Ready or not, here I come," she
said, placing one leg into the water, which had cooled a bit.
She got in and sank down with a sigh of bliss, leaning her
head against the high back of the tub. "If I'm not careful, I'll
fall asleep and drown."

From the sitting room, Clint could hear the sounds of
splashing water. His mouth went dry and his body hardened.
He could picture Delilah's pink, naked flesh glistening with
soapsuds. His heart pounded as all the blood in his body
rushed south. She was humming softly to herself now. The
temptation to try her bedroom door was overwhelming. But
he would give hundred-to-one odds that she had locked it
before she took off so much as her gloves. Besides, they had
an agreement of sorts. So far both of them had managed to
stick to it.

Sighing, he left his gift displayed on the settee and slipped out the hall door. Maybe a good, cold soak would put him right to face the evening. Somehow he doubted it. What had the woman done to him? He was going to endure a perfectly horrid rendition of Shakespeare just for the opportunity to be Deelie's escort. Horace had come up with the crack-brained idea after learning Bismarck boasted an opera house and a troop of actors were in town. Having seen the talent of actors out West, he couldn't help grinning. Horace would cringe the moment the Prince of Denmark uttered his first syllable.

"Serve him right," he muttered as he headed to his room.

Delilah fussed with her hair after her blissful bath, brushing it dry when the hotel maid knocked on the sitting-room door, saying she was there to empty the tub and bring fresh towels. Delilah called out for her to enter. Almost immediately, she heard the girl exclaim from the outer room, "Ooh, niver seen anything so grand, ma'am. Pure beautiful it is!"

Considering the less than *grand* décor of the hotel, she asked, "Whatever are you talking about?" But the instant she opened the door from her bedroom and saw the green velvet gown spread across the settee, she stopped in mid-stride. It was the gown she'd tried on in Hermann and refused to buy because it was too great an extravagance.

"How did that get here?" she asked, just as Sky appeared. "Uncle Horace didn't—no, of course not. It was Clint. Did you put him up to it? Because if you did," she went on, not giving Sky a chance to reply, "it was a useless gesture. It required major alterations."

Sky, dressed in a blue silk creation that matched her eyes, grinned as she walked over to the gown and held it up. "Hmmm, it looks as though it will fit now," she said consideringly. "Why don't you try it on and see?"

"Don't be foolish. It hung on me like a sack. Besides, I refuse to accept such a lavish gift, especially from Mr. Daniels. It isn't appropriate and you know it."

Sky let the rich velvet ripple, catching the light. "Don't be silly. We're in Bismarck, a stone's throw from some of the worst saloons west of the Mississippi. Propriety be damned. Just try it on."

"Sure and it does match yer emerald eyes, ma'am," the maid said encouragingly.

"Look at the lace. It practically drips from the bodice and sleeves," Sky noted as she shook the gown slightly and the paler green folds of handmade lace rustled enticingly.

"I'm not going to wear that dress," Delilah gritted out, itching to touch the silky fabric as it changed colors with every movement.

"You'll really disappoint me. And just think, our next stop will be at Fort Berthold, where I'm rejoining my father's people. It may be a year or more before we see each other again. Please, Delilah." Sky held out the dress cajolingly. "You won't be able to attend the play or have dinner if you don't wear it."

"Of course I will. I'll wear—" She stopped in midsentence and looked from Sky's triumphant face to the maid, who stood between the two women, a frightened expression on her face. "Where is the dress I asked you to lay out?"

"Ma'am, yer uncle, Mr. Mathers, 'twas he who told me ye wouldn't be needin' it. He said 'twas yer wish."

"Everyone conspires against me. Well, it won't work. I shall remain in my room and order a meal sent up," Delilah said stubbornly. Try to trick her, would they? Horace should've known better, even if the arrogant Clinton Daniels didn't.

"I'm afeard that won't work, ma'am. 'Tis that sorry I am, but this establishment has no kitchen." Now the maid was wringing her hands, looking pleadingly at Sky.

Smugly, Clint's little sister said, "Unless you want to eat saloon fare and pack a gun, the only restaurant is the one where we have reservations to dine before the play. You're going to disappoint your uncle as well as Clint and me."

"Then I'll return to the boat."

"Don't you remember? Luellen, Sadie and Beth have taken a well-earned day off, too. They're here in town. Can you cook, Delilah—or do you want to ask one of them to return with you and fix your supper?"

Delilah sighed. "You're making me feel petulant and ungrateful, spoiled as a Philadelphia debutante."

"Oh, I suppose that means you'll wear the dress and join us for the evening then," Sky said innocently, shoving the velvet gown into Delilah's arms.

Against her will, her fingers caressed the incredibly soft lushness of the fabric. "It will hang on me like a tent, but I'll wear it—on one condition only: I must pay your brother for it."

Sky's mischievous grin really broadened now. "You can take that up with him over dinner."

Narrowing her eyes, she asked, "Did Clint teach you to manipulate people, or did it just come naturally?"

"My education was most varied and unconventional . . . but my brother did supervise it."

To Delilah's amazement and perverse aggravation, the gown fit perfectly. Clint must have paid the parsimonious German seamstress in Hermann a great deal to alter it before the boat departed. She walked down the stairs to the hotel lobby with Sky, who had already exclaimed over how perfectly it matched her eyes. By the time they reached the landing, a few women were staring enviously, but their admiring audience was primarily male.

She could see her uncle watching them, smiling gently. *Brutus.* But it was the tall, blond-haired man beside him who held her attention. Pale blue eyes glowed in his darkly tanned face. His overlong hair was tied back in a queue and he wore one of his custom-tailored suits. This one was midnight blue with a snowy ruffled shirt and gold cufflinks. Even his black boots were hand-tooled and gleamed in the light. Clint Daniels looked handsome as sin and he knew it. Delilah could feel the heat stealing into her cheeks as his eyes swept over her and his smile widened in appreciation of the low-cut bodice of the gown.

Clint couldn't erase his grin and knew he must look like a lovesick puppy hoping for a pat on the head. But damn, she was splendid! The lace dripping from the neckline swayed softly with every breath she took. When he focused on the sun-gold skin rounded enticingly above her bodice, his breath caught. He could span her waist with his hands and knew she wore no corset—not that he'd mind undressing her just to make certain . . . no, best not to entertain that thought. His breeches were getting uncomfortably tight already.

He started walking toward the women, making an elegant bow as he reached for their hands to assist them from the bottom step. "Evenin', ladies. Your beauty outshines the morning star." He saluted Sky's hand first, then gave it over to Horace, who made his bow. The two of them swept ahead, leaving Clint and Delilah behind. When he attempted to take Delilah's hand, she pulled back and stepped down by herself.

"There's something we must get straight, Mr. Daniels," she said briskly. "About this gown. It—"

"You can't say it doesn't fit perfectly now, can you?"

"You know quite well it does, but the gift is inappropriate and a gentleman would know that."

"Being no gentleman, as you've often reminded me, I bought it anyway."

"Being a woman of business and independent means, I insist on paying you for it," she countered.

He seized her gloved hand and tucked it into his arm, striding toward the door. Without causing a scene that would embarrass her uncle and Sky, she could do nothing but allow him to lead her across the lobby toward the waiting carriage outside.

"Pay me for it, hmmm." He appeared to consider. "Well, that might be a little rich for your bankroll right now, Deelie, seeing as how the alterations cost as much as the gown."

"The seamstress has a good eye for fitting. I'll pay whatever she asked."

"She didn't take your measurements. I gave them to her. She just followed my orders," he murmured, looking down at the way the velvet and lace hugged her breasts and waist.

Delilah jerked her hand from his arm as they stepped into the cool night air, then fussed with her wrap to keep from throttling him. She could well imagine him describing the way he wanted the gown to mold to her curves. "You, sir, are a sharp-eyed lecher."

"A body needs sharp eyes to play cards, but then you know that," he replied, gallantly, helping to fold the heavy satin cloak over her shoulders.

His fingers seemed to burn through the fabric and she could remember the feel of them, warm and deft, caressing her bare skin. "I insist on paying for the gown, alterations and all," she whispered fiercely as he helped her into the carriage where Horace and Sky sat, chatting placidly.

Observing the two bickering, lovestruck young fools, Horace smiled and actually winked at Sky. Things were going quite well. Serenely, she smiled in return.

"Tell you what," Clint said to Delilah, "when we split up our profits at the end of the trip, you can pay me then. Fair?"

Delilah knew they had precious little cash now and might require it for emergencies. Heaven only knew what that seamstress had extorted from him to do the work in such a short time. "Fair enough," she said, knowing her tone of voice sounded grudging.

The Grand Northern would not have rivaled the finest restaurants east of the Mississippi, but it did offer spotless white linen and sparkling silverware. The dishes were even bone china. If the menu leaned heavily toward steaks and other beef dishes, the meal was as well prepared as any Luellen Colter could offer, and the portions were ample. To her surprise, Delilah found herself enjoying conversation and food away from the dangers and hardships of the river.

"Imagine seeing Shakespeare performed in Dakota Territory," Sky said, her eyes gleaming with pleasure as she sipped a cream-laced cup of coffee. "Although I'm sure it won't be up to the standards of Eastern cities."

"I doubt this rendition of *Hamlet* will fall 'trippingly on the tongue,'" Horace replied dryly, wiping his mouth with his napkin after finishing a large piece of custard pie.

Clint chuckled. "Oh, you'll get a great deal of 'sawing the air too much,' and 'the town crier speaking the lines,' against the Prince's instructions."

Horace's eyebrows rose. "You continue to surprise, Clint, quoting the Bard."

"Hamlet's speech to the players, Act Three, Scene Three, I believe," Delilah could not resist adding. Mr. Daniels had already blindsided her with his self-taught knowledge. Now he was showing off for her uncle.

"Scene Four," Clint corrected, sipping his black coffee.

"I'm certain it's three." She looked at Horace, the final arbiter in all things pertaining to classical education.

He shook his head and chuckled. "I'm afraid I would be as foolish as Polonius to arbitrate this dispute. Let us enjoy the play and then you will find who is mistaken."

"Show off," Delilah said sotto voce to Clint as he pushed her chair away from the table so she could rise.

"Deelie, you're so easy to tease. How could I resist . . . and you're right, it is Scene Three." He loved it when she gave him that startled, caught-off-guard look. It made her appear as innocent as a young fawn . . . although he knew from experience she was quick, clever and ruthless when she wanted something.

Well, so was he. And he wanted her in his bed more than he had ever imagined he'd want a woman again. The question was, what would he be willing to risk to get her there?

Chapter Fifteen

The play was every bit as horrible as they had anticipated, but they all enjoyed it in spite of dreadful actors, collapsing scenery and even an off-key piano during the intermission. "My favorite part was Hamlet stabbing the right side of the curtain and Polonius falling through the left side," Sky said as they walked from the theatre.

"The castle battlement tumbling into the audience in the first scene wasn't bad either," Clint added with a chuckle. "I told you not to expect much, but this was actually fun." What had been most enjoyable of all was watching Deelie laugh out loud, something he had never seen before.

Horace looked about for a carriage, and saw only one pulling up. "I'm afraid it will not carry a foursome," he said, inspecting the small two-seater.

"You had no trouble engaging a large carriage for the trip from the hotel," Delilah said suspiciously to her uncle. Horace looked at her with a twinkle in his eyes. *No doubt he hopes the dim light will conceal his smugness.*

"That was at the hotel. I imagine the larger conveyances have already been engaged. We could put the ladies in this one and walk the distance," he ventured, ignoring Delilah and speaking to Clint.

Daniels shook his head. "Not a good idea, two women alone in Bismarck."

Delilah cursed herself for not bringing her Derringer. "I'm certain Sky and I can fend for ourselves," she said.

"You haven't seen how rough river towns can be. I think it

wise if we each have a male escort," Sky said, sidling over to Horace.

Delilah knew they had hatched this plan well in advance. "Uncle Horace, you and I should walk. Let Sky and Mr. Daniels take the carriage."

"Nonsense, my dear. Clint is familiar with the town and has his sidearm. I have every confidence that you will be quite safe with him for the few short blocks from here to the hotel."

Delilah smiled up at Clint. "Why is it that I feel less safe when I am alone with you, Mr. Daniels?"

"Too vivid an imagination?" he suggested with a grin.

The driver reined in directly in front of them before she could make a retort. Horace moved with startling alacrity, assisting a preening Sky into the carriage, then following her with the words, "We shall see you in the morning."

Delilah turned to Clint. "Were you in on this transparent little arrangement?"

"They're about as subtle as a buffalo stampede, aren't they? But then, I guess everyone on the *Nymph* expects us to pair up. Crew's making bets on how soon."

Delilah stiffened, horrified. "No! You're making that up. Sky and I were so careful when we returned from the pool and—"

"They started talking a long time before that. Just seein' us fight makes it clear what we both want, Deelie. At least I'm honest enough to admit it."

"Don't you mean vulgar and lascivious enough?"

He shrugged. "There goes your imagination—thinking those vulgar, lascivious thoughts again," he said with a grin, offering his arm. "Shall we walk, ma'am?" She stomped ahead, refusing his arm. He let her go for several paces before calling out, "You're going in the wrong direction, Deelie. That way's the saloon district."

On the trip from the restaurant to the theatre, she'd paid no attention to the turns the carriage had made. She'd been too aware of Clint sitting so close beside her, his muscular thigh brushing against her skirts. She had tried to engage in light conversation to keep her mind off how splendid he looked and how luxurious the green velvet gown felt against her skin. Almost as wonderful as his hands . . . She stopped abruptly, realizing that she was being just as lascivious as she'd accused him of being.

She turned and faced Clint Daniels. "All right, you devil. Let's walk—and talk about our situation."

The forthright expression on her face almost gave him pause. Clint knew he was in a high-stakes game holding a pair of deuces. In spite of the cautions his mind gave out, he extended his arm again and tucked her hand around it, then started slowly walking in the opposite direction. "What are we going to do, Deelie?"

"Well, you could begin by not calling me a name better suited for a pet dog," she said mildly.

Clint threw back his head and laughed. "You're hardly a pet. If only this were so simple. A rose by any other name . . ." He leaned toward her and inhaled the soft fragrance of her hair. He could feel her response and knew she was equally sensitive to him as he was to her. "I want you. You want me. And"—he hurried on when she was about to protest his last statement—"we're going to be on that boat, working side by side, for weeks yet—with my little sister and your uncle throwing us together at every opportunity."

"But they expect a different outcome from their match-making than do you or I," she said flatly. "I don't want to marry you, Clint. You don't want to marry me. We both know it would never work out. We're from different worlds, even if we are both gamblers."

"Then I propose a gamble," he said after several strides in silence. He could feel her tense and stop.

"And that would be?" she asked.

"This," he said raggedly, drawing her into his arms and pulling her beneath the shadows of a large storefront entryway. His mouth descended on hers, swiftly and hungrily, but still waiting to see if she would answer in kind.

A kaleidoscope of sensations and muddled thoughts tumbled through her body and brain as she returned his kiss with equal passion. Her arms were suddenly around his neck, pulling his mouth to hers. Her breasts pressed against his ruffled shirtfront, tingling from the aching need for his hands and mouth to be on them. This was madness. This was heaven. This was inevitable.

After a few moments of exchanging fierce kisses and caresses, their bodies molded together until each felt they would melt into the other. Clint broke away, holding her shoulders, laboring to catch his breath. His eyes swept up and down the deserted street. "This isn't safe . . ."

She could hear the catch in his voice and had felt the pressure of his erection even through the heavy velvet of her skirt. That he had the control to stop when she would most probably have lain down on the wooden sidewalk appalled her. Delilah had always prided herself on her self-discipline and coolness under pressure. This was not a gaming table, but it surely would be a gamble—the biggest one she'd ever taken in her life.

In the calmest voice she could muster, she said, "Nothing about the two of us together is ever safe, Clint, but you've made your point. Yes, we desire each other. So, for the duration of the voyage, if we're very discreet, perhaps we can be lovers." The moment she said the words, she could not believe she'd had the courage—or was it insanity—to utter them.

His expression was far from triumphant. If it had been, she'd have slapped him and walked away. But he looked at her with naked desire firing his eyes as if they were glowing coals. "My room is at the end of the hallway. We can use the servant's door in back. Horace and Sky won't expect to see us until morning."

Delilah nodded. "Let's go then," was all she said. She knew she would pay dearly before this was over, but for the moment, that did not matter at all.

They walked the short distance to the hotel quickly, neither of them saying a word. He led her around the back and tried the service door. It was open. He held it, gesturing for her to enter. "You must have a good deal of practice sneaking women into your quarters," she said.

"Never had reason to hide what I was doing before," he replied as they climbed the narrow wooden stairs and he used his key to unlock the end door.

Delilah thought fleetingly of his dead wife. Of Indian customs. Had they simply come together without formal vows? In spite of her extensive education in white society, Sky appeared to have no problem with the morality of sending Clint to the pool, knowing that nature would take its course. Before Delilah could consider that troubling thought further, he swept her into his arms and carried her inside the room, kicking the door closed behind him.

When he put her down beside the bed and reached for the gaslight, she almost asked him not to turn it up, then stopped. She did want to look at his body, just as he wanted to look at hers. No fumbling in the dark, no false modesty. She was not a schoolgirl any longer. Instead, she watched the flickering shadows cast a golden glow around his head. She brushed a long, straight lock of hair from his brow.

Clint took her hand in his and kissed the palm, then placed it against his chest so she could feel the pounding of his heart. "Unfasten my shirt studs, Deelie," he commanded softly as he shrugged out of his suit jacket and threw it carelessly across a chair. Then he reached over and started to pull the pins from her hair.

Delilah did as he asked, a simple task she'd often performed for her uncle since he found it difficult to do with a crippled hand. But this was utterly different. Clint wore no undershirt. Instead, as the ruffles gaped open, she could see that mat of pale hair with the hard muscles tensing beneath, remember how crisp and enticing it had felt when she'd run her fingers through it. Her hands were clumsy at first, and she dropped one of the gold fasteners.

"Let them fall," he said hoarsely when she stooped to pick it up.

With that urging, she worked faster. By the time she reached his belt, she grew bold, tugging the shirt from his breeches, smoothing it from his broad shoulders.

"Cufflinks," he murmured to her, holding up one wrist while his other hand teased light, circling patterns across the bare skin above the bodice of her low-cut gown. When she unfastened one, he changed hands.

"You're driving me mad," she whispered, feeling her breasts ache as his fingertips brushed so near . . . yet so far.

"Oh, I've barely begun," he replied, tossing the shirt behind him. "Now I'll be your maid." His hands cupped her shoulders, turning her so he could reach the buttons running down the back of her gown. As he worked, deftly unlooping velvet-covered buttons, his mouth brushed away her hair and found the bare skin at her nape. He trailed soft kisses around her neck, then down her sensitive spine. A surge of primitive delight filled him when she shivered with pleasure and arched her back.

Delilah tugged the heavy gown down her arms and stepped out of it. Clint took it from her and laid it carefully across the chair. "It really is lovely," she said. "Thank you for the trouble you went to."

"Not nearly as lovely as its owner, but my pleasure," he replied, letting his eyes sweep hungrily down her body, clearly outlined through the sheer silk and lace undergarments she wore. "Now, darlin', your valet services are required once more." He looked down at his breeches, stretched out by his erection. "Damned uncomfortable," he murmured, yanking off his boots and stockings. He stood half-dressed, waiting to see what she would do.

Delilah's mouth went dry as she stared at his belt buckle. Did she dare? How could she not? She reached over and unfastened it, then set to work on the buttons closing his fly. When she inadvertently brushed his straining staff, he gasped an oath of pleasure as it sprang free. He shucked both suit pants and underclothes down his legs. Now he was fully naked, aroused. Her breath hitched. She let her gaze roam over his body, tracing each scar, the patterns of hair, his muscles and sinews, all so magnificently male. "Yes, I do desire you," she admitted, oddly liberated by her confession.

Clint's smile was rueful as he glanced down at himself. "You can see the feelin's mutual. Lordy, woman, you are a sight to tempt a saint—and we both know I'm not one." She stood in her undergarments, silk stockings and high-heeled slippers, not moving back an inch as he stepped closer, picked her up and deposited her on the bed behind them.

Very slowly, he peeled down one stocking, kissing her inner thigh, the sensitive place in back of her knee, even her toes after he tossed the slipper across the floor. His fingers encircled her slender ankle. "Your legs are so long, so lovely . . ." He was rewarded by her little moans and wriggling movements as he repeated the process on her other leg. By the time he completed the task, she was writhing on the mattress. He leaned over her and unlaced the strings holding her chemise, then shoved it down her arms, baring her breasts to the cool night air.

When her nipples hardened into two tiny pink buds, he brushed one, then the other with the heat of his mouth. Her hands drew him closer, locking behind his neck, while her fingers dug into his long, thick hair. He took one hard, pink nipple in his mouth and suckled, teasing it with his tongue until she moaned again. His hand caressed the fullness of the other breast before he replaced hand with mouth.

Delilah arched her spine, letting the exquisite pleasure sweep over her. When she felt the scalding heat of his staff against her thigh, she took the hard member in one hand and stroked it boldly, eliciting a growl from him.

"Better stop . . . before I lose control," he gasped, reluctantly pulling her hand away. He slid down her chemise and pantelettes, pausing to kiss the concave silky skin of her belly and let his tongue swirl around the hollow of her navel before he rid her of the last of her clothing. While it floated to the floor at the foot of the bed, he lay down beside her and took her in his embrace.

She went eagerly, trapping his staff between her thighs and pressing. "Consider yourself my prisoner, sir," she whispered, kissing his ear.

"Oh, Deelie, I think we're both captives." He rolled her atop him so she straddled his hips. At her startled look, he said, "Let me guide you." He took his hands and lifted her above his erection, teasing her soft feminine heat by lowering her just close enough so the head of his penis stroked back and forward.

His eyes glowed in the gaslight, devouring her breasts, moving lower to gaze at the place where they were almost joined. Delilah watched his expression, rolling her hips, uncertain about this strange new position. She felt utterly vulnerable, yet at the same time in complete control. *What a shameless hussy I've become.* She could stand it no longer. "Now," she said through gritted teeth, impaling herself in one swift, hard stroke.

His hands cupped her buttocks, guiding her up and down, until she found the rhythm, improvising on it with rolls and twists of her hips that left them both breathless. "Woman, you're a natural-born rider," he gasped raggedly, his fingers pressing into her hips to stop her before he lost control.

"Please, don't stop," she found herself begging, and knew there was desperation in her voice.

"Anythin' you want, love," he replied, beginning to thrust upward slowly once more, freeing her hips so she could follow his lead. His hands cupped her breasts, thumbs circling and teasing the nipples. She was a glorious sight from any angle, but especially this way. "Let's just take it slow, easy. We want this to last. . . ."

And it did. Each time she began to shudder in culmination, he stilled and held her hips, letting her glide off alone, watching as her head fell backward and a deep rosy flush tinted her body. Finally, with sweat beading his body and face, he clenched his jaw, the sight of her breaking his intense concentration. "I can't . . . wait . . . any longer, darlin'. . . . Hang on . . . for . . . the . . . ride . . . of . . . your . . . life!"

With those desperate words, he began to buck and thrust, waiting for her to begin another climax. When he felt the soft, tight heat of her body again convulse around his staff, he let go with a low, rough cry, echoing her sudden gasp of pleasure.

Delilah flew beyond the vastness of the starry sky outside, yet at the same time was completely centered on the man joined with her. How that could be so, her mind could not encompass during each surge of blinding ecstasy, especially once he gave in and followed her to surfeit. As his staff swelled and released its seed deep within her, she did not—could not—think at all. She only felt.

At last, utterly spent, she collapsed on his chest and nestled her head against his shoulder. She could feel one of his hands gently gliding through her tangled hair while the other lay possessively across the curve of her derrière. His breath came in ragged gasps as did hers, and his heart pounded like a drum in his chest. They lay for several moments without moving.

Finally she stirred, lifting her head as she climbed off him. But Clint did not let her go. One arm wrapped around her waist, pressing her to his side. She seemed to fit so naturally there that she relaxed and let him continue to hold her. Then he reached down and pulled up the covers. The night air was suddenly chilly now that their passion had been spent.

"I shouldn't stay. Sky or Uncle Horace might knock on my door," she protested.

"Not until mornin'. I'll tuck you in your bed safely at dawn."

They lay contented for several moments. Then, sleepy yet emboldened by yet another new experience in making love, she said, "I never imagined a woman could . . . that I could . . . so many times." She could feel the slight rumble of a chuckle in his chest.

"What? No credit for my stamina?" Before she could make an indignant reply, he said, "You're a passionate woman, love. You respond wonderfully."

"I never imagined that a woman could be on top."

"Top, below or any other way. No matter what position, with us it's pure magic, Deelie."

"There are more ways than a man or a woman on top?" The words tumbled out before she could stop them. Delilah knew her face must be red, but she looked up at him, more curious than embarrassed.

He smiled at her innocence, brushing a long strand of dark hair from her cheek as he replied, "Oh, there are lots and lots of possibilities and, er, other things I'll show you. It's a long way to Fort Benton and back."

After he reached up and turned down the light, she snuggled against his side once more, envisioning the weeks ahead and all the delights of new discovery. Before she could consider the price she might pay, sleep claimed her.

After the layover in Bismarck, the *Nymph* pushed on. Delilah dreaded the day after next when her new friend, Sky Eyes of the Ehanktonwon, would leave them. Her father, Talks Wise, had arranged for a party of kinsmen to meet them at a small fort within a day's ride of their reservation. As far as Delilah was concerned, the timing could not have been worse. There was so much to ask Sky about Clint, so much she wanted to know. But perhaps it was best this way. The magic interludes at the pool and in town, even what lay ahead for them as lovers, all would end in a few brief months. Upon returning to St. Louis, she would buy out Clint's share of the boat and he would return to Eva and the Blasted Bud with a handsome profit on his initial investment.

"You look pensive," Sky said to Delilah as Bismarck vanished on the horizon. A smile lit her blue eyes. "Was last night as wonderful as the afternoon at the pool?"

Unable to resist Sky's uninhibited glee, Delilah grinned. "Let's just say it was even better in a bed."

Sky clapped her hands together and gave a shout of joy that was drowned out by the noise of the engines, but several of the crew did look up to where the two women stood on the aft section of the boiler deck, hugging each other.

Unaware of their audience below, Sky said, "Now I'll be able to leave and not worry about my brother. You will be good for him, Delilah."

Delilah knew she meant *be a good wife,* but said nothing to disillusion her friend. "We have a long way to go before we sign marriage lines," she equivocated.

"Oh, I don't know. One member of the party coming to meet me at Berthold will be a priest—or so my father says. He could marry you tomorrow."

Delilah paled. "No—that is, we can't rush this. Clint's a man who can't be pushed."

"And you're a woman who is just as stubborn as he is. That's why you will deal so well together." She sobered. "My sister loved him and he her, very much, but he must remain in the white man's world now. And that means having a white wife. No simpering finishing-school girl would ever suit him."

"I suspect Eva St. Clair is more to his taste," Delilah said before she thought, then realized her gaffe. "I mean—"

Sky laughed. "Oh, you mean that woman at the Bud. I know more than my brother could imagine about his life in St. Louis. Clint would never marry her—and now that he's met you, I know he's not once considered bedding her."

Delilah looked dubious. "There's a very good reason for that. She's well over a thousand miles away."

"No, silly goose, I mean before we even left the city. He never touched her. Not that she didn't try to lure him back. She was really miffed when it didn't work."

"How on earth would you know that?"

A beatific smile wreathed Sky's face. "I overheard Clint talking to Banjo Banks the day before we sailed—you remember Banjo?" At Delilah's rather dazed nod, Sky continued, "Well, Clint was giving him instructions about running the Bud while he was gone and Banjo asked him why Eva had been so foul-tempered with everyone for the past weeks. Clint tried to hedge around the subject, but Banjo can be quite persistent when he wants to know something, especially if it concerns the saloon."

"He actually told Mr. Banks that he hadn't . . ."

"Yep," Sky replied with a satisfied smirk. "Oh, he wasn't happy about confessing it either, let me tell you. You should've seen his face when Banjo asked if that had anything to do with you."

"Of course he denied it," Delilah said with a smirk of her own.

"Of course."

In spite of the inner voice cautioning her that the idea of a permanent relationship with Clinton Daniels was madness, Delilah could not stop herself from hugging Sky again. Both women giggled as if they were fourteen-year-old girls.

When they reached a wide curve in the river late the following day, the remains of Fort Berthold's guard tower became visible upon the shallow bluff on the east side of the Missouri. Clint and Talks Wise, using post and telegraph, had settled on the deserted fort as a safe meeting site. It was a good distance from white army officials and marauding Indian tribes, yet only a few days' ride from their lands. Sky's father had led a large party of her kinsmen and women, as well as the missionary serving on the reservation. With a clergyman to act as intermediary, they would have a safer journey if they ran into any army patrols. Sky was ready to begin a new chapter in her life, standing between red and white worlds.

Delilah and Clint watched as the captain skillfully maneuvered the boat to the shore. It was several hours before sunset, but they would lay over here tonight to have a farewell feast with the Ehanktonwon. She watched him scan the vast open horizon past the dilapidated remains of the fort. "Do you miss it?" she asked, wondering again about his violent past and how great a hold it had on him.

He did not reply for several moments. "Some of it,

yes . . ." The reluctant tone of his voice and posture indicated that he did not wish to discuss the topic.

Delilah did not press. "I see a campfire and people up on the hill," she said, squinting in the bright afternoon sunlight.

"They're preparing the feast. Still a few buffalo around for the taking. They're probably roasting the hump." He turned and looked at her. "Guess you'll get your first real taste of the West. Not quite like Luellen's cookin'."

"I understand it's rather like beef," she said, not at all certain she believed it. At least they weren't boiling dogs in pots! She'd overheard crewmen speak of that practice too.

Clint shrugged. "Beef tastes like beef. Buffalo tastes like buffalo. And nothing tastes like chicken but chicken." Then his expression changed when he saw a tall man dressed in buckskin breeches climbing down the steep embankment to where the boat would moor. "Stands in Water, my brother!" he called out, and the greeting was returned.

The warrior's fringed buckskins were similar to the ones Clint had on, but his upper body was bare except for a breast-plate made of quills. His hair was long, worn in two shiny plaits decorated with beads and feathers. Large gold hoops adorned his ears. Delilah looked at Clint and for the first time noticed, among his other scars, that his earlobes had once been deliberately pierced.

While he and his adopted brother called out to each other in the Sioux dialect, she considered how easily he could revert to being one of these people. He'd worn such primitive adornments and lived this life. Once they'd left behind the dubious elements of civilization in Bismarck, Clint had immediately returned to his buckskins. She could imagine his shaggy hair untouched by a barber's razor, braided in the fashion of the Sioux tribes, his body bare save for loincloth and moccasins, his face marked with stripes of vermillion war paint.

"He could be one of them again. Don't let him, Delilah."

Delilah turned, hearing Sky's voice, and was shocked at the transformation in her friend. Miss Sky, who had read law in

St. Louis, was now Sky Eyes, daughter of Chief Talks Wise of the Ehanktonwon. Her hair was parted in the center and wound in plaits at the sides of her head. She, too, wore large hoops in her ears and a buckskin tunic, elaborately fringed and worked with beads and quills. Under the long tunic her legs were encased in moccasins, knee-high and beaded to match the rest of her clothing.

"My, you look like a princess," Delilah said, shocked at the transformation from finishing-school lady to Indian.

Sky laughed. "There are no Indian princesses. That was just a term the first white settlers used for the daughters of our chosen leaders."

"You're dressed for riding tomorrow?"

"No, this is purely ceremonial for the feast tonight. I'll wear an ordinary tunic with leggings and lace-up moccasins, but not this fancy. It takes our women weeks to work the beads and quills into ceremonial leathers—not to mention the backbreaking amount of labor that goes into tanning buckskins to get them this soft."

"It's lovely. You're lovely," Delilah said. And she meant it. When she reached out, Sky hugged her in return.

"We'll have more time together. I know it in my heart."

"Well, since there's a telegraph near where your people live, every time we make a trip upriver, I'll wire ahead and we'll plan to meet," Delilah said, only praying that it would be possible. She refused to consider whether Clint would be with her. He had already gone ashore and was surrounded by a group of Ehanktonwon.

Sky waved to her father and several of the women, who excitedly returned her greeting. "Come, meet my people." She took Delilah's hand and they climbed down the stairs and headed for shore. But just as they reached the top of the gangplank, Sky stopped to stare at a white man wearing a clerical collar and dark suit. Although Clint was a tall man, the fellow towered above him. He was young, with rusty reddish hair and warm brown eyes. The laugh lines at their corners and the wide smile on his face indicated that he was a gentle giant. He held his hat in one hand and made an elegant bow to the women.

"Oh, my, who is that great red bear?" Sky whispered with a gulp.

Delilah smothered a chuckle. It was obvious that her friend was smitten. "Love at first sight can be quite a trial," she said dryly. *So could lust!*

Chapter Sixteen

"*Y*our foster father is indeed a wise man, just as his name implies," Delilah said to Clint while they stood at the back of the boiler deck, waving to the assembly on the shore as the *Nymph* pulled out into the current following two days of feasting. A lump formed in her throat as she watched Sky, her father and the others grow smaller in the distance.

"You mean because Talks Wise advised me not to try livin' Indian again." His expression was unreadable as he stared at the vanishing figures.

Delilah watched his profile, wondering what he was thinking. Had he taken Talks Wise's words as a rejection? She did not know what the two men had discussed after they'd left the feasting late last night. At first she'd assume it was about Sky and Father Will, the young Episcopal priest who served their reservation. But later she learned that the old chief had cautioned Clint about returning to his former life, reminding him that he had built a new one in the white world and could serve the Ehanktonwon people best by remaining a respected businessman aiding Sky with legal connections in St. Louis.

He remained silent, staring into space for several moments. At length, she said, "Sky and Father Will certainly seem taken with each other. I suspect we'll be hearing about a wedding within the year." She blinked, then asked, "Oh, I wonder— can a clergyman perform his own marriage?"

Clint rewarded her question with a quizzical smile. "Yeah, I noticed the way they were huddled together, too. He'd be an asset dealin' with the government. As to the marryin' part,

I reckon it's possible. Sky's spent too much time with whites not to want marriage lines, all proper."

Left unsaid, Delilah knew, was any mention of their own situation. "Sky also expects that we'll marry. I had a difficult time explaining that neither of us wants that."

He snorted, half laughing. "She came to me last night, riled as a mama bobcat with new kittens. Tellin' me I was taking advantage of you." He looked down at her, watching the wind blow her curly hair, partially obscuring her face. "Well, am I, Deelie?" he asked in a husky voice.

"No, Clint. We have an understanding," she replied calmly. Then, to cover her own unease, she added, "Besides, I'd never marry a man I couldn't trust not to steal my boat."

He threw back his head and laughed.

Rising early had become a habit since Captain Dubois blew the whistle at dawn each day as warning before they left the shore. He was tireless, always early at his place in the wheelhouse, studying charts and measuring them against what the river's new twists and currents revealed to his keen eyes. Breakfast was usually brought up to him by the boy, Currie.

Delilah rubbed sleep from her eyes. It had been a week since they'd left Sky and her family. They had crossed from Dakota into Montana Territory. In spite of rainstorms, tornados and boiler break-downs, they were making good time. She watched as a big slope-shouldered roustabout carried the captain's tray up to the wheelhouse. She wondered idly why Currie had not performed this task, but one of the crewmen approached her with a tally discrepancy on the buffalo hides that they'd purchased from Sky's people. As clerk, it was her job to check, so she spent the next hour searching until the last of the cured skins were located.

Then she started thinking about the winsome boy who wanted to be a pilot. Had he fallen ill? The lad was devoted to his duties aboard the boat and would never shirk any assignment. She went in search of him on the main deck.

"Where's Currie? Why didn't he take the captain's breakfast to him?" she asked Todd Spearman when she found him in the kitchen, flirting with Sadie, the pretty Irish cook's helper.

Todd's ruddy face appeared puzzled. "He picked up the tray, same's usual, a couple hours ago."

"We have to find him," she said without further explanation. Obediently, if reluctantly, he left Sadie kneading bread dough and followed his boss lady around the deck until they located Currie with Zeke Hagadorn, the second pilot, who was teaching the lad how to take depth readings with a lead-weighted line.

"Why didn't you take Captain Dubois's tray up to him?" Delilah asked.

Currie's eyes grew round with alarm. "I started to, honest, but Lew Flowers, that big rooster, he said capt'n ordered him to do it. I . . . I slipped on the steps 'n spilled some coffee in his eggs yesterday. Lew said the capt'n was powerful mad," the boy stammered, rubbing one foot against his ragged pants leg.

"That doesn't sound like Captain Dubois. I'm going to ask him about this," Delilah replied.

Zeke and Todd nodded in agreement. Jacques Dubois would never be short with a boy for such a simple mistake. Carrying a tray up the ladder when the boat hit a shift in current could often result in a mishap. She headed for the wheelhouse, but when she called up to the captain, she received no reply, nor could she see him through the windows that wrapped around the small room. A sudden premonition of unease swept over her.

When she opened the door, she found him holding onto the wheel, struggling to reach the whistle, no doubt to stop the boat. His normally café-au-lait complexion was ashen. Delilah tried to yell for help, but the noise of the engines drowned her cries. What was the number of blasts for pull to shore? She began to yank on the cord, sending a frantic cacophony of whistles, sure to call attention.

Below, Clint heard the racket and ordered the engineers to stop the boat and drop anchor in deep water. Then he took the stairs to the boiler deck two at a time and raced to the wheelhouse. He saw Delilah at the door, a look of grave alarm on her face. He was up the stairs before she could finish saying, "Captain Dubois is unconscious, gravely ill! We need Mr. Hagadorn to pilot the boat to shore."

"I'll carry him down to his cabin. You send for Hagadorn," Clint said, kneeling and hoisting the smaller man over one shoulder. She scrambled down the stairs, with Clint moving more carefully behind her.

By the time she reached the stairs to the main deck, she remembered Currie and the big rooster who'd taken the breakfast tray away from him. "Riley's man!" And Currie was with the second pilot right now! She reached into her pocket for her Derringer. Since the incident with Riley's assassin, she'd taken to carrying it with her at all times. She hiked up her skirt and raced down the steps in the most unladylike fashion imaginable, then ran toward the back of the deck, where she'd left the second pilot with the boy.

Zeke Hagadorn was nowhere to be seen but the burly roustabout had Currie cornered between the wall of the engine room and the hog chains. "Now it's yer turn, ya little turd," Lew Flowers said, lunging forward and grabbing hold of the boy's shirt collar as the nimble youth tried to slip past his far larger foe.

"No, it's your turn, Flowers," Delilah yelled just as the deafening noise of the engines began to abate.

The giant turned around without relinquishing his hold on the boy. Instead, he threw Currie overboard and advanced on her with a feral growl, big yellow teeth showing when he laughed at her small pistol. She fired point blank, though not at his chest, which might not stop the brute quickly enough. Instead, she aimed for the bridge of his nose.

Delilah did not miss.

With a look of amazed consternation twisting his features, Flowers collapsed backward as blood spouted from his ruined face. He crumpled to the deck. She screamed, "Man overboard! Man overboard!"

From above, Clint heard the shot and her cries as he laid Dubois on the bed in the captain's cabin. Turning to Todd Spearman, he said, "Fetch Luellen and have her bring Mrs. Raymond's medical kit from her cabin."

With that he dashed out the door and leaned over the railing near where he heard Delilah's voice. She was pointing to a head bobbing in the swift current about a dozen yards off the port side. He yanked off his boots and gun belt, then vaulted the rail. At this stretch of river the bottom was uncharacteristically deep. He only prayed it was deep enough for him to come up without breaking his neck—or miring himself in silty mud while the crewman was swept to his death.

With her heart pounding madly, Delilah watched Clint leap from the upper deck. *Please let it be deep enough!* She could see the boy growing smaller in the distance as he struggled ineffectually against the strong, swift water. But Daniels surfaced quickly and stroked powerfully downriver. In moments he reached Currie and began swimming slowly back toward the stopped boat.

"Zeke Hagadorn is missing," she said to Horace, who had heard her screaming and rushed to see what was wrong. "I think this offal—" she shuddered, pointing to the dead man at her feet—"must be responsible. He threw Currie overboard."

"Riley's man, no doubt," her uncle said, quickly assuring himself that she was unharmed.

Horace immediately ordered several of the crewmen to lower the yawl over the side and begin searching up and down the banks for the second pilot. Delilah and Todd assisted Clint after he swam to the boat with Currie. They pulled the boy over the railless, foot-high side of the main deck while Clint hoisted his dripping body beside them, panting from the exertion of the swim.

"Zeke Hagadorn's missing," she said to Clint.

"He . . . h-he k-killed 'im, ma'am," Currie hiccupped, gulping for air and coughing as he pointed to the dead rooster. "He sneaked up back of us with a b-blackjack 'n split his skull, then shoved him overboard afore I cud do anythin'."

"You all right, son?" Clint asked. Currie nodded.

Clint looked at Delilah. "How did you—"

"I was suspicious when Flowers took the captain's breakfast tray away from Currie. I suspect he put poison of some kind in the food."

"Luellen's taken your medical kit to his cabin. Best you help her tend him," he said, peeling the soaked shirt from his broad shoulders.

Any other time she would have stood transfixed at the sight, but now she turned quickly and did as he told her, eager to get away from the bloody corpse. She had known when they tricked Riley and took the *Nymph* into the upriver trade that it would be dangerous. But she had never imagined watching men die, much less killing two herself.

When she reached Captain Dubois's cabin, Luellen looked up at her. "Capt'n don't look too good, but he says he's gonna be at the wheel tamorrah."

"Lew Flowers must've poisoned your meal after taking the tray from Currie," Delilah explained.

"I hate to give a backhanded compliment, but I am most grateful you served grits this morning, Mrs. Colter," Dubois said. "I detest them so ate very sparingly—and your normally excellent coffee tasted a bit off. I took one taste and no more."

Luellen slapped one plump knee and chuckled. "Reckon I'll recomember not to serve yew grits no more, but I shore am glad I did this mornin'."

"Just to be certain you'll not suffer any lingering effects from the poisoning, let me check your tongue and eyes," Delilah said, opening her medical kit. She turned to the cook. "Please brew a tea from these herbs," she said, handing Luellen a cloth-wrapped packet. "It's a soothing aid for digestion. Some plain bread would be good, too. That is," she asked Dubois, "if you think you can hold down solid food?"

"*Mais oui,* anything to get out of this bed. Have Mr. Hagadorn restart the engines. We have all day to run and hours before we reach the next wood stop."

Delilah explained about Zeke, whom she knew the captain

had worked with for many years. "My uncle has the crew searching for him, but Currie said he was thrown in the water after a strong blow to his head."

Dubois's eyes grew hard with anger. "In this stretch of the river, so wide, so deep . . ." He sighed in resignation.

But in spite of their fears, Zeke Hagadorn was located clinging, semiconscious, to a sawyer nearly a mile down the river. Although Delilah had to put seven stitches in the gash Flowers had made on his head, he appeared little the worse for his ordeal.

"We were very lucky," Delilah said to Clint when all the commotion had died down.

"*You* were very observant. If you hadn't been suspicious of Flowers and gone looking for the captain, we could've lost him, most certainly would've lost Hagadorn and Currie. Probably wrecked the boat and lost half the crew and passengers to boot." He looked at her with genuine admiration. "You're one hell of a partner, Deelie."

Visions of Flowers's ruined face flashed through her mind. She hugged herself. "I never imagined having to kill men to survive. Is that the way it has to be out here in the wilderness, Clint?" She searched his face, which had grown expressionless . . . all except for the graying of his pale blue eyes. She knew that he was remembering the tragedy Sky had told her about.

The stars shone brightly that night, countless millions of pinpoints of light. Mr. Hagadorn had been able to guide them to shore for the night's berthing. Now both he and the captain slept, recovering from their respective ordeals. Although she was grateful both men were mending, Delilah's thoughts were not on the *Nymph*'s near brush with disaster but on Clint and how he'd looked that afternoon.

She waited for several hours, making certain her uncle was soundly asleep before donning her wrapper and leaving their quarters. Starlight illuminated her way down the deck to Clint's cabin without need for a lantern. She paused for a moment before she knocked softly, praying no one would see her out this late.

For what seemed like an eternity there was no answer. Just as she was about to slip away, Clint opened the door. He was barefoot, practically naked, wearing only a short robe that draped open, revealing his chest. She was certain he had nothing on beneath the blue cotton. His expression was once more unreadable as he extended his hand and she placed hers in it so he could pull her inside.

"I wondered if you might come to me tonight . . . no, I hoped you would, Deelie," he said, closing the door silently.

"I . . . I couldn't sleep. I keep seeing that man I killed. I shot Pardee after a long, frightening ordeal. I acted instinctively, but Flowers . . ." She shuddered, remembering how she'd deliberately aimed for his face to stop him.

"You did what you had to do today. Saved Currie's life with your quick thinking—else I'd've had to choose whether to save him or you from the river," he said with a crooked grin, smoothing a long strand of hair away from her cheek.

"I could swim for myself," she whispered. "When I saw you leap into the river, I was so afraid." She laid her head against his chest and felt the reassuring beat of his heart.

"I could've buried myself in mud instead of water. Fool way to die."

She raised her head and touched his lips with her fingertips. "Don't say it. You didn't die. It was very brave if reckless, just like you . . . and then, when you climbed back onto the boat, dripping wet . . ."

"Come," he invited, leading her to his bed.

Although it was unmade, she could tell he had not been sleeping. A book of Shakespeare's sonnets from her uncle's collection lay beside a lantern turned up high. He lowered the flame, then drew her into his arms. Delilah went eagerly, untying the belt to her wrapper as he slid it off her shoulders, tracing soft, wet kisses along her arms and breasts. She could feel the heat of his mouth through the sheer batiste of her night rail and wanted no barriers between their flesh.

When her hands moved to the belt of his robe, he plucked her loose gown up and over her head in one swift, graceful motion, then shrugged out of his robe. "Do you always sleep in the altogether?" she asked breathlessly.

"Always," he said, scooping her into his arms and laying her on the narrow bed. He sat beside her, spreading her hair across his pillow, then lifting it with his fingers, letting it fall like silk, gleaming russet in the shadows cast by the lantern. "The light catches your fire, Deelie," he murmured, lowering his head so his stubbled chin brushed her sensitive breasts.

Prickles of delight shuddered through her at the faint scratchiness, but she wanted his mouth on the aching tips and guided his head until he took one nipple between his lips, then the other. She writhed, reaching for his straining staff at her thigh, but he moved lower, eluding her grasp, trailing kisses down to her belly and around the curves of her hips, his hands following where his mouth led.

She expected him to kiss her legs as he'd done last time, but now he paused by the dark russet curls at the juncture of her thighs. Delilah squirmed, uncertain whether or not she wanted this shocking intimacy. His mouth brushed across the tops of her thighs. "No," she whispered.

"Oh, yes," he answered, lying on his stomach on the bed, spreading her legs, caressing her inner thighs until they fell apart of their own volition, even though her mind said this was . . . was . . .

"This is . . ." Again her thoughts faded into pure sensation, her mind fuzzy and lost.

"Wicked? Forbidden?" He chuckled softly. "Oh, Deelie, you have so much to learn. Let me teach you?"

He did not give her the opportunity to reply but lowered his head once more to her soft, feminine heat and tasted of her. When she moaned and offered herself to him, he cupped her derrière in his hands and raised her lower body up to feast, laving gently with his tongue, swirling, tugging, ever so softly, gently caressing.

Delilah gasped at this scalding new pleasure. How

strangely, wonderfully, wickedly delicious it felt. Her fingers sank into his straight dark gold hair, urging him on until she could feel the beginnings of what she had come to know meant culmination. Her breath gathered to emit a cry of keening ecstasy when the waves crested.

But before she could do so, he slid up her body, plunging his hard staff deep inside her while his mouth found hers in a fierce, possessive kiss, smothering her cries lest they be heard through the thin walls of the cabins.

She could taste herself on his lips, although there was no room for thought of it now. He stroked hard and fast, drawing from her his own desperate pleasure, mindless as she, feeling her clenching heat surround him. Then he, too, surrendered to the bliss.

They lay entwined, sweat-soaked and panting for breath in the afterglow. The soft lantern gave its golden benediction.

"It's the Liver Eater's camp! Ole man Johnson hisself," one of the roosters called out as they approached the wood stop the following afternoon.

"I ain't a goin' into his place. Seen it once't 'n that were 'nough fer me," a second said, shivering. "'Sides, he's got some fancy-ass gunman workin' fer 'im now, has ole Jeremiah. Word is that killer'd jist as soon shoot a feller as spit."

Delilah listened to them and turned to Horace. "Who is this woodhawk, Jeremiah Johnson? Have you heard of him?"

Horace shrugged. "Only vague rumors, probably greatly exaggerated, as are most tales on the Missouri. His name is either Jeremiah or John. Nobody knows which. It's said he's killed scores of Crow Indians in revenge for the death of his Flathead wife."

"And he ate their livers?" she asked, horrified.

"As I said, probably a tall tale," Horace replied dismissively. *Just like Sky's tale of Lightning Hand's scalp poles*. But she knew her friend would never invent such a terrible story about her beloved brother. Delilah said nothing more to her uncle, only nodded, watching the shoreline as they drew closer.

As the boat stopped, Delilah could see a tall, gaunt man of indeterminate years with a matted beard and thinning, gray, shoulder-length hair standing at the top of the steep embankment. He wore only a filthy red flannel nightshirt that stopped barely at midthigh, revealing long, sinuous, hairy legs. "So that's the fabled Mr. Johnson. He looks dirty and disheveled, but I'd scarcely say all that dangerous."

"You are most probably correct, my dear. Nevertheless, I'm going to accompany Clint while he negotiates for wood. You note the unsavory fellow in Mr. Johnson's shadow? His name is, rather bizarrely, Mr. X. Biedler, a hired killer, apparently of some repute. Because of Mr. Johnson's, er, exploits among the various Indian tribes in the territory, Biedler's gun provides protection for Johnson's wood business." Horace held his telescopic rifle at his side.

She watched her uncle and Clint stride down the gangplank. The old man at the top of the hill stood like a malevolent sentinel, arms crossed, bare feet firmly planted on the grassy slope, as if defying them to enter his fiefdom. Some instinct made her suddenly uneasy. "Todd, have the crew staying aboard arm themselves and be prepared for trouble," she said to Spearman.

"Mr. Daniels already done tole us," Todd replied. "We hear any ruckus, we come on the double."

Delilah watched intently as Johnson called out to Clint, "Wall, if'n it ain't the great Pawnee Killer, Lightnin' Hand, come back from th' dead. How be ye, white Injun?"

She could not discern Clint's reply but sensed the tension in his body. He wore buckskin breeches and moccasins as usual, but this morning she'd been surprised to see him without a shirt. Instead he had a sleeveless leather vest laced across his broad chest, making him appear all the more savage. After their breathlessly wondrous interlude last night, his apparel distressed her. She was no closer to understanding him than she had been the day she met him. It seemed with each passing mile upriver, he became more Indian, less white. Was this the gentle, teasing man who quoted Shakespeare and made such delicious love to her? Or was he once more Lightning Hand, the white Sioux?

Suddenly, Delilah felt some perverse compulsion to know what was going to happen between the two antagonists. She felt the weight of the Derringer in her pocket, reassuring her as she waited for them to disappear over the embankment into the Liver Eater's camp. Then she walked down the gangplank. But instead of following them directly to the camp, she walked along the bank a couple of dozen yards upstream, moving around to the side, where she could watch what went on without giving away her presence.

She had slipped from Clint's cabin near dawn, undiscovered. Other than one last, lingering kiss, he had said nothing, promised nothing to her. But that had been their agreement. She would not settle for this enigma, a man standing between two worlds, yet invading her bed, her thoughts, her very soul. That realization frightened her, and Delilah Raymond resented being frightened. She refused to consider that she had been the one to go to him last night.

Why had he dressed like a savage after such a tender interlude? For this man whom he'd known he would meet today? What was their past history? The awful woodhawk obviously knew Clint from his time with the Ehanktonwon. She crept up the bank and sneaked nearer to the sounds of their voices, braving the prickling thorns of wild blackberry bushes and other low-growing, scratchy prairie grasses, still dry from the last brutal days of winter on the high plains.

When she saw the camp, her breath caught in her throat. She suppressed a scream of revulsion, unable to tear her eyes away from the horror. Delilah swallowed hard, trying not to cry out.

Chapter Seventeen

A long corridor stretched from the lip of the hill downward like a throne-room entry hall. Human skulls hung from the poles that lined the sides of the dirt walkway leading to Jeremiah Johnson's large, crude log house. Some of the bones gleamed, bleached white by the sun, the jaws clamped in a rictus of what looked like obscene laughter. Others were fresher, with bits of rotting flesh and hair still marring what would become a death-white patina. There must have been— her mind shut down, unable to count the number. They swayed in the wind from the river, suspended on long ropes.

It was a savage scene, straight from the fiendish imagination of an utter madman. Delilah remained frozen behind the bushes, unable to turn away. Her uncle stood at the bottom of the slope, observing from a distance, his rifle at the ready. They both watched as Clint walked up the hill through the hideous gauntlet, seemingly oblivious to the demonic horrors surrounding him. She could not envision what a civilized man such as Horace Mathers must think of this barbarity.

She wondered what Clint thought. He knew this insane old murderer, had dealt with him before. Now he approached Johnson, who had retreated to the front of his lair as if to make his visitor walk past his grisly trophies. She could see the crazed light in his rheumy eyes, even smell the incredible stench emanating from his body—or the death heads rotting all around him; it was difficult to tell which. She swallowed down her gorge as Johnson spoke.

"Good ta see ye, Lightnin'. Heerd ye'd gone back ta bein' white agin, but it don't much look like it." He surveyed

Clint's buckskins and long hair and then spit a gob of black tobacco near Clint's moccasins.

Daniels did not move. "I've come to buy wood, Johnson. What's your price for a load?" he asked in a flat voice.

"See ye got ye a fancy stern-wheeler. Come up in th' world, ain'tcha? Think thet makes ye better 'n a ole woodhawk?"

"I'm not thinking about anything but loading up and pulling out, Johnson. How much?"

"Now, thet ain't sociable." He took a menacing step forward, hands at his sides as if ready to throw a punch. "Ye and me, we be cut from th' same cloth—don't ye be fergittin' it. We done th' same. Tuk vengeance fer our wimmen. Ain't nothin' wrong in thet."

Delilah had watched Clint's back stiffen during the exchange, his anger palpable. Now he clenched his fists and spoke through gritted teeth. She noted that her uncle had raised his rifle from his side and cradled it in his arms.

"We're nothing alike, Johnson. I'm no cannibal."

Johnson laughed, a high-pitched, screeching sound that sent a new shiver down Delilah's spine.

"Oh, I et me some Crow livers, right 'nough. Tuk their heads 'n made me some real purty de-cor-ations." He drew out the last word, relishing it as he looked up and down his walk of infamy. "Ye tuk Pawnee scalps. Filled a couply mighty tall lodge poles, way I heerd it. Don't rightly see whut's so differ'nt jest 'cause ye didn't taste 'o their innards. We're th' same unner th' skin."

The blow landed so swiftly, Delilah scarcely saw Clint move. In an instant, the rangy old giant was flying onto his back in the dirt. The small, swarthy gunman materialized from the side of the cabin, his Remington .45 halfway out of his holster. Horace raised his rifle, but before he could aim it, Clint wheeled around and drew his revolver. The little killer's black hair bounced in oily ringlets as he shook his head, letting his weapon drop back into its holster.

"No, I got no fight with you, Yankton. You come to buy wood, we'll sell it. Ole Liver Eater, he's a mite tetched."

Biedler's forced grin revealed tobacco-stained teeth as he jabbed the fingers of one raised hand against his head to indicate Johnson was crazy.

Clint's hand remained steady, his Army Colt aimed at the gunman's heart. Delilah could see his finger whitening on the trigger. She almost cried out, afraid he would shoot the man in cold blood, so great was his rage. Then, ever so slowly, he exhaled and slid the gun back into his holster. Neither he nor the hired gun seemed aware of Horace standing in the distance. Clint deliberately turned his back on Biedler and walked away, daring the killer to try again.

After a dozen paces, he called out, "I'll send my men for the wood. The goin' rate, not a penny more." He pulled a sack of coins from his belt and tossed it over his shoulder.

Delilah watched Clint's face. His eyes looked cold, dead as the Liver Eater's hideous trophies that surrounded him. He stared straight ahead toward the river and never looked back. He passed Horace without acknowledgment, half walking, half sliding down the bank. *Fleeing memories so terrible he cannot bear them.*

Johnson got to his feet as Biedler picked up the money from where Clint had thrown it. The giant shook his grizzled head and rubbed his jaw. She half expected him to yell out after Clint, but he held his peace. The two men conferred for a moment. Then Biedler disappeared inside the cabin. Johnson shambled toward the huge woodpile in the clearing on the other side of his cabin to wait for the roosters.

Delilah worried that Clint might notice she had left the boat, but when she came around the bank from her hiding place he was nowhere in sight. Todd informed her that he had ordered the men to load up the wood, then gone directly to his cabin. Wilted with relief, she went to her own cabin and sat down on rubbery legs. She knew he would be furious if he ever found out she had eavesdropped on his exchange with Johnson—heard the Liver Eater's accusation that they were brothers under the skin.

"His guilt must eat at him like a cancer," she murmured,

torn between wanting to go to him and offer comfort . . . and her own revulsion at what he had been, had done. An educated white man had no excuse to behave so barbarously. But then, as she turned the whole ghastly episode over in her mind, she realized that it was unfair to judge Clint as harshly as Johnson.

Sky had explained how her brother had buried his trophies and spent days in silence, grieving for what he had done. This confrontation explained why his Ehanktonwon family knew he could not stay with them. She had seen how his reckless disregard for his own life had grown the farther upriver they traveled. Some part of him wanted to die. Delilah knew that her friend Sky expected her to redeem him.

If only she knew how.

Clint never left his cabin until they reached Fort Benton. On the three-day journey from Johnson's camp to their final destination, he had his meals and a bottle of whiskey left outside the door. He consumed the whiskey but left the food mostly untouched. Delilah made several overtures, but he refused to say anything except to order her to leave. At first she worried and paced the floor nights, fearful about what he would do when they arrived. But by the time the flat, muddy expanse of riverbank dotted with hastily erected clapboard buildings appeared, Delilah was angry. How dare he hide from her and shirk his responsibilities?

She looked at the desolate waterfront where half a dozen other stern-wheelers were busily disgorging their cargoes. Teamsters goaded stolid oxen or sturdy mules through the muck with curses and bullwhips, awaiting their turn to pick up the bales, boxes, barrels and crates filled with goods for the gold camps. Local merchants haggled prices with steamer captains, and warehouse owners dickered storage rates for consignments already spoken for by gold-camp traders not yet present to accept shipments.

Here and there, the denizens of the local saloons lining the waterfront spilled out to observe and comment upon the latest arrivals. Some were newly returned from the camps, laden with gold dust and eager to drink up their hard-earned profits. Others had struck out at panning for gold and hung on the periphery like vultures, waiting to rob or cheat their drunken compatriots. Slick, hard-eyed card sharks and even harder-looking saloon floozies trolled for customers. The stink of gold and the corruption that accompanied it hung in the air.

"We require Clint's assistance, I do believe, my dear," Horace said to his niece. "Perhaps if I spoke with him—"

"No. He forced us to take him on as a partner. He can damn well sober up and do his job!" Delilah stomped down the deck to Clint's door and pounded on it.

Clint had awakened at dawn long before the captain stopped the *Nymph's* engines. Todd Spearman had fetched him the hot water he'd requested, as well as a large pot of coffee. When he heard the ruckus on the riverfront he knew they were in Benton. He grimaced at his appearance in the mirror. He had not shaved in days. A thick, dark stubble of beard combined with bloodshot eyes and shaggy, unkempt hair made him look as bad a customer as any hanging out at the rowdy saloons in town. He set to work making himself as presentable as possible before disembarking.

When he heard the click of her high-heeled slippers approaching, he knew it was Delilah. Mad as a scalded hen. He couldn't blame her. Wiping the last traces of shaving soap from his face, he slipped on a shirt while she pounded on the door. After tucking it in the waistband of his buckskins, he opened the door, amused to see her small fist raised in midblow. Her lips rounded in a surprised *O* when she looked at him.

"You fixin' to knock on me or the door?" he asked with a shaky grin.

"If I was 'fixin' to knock on you, I would've brought a hammer. Your skull is harder than the door." She lowered her fist. "Your eyes look dreadful, like two burned holes in a bedsheet," she blurted out.

"You should see them from the inside," he replied, reaching for his gun belt.

She stood in the doorway of his room, feeling awkward, her eyes sweeping past him as he fastened the weapon around his narrow hips. She could see the bed where they'd made love. He'd been a different man then . . . or had he? She honestly did not know, but this was not the time to consider personal matters. There was business to conduct. "Are you ready to begin unloading? You're in charge since Mr. Iversen's gone," she said, blotting the perspiration on her forehead with her handkerchief.

Clint noted the freckles dotting her nose and touched the tip of it. "Looks like a sprinklin' of gold dust."

"Let's just see about getting some real gold dust. It's worth more," she replied, backing away from him. "The town is filled with miners spending like drunken sailors."

"Always the mercenary little soul, aren't you, darlin'?" he drawled, trying to get her into a better mood.

She ignored him. "We need to collect return passage money from them before they whore, drink and gamble it away. You are in charge of disposing of that illegal whiskey before any of the soldiers from the fort learn of it."

"I'll handle the whiskey deal. The captain knows a couple of merchants who'll give top dollar for it."

"Which will have to be handled in the dark of night?" she asked.

"You can count the proceeds by lamplight," he replied dryly.

"Just as long as we don't end up in an army prison cell." She turned and headed for the stairs on the hurricane deck.

He walked beside her. "I'll never spend another day in a bluebelly prison."

His grim tone made her pause at the top of the steps and look at him. "I know you were a galvanized Yankee during the war—and the reason why. Don't permit your dislike of the army to lead you to any irrational acts," she said, placing her hand on his arm.

He gazed at her for a moment, then smiled his old sharkish grin. "I wouldn't say I *dislike* the bluebellies. More like I hate 'em, but don't fret, I never let my feelings interfere with business."

"Splendid," she said sourly, not at all certain she could trust him. "But I believe I'll handle any dealings we have with the army. You just oversee the whiskey sale and the unloading of the rest of the cargo while I tally."

"Yes, ma'am," he replied, giving her a mock salute. "You do own 51 percent, after all."

By the end of the day, the captain had arranged a meeting with several bidders interested in purchasing the whiskey. No one appeared to be much troubled by an army detachment that knew damned well whiskey was being habitually shipped to the miners. Clint posted a notice for an auction of their legal cargo, inviting all the local merchants and drummers serving the gold camps. It would take the best part of the week to assemble enough competitors to get top dollar for everything. The roosters unloaded about half the goods onto the wide, muddy riverbank and were securing it against inclement weather by lashing it down with waterproof sailcloth.

"We'll need to post armed guards for our cargo, I do believe," Horace said to Daniels as they both surveyed hard-eyed frontiersmen ambling along the riverbank, armed to the teeth.

"I've handpicked the most trustworthy men, those the captain can vouch for. I figure you and I can take turns supervising them. After Lew Flowers, we can't afford any more mistakes."

Horace nodded. "Indeed. Let us hope he was the last of Riley's ruffians." He turned back to the boat and looked at the group of passengers waiting their turn at the table Delilah had set up forward of the now idle boilers. Each paid in advance for the return journey when the *Nymph* had finished selling all her cargo. The downriver trip would be far swifter, months transformed into days because they would be moving with the current. He chuckled. "With fares up to two hundred dollars apiece, my niece has been delighted with the passenger money."

Clint grinned. "I can imagine. There'll be lots of others once word reaches the camps. Then more miners who've struck paydirt'll drift in."

"How long do you imagine we will be here?" Horace asked.

Clint shrugged. "Hard to say. Longer we wait, the better the profits. Now, I reckon I'll head over to the Nugget and see a couple of men about our whiskey. Once the captain and I collect six or seven hundred a barrel for it, I think Deelie's snit over carryin' it will plumb vanish."

Horace laughed as Daniels sauntered toward the clapboard saloon where Dubois was waiting for him. *If only the ghosts haunting you would so easily vanish.*

Delilah stood on the hurricane deck late that night as her uncle walked around the cargo, speaking with their guards and making certain all was secure. The captain had returned from town after the conclusion of their deal for the whiskey. Clint had yet to appear. She chewed her lip in vexation. Surely he would not spend the night with one of those diseased whores she'd seen displaying their garishly painted faces from the upper stories of the saloons, calling out enticements to passersby.

"I'm being a jealous fool. He'd never do that, no matter how things stand between us," she murmured to herself, remembering the beauteous Eva St. Clair. At least his taste was high, if not his moral standards. Of course, what did that say of her own? She had been carrying on a passionate affair with a man she neither trusted nor intended to marry.

Damn you, Clinton Daniels! Delilah feared for him . . . yes, and cared a great deal more than she had been willing to admit. His wild, self-destructive actions with the Tetons and the confrontation at the Liver Eater's camp proved that he still carried the burdens of his bloody past. And, sadly, she had not been able to free him. Perhaps no one ever could, but back in St. Louis, he functioned as a civilized, rational man. Out here . . . out here lay only danger and death.

She had to get him safely home. If that meant relinquishing him to Eva, so be it. At least he'd be alive. Then, as if con-

jured from her worried imagination, she saw his tall, lean figure approaching. He was none too steady on his feet. Doubtless he'd been sampling his own wares with their buyers.
After a brief word with her uncle, he climbed the gangplank.
Surprisingly he managed to make it without a dunking in the
cold, muddy water. She turned and quickly slipped into her
cabin before he saw her.

Clint climbed the stairs to the hurricane deck, then mean-
dered toward his cabin. He had not told Horace what he'd
learned in town from a miner with a Teton wife. The rumors
would spread like wildfire all too soon. That damned suicidal
idiot Custer had split his command and led a few hundred
men against thousands of Sioux, Cheyenne and Arapahoe
camped along the banks of the Greasy Grass. All his soldiers
had been wiped out with Custer.

The army's retribution would be swift and terrible. He
only prayed the Ehanktonwon, being part of the Sioux Nations, would not be swept up in the coming decimation.
They were far away, living peacefully on a reservation. With
Father Will and Sky to speak for them, surely they would escape this time, but he knew the public outcry for vengeance
would deprive them of yet more of their land. The army
would see to that, too.

"Civilized progress," he muttered. All because one arrogant madman had been loosed to destroy the high plains Indians and then disobeyed orders from his own commanding
officer. But now the Long Hair would become a hero. The
lieutenant colonel would go down as *General* Custer in the
history books, even though it was only a brevetted rank for a
brief period during the late war. Clint knew it in his gut. And
it made him sick.

He walked down the narrow passage between the cabins
and the railing, angry, fearful and quite suddenly unbearably
lonely. When he passed Delilah's door, he heard her stirring
inside and caught the faint essence of her rose perfume on the
air. Was she hiding from him? With the liquor to fuel his
nerve, he turned the handle and opened her unlocked door.

Delilah turned, startled by his sudden appearance. He stood silhouetted in the doorframe with the dimmed lantern on the outer deck casting his face in harsh shadows. "You're drunk," she accused.

He took a step inside and closed the door. "Appears so," he drawled, pleased when she did not back away from his advance.

Her heart pounded and her mouth went dry as he came closer. She could smell the whiskey fumes. "You can't believe you'll . . . you'll be able to . . ."

A slow grin split his face. "Oh, yeah, Deelie, I can—and I will . . . if you want me to." He reached out and ran his fingers down the lapel of her silk robe. "Your call, ma'am."

His fingers did maddening things to her heartbeat when he brushed them softly across her collarbone, then slipped his hand inside to let it graze the tips of her already sensitive breasts through the thin fabric of her night rail. She could see the need in his eyes, unspoken yet clearly visible—to her. Perhaps only to her. "I call your bet, Mr. Daniels, and I raise," she whispered, wrapping her arms around his shoulders and pressing her body against his.

"I like it when we both win," he murmured against her throat. He kissed her hungrily, a deep, devouring kiss that she returned with equal fervor.

When they finally broke apart, breathlessly, she guided him to her bed. "Sit," she commanded, shoving him down. "You'd never manage without toppling over."

"Anythin' for a lady," he replied, plunking himself on the edge of the mattress. He watched as she tugged off his boots, a concession to conditions on the riverfront and streets of the rough town; moccasins would have been sucked into the foot-deep mud within three steps. His lips split into a lopsided grin when she dropped the footgear by the door and made a moue of distaste over her dirty hands. Clint loved watching her wash them with scented soap, then briskly dry them on a spotless white towel.

By the time she turned around, he'd pulled off his shirt and was working at the lacings on his buckskins. She had felt his eyes on her as she acted as valet. Now she swallowed for courage and untied the sash of her robe, letting it fall across the chair behind her. His gaze, gleaming like blue ice in the lantern light, penetrated the sheer batiste of her night rail, raking the curves of her body until she felt on fire.

She looked at his broad, lightly furred chest, enjoying the flexing of his muscles when he stood and pulled down his breeches. He kicked them away without losing his balance. "Are you sobering up?" some imp made her ask.

"Hell, yes. You could raise the dead, Deelie," he said raggedly as she walked over to him. "Not to mention this." He looked down at his stone-hard erection ruefully.

Delilah took it in her hand and stroked it delicately, eliciting a low growl of pleasure from him. Her own boldness pleased her. So did having a dangerous man such as Clint Daniels utterly at her mercy. "Now, I think it's time for bed."

"Just so it's not for sleeping," he murmured, sweeping the wisp of sheer cotton from her body. It floated across the small cabin and landed on his muddy boots. Neither of them noticed, nor would they have cared. . . .

Early the next morning, as Clint directed the roosters about where to place the last of their cargo, he cursed his foolish celebratory drinks with Toots Messinger, owner of the largest freighting outfit that hauled goods—especially whiskey—to thirsty miners in the gold camps. Messinger's men had unloaded the barrels before dawn this morning and paid in hard currency, which he'd given to Horace to deposit in the bank until they were ready to leave. It was an astounding amount of money.

Clint grinned, thinking of how delighted Deelie would be with the profit—in spite of her outrage over the risk. He knew the pounding in his head was not solely due to overindulgence . . . at least not in drink. It was Delilah Raymond's fault that his head spun. She had swept into his life and turned it upside down, right from that first night aboard the *Nymph*.

What was it about the woman? Yes, she was beautiful . . . and highly intelligent . . . and wonderfully responsive in bed. But she had a shrewish tongue and the devil's own temper. Not to mention that she was stubborn as a mule, spoiled as a debutante and came from an upper-class, monied background that he had despised all his life. But she stuck in his craw like no other woman he'd ever known.

The image of his docile and loving Teal faded from memory in spite of the hole her death and that of their unborn child had left in his heart. He'd sworn never again to love another woman, to risk that kind of all-consuming agony and emptiness. *I do* not *love Deelie, dammit!* But somewhere deep inside him a mocking voice called him a liar.

His troubling ruminations were suddenly interrupted when a spit-and-polish captain with gray sideburns, a soft belly and a self-important manner came walking up the riverfront. The bluebelly was followed by a contingent of soldiers, marching in formation. Clint could smell trouble closing in. Apparently Horace could, too, because he came ambling down the gangplank.

"Take over the unloadin', will you?" he asked Horace, who nodded and turned his attention to the roosters' careful placement of boxes of dynamite on the soft riverbank. Nevertheless, he kept one eye on Clint's stiff back as he sauntered toward the army officer. When Daniels was out of hearing, he told one of the roustabouts to fetch Mrs. Raymond.

"Mornin', Captain," Clint said, his tone none too cordial, as the potbellied man stopped directly in front of him.

"I am Captain Dwight Andrews. Are you the owner of this vessel?" he inquired.

"Part owner," Daniels replied noncommittally. "Why?"

"And you are?" the captain asked, tipping his head to indicate Clint's lack of manners.

"Clint Daniels." The reply was curt.

Ignoring the hostility, the officer nodded. "Perhaps you heard in town last night about the catastrophe visited upon our Seventh Cavalry under Lieutenant Colonel Custer's command last week?" he asked gravely.

Clint nodded. "Don't rightly see what I can do about it, though," Clint drawled.

"Actually, quite a service to your country, sir," the captain replied sternly, then turned to doff his hat when he saw Delilah coming down the gangplank.

Every man on the riverfront paused to stare at her. She was a vision in yellow dimity, a simple dress for a warm day, but one that showed off her golden-hued skin and lovely curves to great advantage. Her hair was caught in a white ribbon and waved gently on the breeze.

"Good morning, Captain," she said briskly, offering her hand in a businesslike manner. "I'm Mrs. Raymond, Mr. Daniels's business partner and half owner of *The River Nymph*." She hoped to defuse any conflict between Clint and the officer. Horace had assured her the whiskey was off the *Nymph*, and the money for it already in the bank. That could not be the reason for the captain's presence. "To what do we owe the pleasure of your visit?" she asked as he made a show of saluting the back of her hand with a very proper kiss.

"As I was explaining to Mr. Daniels, there was a most tragic—"

"Custer and his men wandered into a camp of three thousand or so Indians and attacked them," Clint cut in. "Long Hair and the Seventh are gone."

Delilah's face registered horror at the news. "All of them?" she asked.

"Not quite all," Captain Andrews replied, clearing his throat. "Er, the colonel split his command. Some of Major Reno's and Captain Benteen's companies found places to make a stand and survived."

Clint muttered something about fools being lucky beneath his breath, but Delilah covered it up by asking, "How many survivors are there?"

"We don't know precisely yet, but we were just informed

by telegraph that Grant Marsh's *Far West* is bringing nearly three score down to Fort Abraham Lincoln. Some of these brave soldiers are so gravely wounded that we must have them sent to Jefferson Barracks for better medical treatment than is available above St. Louis. Since Captain Marsh's steamer is needed to supply the troops as they pursue the hostiles, we require another boat to pick up the injured soldiers at Lincoln posthaste and transport them downriver—yours, ma'am."

"And I require that you get the hell out of here before I throw you in the river, bluebelly," Clint said tightly, taking a step toward the bug-eyed officer.

Delilah quickly interposed herself between the two men as Horace walked over and stood beside Clint. "But surely, Captain, there are other boats that would serve as well as ours," she said, gesturing to the six stern-wheelers lining the riverbank above and below them.

Andrews shook his head. "I fear not, ma'am. None of the others have fully unloaded their cargoes. Yours is in prime condition and ready to move immediately. And Captain Marsh informed General Terry that your Captain Dubois is as fine a pilot as he himself—high praise, indeed. The general wants *The River Nymph* and its captain. You will be carrying a very precious cargo, and the army will reimburse you generously for your effort."

"If we wait until the end of summer, we'll make a fortune taking miners downriver. They pay gold—up front," Clint snarled.

For once, Delilah could not feel mercenary, even though she knew how slowly the army paid and that they would not receive as much as they'd make from private passengers. "Clint, I know how you feel, but we can't just—"

"Yes, we can. Get another boat," Daniels said flatly to Andrews.

The captain stiffened and pulled a sheaf of papers from his jacket, thrusting them at Mrs. Raymond, knowing if he tried to hand them to Daniels, the Southerner would grind them into the mud. "I regret to inform you, ma'am, that you and your associate—" he paused to give Clint a triumphant look—"have nothing to say about the matter. I have direct orders from General Terry to commandeer this boat if necessary. Captain Dubois will depart forthwith for Fort Abraham Lincoln to board the injured soldiers. A contract for *The River Nymph*'s services will await you there."

"And if we don't *depart forthwith* . . . ?" Clint said through clenched teeth.

"I've been authorized to use all due force to see that the orders are carried out. If you refuse to cooperate, I have thirty infantrymen at my disposal." He now gestured to the line of armed soldiers encircling the boat's cargo. "Rest assured they will shoot if they have to. Be prepared for boarding. We leave by two this afternoon."

Delilah and Horace each seized hold of one of Clint's arms as the red-faced little captain marched smartly off. His men remained in position, their Springfield rifles at their sides.

"Well, it looks as if you've just enlisted," Clint said flatly. "But I haven't."

Chapter Eighteen

"*W*hat do you mean, *you* haven't?" Delilah asked, frightened at the look in his cold gray eyes as he stared at the sergeant left in charge of the soldiers. "You heard Captain Andrews. There is no choice."

"Way I figure, there are always choices, Deelie. Sometimes they aren't the ones a man wants . . ."

"I fear the officious little captain has commandeered the boat. The issue now is who among us will remain behind to sell our cargo while the *Nymph* heads downriver on its mission of mercy," Horace said, attempting to interject the practicalities of business, something Clint and his niece could discuss without coming to blows.

"I'm staying here. I'll conduct the auction. You two go." Clint's tone and granite-hard expression indicated there would be no discussion. He started to walk away, then paused and said, "Oh, don't take less than three hundred a day from that damned bluebelly Terry for the use of our boat."

"No!" Once again she seized hold of Clint's arm and stepped in front of him. "Uncle Horace can auction off the cargo and arrange passage downriver for himself with the money. I need you to negotiate with the army so we get the best deal we can."

He cocked his head and looked at her, then laughed bitterly. "You still don't trust me, do you, Deelie? What do you expect I'll do—take the money and run off to Chicago or New York with it?"

Delilah looked stricken. "That is hateful. I know you

wouldn't steal our money. I want you with me, Clint," she said simply, looking into his cold eyes unflinchingly.

"Darlin', I don't give a damn what you want. I'm not goin' on a boat ride with a bunch of bluebellies." He stalked away, shaking off her hand as if it were a snake.

Horace saw her shoulders slump in dejection. He walked over to her and placed his arm around her. "Tut, child. We can straighten this out. Only remember Clint was forced into the Union army once before with disastrous results. It's natural he would resent the way this has been thrust upon him."

"He's headed for the saloon," she said, watching as Clint climbed the crude plank walk in front of the closest establishment lining the street. "We can't leave him this way. He won't take the money. He probably won't even sell the cargo. He'll . . ."

"Return to his adopted family?" Horace supplied.

"No, Sky and Talks Wise would never let him go wild again. You've seen it, how he's reverted the farther upriver we've come. He'll either drink himself to death or join the Sioux fighting to escape the army's vengeance. He'll die, Uncle Horace!"

Horace nodded sadly, knowing that she was most probably right. "Then we must act quickly to stop him. There is a way, although it would best be implemented by you, I believe."

Moments later, Delilah approached the sergeant in charge of the soldiers. "I need your help with a problem." She fluttered her lashes and wrung her hands. What man—besides Clint Daniels—could resist a damsel in distress?

When she finished telling her story, Sergeant Jamie Finn was putty in her hands. The big man had a large nose that bore the hallmarks of having been broken multiple times, as well as scars over much of his beefy, weathered face. But there was kindness in his dark brown eyes. "I'll have to clear this with the capt'n, ma'am, but don't ye be a worryin' about it. We'll have your husband back aboard the boat before it's time to shove off."

Approximately two hours later, after Finn had cleared the matter with Andrews, he and three of his men approached the boat with Clint. The sergeant led the way, two troopers walked beside Daniels and a third followed behind him. Clint's hands were shackled behind his back, his shirt torn and bloody and his face bruised, with one eye starting to swell. A thin trickle of blood came from one nostril. Delilah knew his knuckles must be as bruised and bloody as his face. But he was intact and able to walk under his own power, thank heavens.

The sergeant beamed with admiration as he walked up the gangplank to where she stood. "Niver saw a man fight like that since I left the old sod. Are ye certain he's not Irish?"

In fact she had no idea what *her husband's* heritage was, but Delilah merely said, "I fear not," as she inspected the sergeant. His lip was split, his nose newly displaced and he, too, was sporting a fresh shiner.

"Best barroom brawler ever, that man of yours. It took eight of us to bring him down. Four of me troopers, they're getting patched up at the fort infirmary. And this after we waited until himself had a belly full of whiskey to slow him down." There was awe in his voice.

Clint stared past Delilah as if she were invisible. His eyes were flat, his face emotionless. As she thanked the sergeant for returning *her husband,* she wished Clint would rage at her, show some feeling, even if it were hatred. *He's all Indian, now. What have I done?* But what else could she have done?

"I'll be shacklin' him to a bunk, if that's all right with ye, ma'am?" Finn said, sensing that much was amiss between Mr. and Mrs. Daniels.

"My uncle's on the hurricane deck. He'll direct you," she replied as Finn handed her the key to the irons and Clint's weapons.

"It might be for the best if ye'd be keepin' him under lock 'n key until we're well on the way."

Delilah nodded as the three troopers led the prisoner toward the stairs to the upper deck. She clutched Clint's gun belt as Finn followed his men, still muttering about a man who loved to fight so much he'd take on eight-to-one odds. She was just grateful no one had been seriously hurt, especially Clint. Finn had assured her that he knew the proprietress of the Gold Nugget. At his request, she had insisted that Mr. Daniels remove his firearms before she served him any whiskey.

Delilah stood by the railing, staring out at the cargo on the bank, her mind a muddle of conflicting emotions. Horace joined her shortly. "He'll come around, my dear. I'm certain of it, although," he chuckled ruefully, "it might take some time . . . and feminine wiles."

"Will you be able to sell the cargo and make it all the way home safely?" she asked, realizing what a huge responsibility she was asking her uncle to assume. "All of this, deceiving Red Riley, converting the boat for upriver trade, it was all my idea, but now—"

"Delilah, child, you know I've wanted this as much as you. And I am certainly capable of dealing with the ruffians masquerading as merchants here. Never fear, I shall book passage aboard the first steamer heading home as soon as I've made us a sizable profit and retrieved our whiskey money from the bank. You see to Clint. I suspect that will prove the more daunting task."

Delilah kissed his leathery cheek. "I suspect you're absolutely right."

"Excellent. Now, while Captain Dubois and I discuss how to conduct the auction of the cargo, I suggest that you gather your medicinals and tend to your patient."

Delilah stood outside the door to Clint's cabin, clutching her basket of medical supplies with a white-knuckled grip. Swallowing for courage, she opened the door and stepped inside. He lay on the mattress on which they had made love, but this time his wrists were chained to the frame of the bed. He stared at the ceiling above him in stony silence, not turning to look at her when she approached.

Well, if that was the way he wanted to play out the hand, she could act as dispassionate as he, damn him! She walked over to the bed and pulled up a chair beside him. Willing her hands to cease their trembling, she took a soft napkin from her basket, soaked it in the basin of clean water on the nightstand, then sat and began to cleanse the cuts and abrasions on his face and hands with nurselike precision.

His lip was split, but fortunately no teeth had been loosened. When she inserted her fingers in his mouth to check, she half expected he'd bite her, but he did not. His long, dexterous gambler's hands were a mass of bruises and cuts, the knuckles swollen horribly. It was all she could do not to bend over and kiss them, remembering how he had used them to caress her body so exquisitely.

As she worked, he did not flinch or in any way acknowledge her presence. "I could use the carbolic solution on you again," she murmured but received no response. "Very well," she said softly, soaking another cloth with plain alcohol.

Very gently she disinfected his cuts, then applied a cold compress to his swelling eye. Still, he did not move. When she had done all she could for his injuries, she left the cabin, shaken and close to tears that she refused to shed. She would not show him how he'd hurt her. At this point, who knew how such a revelation would affect their relationship? Delilah certainly had no idea.

He'd accused her of not trusting him. She did not. But not for the reasons he assumed. Her greatest fear had not been for the money but for his life, that he'd turn wild red Indian again and die. Then she would own the *Nymph* and collect all the profits. Delilah laughed bitterly to herself. She would never have imagined that freedom, respectability and money would mean so little to her as they did now.

Horace was waiting with Captain Dubois in the dining room when she composed herself and went in search of them. Her uncle explained that several merchants who dealt with the gold camps had already come calling after receiving word about the auction.

"It should not take more than a week at most to dispose of everything on the riverbank for a handsome profit, Madame," Dubois said with a reassuring smile.

Horace could see the haunted look in her eyes and knew things with Clint had not gone well. As he pulled out a chair for her to take a seat at the dining table, he said, "The captain has graciously agreed to provide four of his most trusted roustabouts to act as guards until the transaction is complete. Then we'll take the first packet downriver for St. Louis. There should be no problem arriving in plenty of time to pay off our note at Consolidated Planters Bank."

Delilah smiled at the captain. "I do thank you, sir. We had not expected to have this sort of difficulty with the army."

Dubois gave a Gallic shrug. "I fear I am partially to blame. If Grant Marsh had not been so laudatory about my skills, General Terry might not have telegraphed here to commandeer your boat. Although it will take considerable time, you will be handsomely reimbursed for transporting the wounded soldiers. Captain Marsh has told me what his going rate is. If I am so fine a pilot as he says, then they must pay you that same rate."

Delilah and Horace had both heard of Marsh's lucrative deal with the army. "Do discuss that fee with Clint before you reach Fort Abraham Lincoln," he said to his niece.

Now Dubois looked a bit uncomfortable. "I know how he feels about the Union army, and several of my crew have given me a grisly description of how the soldiers returned him to the boat. Is he feeling . . . well?"

"As well as can be expected," she replied calmly. "Sergeant Finn was quite in awe of the fight he gave them."

Jacques and Horace chuckled over that and the tension was broken. But Delilah knew she would have a difficult task getting her galvanized Yankee to deal with General Terry . . . and to forgive her.

After a final wave at Horace standing on the muddy riverbank, Delilah watched as his figure grew smaller in the distance. It was quite amazing how swiftly a boat moved with the current when one was used to laboring upstream against it. The journey to Montana Territory had taken well over two months. Even if their stop at Fort Abraham Lincoln held them up for a few days, they would still make St. Louis in as little as three weeks.

She trudged to the kitchen, where Luellen was overseeing dinner preparations. Clint had not been given a noonday meal. Delilah knew he'd refuse to eat. Well, if she had to starve him into submission, so be it. She knew that the rot-gut whiskey he'd consumed on an empty stomach would make him utterly miserable by the time they moored for the night. That morning, Luellen had purchased a dozen fat live hens from the boat moored next to them, then enlisted Todd, Sadie and Beth to help her kill, pluck and clean them for a feast. Delilah intended to take Clint a tray of delicious fried chicken, mashed potatoes and gravy. If he could resist such a treat, he would indeed win a contest of wills.

"We'll just see who folds," she said with steel in her voice.

The *Nymph* pulled up against a stretch of shallow embankment around dusk that evening. The smells of Luellen Colter's cooking wafted on the warm evening breeze. The officers in the dining room gave lip-smacking approval. Even the captain, with his fine New Orleans palate, complimented the cook effusively. Delilah ate sparingly, too nervous to really do justice to the excellent meal.

Luellen watched her picking at her food as Sadie and Beth served coffee. When Delilah rose and started to leave the room, the cook caught up with her. "Yew feelin' poorly?" she asked, knowing her young friend's lack of appetite had little to do with physical health.

"I'm fine . . . no, that's a lie. I'm not fine at all. My uncle has been left behind in that horrible town of cutthroats, the army's commandeered our boat and Clint is chained up in his quarters."

Luellen let out a hearty laugh. "Chained up, huh? Whut

better way kin a woman have a man? Sounds like jest the ticket. He ain't et today neither, has he?"

"What are you saying?" Delilah asked, half afraid of the answer.

Luellen's warm brown eyes stared into Delilah's cat-green ones. "Git yerself all decked out in some fancy, lacy rig. I'll fix a tray fer yew ta take ta the mister's cabin."

"Does everyone aboard this boat know that Clint and I have . . . that we . . . ?" She sighed and shook her head. Of course they did. But surely her uncle . . . Delilah was not certain of anything these days.

Luellen patted her on the back in a motherly fashion. "Naw, not th' capt'n er crew er yer uncle, if that's whut yer afeard 'o. But Miss Sky 'n me, we knowed right off. Wimmenfolk, we got us a way. Now, don't fret, jest do like I say." With a wink, she turned and waddled back toward the kitchen, calling out, "I'll fetch th' tray ta yer room in ten minutes er so."

Delilah put on a pale green silk night rail with delicate embroidery across the low, rounded neckline. The garment was so sheer, it revealed far more than it concealed. She had bought it because it was cool, but now utility took second place to seduction. Just as she belted the matching satin robe at her waist, Luellen knocked on the door. Delilah took the tray as the cook inspected her outfit.

"Set that down," she commanded. When Delilah did so, Luellen pulled the collar of the robe open so it gaped loosely, revealing the night rail and what lay beneath it. "Now, thet's more like it," she said with a big grin. "Jest remember, keep him tied up till yew got 'im eatin' outta yer hand."

Chuckling at her own jest, Luellen left. Delilah picked up the tray. Her hands trembled so badly that the dishes clattered and the coffee sloshed over the side of the cup into the saucer. She took a deep breath and willed herself to be calm. After a moment, she slipped from the room and down to Clint's door. By the time she balanced the tray against one hip and used her free hand to turn the knob, Delilah felt her self-confidence return.

I can do this.

The interior of the room was dim, with fading sunlight filtering in the sole window. Two of the roosters, under the watchful eyes of the sergeant, had taken Clint to the privy that afternoon, his only break from the isolation of his makeshift prison. Now he was again shackled to the bed. As before, he did not turn, but continued to stare straight up.

Clint could smell the essence of roses and hear soft footfalls. Deelie. Her own delicious scent combined with the heavenly aroma of Luellen's fried chicken. His stomach twisted with cramping hunger and the burn of raw whiskey. Damn her for siccing those soldiers on him! He tried to concentrate on his anger, hold it fast. But then she stood beside the bed, and the slither of her robe brushed against his bare arm. If a direct lightning strike had just hit him, it would have had less impact.

She placed the tray on the small table beside his bed, then surprised him by sitting on the side of the mattress, facing him. His breath hitched when she reached for the lantern. Her robe gaped open, revealing the incredible bounty inside. Gold and green, her flesh and clothing were all pale and shimmery in the twilight. After lighting the lantern, she sank a fork into the mashed potatoes glistening with thick brown gravy and brought them to his mouth, letting the tantalizing smell tease his nostrils.

He tried to turn his head away, but his stomach emitted a loud growl. Other, lower parts of his anatomy were also letting him know their hunger. Better to eat than think of sinking into Deelie's silken flesh, not when he was chained here because of her. He took a bite. She offered a second forkful. He ate.

They continued in silence. He watched as she picked up a large chicken leg and began tearing the meat into bite-sized pieces that he could chew in spite of his sore mouth. The consideration almost brought an unwilling smile. She had been brought up with delicate table manners, yet here she was with greasy fingers . . . delectable fingers he wanted to feel gliding across his aroused flesh.

He suppressed his treacherous thoughts and took the first bite she offered. Feeling her fingertips on his mouth sent shockwaves through him. If she had noticed the bulge in his breeches, she gave no indication until now. But once their flesh touched, she let out a tiny gasp and pulled away before recovering. Doggedly, she picked up another bit of meat, this time using the fork.

"You aren't planning to stab my poor mouth with that are you?" he asked.

"Well, he speaks," she said dryly, offering the meat again.

He raised his head from the pillows and wolfed down the chicken. "Just like a trained seal in the circus—only they don't chain them."

"But they do chain lions and tigers," she retorted, offering another bite.

"Then you'd best beware, Cat Eyes." He appeared to consider her words as he ate. "I'm more wolf than lion."

"I've sensed a certain lupine quality in you," she retorted, offering another bit of meat, doused in gravy.

He ate, then swallowed and said, "You told the sergeant we were married. You still thinkin' along those lines?"

Delilah dropped the fork with a clank against the plate. "Certainly not, nor have I ever! It was simply the most expedient way of convincing him to bring you back with as little bodily harm as possible."

"Yeah, you do need me to act as your mate on the downriver run," he replied, eyeing her pebble-tipped breasts, barely veiled inside the gaping robe.

Delilah knew she should be insulted at the double entendre, but wasn't this exactly what she'd come here to elicit? "So, you can still perform verbal gymnastics. At least your sense of humor hasn't been totally battered out of your head."

"I can perform all kinds of gymnastics if you unlock these shackles. Want me to show you?" he dared.

She could see the faintest hint of the old Clint gleaming in his eyes now. A lopsided smile tugged at the corners of his lips, and those pale blue eyes hungrily moved from her face to her breasts and back upward. His erection stood like a tent pole in his breeches. She couldn't resist brushing it with one arm as she resettled herself on the mattress and dished up the last of the potatoes.

"Open wide," she said.

"Isn't that supposed to be my line?"

"Don't be crude, Mr. Daniels." She shoved the fork at his mouth and he accepted the potatoes, but a drop of gravy dripped onto his chest.

"My apologies, Mrs. Raymond," he said through a mouthful as he chewed. "I've been too long away from the niceties of the officer's dining table."

Delilah couldn't take her eyes away from that tiny brown spot.

Noting the way she stared, he chuckled and said, "Out, damn'd spot?"

"I don't think Lady Macbeth was talking about a gravy stain," she retorted, beginning to enjoy their repartee.

"Gravy's a lot easier to remove than blood, Deelie. And a lot tastier, too."

"You think so?" she asked, leaning down and licking the small drop with her tongue. "You're right." She made a show of licking her lips with her tongue.

"Boldly wicked," he said, his breath catching as his heartbeat accelerated. "Now, let me out of these damned shackles so I can—"

Delilah shook her head. "I don't think that will be necessary . . ." A truly wicked grin danced across her mouth and her eyes gleamed cat green in the lantern light. She stood up and unfastened the belt of her robe, letting the satin slide to the floor. When he gasped, his eyes raking her body, wrists straining against the shackles, she returned his fiery gaze, her body equally on fire.

Slowly, very slowly, she began to raise the sheer night rail until she had it bunched in her fists at shoulder height. With a swift motion, she pulled it over her head and let it float to the floor, landing in a soft pile atop her robe. She walked to the foot of his bed and tugged off his boots and socks, tossing them in the corner.

Then she climbed onto the mattress and crawled between his legs, reaching toward the lacings of his buckskins. "Now, open wide . . . again," she repeated. His legs parted with a will of their own. She moved closer and started to work.

"If you don't hurry, I'll explode," he gritted out, desperate for her to remove the last impediment between their flesh.

She finished unlacing the buckskins and pulled his phallus free, then leaned back on her knees, arms crossed beneath her breasts, gazing at its pulsing length. He was rock hard and straining against the irons holding his arms to the bed. "Mmmm, I think I like this. Perhaps I'll keep you in chains until we reach St. Louis. Pity the trip will be so brief . . . maybe next year when we go upriver . . ."

Clint's hips rose and his knees bent, trapping her between his legs. "Stop foolin' around and do what you know we both want you to do," he said in a raspy voice.

"I like fooling around," she murmured, slipping from his leg lock. She lowered her body to his, allowing her breasts to brush his chest. The contact sent a sizzle of sudden pleasure jolting through her, but she suppressed the desire to move quickly. Instead, she offered one breast to him, while at the same time letting the soft curls at the apex of her thighs press against his straining erection.

With an oath of pleasure and frustration, he took the offering in his mouth and suckled, then gave her a small, swift bite. She jerked away, touching her breast in amazement, making sure it wasn't injured. "Why did you—"

"Just payin' you back a little for our first kiss." A lazy grin spread across his face now. "Notice, I didn't even draw blood."

"I'm going to make you pay for that, Mr. Daniels," she said, scooting down the mattress and taking his shaft in one hand. She teased it with her fingers, knowing she was playing with fire—a liquid flame that had ignited in her own belly and pooled between her legs. How long could she resist? When he strained at the shackles, the muscles of his arms and chest stood out, sweat-sheened in the soft light, tan and rippling, powerful. She moved away from the instrument that was causing her—as well as him—to lose control, and let her hand splay over his chest, feeling his heart pound. Then she grazed her nails slowly down, tracing the narrowing vee of gold hair that traveled back to the inevitable.

"You must've been a Spanish Inquisitor in a previous life," he said through gritted teeth.

Delilah cocked her head, considering. "Perhaps. Some kinds of torture are great fun." Without warning, she climbed higher and swung one knee, then the other, outside his hips and moved over the rigid staff begging for attention. She brushed back and forth, just enough for her moisture to wet the head of his phallus.

"How long are you going to keep this up?"

"Oh, I don't know. How long can you keep that up?" she replied, breathlessly.

"St. Louis?" he ventured, positioning himself as she swayed over him.

"That long?" she asked, with a roll of her hips. "I am impressed."

"You should be." He gasped, raising his hips and plunging upward, impaling her with a hard thrust. "But, I . . . am . . . a very . . . impatient man," he said, feeling her moist heat surround him. He rotated his hips, then began to withdraw.

Delilah followed him down as he lay against the mattress, placing her hands on his chest. "I was impatient when you first taught me this game, remember?"

"I never figured on bein' chained to a bed to practice," he replied, waiting for her to move as he arched high inside her.

"I never figured on having to chain you for practice." Finally, unable to resist, she began the familiar ride, slowly at first, then quickly escalating to a desperately swift pace that sent her spiraling out of control, her body convulsing with spasms of pleasure that shook her soul. *I can't ever lose you, Clint, never!* Delilah waited as the storm subsided. Then feeling him yet rock hard inside her, she began again . . . and again . . .

Finally, he knew his endurance was ending. He tried to think of something, anything besides his cat-eyed woman with her silky flesh pressed so close to his, her scent heavy in his nostrils, her fiery hair brushing his shoulders while her breasts burned against his chest. She was his in a way she'd belonged to no other, and that pleased him more than he wanted to admit. She had betrayed him, sent bluebellies after him, had him dragged here in shackles—hell, she'd even taken his boat!

But none of that mattered now. All he could think of was their joining and how much he desired to have her by his side always. That thought forced an end to his control. He spilled himself in deep, wrenching pulses, filling her, feeling her cries as she came to culmination yet again. For all her skill in hiding her feelings across a card table or in a business negotiation, Deelie could never hide this. This was primal truth.

The truth was he loved her.

As she collapsed on top of him and nestled against his shoulder, the unalterable fact rocked him to his very soul. He could not travel down this road again, had sworn never to allow such pain in his life again. Yet here he was, in love with a woman once more. A woman who didn't even trust him. *Fool!*

Unable to stop himself, he asked, "Deelie, why did you send the soldiers after me?"

She grew very still, her hands cupped around his shoulders, motionless for several moments as the silence thickened. Finally, she sighed, letting out a long, slow breath. Then she rose up and looked down into his face, meeting his gaze, as if measuring her response.

What would it be?

Chapter Nineteen

$\mathcal{I}$t was not that I didn't trust you," she began hesitantly, then bit her lip and continued, "well, maybe I didn't—but not for the reasons you think. I wasn't afraid of losing the money. I don't believe you'd run off with it—not . . . not any longer."

"Then what?" he coaxed, utterly confused as he saw his own tumbling emotions mirrored in her eyes.

"Sky told me about your wife and child . . . what you did . . ." She felt his whole body stiffen with outrage. "Please, don't be angry with her. I saw the way you began to change the farther upriver we traveled, your clothes, your hair . . . your . . . manner. Then the incident with the Tetons and the dynamite . . . that ghastly woodhawk's camp . . ."

He almost wrenched his shoulders from their sockets as he came up off the mattress. "You followed and spied on me at Johnson's lair! Well, I reckon it's a good thing you did have the bluebellies shackle me. Who knows what a savage like the Liver Eater might do to you," he said tightly. "Tell me, did you enjoy the show we put on for you?"

A bright spurt of fury swept through her, amazing her as she seized his shoulders and shook him, digging her nails into the muscles. "Don't you ever dare compare yourself to that—that animal! You're nothing like him—nothing, do you hear me!" When he turned his head away, she cupped his jaw in her hand and caressed it, letting her thumb rest on the cleft in his chin. "You mourned over the vengeance you exacted— you didn't revel in it. Sky told me how you drank and grew suicidal with grief and guilt. Then when Talks Wise finally brought you back from the abyss, you returned to civilization and took care of your sister."

"That's me, purely noble," he snarled. Humiliation swept away reason. She had seen him in that hideous place, that very heart of darkness.

"Clint, if I hadn't brought you back to the *Nymph,* I was afraid you'd sell our cargo and wire me the money, then join the Sioux who are being hunted down by the army. You'd be killed for certain. I . . . I couldn't let that happen."

"You couldn't let that happen." He parroted her words in a harsh, angry burst. "Well, I surely appreciate your concern, ma'am, but it was my decision to make, not yours."

Delilah slipped quickly from the bed and seized her robe. With her back turned to Clint, she jammed her arms into the sleeves and tied the sash, then scooped up her night rail. She walked to the lantern without looking at him and turned down the wick so he could not see the tears trickling down her cheeks. Once the room was dark enough, she pulled the key to his shackles from her pocket and unfastened his right arm, then tossed the cold steel on his chest.

"I don't believe you'll cut off my head for a trophy, Clint. You're free. If you want to break your family's heart, then go off and join those poor people the army will decimate, leave behind the life you've built in St. Louis. Try to expiate your imagined sins by killing yourself on a battlefield." *I'll die with you, my love . . .*

She could hear him unlocking the other chain and heard the soft rustle as he picked up his buckskins and started to pull them up his legs. Delilah let herself out of the room, leaving him alone in the dark.

Clint stood on the hurricane deck as they loaded the soldiers on the boat. He had refused to go ashore with Delilah and Jacques when they met with the commandant at Fort Abraham Lincoln that morning. As he knew she would, Deelie played her poor widow card, and the army agreed to pay them four hundred a day for the services of Jacques Dubois and *The*

River Nymph to transport the wounded back to Jefferson Barracks in St. Louis. The money would arrive eventually.

After she'd unlocked Clint's shackles four days ago, Sergeant Finn's troopers had kept a close eye on him. The river was high and very swift-moving, but he knew that even if he jumped overboard, he'd be as likely to get stuck in mud as swim to shore—and that was if they didn't shoot him either way. When they moored at night, he was not confined to his cabin, but sentries were always posted along the shoreline. In truth, he was not certain if he wanted to escape. He went about in a daze of confusion, humiliated and guilty, trying to sort out what to do with his life. So far answers had eluded him.

And Deelie avoided him. *Well, hell, why wouldn't she?*

He continued his duties as mate, keeping order on the main deck and supervising the crew for the captain. When occasional fights broke out between passengers over sleeping space, the angry yellow-haired man with the gun quickly put an end to them. Perhaps it was something the combatants saw in his eyes . . .

Although Deelie's betrayal still stung bitterly, his anger toward the wounded men he saw now began to evaporate. They were just ordinary soldiers, following the orders of an egotistical madman whose craving for fame and power knew neither conscience nor bounds. He watched as they were carried up the gangplank on crude litters, bloody bandages and crude splints covering shattered limbs—and those were the ones fortunate enough not to have been gutshot or hit in the face.

"Poor devils," he said quietly, remembering his days in that Union prison in Alton, Illinois, when Confederate soldiers lay with their wounds festering until cholera finished off many who might otherwise have survived with decent medical care. Blue or Gray, men such as these paid for the stupidity of their leaders. That was the insanity of war. He had experienced enough of senseless violence. His life had been destroyed twice because of war. Perhaps he lacked the spirit to rebuild it a third time.

Clint watched Delilah and Luellen overseeing the placement of the wounded. During the time when the majority owner and the captain of the *Nymph* signed papers at the fort, the formidable Mrs. Colter had enlisted a dozen soldiers to cut fresh buffalo grass and make soft pallets of it on the main deck. Since the cargo had been offloaded and they had not been allowed sufficient time to fill the space with return passengers, there was plenty of room. Luellen selected the coolest places away from the boilers, well-shaded from the harsh July sun.

Delilah and the doctor from the fort stood directly below him, discussing the care and treatment of the patients during the voyage. Clint watched him hand her a black leather case filled with medicines and a large drawstring cloth sack of bandages. After the medical officer left, she paused, as if feeling his eyes on her from above, then quickly walked away from the gangplank and disappeared on the floor of the main deck.

Clint tried to tell himself her avoidance of him was for the best. She had seen Johnson's lair. She had overheard their vile exchange of insults, Johnson's accusation: *What makes you think you're better than me?* Just because he'd taken scalps instead of heads did not exonerate him from the soul-staining savagery of his acts. He shuddered in self-loathing as he remembered his response to the Liver Eater—a swift punch, knocking the big old bastard to the ground. As if that could silence the demons lurking inside his head. Perhaps that was why he then nearly killed Johnson's hired gun . . . or dared Biedler to kill him.

Perhaps he should dive into the river and let Finn's men shoot him. End it. But then he thought of Sky and Talks Wise and all the rest of his Ehanktonwon family . . . and, insidiously, of Deelie. She'd done her best to hide her tears from him when she freed him, but he'd seen them. He knew he had hurt her as much as she had unwittingly hurt him. But that was all he would do—hurt her again and again if they continued their relationship.

Clint stared out at the water rushing swift and brown, twisting treacherously around sandbars and rocks, filled with hidden surprises—the joy of gliding over smooth water could abruptly end in a crash of splintering wood. "The Missouri as metaphor for my life," he muttered, laughing at his circling thoughts. Blind Owl had been right: He'd spent too much time reading white men's books!

If only they could teach him how to handle his volatile affair with Delilah Raymond. He'd already broken his sworn oath never to fall in love with a woman again. But that did not mean he would soil her with the sickness buried deep inside him, one not even her skilled nursing could cure. Once they reached St. Louis and completed their contract with the army, he'd sell her his 49 percent of the *Nymph* and return to the Blasted Bud. And Eva. That was the only way to convince Deelie to get on with her life. Somewhere traveling up and down the river, she would find a man worthy of her.

But that man would not be Clint Daniels . . . the man she now knew as Lightning Hand, the Pawnee Killer. The thought left a hollowness in his gut. Swallowing the bitter taste in his mouth, he pushed away from the railing and went to his cabin to wait until Deelie left the main deck.

Delilah knelt beside the pallet of a soldier who had lost an arm and was running a fever. "Just let me raise your head and give you this medicine, Private Simmons," she said to him. He was little more than a boy, with blue eyes and yellow hair. She wondered if Clint had ever looked so young or helpless. She doubted it.

"You're an angel, ma'am," the young soldier said in a voice raw with pain. He grimaced at the taste of laudanum.

"It will ease the pain, help you sleep," she said, urging him to swallow the rest. "Now, some fresh, cool water."

He looked up at her. "It ain't from the river, is it?" he

asked, almost pleadingly. "If it is, I'll have to chew it." At the fort, river water had been used for drinking.

"No, it's from a fresh stream. We fill barrels with it every chance we get."

He murmured thanks as his eyelids slowly closed and he drifted off to sleep.

Delilah found herself fighting tears. He was so young, maimed for life. The army had been his only career and now that was ended. She prayed he had family who would care for him and that he and the others would find a way to earn a living. Without that, all the medals and honors Washington intended to bestow on them would be meaningless.

"Yer all tuckered out, Missus. Best let me take over," Luellen said, reaching for the wet cloth Delilah was using to bathe Private Simmons's face. "You been at this fer days 'n hardly slept."

"So have you, besides cooking for everyone on the boat," Delilah replied, continuing her task. "I'll manage. Although I don't know how we would've done it if the army had been forced to send all the wounded back with the *Nymph*. As it stands, nineteen are too many for only four women to provide the care and company they need. Todd and a few of the crew do what they can, but wounded men respond better to a woman's touch."

"Someone else needin' a woman's touch—yers, 'n he's hidin' out in his cabin," Luellen said, her shrewd gaze fixed on her young friend.

"Mr. Daniels is well able to fend for himself," Delilah replied softly, trying to keep the pain out of her voice, knowing she was not succeeding.

"Sooner 'er later, yew two gotta set down and talk. I don't rightly know whut's happened betwixt yew, 'n it's none 'o my bidness, but this boat's not big 'nough fer yew ta hide one from 'nother."

Delilah watched Luellen trundle away with a pail of water and knew she was right. They had been hiding from each other since the night they left Fort Abraham Lincoln. As she picked up the medicine case and her other supplies, she scanned the open deck to be certain every man was resting as comfortably as possible. The sun was a hazy orange ball sinking toward the horizon. Dinner would be served in an hour or so. If she hurried, she might have time for a cool bath to wash off the stench and blood clinging to her hands and clothing.

After asking one of the roustabouts to fetch her some water, she climbed the stairs wearily. Days such as this brought back horrible memories of the late war and working at the hospital in Pennsylvania. "Just place one foot in front of the other and you'll get through this," she murmured to herself. But her exhaustion had less to do with the men below than it did with the one in the cabin at the end of the second deck. Luellen was right: They should talk . . . if only she had the nerve to face him after the ugly end of their last meeting.

Since every surface in her cabin was covered with the medical supplies she had carefully laid out in order to keep track of them, she asked Luellen to have Todd set up her tub in her uncle's empty cabin, which adjoined hers through the small sitting room they had shared. How she missed his calm, sensible advice and dry wit. He would know what to do about Clint. When they reached Yankton, she would telegraph Fort Benton to find out when he'd departed. With any luck, he might actually beat them home on a small packet, since they had lost two days to army paperwork and loading the wounded at Fort Abraham Lincoln.

With that comforting thought, she laid her head against the back of the tub and began drifting off to sleep, utterly exhausted. The water had been filtered to remove as much of the river's silt as possible. Drinking water was far too scarce to waste on such frivolities as bathing, so she added a bit of her expensive bath oil to sweeten it. She smelled the scent of roses as her eyelids fluttered closed.

Clint paced like a caged tiger in his small cabin, looking around at four bare walls. He had been taking his meals with the roosters rather than in the dining room with the officers and Deelie, then retiring, not wanting the suspicious and hostile stares of Finn's soldiers on him. But the nights were damnably long and boring. He stared at his bed and remembered being shackled to it, Deelie coming to seduce him . . .

He forced the lovely idyll and its ugly aftermath from his mind. *Think of something else.* But what? Then he remembered the volume of Shakespeare Horace kept in his cabin. That would provide diversion. On silent moccasined feet, he slipped out and walked down the deck to his friend's door. Clint wondered if it would be locked. If so, he would not ask Deelie for the key. But, to his relief, it opened quietly. He blinked, allowing his eyes to adjust to the dim lantern light.

Clint blinked again, certain he was losing his mind. But no, there she lay up to the tips of her lush breasts in a tub of bubbles, her hair pinned on her head, which lay against the back of the big copper bathtub. Deelie was sound asleep. He had watched her on deck with the wounded men, working herself to exhaustion every day. Small wonder she slept so soundly. His mouth went dry as he studied her beautiful face in the faint golden glow from the lantern.

Every fiber of his being urged him to kneel by the side of that tub and beg her to forgive him, to let him make love to her . . . to take him back into her heart once more. His jaw clenched when he gritted his teeth in denial. He could not be that selfish. She deserved better. After allowing himself one lingering, painful last look, he slipped silently from the room. Clint knew the image he carried of her so innocently sleeping would remain with him for the rest of his life. If it was all he had left of his time with Delilah Raymond, he would treasure this memory.

"No! Please, no! Don't do it. I'd rather die . . . please . . ." The voice of the sobbing man on the table faded, as did his desperate thrashing. The poison of his wound robbed him of strength for the moment.

Delilah trembled, almost biting through her lip as she examined the red streaks starting to snake up the young corporal's lower leg toward his knee. She had seen firsthand what happened after the streaks reached the large arteries at the top of a man's thigh. Blood poisoning . . . and certain death. She turned to Luellen, who stood across from her. The two women walked out of earshot, leaving the moaning man with two soldiers standing beside the table they'd placed him on after Delilah had checked the dressing on his shattered leg that morning and discovered his critical condition.

"Yew know whut's gotta be done," was all the older woman said.

"Yes." Delilah's voice was a harsh whisper. "I've assisted doctors in military hospitals when they performed amputations a few times, but I've never done one! And we have so little ether—what if he awakens during the cutting?" She shuddered, recalling one time when soldiers had been ordered to hold down their comrade while the surgeon sawed without anesthetic because they had run out. "I . . . I don't know how fast I can get through this—or even if I'll know how to stop the bleeding once I do."

"But he'll die fer sure if'n yew don't take the lag." It was not a question. Luellen had seen enough blood poisoning to know what the red streaks meant.

"If only one of the forts we've passed had a surgeon," Delilah said. But the campaign mounted in retaliation for Custer's death had sent every doctor along their route out into the field with the army. "And Yankton's another day away." She'd been monitoring the soldier's injury since he was brought aboard.

Corporal Pierce wouldn't last another day.

Delilah headed toward the wheelhouse. When she explained the situation to Captain Dubois, he sounded the shrill whistle signaling that they were pulling to shore for an emergency. As the rumbling steam engines quieted in the lapping water, she returned to the main deck for the ordeal ahead.

Swallowing for courage, she explained to Luellen about

sterilizing the instruments she would need. But when she told Sergeant Finn what had to be done, he and the two men behind him turned distinctly green and looked away.

"I niver watched 'em cut on one of me boys, ma'am. But I've heard their screamin', that I have." He paused, as if gathering courage. "I'll help . . . if ye can't find another to volunteer. I could order one of me men—"

"No, I can't have someone pass out in the middle of the operation. Actually, it would be best to have two strong men to hold him steady while Mrs. Colter administers the ether and I . . ." she swallowed, "I do the surgery." Delilah was grateful the wound was below the knee. She was not sure she possessed enough physical strength to use a bone saw on a femur. At least this would be the smaller tibia and fibula bones in the lower leg. But the procedures to stop the bleeding during and after blurred in her mind.

Please don't let me kill him! "I need another man to assist us." She looked past the sergeant to the privates, both of whom backed up as if she were thrusting a live rattler at them. "Please," she entreated as Pierce moaned. She swept the crowd, soldiers, passengers and crew, searching desperately for a volunteer. Heads shook and men looked away, unable to meet her eyes.

"Aw, hell, I'll do it." Clint emerged from the side of the boiler, where he'd been silently watching the scene play out.

"He's a damned Reb. Why'd he help one of us live?" a private said from the back of the crowd.

"If I don't, 'pears to me he'll die for sure," Daniels drawled, then looked at the grizzled sergeant. "Well, Finn, looks as if we'll be on the same side this time 'round."

The two men took each other's measure. Sergeant Finn nodded. "If ye'll be standin' it, so will I."

They looked at Delilah, who nodded. "I'm grateful to both of you." She turned to Luellen. "Have Beth and Sadie bring the kettles of boiling water with the instruments. Then I'll show you how to use the ether."

"How much of that do you have?" Clint asked her in a quiet voice when the cook walked away.

"Not as much as I'd like. That's why I need strong men to hold him steady . . . just in case . . ."

His hands gripped her arms and he gave her a tiny smile of encouragement. "You can do this, Deelie. I know you can. We'll back you. Just dose him up good with laudanum before we start. It might make the ether last longer."

"I've already given him quite a bit. . . ." She hesitated, knowing they would need it for him later—and for other patients who were also in terrible pain.

"We'll be in Yankton tomorrow. There's a doc there named Morrow. I know he'll have laudanum for sale."

She looked up into his eyes, gathering strength from his touch. "All right. Then let us begin."

Clint watched her walk resolutely over to the corporal and speak soothingly to him, giving him another dose of the narcotic. After Luellen's kitchen helpers brought the pots of boiled water filled with instruments, both girls fled, as had most of the others in the crowd. Delilah laid out a clean white cloth and extracted the tools she would use, lining them up as she watched Corporal Pierce's eyelids close.

Daniels was certain when she paused and closed her eyes that she was trying desperately to envision the surgeries she'd seen during the war. He'd seen a few himself. Not something anyone wanted to recall voluntarily. He studied Finn and found the sergeant looking steadier than he had a few moments earlier. The tough Irishman would do all right. He had to admit to a grudging admiration for the bluebelly's grit— and decency. After Finn and his men had subdued him in that bar in Fort Benton, the sergeant could've let the soldiers bust him up, but he hadn't.

When everything was ready, Delilah examined Pierce, who was dozing from the effects of the laudanum. But when she began bathing the area above his smashed leg with alcohol, he awakened and began sobbing incoherently. She nodded to Luellen, who stood at Pierce's head.

"Jest yew lay back now, n' everthin'll be right as rain," she crooned, stroking his soft brown hair as she let a few drops of the clear liquid fall through the folded thicknesses of gauze. Then she laid it gently over his nostrils and cupped his jaw. When he tried to move, the sergeant leaned over his upper body while Clint secured his uninjured leg to the table, then held the one to be cut for Delilah.

"You can do it, Deelie. Get it done, now," he whispered with conviction.

He watched as she worked, amazed at her steady hands and deft fingers. Those same smooth, white hands that had flipped cards with such skill now held a man's life in their grip. Gory with blood, she worked as swiftly as she could, plying the crude instruments the doctor at Fort Abraham Lincoln had given her. Old and well used, they had doubtless been replaced for the campaign ahead. Of course, the army wouldn't be wasting any healing arts on the *savages* they pursued.

Just as she was cauterizing the bleeding stump, Pierce suddenly jerked to consciousness and began to moan and thrash. "I run out 'o ether," Luellen said, cradling the boy's head in her hands. Both Finn and Daniels increased their hold on him, steadying his body.

"Dose him with more laudanum," Delilah ordered the cook, then hurried on with her awful task.

When it was finally complete, she inspected her work, noting the amount of blood lost—more than she would have liked— but far less than she'd seen men lose and still survive. "I'll give him more laudanum in an hour," she said, dropping her tools back into the pot, whose water was now pink from blood. "Sergeant, please dispose of that," she said. Without a word he wrapped what was left of the ruined lower leg in some bloody cloth and carried it to the starboard side of the boat. He tossed it into the rushing brown water, where it quickly vanished.

She stepped back and swayed on her feet, then forced herself to stand upright. "As soon as he's still, tie him securely to the table so he can't move much. It could start the bleeding again," she said to Luellen. Clint continued to hold the semiconscious Pierce while she covered his lower body with a clean white sheet.

Clint released the corporal's leg when he felt the muscles go slack as the drug did its work. Finn returned, watching Luellen complete the task she'd been given. The sergeant looked across at Delilah. "Ma'am, did ye ever consider becomin' a doc? 'Tis that fine ye'd be at it."

She shook her head. "God, no. I've seen enough already to last a dozen lifetimes, but I do thank you for your help."

"Corporal Pierce is me own soldier. Me own responsibility. 'Tis the Reb here we both should be thankin'."

But when they turned to where Daniels had been standing, he was no longer there.

"Where in the divil?" Finn muttered.

Delilah thought of Clint swimming across the river and vanishing into the brush along the riverbanks, but Luellen said calmly, "He jest hightailed it up the steps ta the hurricane deck. If yew hurry, yew kin catch up ta him." She looked at Delilah.

Without a word, Delilah peeled off her bloody apron and dashed toward the stairs. None of the soldiers was paying attention. Everyone had returned to look in on Pierce now that the worst was over.

Clint wouldn't run away now . . . would he?

Chapter Twenty

$\mathcal{D}$elilah found him standing on the hurricane deck, staring out at the landscape of distant purple hills and rocky ground covered with dense sage. She had never seen another human being look so alone. Hesitantly, she stepped to the railing and looked up at his face. In profile it appeared chiseled from granite, so striking and bold, yet desolate. "Thank you for what you did down there," she said, aching to touch him but not quite daring.

"Someone had to help." He shrugged, still not looking at her.

She smiled softly and touched his arm. "Even if it meant working with a 'bluebelly'?"

He turned then, and bestowed one of his old grins on her. "Finn isn't a bad sort . . . for a bluebelly. And that kid . . . I saw too many like him in the war, on both sides. Left to die by their so-called leaders, who don't give a damn what happens to them."

"Yes, so did I," she replied quietly.

Clint could read a wealth of suffering in her eyes. "You know, Reb and Yank aside, we're kinda alike in some ways."

"We both hate war," she said hopefully.

He nodded. "That's the truth. A man oughta have the right to pick his day to die, not have some idiot general do it for him."

"And you want to die?"

He resumed gazing out at the vast, rolling hills beyond the river. "Sometimes." Then he looked back at her. "Other times, I'm not so sure."

She studied him for a moment, knowing her heart must appear in her eyes. "Dare I ask if I have anything to do with that?"

He placed two fingers beneath her stubborn little chin and tipped it up, giving her a lopsided smile. "Cat Eyes, you've given me nothing but trouble from the first time I met you . . . but—"

A shrill whistle from the wheelhouse drowned them out as the captain gave the order to pull out into the current and resume their trip downriver. The spell was broken. Clint lowered his hand and stepped back. "I promised Zeke Hagadorn a chance to win back some matchsticks before he goes on duty."

She stood and watched him saunter down the stairs. Delilah would've given anything to hear what he was going to say after that pregnant *but* . . .

Perhaps because of that interrupted conversation, Clint avoided Delilah, keeping busy overseeing the crew on wood stops and breaking up fights between bored roustabouts. She, too, was consumed by nursing duties. Corporal Pierce rested fretfully, but no further signs of blood poisoning or other infection appeared on his leg. They lost another half day when a badly gutshot man died and had to be turned over to the army at Fort Randall for burial.

As soon as they pulled into Yankton, Delilah rushed to the telegraph office and wired Fort Benton. Horace had left her an incredible message. He'd sold their cargo for a good deal more than they'd anticipated and taken a packet for St. Louis. He promised to greet his niece at the levee with a bank deposit note for over forty thousand dollars—and that did not include the profit from the whiskey sale! She rushed back to the boat and found Clint with the first engineer, inspecting one of the boilers after two crewmen had shoveled out the river muck.

Giddy with excitement, she threw herself into his arms as he turned toward the sound of her running footsteps and cry. "Clint! We did it! We did it—forty-two-thousand-dollars profit on the cargo!" She did not mention the substantial sum the whiskey had brought.

His eyes crinkled at the corners and he grinned broadly as he swung her around in a circle. "Your uncle missed his callin'. Horace Mathers should've been a drummer. That's more than I figured we'd make, Deelie."

Laughing and yelling with joy, they kissed without consciously intending it. When she would have kissed him again, he gently pulled back and released her. As she slid slowly down his body with her eyes gleaming bright green in the sunlight, everyone on deck watched them, some with a mixture of chuckles and cheers, others with knowing smirks. They all could see the owners had feelings for each other.

Clint cursed to himself as she backed away a step. Damnation, she wanted to be a respectable businesswoman in the city. The passengers and crew would spread gossip as soon as their feet hit the St. Louis levee. Now she looked hurt, her bubbling joy turned to resigned sadness. "You're rich now, Mrs. Raymond," he said softly. "An independent woman, free to make her own way in life. Let society be damned."

With that puzzling pronouncement, he walked away as crewmen and passengers slapped him on the back and offered congratulations to both of them. Delilah smiled determinedly and accepted good wishes from everyone crowding around her. *I'm rich. I'm independent. I'm free.* She had everything she had ever wanted since the war took it all away. Then why was she so blessed miserable?

Damn Clinton Daniels to perdition. She would find a way to win him back once they were home . . .

When the St. Louis levee came into view, the men on deck began to cheer, but the rows of side-wheelers and stern-wheelers lining the waterfront, backed by big brick warehouses stretching up the hill, were not their first destination. Everyone knew the *Nymph* had to discharge its precious cargo of wounded cavalrymen at Jefferson Barracks, where some of the army's finest doctors waited to treat them in preparation for a trip to Washington, D.C. The old army post was situated several miles south of the city on a scenic bluff of gold sandstone surrounded by trees and rolling hills.

Sergeant Finn watched the shoreline as the fort came into view. "It's a debt we'll niver be able to repay ye . . . the kindness of a woman's touch for these wounded men, ma'am," he said to Delilah and Luellen, giving each an awkward but gallant bow and kissing their hands with proper formality.

"The army will pay us, but the most important thing is that these men make as full a recovery as possible," Delilah said as soldiers filed past her with litters to carry off their comrades.

"We only done whut any good Christian would'a done," Luellen averred, her cheeks a bit pink when the grizzled Irishman took her work-roughened hand and kissed the back of it.

Delilah had seen the two of them speaking together often during the voyage and smiled to herself. "Will you be stationed here in St. Louis now, Sergeant?" she asked for her friend.

"That I won't be knowin' 'til the army gives me orders. But if there be a way on the Lord's green earth to make it back to St. Louis, I'll visit ye. Th' barracks has a rail line straight to the city, don't ye know?"

Delilah noted with satisfaction that he directed his reply to the Widow Colter, whose address he must already have. As he strutted down the gangplank and saluted the commander, she said to Luellen, "A fine figure of a man, is himself."

Luellen snorted. "Yer Irish accent ain't thet good, but I reckon I agree with ye though." She smiled broadly now.

The commandant of the barracks sent his aide aboard with more paperwork for Delilah and Clint to sign. "The army is greatly in your debt," he said with a brisk salute.

"Just so the debt's repaid in Yankee dollars, then we'll be square," Clint drawled.

Delilah could see the tension between the young lieutenant and Clint. "Please forgive my business partner, sir. Every time he sees a blue uniform, I fear it brings out the very worst in him." She gave the sandy-haired young man a blinding smile.

Clint watched the shave-tail melt under her charm. *The woman's a witch. She could make a blind man see, just listenin' to her voice.* While Deelie and the bluebelly talked, he slipped quietly up the stairs.

When the men Delilah and Luellen had nursed for several weeks were carried down the gangplank, the two women bade each one farewell and wished him good fortune in the future. Corporal Pierce, looking considerably better than he had immediately after his ordeal, clutched Delilah's hand with both of his own.

"You saved my life, ma'am. I'm sorry I was so ungrateful before, but I been thinking about what I'll do once I'm out of the army. My father's got a cabinetmaker's shop up in Hannibal. He always wanted me to come in with him. Now I reckon I will." He managed a weak smile. "He can even make me a wooden leg to get 'round on. I wouldn't have made it this far without you. Thank you."

Delilah fought back tears and the lump in her throat and said, "You will do just fine, I'm certain." She was immensely relieved that he had come out of his depressed state and had family to help him rebuild his life.

The wounded soldiers, green youths and battle-scarred veterans alike, were shyly grateful to their nurses and thanked them profusely. A full military color guard had been turned out to honor the heroes of the Little Big Horn and a band played the Seventh's fight song, "Garry Owen."

"Lots of pomp and glory. I hope the poor devils live long enough to forget what they've been through," Clint said softly as the last of them disappeared from view over a rolling hill.

Delilah had not heard his return over the babel of voices and music. "You still carry scars—and I don't just mean the ones I've seen on your body. The nightmares will end—if you'll just let go, Clint."

He snorted. "You can't amputate my head, darlin'. There are some things even you can't heal."

"No, *I* can't . . . but *you* can," she replied stubbornly. "It's why you've been avoiding me—because of your precious guilt. While I've been nursing wounded soldiers, you've been nursing your wounded soul."

"Maybe so . . . or maybe I just want better for you, Deelie." He turned away and strode down the deck, leaving her alone to ponder what he had said. And not said.

The ten-mile trip up the Mississippi back to St. Louis took another day. As soon as they pulled into a berth on the levee, Delilah and Clint were the first to disembark, searching the melee for Horace.

"Surely he must've heard that we steamed by yesterday," she said, looking for his tall, thin figure but not seeing it.

"I'll head up to the Eagle Boat mercantile and see when his packet came in," Clint said. "You wait here."

She had a twinge of unease as he hailed a hack and climbed in. Where was Uncle Horace? Deciding she was just being a worrier, Delilah returned to her cabin to pack. They would be able to afford a decent hotel now, and the thought of moving off the constantly rocking steamer and sleeping in a real bed sounded like heaven to her. Perhaps her uncle had already secured them rooms at one of the city's best. With that comforting thought, she set to work.

But an hour later, Clint knocked on her door. "Bad news, Deelie," he said grimly when she opened it.

"What's happened?" she said, grasping his arm. "Has my uncle been injured or—"

"No. He just hasn't arrived yet. A half-dozen packet boats from upriver have left off passengers over the past week, but he wasn't on any of them." Seeing the stricken look on her face, he added, "Don't fret. Those little boats sometimes break down and fall behind schedule, just like big steamers. Maybe he'll arrive tomorrow. Meanwhile, the captain's invited us to his home for dinner tonight. You get gussied up and I'll be back to collect you in a couple of hours."

With visions of Horace's packet smashed on rocks or a

sawyer in the swift Missouri current, Delilah had little desire to eat, but she nodded woodenly. "I'll be ready." At least it would be good to see Mrs. Dubois again, and to meet their daughter, who would be home from boarding school now.

When she opened the door almost three hours later, Delilah emitted a small gasp of delight upon seeing the transformation in Clint. "You've gone to a barber," she said approvingly as her eyes swept over his freshly shaved face. The ragged shoulder-length hair was once more trimmed with clearly delineated sideburns. Her eyes swept down from his ruffled white shirt and perfectly tailored dark blue suit to the polished black boots on his feet.

"Do I look civilized enough, Deelie?" he asked, raising his scarred eyebrow mockingly.

He looked good enough to eat, but she wasn't about to tell the handsome devil that. "I'm happy the old Clinton Daniels has returned," she said as she took his proffered arm.

He looked at her and gave her that, butter-wouldn't-melt-in-his-mouth grin. "Deelie, you set too much stock on outer appearance. You can't know what I'm like inside."

She returned his smile with a dazzling one of her own, pushing her worry about Horace to the back of her mind for now. Clint was back; Lightning Hand had been banished. "I believe your outer transformation signifies an inner one, too." Before he could remonstrate, she said, "Let's enjoy an evening of celebration with Captain Dubois and his family upon completion of another safe trip from the wilds of the upper Missouri."

They both knew that the escape from Montana Territory had more to do with his problems than with the captain's perfect record. Clint merely nodded and escorted her to the hurricane deck and down the stairs. As he helped her into the carriage he'd hired before returning to the levee, he feasted on her loveliness. She wore a copper-colored silk gown that molded to her upper body and flattered her sun-kissed skin and the more pronounced reddish highlights in her hair. When she raised her skirt to step up, he could admire a glimpse of slender ankle and foot encased in a matching high-heeled slipper. Hell, even if she hadn't known a club from a diamond, any man would lose his shirt to her in a card game! *And his heart . . .*

Their dinner with the captain and his family proved delightful. But on the carriage ride back to the boat, Delilah could not help returning to the worry gnawing at her ever since they had learned Horace was not in St. Louis.

"He was carrying a great deal of money. You don't suppose one of the crew—"

"Jacques handpicked those men. He's worked with them for years and is a passin' good judge of character. No, no one's robbed him and left him for dead, Deelie," Clint said soothingly.

She could see a worried look on his face in the bright moonlight. In spite of his reassuring words, something was wrong. "You say one thing, but I detect something else. Surely you don't believe my uncle would steal our money?"

He shook his head emphatically. "No, of course not. I'd trust Horace Mathers with my life."

"But . . . ?" she prompted.

"Well, you'll find out soon enough, so I might as well tell you now." Clint sighed. "Jacques didn't want to worry you. That's why he didn't mention it. He's willing to wait, but his crew will expect to be paid within the week. Lots of them live up and down the river and have hungry families to feed. And Herr Krammer knows that we've returned and we owe him three thousand, too, although like the captain, I expect he can afford to wait longer."

Delilah sat very still for several moments, dreading what she had to tell Clint. He sensed her unease. Taking her hand in his, he removed the glove and pressed a kiss on her bare palm. "All right. Tell me what's goin' on in that devious little mind of yours."

Now it was her turn to sigh. In a very small voice, she replied, "Mr. Krammer isn't the only one we owe. Before we were able to begin outfitting for the trip, I took out a ten-thousand-dollar loan on the *Nymph* from Consolidated Planters Bank in St. Charles. It will come due the end of the month."

"Damn, Adam must've done somethin' really skunk rotten for the Lord to have created woman," he muttered, combing his hands through his hair.

Delilah bristled. "It was the only way I could manage. You were the one who cheated, tricking me with that low card— and . . . and walking off the boat stark-naked! No one would work for us!"

"Oh, so now it's my fault!" He threw up his hands, as if imploring the heavens for an explanation of the inexplicable nature of feminine logic. "You had no idea about what it cost to pay a crew or fit out a steamer. I suppose that was my fault, too, hmmm?"

Delilah struggled not to rip out his eyeballs. "What's done is done. There is no sense in recriminations," she snapped.

"Recriminations? Sounded a lot more like you callin' me a card cheat."

"Uncle Horace saw you palm that deuce!"

"And had the good sense not to say anything. Of course, he expected I was cheatin' to win the thousand, not lose the clothes right off my backside," he said with a chuckle. "Admit it, Deelie, you had that coming and I outsmarted you."

"You forced yourself into a partnership on the *Nymph* and now we're both in mutual debt," she replied smugly, regaining control of her temper. "We must look at this logically, Clint. If you're right—and you *must* be—then my uncle will be here in a few days with plenty of money to pay what we owe and have a fat profit left to split. All we need to do is stall for time."

He slouched back against the seat of the carriage and regarded her. She sat ramrod straight on the edge of the seat, as if ready to jump if a feather touched her. "You're still worried about Horace, aren't you?"

"Yes," she replied in a small voice. "More than anything else. If something's happened to him—"

"Shhh, nothin's happened to him," he said, leaning forward and taking her in his arms. He rubbed her back softly. "Tell you what, in the mornin', I'll talk to the crew. Get them to wait for their pay. You explain to Mr. Krammer about what's happened. I imagine he'll be happy to extend your loan. We have enough time for the bank note. It'll all work out, Deelie."

She squeezed her eyes closed and inhaled the smell of fresh starch from his shirt. It felt so natural and comforting to be in his arms. She wanted to be held this way for the rest of her life. When she raised her head and her eyes met his, she searched for the answer to her unasked question, but he looked away.

"And after that, Clint—then what?" she dared to ask.

He sighed as the carriage pulled up in front of the *Nymph*. "Hell, Deelie, I don't know . . . I just don't know. I reckon our creditors aren't the only ones needin' more time. A woman like you deserves better than the devil's bargain we made upriver. I'm just not sure I can give you what you're entitled to have."

Delilah deflated. Pulling away from him and gathering her skirts, she quickly stepped out of the carriage before he could assist her. He caught up to her at the top of the gangplank. "Deelie, wait!"

"For what, Clint? I thought tonight . . . the way you looked, the way you acted . . . I thought you were through with your old life, that you'd put it behind you. But it seems as if I made a mistake."

"I told you, appearances can be deceiving. Just because I clean myself up and put on fancy duds doesn't mean the past goes away. It's still inside me."

"Well, hang on to your blessed guilt and grief and never let them go. See how happy that makes you—or better yet, go back to Eva and let her console you!"

He stood and watched her stomp off, trying to convince himself it was better this way. Better to make the cut clean and quick now that they were back in St. Louis. But the thought of returning to Eva's bed made him feel hollow. If he did that, it would be no more fair to his old partner than he'd been to his new one . . . the one he had so foolishly allowed himself to fall in love with.

"Deelie, Deelie, what are we going to do?"

The quietly lapping waters of the Mississippi had no answers for him as he slowly climbed the stairs to his cabin.

The next day Delilah watched from her cabin window as one of the roosters hauled the last of Clint's belongings down the gangplank and deposited the two bags on a wagon. So, he was taking her advice and returning to Eva at the Bud. Good riddance. If the man wanted to wallow in guilt, who was she to think she could change his life? Did she believe that he could love a woman who had taken his boat and run him into debt? Or did Clint really think her uncle had stolen his share of the money and was waiting for her to sneak out of town to join him?

Surely not. He knew them both better than that . . . which left his stupid, stubborn guilt blinding him to the possibilities of their making a life together. This was one game she could not control. Fate would deal the cards and she was powerless to do anything to change the outcome. She turned and looked in the mirror.

"The hell I can't!" she muttered to herself. If she had to claw off Eva St. Clair's face and drag him from the Blasted Bud by the front of his ruffled shirt, Delilah Raymond would have Clint Daniels!

But first things first: Until Uncle Horace returned, there was business to attend. Clint would do his part by speaking to the crew. Now it was up to her to get Mr. Krammer to agree to defer payment. Thank heavens they had nearly a month until the bank in St. Charles foreclosed. She dressed in her best dark green linen business suit, fixed her hair into a sleek chignon and jabbed a pin through her feathered hat, setting it at a rakish angle just to give herself confidence. After a final inspection of her appearance, she sent word to Mr. Hagadorn to summon a hack for her.

Within a quarter hour she reached Krammer Mercantile. Smiling when she saw him through the window arranging bolts of calico on a table, she entered the large, dim emporium. "Good day, Herr Krammer. It's good to see you again."

"Ach, Frau Raymond, it is happy I am to see you also. Last night I hear your boat has returned safely," the short, stocky man said, shaking her proffered hand as if priming a water pump. But the normal sparkle in his blue eyes was not there. He stammered, "Something there is . . . I must explain . . ."

Delilah could tell he was upset, and here she was with more bad news. "Please, my friend, what's the matter?" she asked gently. "Have you heard that my uncle has not returned yet with the money we made upriver? I promise we will—"

"*Nein, nein,* never would I doubt your honesty. I know you would pay." He sighed, running his hands over the top of his pink scalp. "To tell you this is very difficult. It is not me you must pay. It is Red Riley."

Chapter Twenty-one

$\mathcal{R}$ed Riley?" she echoed, appalled. "How could we owe him?"

"I was late on a payment at my bank. This, it happens now and then. Never before was there a problem. Until now. Herr Riley buys my note from Herr Brinker at the Boatman's Bank. He forecloses. Now Riley owns this business . . . and I do not believe an extension on your debt he will allow."

Delilah felt as if one of the teamsters on the levee had just run over her with a load of quarry rock. "How soon will we have to make good on that note?" she asked, resisting the urge to twist her handkerchief into shreds. Riley would be merciless.

Krammer chewed his mustache, shaking his head hopelessly. "Next week, the first day."

"Monday?" she echoed numbly. That gave them only five days. Would Uncle Horace return by then? "My uncle is bringing a huge amount of money from the sale of our cargo. He should be here any day now." She tried to say that with conviction, but a premonition of dread began to settle over her. What if Riley had sent men upriver after them, waited and waylaid Horace? Not only might the money be lost, but her beloved uncle as well. The thought was too horrible to contemplate.

"Do not fear, *leipchen*," Krammer said, patting her arm in a fatherly fashion. "He will be here, I am certain."

Delilah's eyes narrowed as she considered Riley and his vengeance. One way or the other, she would beat the vicious bastard. If one hair on Horace Mathers's head was harmed, she would see Big Red Riley begging in the streets before she was finished with him. "I'm sure we'll be fine—oh, yes, and when this is over, you'll own this mercantile again. I swear it!"

Clint and the captain called a meeting with the crew of the *Nymph*. The men assembled restively that afternoon, milling about the main deck. Daniels explained that until Horace arrived with the money, they would be strapped to pay unless they sold the steamer, which would guarantee that the men would not have a job the following spring unless they signed on with one of the large companies gobbling up independent owners. These larger lines had already driven down crewmen's wages.

He promised a bonus to every man content to wait for another week. Of course, what he would do if Horace didn't show by then with the cash, he did not know. They would have to sell the *Nymph*. Hell, to make good on their other debts, he'd have to sell his share of the Bud, too! But he'd cross that river when he came to it. For now, the men, at the captain's urging, agreed to wait.

Clint knew that word of this meeting would spread like wildfire on the levee. By the time he reached the Bud that afternoon, Banjo Banks confirmed his surmise. That and other things far more alarming. He'd no more than walked in the door when his pear-shaped partner came barreling toward him.

"Boss, heerd you was back! I wuz just fixin' to fetch ya from the *Nymph*. Everybody in town's talkin' 'bout them bluebellies taking over the boat . . ." He shuffled around from one foot to the other for a moment, removing a greasy, high-crowned hat to scratch his straggly hair into further disarray.

"Spit out the bad news, Banjo," Clint said in resignation. His gut tightened.

"Wall, everybody knows 'bout yer partner's uncle stayin' behind to sell the cargo 'n fetch the cash back here. 'Pears a packet bound from Fort Benton ta St. Louie got smashed up jest above Sioux City last week. Hit by river pirates, looked like. Rumor says that Mathers feller and four of Cap'n Dubois's men was aboard. Capt'n of the *Greyhound*, ole Foxy Whitfield, he says he passed the wreck of *The River Race* a day 'er so after it happened. Stopped to look 'round fer survivors. Said he didn't find none."

Daniels's heart skipped a beat. "Foxy Whitfield wouldn't slow his packet run to rescue the Queen of England unless she waved the crown jewels from the riverbank."

"They's more . . ."

Clint saw the hard, angry expression on Banjo's face and braced himself. "This have anything to do with Riley?"

Banjo nodded. "Looks like Mathers 'n his men're dead, Boss. . . ."

As he relayed the rest of what he'd heard, Clint walked over to the bar and poured himself a stiff bourbon. "Yeah, Banjo, the smart money'd bet on Riley hiring river pirates to kill all of them." His friend Horace was gone. The loss of their money didn't even register as his thoughts raced to Deelie. Horace was all the family she had left in the world. What would she do now? Life had once again left her alone and penniless. He tossed back his whiskey and felt the burn. It matched the one in his eyes . . . and his heart. He would have to be the one to tell her.

" 'N thet ain't all."

Clint turned, unbelieving. "What more could there be?"

"Big Red bought the note on Krammer's Mercantile not long after you took off upriver. He'll be 'round to gloat and collect his money real soon."

Clint poured himself another drink, cursing beneath his breath. He would have to kill Riley somehow without getting Deelie involved. With the glass halfway to his mouth, he was interrupted by a familiar voice.

"Welcome home, baby," Eva said in a sultry drawl as she posed artfully on the stairs. Her silver-blond hair lay like polished sterling around her shoulders. She leaned forward just enough for her silk wrapper to show off the creamy curves beneath. One slender ankle showed when she bent her leg on the step. "I've missed you."

He had, in fact, barely given a thought to Eva since leaving St. Louis with Delilah and Horace. When he turned and nodded to her, she sensed something was wrong.

Deserting her position above him, she rushed down into the deserted bar, which would fill with customers in a few hours. "What's wrong, Clint? Did that Yankee bitch and her uncle separate you from your money? You still have the Bud . . . and me."

The high heels of her lavender silk mules stopped midclick when she saw the icy glint in his eyes. He set the glass carefully on the bar without drinking. "Mrs. Raymond and her uncle didn't steal my money. Riley's most probably killed Horace and left Delilah destitute."

Eva approached in spite of his hostile stance. "I'm sorry, Clint. You've fallen for her, haven't you?"

"Horace Mathers was my friend. He'd never cheat me," he said, evading a declaration of his feelings for Deelie. "Now I have to tell his niece that she's lost the only living relative she had left in the world." With that, he turned to Banjo, who had stood motionless during their conversation. "Is Samson in the stable out back?" he asked.

Banjo nodded, his Adam's apple bobbing with his head. "Shore is. I kin saddle him fer you pronto."

"I'll do it myself," Clint said, heading for the back door of the Bud. En route, he paused and told Banks, "Keep your ear to the ground about those thugs Riley hired to go after Horace. Probably river pirates. They might have stolen the money and hightailed it. Mrs. Raymond will need a stake to carry her through if her uncle's gone. We have to find them."

"I'll do thet, boss. Got me an idee or two 'bout who they might be."

"Find out for certain and let me know."

When Clint reached the levee, he reined in the gelding and let the great black beast's reins lie across the pommel of the saddle. No one on the riverfront would try to steal the valuable animal. Everyone knew the horse would allow no one but Daniels to ride him. As Clint walked up the gangplank, he rehearsed for what seemed the hundredth time how he would tell Deelie about Horace.

There was no good way. He would just have to give her the awful news straight out. He only prayed no one in town had beaten him to it. Krammer might not have heard the waterfront gossip that Banjo was assigned to monitor. He climbed the stairs to the second deck and walked to her cabin. When he knocked, he could hear her stirring within. She opened the door with an expectant look on her face that broke his heart.

"Is my uncle here?" she asked.

He took her arm and stepped inside, then closed the door. "I have some bad news, Deelie. Banjo's heard rumors on the levee. His sources say Riley sent thugs to wreck the packet your uncle and the captain's men were on. Make it look like an accident. Kill them and steal their money."

She swallowed hard. "Did they succeed?" she asked, her voice almost breaking. She knew the answer.

Clint spread his hands helplessly. "No one knows for sure. Banjo's been trying to find out if Riley's come into any large amount of cash. So far, nothing, but the thugs may have failed—or double-crossed Riley. Banjo'll keep after it until we know what happened. I'll take care of Riley." His voice was flat and cold.

Delilah sat woodenly, no tears, no more expression on her beautiful face than she'd had sitting at a poker table. He got up and poured a shot of brandy—Horace's good stuff—into a glass. "Drink this," he said gently, holding it to her lips as he knelt beside her.

With a surprisingly steady hand, she took the glass and sipped. "I knew something was wrong. He should have arrived days before us. I thought Riley might have been responsible."

Now he could see the icy calculation in her eyes. Anger was better than the numb shock she'd first exhibited. "If he knew Horace was aboard *The River Race,* it wouldn't be hard to have it sabotaged," he said.

"Riley would do anything to break us . . . even kill my uncle."

Clint took her ice-cold hands in his. "Two things seem sure: Riley would never let all that money be swept down the Missouri, and he would've told the cutthroats he hired to leave no witnesses."

Delilah stood up, clutching the glass in her hand so tightly that she might have broken it if Clint hadn't pried it from her fist. "I'm going to make him pay, Clint. It's the least I can do to honor my uncle's memory. For his whole life, Horace Mathers paid his debts—and we owe Captain Dubois, our crew and Mr. Krammer. I promised him his mercantile back, and by heavens, he will have it! And I will have a marble grave marker for my uncle placed at the front of Bellefontaine Cemetery. Red Riley won't be king of the levee for very much longer. I'll make him crawl."

He could see her dark cat-green eyes narrow. "What are you thinking, Deelie?" Already he knew it would be dangerous.

"Arrange a meeting with Riley for first thing tomorrow morning."

"To talk about what? You know he'll demand the money we owe immediately." He studied her as she walked over to the open door into Horace's room.

She picked up a volume of Blake's poetry and turned to a well-read page. "'Songs of Experience.' I know all about that," she said bitterly.

"You also knew about 'Songs of Innocence,'" he said softly. "Horace wouldn't want you to risk—"

"Risk what? All I have left is 51 percent of this boat and a fortune in debt," she said, then immediately calmed herself.

"So you figure to tempt Riley into a card game using the boat." It was not a question.

She looked up at him, clutching the volume of poetry to her heart. Now her eyes brimmed with tears that she refused to let fall. He crossed the room and took her in his arms, rubbing her back and pressing her head against his chest. But he knew she would not cry. Not now. Not until it was finished.

She let him hold her for a moment, composing herself, then looked up and met his gaze. "If I sold my share, there still wouldn't be enough to cover our debts. A card game is our only chance."

"Riley will hire a card shark to play for him, you know that."

A mocking, almost cruel smile barely touched her mouth. "Yes, I expect he'll get the best he can find between St. Paul and New Orleans. Uncle Horace could beat any one of them. So can I."

Clint knew there was no way to reason with her in her present emotional state. And she was right about being one of the very best players he'd ever faced. "Then let's see if Riley will bite," he said, pressing a kiss on her forehead before releasing her. One way or another, Big Red Riley was a walking dead man. When he reached the door, he turned and added, "If you're sure about risking the boat, it'll be the whole damn shootin' match. I'll throw in my 49 percent to sweeten the bargain."

Suddenly, the tears escaped, gliding crystalline down her pale cheeks, but she did not make a sound, just swallowed hard and nodded. As he closed the door behind him, he thought he heard her say very softly, "Thank you, Clint."

As Clint expected, Riley refused to come to the boat or to the Bud. If Mrs. Raymond and Mr. Daniels wanted to talk to him, they could come to his establishment in town. At ten the following morning. The man known on the levee as Rat Turner delivered the reply to Clint's message. Riley's small, stoop-shouldered messenger had a narrow face, close-set eyes and an elongated nose. Some said that was the reason for his unfortunate nickname, but others said it was because he was sneaky, mean and would kill anyone, then gnaw on the carcass.

"We'll be there, Rat. Tell Riley to be punctual," Clint said, knowing the little thug had no idea what the last word meant.

In the morning, Clint and Delilah rode from the levee through the more elegant red-light district and headed toward the rail yards, passing some of the roughest parts of the city. "It looks like a far larger version of Fort Benton," she said, appalled at the offal strewn on the streets and the shifty-eyed men lurking in the shadows of doorways. She thanked heaven it was too early for the whores to be up, cat-calling from the open windows above them.

Clint shrugged. "Wait till you see Red's place," was all he said.

The saloon and bordello was made of brick and took up a city block. Big Red had obviously spared no expense in building his palace. The pity of it was that he had far more money than taste.

"Crenellated towers?" Delilah said as the carriage pulled up in front of the pseudo-castle.

"He wanted a moat, but the mayor and city council balked at that. Said it would breed insect pests," he replied as he helped her down.

She paused, looking at the garish doorway but speaking to Clint. "Are you certain you want to risk your share of the boat? I don't want to—"

He placed a fingertip on her lips and smiled sadly. "Yes, you do. You want to avenge Horace and so do I. Besides, we're kinda joined at the hip . . . financially speaking. The only way Red'll go for a game is if he can get full ownership of the boat."

They entered the front door of the saloon and smelled the stale acridity of tobacco chaw mixed with cheap whiskey. Spilled beer had soaked into the wooden planks of the floor, swelling them so they buckled and creaked. Above the bar a garish painting of a voluptuous nude stared down at them with heavy-lidded, knowing eyes. Delilah blinked and looked away. There was absolutely nothing left to the imagination when the artist had finished his masterpiece.

Although the room was cavernous and filled with expen-sive fixtures, the overall effect was one of clashing colors and textures, reds and purples, rough wood and garish velour upholstery. A man with hideously large liver spots disfiguring his face stood behind a bar carved with gargoyles. He busily rubbed a soiled rag over a row of smeared glasses, ignoring the newcomers until Clint spoke.

"Howdy, Leo. We're here to see your boss. Go fetch him."

Leo "the Leopard" Lewinski looked up, and his mottled face grew red with anger. "I ain't yer errand boy, Daniels. Boss is down thataways," he said, gesturing carelessly to the long hallway at one side of the barroom.

"Into the lion's den," Delilah said softly.

"More like a rattler's pit," Clint replied, guiding her down the hall.

Daniels knocked on the door, and Riley's nasal voice echoed from the other side, "Drag it in. Door's open."

The little man sat behind a desk that dwarfed him, feet up on the top, which was littered with legal documents, over-flowing ashtrays and dishes with various stages of green mold growing on them. He sipped a whiskey, even though it was midmorning, and puffed on an Elegant Gent cigarette. When they stepped inside, Delilah nearly gagged at the stench.

Raising his glass as if for a toast, Riley recrossed his boots, shifting ankles, and leaned back until his spring chair squeaked. "You'll forgive me if I don't stand up. Only do that for ladies," he said with a nasty smirk, as if waiting to see what Daniels would do.

"You wouldn't recognize a lady if one were desperate enough to clean her boots on you, Riley," Clint replied as Delilah put a cautioning hand on his arm.

Her voice was cool and even, without a trace of the hatred she felt for the cowardly murderer. "We won't waste our time by taking a seat," she said, looking contemptuously at the low, grimy crimson chairs placed like kneelers in front of the altar of Baal. "We're here to discuss a business proposi-tion with you."

"Z'at so?" He puffed more, letting the vile-smelling to-bacco smoke fill the stale air.

It made a potent blend with his macassar-oiled hair and unwashed body. She could see the greasy gray edge staining his shirt collar. "We'll put up the *Nymph* as a stake for a poker game. It's in prime condition now, worth well over forty thousand. Me against you." She expected him to haggle about bringing in another player, but he merely hooked his thumbs in his vest pockets and chuckled.

"Honey, I don't have to play tiddledywinks to get my boat back. All I gotta do is wait. You owe my mercantile three thousand, due next week. Oh, and that there loan from Consolidated Planters for ten thousand? Soon as you default, I'll just buy the note and have the *Nymph* free 'n clear. See, no risk . . . no nothin' . . . no deal." He bit off the words between puffs from his nasty cigarette, smirking at them with hard dark eyes.

Clint was not taken by surprise nearly as much as he knew Deelie must be. The king of the St. Louis levee had spies everywhere. But she stood calmly, her outer facade unshaken as she nodded to him.

"You win this hand, Mr. Riley. But the game is far from over." With that she turned and walked out.

Clint waited until they were outside on the street before he spoke. "I'm sorry, Deelie. I should've figured Riley would find out about the bank loan in St. Charles."

Delilah took a deep breath. "I will find another way to entice him into a game. Perhaps if I went to the owner at Consolidated—"

"No, that wouldn't work. Word of our predicament's reached him now. Riley will have seen to it. Consolidated would never give an extension. Hell, we can't even get one for the cargo since Riley ruined Krammer. But there may be another way I can light a fire under the little big man."

She looked at the cunning grin shaping his lips. It did not reach his cold gray eyes. "What are you going to do?" She was dragging him into her personal vendetta. He still owned a viable business and had built a successful life here in the city. She had no right to ask him to risk it.

"Just let me handle it. Riley's greedy as a hog hip-deep in swill. If we're goin' to lose the *Nymph* anyway, let's see if we can convince Red we're selling it before the note comes due."

"But that won't do any good. What we owe is still more than what we can get for the boat under these conditions," she protested.

He assisted her into the carriage and took his seat beside her as he murmured, "Just trust me, Deelie, all right?"

She studied him for a moment. "Clint, I don't want to wreck your life—"

"Darlin', the minute I laid eyes on you, I knew you were bound to do just that."

Clint entered the telegraph office and wrote out his message in bold, slashing strokes, then handed it to the telegrapher. It read:

> To Strickland Freighting:
> Hear you are buying stern-wheelers for Fort Benton trade. Will sell *River Nymph* for thirty thousand cash. Boat appraised by Consolidated Planters at forty-two. Response required within forty-eight hours.
> Clinton Daniels, Delilah Raymond, owners.

He paid the operator, then walked out without waiting for the clerk to send it. Clint knew Buddy Sanfield sold information to Riley. No message went through the Western Union office without first being given to Big Red. He slipped quickly into the alley behind the office and waited a moment. Sure enough, Sanfield, without his green eyeshade, scurried from his office and headed toward Riley's saloon.

Grinning grimly, Daniels mounted Samson and rode back to the Blasted Bud to await developments. Old man Strickland was a shrewd businessman who would probably consider the remarkably generous offer, but he would also first check to see that the stern-wheeler was indeed worth the investment. Clint was certain Riley would not let the boat slip from his grasp again. He'd offer Delilah her poker game before any reply could come from the Strickland office in Bismarck.

Clint had no sooner ridden his black into the stable behind the Bud then Eva came rushing toward him, her usually artful morning dishabille not in place. Her hair was uncombed and she was wearing scuffed old carpet slippers. "Eva, what's happened?" he asked, fearing Riley had done something to Deelie.

"You ain't gonna believe this, Clint, honey," she said, breathlessly.

He barely did when she explained, but a sharkish grin spread across his face as he followed her inside, where Banjo Banks was writing out directions to his cousin Clem's place in the old settlement around Spanish Lake, north of the city.

By late that afternoon, word had spread across the levee and throughout the sporting district of St. Louis. Clint Daniels had sold his 60 percent of the Blasted Bud to Eva St. Clair and Justus Brummell for eleven thousand dollars. Both of them had been so frugal with their money that they could pay him in cash. Daniels was out of the saloon and fancy house business!

What would he do now? Rumors were quickly substantiated that he'd ridden that big black horse of his out of the city. No one knew where he was bound. Some said his skill with cards would lead him to use the cash as a stake. He would end up gambling on the big side-wheelers running up and down the Mississippi. A few others speculated that he would head back to Dakota Territory to live with the Sioux, since stories about his violent past had followed him downriver.

When Luellen Colter brought a dinner tray to Delilah's room that evening, she placed it on the table, then stood, wringing her work-reddened hands until her friend asked, "What is it, Luellen? I know everyone's upset about the pay we owe them, but—"

"No! No, Delilah, that ain't it. Oh, tarnation, I hate to be the one to tell you this, but better me than you hear it someplace else. Mr. D, he's up 'n sold his share of the Bud 'n left town. Nobody knows where he's gone."

Delilah sat back in her chair, utterly stunned by the information. "But . . . but, why would he . . . ?" She had seen his set face when he'd asked her to trust him and told her that he had a plan to lure Riley into that poker game. Was this a part of his ploy? She had no idea. She could see the sympathy in Luellen's face and knew the older woman thought she was a jilted lover.

"Mr. Daniels and I were business partners . . . and friends, nothing more." Even as she spoke the words, Delilah knew they rang false.

"Maybe he'll be back," Luellen said, but her words sounded equally uncertain.

"Please excuse me. I don't feel like eating just now, Luellen," she said, rising and stepping inside her small bedroom, closing the door behind her. She could hear the cook's understanding voice saying she'd be back to check on her later that evening, but Delilah did not reply. What was there to say? She was utterly alone, hopelessly in debt . . . and the man she loved might have simply cut his losses and ridden off.

Chapter Twenty-two

$\mathcal{D}$elilah awakened red-eyed in the middle of the sleepless night after two glasses of brandy—she was quickly depleting Uncle Horace's supply—to hear soft knocking on her door and a familiar voice urgently calling her name.

"Deelie, let me in!"

Dazed, not quite daring to believe it wasn't some cruel dream, she yanked on her robe and stumbled to light the lantern before opening the cabin door. Clint was not at the outside door but the one to her bedroom. He must have entered the sitting room through the door adjoining her uncle's cabin. "Where have you been?" she asked, trying to read his expression in the dim light.

"Deelie, you aren't goin' to believe me when I tell you. Just sit down . . ."

When he finished explaining what he had learned, they finalized their plans for the destruction of Red Riley's empire . . . or, at least, what they hoped would lead to that end. Delilah knew that if their plan failed, Clint would challenge Riley with a gun and perhaps the cowardly king of the levee would have his men shoot his enemy. Or, if he succeeded in killing Riley, Clint would hang for it.

She had to make certain it never came to violence. And there was only one way to do that: Delilah Mathers Raymond had to be the best damn poker player on the Mississippi. She could do it. She had to, not only for Clint, but for Uncle Horace, too.

"I'm going to wake up our notary friend 'n have him make arrangements for the game tomorrow night. Will you be all right?" he asked, taking her chin in his hand and tip-ping her face up to his.

"I've never felt more in control, Clint. Never."

He studied her for a moment, then nodded. "Good." With that he slipped out the door and vanished into the darkness.

During their long and earnest conversation, he'd never said a word about what would happen if their plan worked. He'd sold the Bud. Would he head back upriver? Would he leave her? Delilah still did not know. Clint Daniels was every inch as good a poker player as she was.

But once this was over, she intended to call his bluff . . .

Excitement crackled in the open air on the main deck of *The River Nymph*. With the space cleared of cargo, there was enough room for a large crowd to assemble around the single green baize table set up between the now idle boilers and the engine room. The fecund odors of river mud and rotting wood mixed with human sweat and perfume worn by various sporting women who had come to see the big game.

The levee had been buzzing all day since word had gotten out that Big Red Riley and the female gambler who'd won the *Nymph* from Clint Daniels were going to have a high-stakes game in which Riley might reclaim the boat. That af-ternoon Brad Sutton arrived on a fast packet from Quincy, Illinois. He was reputed to be one of the best players between St. Paul and New Orleans. Riley had hired him to play against Mrs. Raymond.

She had beaten Daniels. Could she also beat Sutton? Side bets were placed all afternoon and evening as the level of ex-pectancy rose to fever pitch up and down the riverfront, spilling into the city. From high society to levee low life, rich and poor, prominent and notorious, everyone wanted a piece of the action. Many wanted to see the nasty little Riley re-ceive his comeuppance, but lots of the smart money was on Big Red. He had not made a fortune by repeating mistakes.

Bill Holland, the banker and notary, stood like a stooped sentinel at the side of the table, his balding head shiny with sweat in the sultry evening air. In deference to the heat of summer in St. Louis, the game was not scheduled to begin until an hour after sunset, when the breeze from the river would lower the temperature. However, the standing-room-only crowd, pressed shoulder-to-shoulder, gave off enough body heat to make the table as hot as a boiler on an upriver run.

Clint Daniels stood beside Holland, wearing a ruffled white shirt and a tan linen suit with tiger's eye studs and cufflinks. His only other accessory was the Army Colt strapped low on his hip. As he watched his business associate approach the table, he looked calm, debonair . . . and very dangerous.

Delilah, dressed in a low-cut gown of moss-green silk, made her way through the crowd. She looked as cool as an April garden. Her hair was piled in a tumble of curls atop her head, held in place by ivory combs. Square-cut emerald studs in her ears and a matching bracelet on her right wrist were the only jewelry she wore. The slim gold wedding band was missing from her finger, but the crowd was too caught up in the excitement to notice.

Clint was not.

He eyed her bare hand and wondered why she had taken it off—for the first time since he'd met her aboard their boat. *No, make that my boat—before she won it away from me.* He felt the warmth of a smile begin deep inside him before it spread visibly to his mouth. Realizing what he was feeling, he assured himself it only signified that she was going to win again tonight.

The crowd parted as if she were Moses leading the Israelites through the Red Sea. She offered her hand to Clint for a proper salute, then did the same for Holland. In spite of the formality of the gesture between Daniels and the widow, Eva St. Clair watched the display from the sidelines with a pained expression on her beautiful face. That was when she, too, noticed the wedding band was missing.

Coming up the gangplank, Red Riley and Brad Sutton had their path cleared by several riverfront gunmen in Riley's employ. Silver-haired and patrician, Sutton was well-built and significantly taller than the scrawny Riley, a fact that was noticed and commented upon by many—but not within the king of the levee's hearing. If Riley was willing to hire a man taller than himself, the fellow must certainly be an excellent player.

There were no polite formalities among the opponents, other than Sutton's nod to the lady when Holland cleared his throat and started to speak. An expectant hush quickly fell over the rowdy onlookers as he said, "This will be five-card stud, St. Louis style. First and last card down. I will deal." He glanced between Delilah and Sutton. Both nodded. He continued, "Only funds already on premises can be put into play."

"We don't want you runnin' back to your office safe, Red," Clint said to Riley. Daniels's hand rested lightly on the handle of his Colt.

Red smiled expansively. "Since I already advanced the little *lady*—" he leered insultingly at Delilah—"ten thousand against this here boat, I reckon there ain't no reason to be worried. You got the deed?" he asked Holland.

The notary pulled a sheaf of documents from his jacket and handed them to Riley for perusal. "I trust this is in order. If your player wins, you shall have the title to *The River Nymph* signed over and notarized, free and clear. However, if you lose—"

"We ain't gonna lose, are we, Sutton?" Riley asked with a nasty sneer. He handed the gambler a hefty stack of bank notes.

Sutton's expression was serene, unaffected by his employer's crude remarks. "I surely do expect to win, ma'am," he said to Delilah.

"Just to sweeten the pot," Clint interjected, "I'm placing an additional vote of confidence in my associate. Eleven thousand dollars' worth." He plucked a large wad of bills from the wallet in his jacket and laid them in front of Delilah. A chorus of oohs and ahhs echoed around the crowded deck, and one fellow standing on the periphery called out to those standing on the levee, "Daniels just gave her all his money from selling the Bud!"

At the table, Delilah said, "Why, Mr. Daniels, how you do flatter a *lady*." Like Riley, she emphasized the word, giving Clint a dazzling smile. Then she nodded coolly at Riley as if he were a particularly insignificant species of dwarf cockroach. "The time for talk is over. It's time to play poker."

Riley smirked and counted out another stack of bills, slapping them down on the table in front of Sutton. "Like the *lady* says, let's get to playin'."

And play they did, for several hours without a break. Sutton lived up to his reputation. The balance of cash on the table shifted from him to Delilah and back. The ten thousand Riley had advanced to her for a table stake and Clint's eleven thousand from the Bud were all in play, lost and won again repeatedly until Holland called for a break. Delilah retired to her cabin while Sutton and Riley smoked on the aft section of the boat. Clint remained with Holland at the table under the gimlet eyes of Riley's minions, both armed to the teeth.

When the game resumed a quarter hour later, it appeared that the tide of victory began to move in Sutton's direction. Twice Riley threw in another few thousand, allowing Sutton to meet Delilah's bets and raises. With this help, the money in front of the lady gambler began to dwindle. But Delilah appeared as cool and collected as ever. The heavy night air wrapping around the assembly like a coil of wet rope appeared not to disturb her one whit.

With little more than twenty-five hundred dollars in front of her, she looked at her first up card, a jack of diamonds, and gave no indication of whether it boded well or ill. Sutton did the same when he was dealt an ace of diamonds.

"I bet five hundred," he said.

"Call," she replied, shoving the money to the center of the table.

The second card up was a nine of diamonds for her and a three of hearts for Sutton. His ace still being high, he again bet five hundred. She again called.

The third and last card up was a king of diamonds for her

and an ace of spades for Sutton. He increased his bet to a thousand. The crowd began murmuring now as it appeared the Illinois gambler was ready to pounce for the kill.

Unperturbed, Delilah again met his bet. But now she had only five hundred dollars left in front of her.

Holland dealt the last card down to both players with considerable deliberation. No one on the boat made a sound until Brad Sutton said, "I believe I will bet my pair of aces for all they are worth. Five thousand dollars."

A collective gasp rose, some people in indignation, others with satisfaction. Without enough money to call his bet, Delilah would automatically forfeit the game . . . and the boat. No one saw the tall man hidden in the shadows at the top of the stairs as he slowly began to descend. Clint looked into Delilah's expressionless eyes. He nodded as if confirming something for himself. "Mrs. Raymond calls and raises."

"Ten thousand," she said coldly, staring at Riley, whose head jerked back in amazement.

"You can't call with what you ain't got, gal," Riley sneered. "Remember rules 'o the game—only what's brung to the table can be bet. 'N you got squat."

"No, only what's already on the premises, according to the rules you agreed to," Clint said. "Uncle Horace, time to bring in the reserves." The crowd parted to admit two men who had just descended the stairs from the hurricane deck.

"It's Banjo Banks 'n thet bodyguard feller 'o the widda's," one man said.

"Damme, I heerd he wuz kilt by river pirates," another added.

"Er, Riley's men," a third witness whispered.

"Don't look half bad fer a dead man," the first said, with a nervous laugh.

"Don't look thet good neither," replied a new voice, this one female, as everyone noted the cuts and yellowing bruises on Horace Mathers's face and the splint on his left arm.

Horace limped slightly as he approached his niece. For the

first time that night Delilah Raymond allowed her face to reveal emotion. She gave her uncle a warm smile. "Once again, you've come to my rescue!"

She squeezed his uninjured hand as he tossed a well-worn leather satchel on the table. "There is more than sufficient to meet Mr. Sutton's bet and my niece's raise," Horace said, while the crowd once more hushed, everyone expectantly waiting to see what would happen next.

"You can't let him git away with this!" Riley sputtered to Holland. "He warn't part 'o the game."

"But, as Mr. Daniels already said, you agreed to the rules. This money has been on the premises. Nothing was said about who brings it into play," Holland replied primly.

Riley glared at Sutton. "I near shot my wad bankrollin' you. You sure you got a winner?"

Sutton nodded gravely. "Yes, I believe I do."

Riley dug into the pockets of his garishly tailored suit and pulled out a final bundle of cash. "Go fer it."

"I raise another ten thousand," Sutton said calmly.

"Call and raise ten thousand more," Delilah said as she counted out thousand-dollar bills from the huge bundle of cash inside Horace's satchel.

Sutton looked at Riley, who almost choked. He let out a foul string of oaths and pounded on the table. "I ain't got me no more cash money 'on the premises,'" he said through gritted yellow teeth.

"Rather shortsighted of you," Horace said dryly as his eyes fixed on the king of the levee. The gaze sent a shudder through the crowd. It was as if someone had just walked over Big Red Riley's grave.

"I may have a solution to your problem, Riley," Daniels said quietly. "We might be willin' to waive the rules for this final raise. You foreclosed on Mr. Krammer's mercantile." He turned to Delilah. "Would you be willin' to take a notarized deed as call for your raise?"

"Yes, I would," she replied, still icy calm. Once again, there was no hint of emotion in her cat-green eyes.

Sputtering oaths, Riley sent one of his gunmen to fetch the deed from his office. "Now, with all these here witnesses, can we git on with the game? I'll make good on the deed . . . if'n I have to," he said, glaring at Sutton. Then he crossed his arms over his banty chest and stuck out his chin defiantly, after pausing to spit a glob of snuff on the deck near Delilah's silk skirt.

Many in the crowd murmured about his lack of social graces, although no one phrased it in those words. Neither Delilah nor Clint reacted in any way. Horace, having already made his chilling visual inspection of Riley, stood stone still.

"Sign over the mercantile with all its stock and both our players can turn up their cards," Clint said after allowing Riley to stew for a moment. "We'll collect the deed later."

Riley snorted in disgust while Holland obligingly offered blank paper and a pen. In his semiliterate chicken scratching, Big Red did as Daniels had suggested, eager to get his hands on the boat. Wasn't Brad Sutton the best on the rivers? *He damn shittin' well better be!*

Without a trace of condescension, Sutton turned over his down cards. The ace of clubs and ace of hearts. Echoes of "Four of a kind!" spread through the crowd.

"Four aces! Damn, no wonder he was sure he could beat her!" Teddy Porter crowed triumphantly. "Riley's done won back his boat!"

But before the noise grew any louder, Delilah calmly flipped over one card. It was the ten of diamonds. The last hole card was the queen of diamonds. "I believe a straight flush beats four of a kind," she said gently to Sutton.

"If that don't beat all," Porter muttered. "King-high-diamond straight flush. Damned female's a witch."

Brad Sutton nodded politely to her. "It most certainly does, ma'am. You are a most skilled and fortunate player."

"Sutton, yer through in this town!" Riley yelled, leaping to his feet and pounding on the table. "Yer through from St. Paul to New Orleans, by damn! Time I'm through with you, you'll be haulin' shrimp on one of them stinkin' scows in the Gulf."

The distinguished-looking gambler gazed at his employer much the same way Delilah had when Riley had neared the table at the beginning of the evening. With a shrug, he said, "The odds were in my favor. I regret both our losses." With that he watched Riley stomp toward the gangplank, where he collided with the gunman he'd sent to collect the deed.

"I think when you disembark, you will find a most unwelcome welcome committee awaiting you on the levee, Mr. Riley," Horace Mathers said. "The men whom you employed to wreck the packet on which my companions and I were traveling have confessed everything. You see, after they left everyone for dead, a handful of survivors followed them into the next town, where they had commenced to celebrate with Mr. Daniels's and my niece's money. They retrieved the additional stake for this game that I was able to provide." As an aside for only Delilah and Clint to hear, he whispered, "The whiskey profits alone were sufficient."

"The police are waiting to arrest you for murder and robbery, Little Runty Riley," Daniels said with a grin slashing white on his tanned face. A raucous chorus of laughter followed. The king of the St. Louis levee had just been dethroned.

"Damn, wonder if'n she'll make 'im strip nekked like she done Daniels," some wag speculated in a stage whisper.

"Red Riley nekked? Lordy, I hope not! That'd scare half the catfish in the river plum to death. Whooee, ugly!" his companion responded, eliciting more laughter.

Riley's face grew redder than his frizzy hair as he hissed orders to his men, then whirled and pulled his gun. They did likewise, but the winners were prepared. A bullet from Delilah's Derringer found the place where Riley's heart supposedly resided. As he crumpled to the deck amid screams from the terrified crowd, an amazed expression came over his face, then faded to nothingness.

Horace hit the man to his left and Clint the one clutching the deed. Several others of Riley's men scattered through the crowd had begun to draw their weapons but quickly reconsidered when their boss and his best guns went down. "I would

suggest everyone remain calm," Horace announced in a sten-
torian voice that somehow carried over the cacophony. The
assembly began milling around as onlookers gawked at the
dead men and the cool lady gambler who had shot Red Riley.

"I swore I'd make him crawl. I never intended to kill
him," she whispered quietly.

"You had no choice, dear one," Horace said, wrapping his
uninjured arm around her shoulders.

"Everyone all right?" Clint asked Delilah, Horace and
Banjo, as the shrill of police whistles drowned out everything. Visually he noted Deelie's pallor and mouthed to Horace, "Take her to her cabin. I'll handle things down here."

Horace nodded and did as Clint suggested.

"Dang, Boss, thet wuz some shootin'!" Banjo said.

"Clean the money and papers off the table before folks get
the idea they can help themselves to our winnin's," Clint ordered his companion while his eyes swept the crowd to see if
any of Riley's supporters might yet cause trouble. No one
did. But Brad Sutton approached Daniels and tipped his hat.

"You, too, are a most skilled and fortunate player, Mr.
Daniels. I don't think I'd care to challenge you with a
gun . . . though perhaps at a card table?"

Clint shrugged uncertainly. "We'll see, Mr. Sutton, we'll
see . . ."

"There, that's all of it. Your eleven-thousand-dollar stake
from the game, in addition to 49 percent of the cargo profits
and passage fees . . . minus your share of what we owe our
creditors, and the pay and bonuses for the captain and crew. It
comes to . . ." Delilah hesitated, rechecking her figures one
final time.

"Forty-three thousand eight hundred, give or take some
change," Clint replied, doing the math quickly in his head.

She looked up abruptly. "Why, yes, that's within two dollars of my computation. Her eyes narrowed on him. "If
you're so good with figures, why didn't you say so when I
agreed to take over the clerking?"

"Oh, I'm good with figures, right enough," he said, grinning as his eyes swept over her crisp white lawn blouse and slim navy blue skirt, "but we both know you'd never have trusted me to keep the books when we started out. Besides, I had plenty to do workin' with the crew, especially after Iversen left us."

She felt the heat of his gaze and swallowed nervously. They sat in front of the large table in the *Nymph*'s dining room with an obscene amount of cash piled on the table in neat stacks. Overhead the simple brass chandelier cast a soft glow around the deserted space. Horace and Banjo stood guard at the fore and aft sections of the boat, watching for intruders, while the partners divided the profits.

Delilah was prepared to take the biggest gamble of her life. She was not certain she could win . . . but she knew she had to risk it. Moistening her lips, she said, "I have some plans I'd like you to consider . . . that is, if you don't want me to buy you out so you can return to your saloon? I'm sure Miss St. Clair would be happy to have you back." She waited with her heart in her throat.

Like the consummate card player he was, Clint did not give away anything, but shrugged neutrally. "I haven't rightly decided what to do about my share of the boat yet . . . but I don't intend to go back to the Bud." Then he smiled, his eyes never leaving hers. "Why, Deelie, are you jealous of Eva?"

"Certainly not," she replied coolly. "We had an understanding for the duration of the voyage, which is now over."

"So it is," he agreed. Did she move slightly nearer the edge of her seat? For a woman who'd bluffed one of the best players on the river without turning a hair last night, she sure was off her game now. "What is this *plan* of yours?"

"Well," she said, inwardly cursing the man who leaned back, his big body draped negligently over the chair across from her, "my plan involves some rather extensive remodeling of the *Nymph*. We made a decent profit from main-deck passengers this trip. If we refitted the cabins on the upper deck, we could make considerably more from rich miners who want to travel home in style." She waited a beat, but he said nothing, just nodded noncommittally. *Damn you, Clint Daniels!* "Well, are you interested in continuing our partnership in the Fort Benton trade or not? If so, you'll have to move off the boat while the carpenters do their job, as will Uncle Horace and I, of course."

"Of course," he echoed. "I reckon while I'm makin' up my mind about the boat, I'll take a room in town."

If that was the way he wanted to play it, so be it! At least he wasn't going back to Eva St. Clair, a small consolation. Of course, if he had, she might have had to kill Eva as well as him, she thought savagely. She shoved one large pile of bills toward him. "Here's the money for the crewmen. If you'd be so kind as to pay them, I'd be grateful. I'll pay Luellen, her helpers and Todd. Oh, and, Clint, I'd like to sell Mr. Krammer back his store for the three thousand we owe him, if that's all right with you."

Clint nodded. "Sure is. It'd be a good deal for the old man. He'll have no Red Riley to worry about ever again. That make you feel better about what happened last night?" he asked, remembering her deathly pallor after the shootout.

"I've had time to consider it . . . and talk it over with my uncle. If I hadn't shot Riley, Uncle Horace or you would have, and then those far more dangerous gunmen might have hit one of you."

"Good. I knew Horace could talk sense to you," he said, greatly relieved. "He said you wanted to take Captain Dubois his money. Give him my best."

"I hope to convince him to sign on for another voyage next spring. Do you concur?"

"No argument there. He's the best. Better than Grant Marsh, far as I'm concerned," he replied, scooping up his share of the profits in addition to the money to pay the crew. "I'll have Banjo spread word for the men to come collect their pay."

He left Delilah sitting at the table, gritting her teeth as she watched him saunter toward the door. "Just don't get your thick skull cracked by riverfront thieves before you pay what we owe," she said sweetly to his back.

The next morning Delilah and Horace hired a carriage to take them to the Dubois place outside town. As always, their welcome was warm. Dawn Woman had a lovely luncheon prepared and they enjoyed dining with the couple's son and daughter, now returned from a private academy in New Orleans for the summer.

Dubois readily agreed to pilot *The River Nymph* the following spring. "You and Clint are the folks I would choose to work for above any others," he said, a discreet question about their partnership left unspoken.

"We have been friends with Clint for many years," Dawn Woman said as she passed Delilah a slice of fresh peach pie.

It was the opening Delilah had hoped for. "If it isn't too impertinent . . . well, I am curious about your friendship with a former Confederate soldier," Delilah said, glancing at the Dubois children, Bernadette and Etienne, who looked expectantly at their father.

"Little pitchers have big ears," he said with a twinkle. "After they've finished their pie, we'll have coffee outside overlooking the river. Then I will tell you of my friendship with Clinton Daniels."

As Dawn Woman poured New Orleans–style coffee laced with hot cream for the four of them at an outdoor table with an incredible view of the Mississippi below the bluff, the captain began. "As you have probably heard, I served in the Union army during the late war."

"Running the Confederate blockade at Vicksburg before Grant opened the Mississippi for the Federals," Horace supplied. "You served with some distinction."

Dubois waved away the praise. "I once told you that Clint and I met upriver while he was living with the Sioux, which is true . . . but what I did not tell you was that we knew each other long before that."

Now he had both Delilah's and Horace's attention. "But

you're from New Orleans and Clint's a Missourian," she said, confused.

"My uncle Clarence owned this property before I inherited it. I spent summers with him during my formative years, which is how I learned that he was active in the underground railroad, moving runaway slaves across to freedom in Illinois."

"So, you helped him," she supplied.

"Yes, I did, although if my father had ever found out about it, he would've caned me within an inch of my life for taking such risks," Dubois said with a soft smile. "One of the people he worked with in this dangerous endeavor was a widow named Dorcas Niemeier. She was childless but had taken in her ne'er-do-well brother's young son after his mother died."

"Clint," Delilah said.

"Yes. She was a kind and loving soul and raised him well—until the raiders came. They killed her and then looted and burned her deceased husband's lovely home while Clint was away."

Now Delilah was more confused than ever. "Southern slavers?" she asked. It made no sense.

Dubois shook his head. "No, they were just plain thieves, cutthroats taking advantage of the unrest in a slave state that did not secede. They called themselves Union sympathizers, claiming they were after Southerners guilty of treason." His expression hardened. "That was only an excuse to steal and kill."

"And Clint's natural reaction was to fight against these men," Horace said.

"Since coming to Missouri, you have perhaps heard of Colonel John Singleton Mosby?" Jacques asked.

Horace nodded. "Called 'the Gray Ghost,' a Confederate guerilla fighter."

"Just so. He had men recruiting along the Missouri River the day Clint returned and found his aunt dead and the Niemeier family farm destroyed. Everyone knew the offal who had done it, that they were Northerners."

"Murderous brigands of any geographic designation remain yet thieves and killers," Horace said.

"But a grief-stricken young man saw only what had been done to a woman he loved. It must have been an unbearable loss. He spent a year with Mosby before being captured and sent to a prison in Alton."

"We know the rest of the story," Delilah said quietly. _My mother died when I was just a tadpole and my father was the town drunk._ He had lost his mother, his aunt, his wife and unborn child. Every woman he had ever loved . . .

Do you love me enough to risk happiness one more time, Clint?

Chapter Twenty-three

The following day the workmen arrived at the *Nymph*, and Delilah gave them instructions about the special remodeling project they were to do. Clint had already removed his possessions from his cabin and taken a hotel room in town. She and Horace took rooms in a slightly less lavish establishment a few blocks away. Although she traveled to and from the boat daily to oversee progress, she never encountered Clint.

He kept his distance. But she did notice that Banjo Banks, his eyes and ears on the levee, hung around, doubtless reporting back to him that carpenters were tearing out walls and doing extensive work on the second deck. However, the exact nature of that work remained a secret. She had promised a substantial bonus to Ed Taubmann and his men for keeping mum.

The second half of the summer grew even more sultry and warm . . . and seemed endless to Clint. He played cards and bet on horse races to keep boredom at bay. Mostly he won, even though he did not really care. After all, he was a rich man and the money he had invested yielded sufficient income for him to retire comfortably.

He damned himself a coward for avoiding Delilah. And for not being able to break things off cleanly by selling his share of the *Nymph* to her and leaving the city. She had not pressed him about the matter and he felt gut certain she wanted him to retain his ownership . . . and more. But he was damned if he knew whether he dared to make that commitment.

One evening early in August, as he sat in the Planter's House bar nursing a bourbon garnished with mint leaves and ice, Horace Mathers's tall, cadaverous figure approached his table. "Howdy, Horace. Glad to see your arm's out of the splint. It heal all right?" he asked.

"Well enough to soundly thrash you, if I thought it would do any good," the older man said dryly, pulling up a chair uninvited.

Daniels laughed mirthlessly. "Yeah, I'm the proverbial horse led to water. How's Deelie?"

"Quite busy, as I'm certain you've been informed by Mr. Banks. My niece is unaware I am here. I trust that will not change after I have spoken with you."

Clint nodded. "You want to know if I'm goin' to sell my share of the boat."

"Of far greater significance is whether you intend to remain in her life. The business arrangements are quite beside the point." He paused, his eyes drilling Daniels's face before he resumed. "I will speak bluntly. Delilah is in love with you . . . and you, I believe, are in love with her. The question is, what do you intend to do about it?"

Clint tossed down the rest of his drink and motioned the waiter for a refill. "Damned if I know what to do. Hell, Horace, she's a rich woman, a beautiful, intelligent, good-hearted rich woman. She can do better than me."

"To very loosely paraphrase the Bard, methinks the gentleman doth protest too much. My niece is indeed wealthy, intellectually keen, attractive and generous. She is also headstrong, hot-tempered, stubborn and, above all, exceedingly devious."

Clint didn't like the direction in which this conversation was going. When the waiter placed the refill in front of him, he interrupted Horace to ask, "You want a drink? I sure need this. It's on my bill."

"Ah, generous of you, my boy. A trait you have in common with my niece. Yes, I will imbibe whatever alcoholic libation my friend is enjoying," he said to the waiter, who looked blankly at Clint.

Daniels waved his hand. "He says he'll have one of these,"

he translated, pointing to his glass. After the waiter scurried away to fetch the drink, Clint asked, "All right. What has our devious little schemer done to bring you to me?"

"As I said, Delilah knows nothing of my being here . . ."

"But?" Clint prompted, fortified by another swallow of minty bourbon.

"This afternoon she paid a visit to Miss St. Clair at the Blasted Bud."

Clint nearly spit out the mouthful of bourbon. Choking it down, he sputtered, "She went to face off against Eva! Damn, they'll kill each other!" He jumped up, nearly overturning his chair before Horace placed his hand on Clint's arm.

"No blood was spilled, I assure you. Delilah returned to our suite at the Marsden quite unscathed."

"Why in tarnation would she visit Eva? I haven't . . . that is, well, damn, let's just say we haven't been 'partners' since I bought into the *Nymph*. She and Justus own the Bud now. I have nothin' to do with it."

Horace allowed his austere face a rare beautific grin. "I know. But until this afternoon, my niece did not."

Clint combed his fingers through his hair and sighed. "Eva and I had it out when I made the offer to sell my interest in the place. She told me either to stop drinkin', start wearin' a bib . . . or marry your niece."

"Capital advice if ever I've heard any," Horace said, sipping the drink the waiter placed before him. "Captain Dubois has agreed to take the *Nymph* upriver again in the spring. With Riley gone, men are clamoring to join the crew. Profits should be better than ever."

"You're assuming I'm stayin' aboard," Clint said, irritation in his voice.

Horace finished his drink and rose magisterially above the seated gambler. "Yes, I am. As I said, Delilah is stubborn to a fault and quite single-minded. She wants you. Be warned: She shall have you. Good evening, Clint."

Daniels sat and fumed for another hour, drinking more than he knew he should, remembering his last conversation with Eva. She hadn't actually couched matters in the terms he'd related to Horace. In fact, she had at first been incredulous, then angry, then resigned when he'd offered to sell the Bud to her and Justus Brummell. He could still hear her parting words to him:

"I knew from the minute she walked into our place that she'd be nothing but trouble, baby. Still, I hoped you wouldn't fall for her. Now that you've gone and done it, you might as well make it legal." Justus had seconded the idea, the traitor!

He was sick and tired of everyone giving him unsolicited advice—the *same* unsolicited advice. Even Banjo had played pear-shaped Cupid a week earlier when he'd made his report on the remodeling. "Boss, yew gotta see her givin' them men whut fer 'bout how they's doin' their jobs. One hell of a woman yew got there. Don't go do nothin' dumb like lettin' 'er git away."

"If one more person says I ought to marry Deelie, I'll shoot him," he muttered as the ever-patient waiter hesitantly approached, bearing a note. The moment he handed it over and hurried away, Clint recognized the soft fragrance of roses.

It was from Deelie, dammit!

Delilah looked around the spacious room, still aromatic from freshly cut lumber and newly purchased furnishings. She ran her hand over the rich, dark green brocade upholstery on one of the chairs and admired the gleaming polished mahogany of the table. She'd had Luellen make up a cold feast of fried chicken, fresh garden vegetables in vinaigrette, deviled eggs and a lush peach cobbler. A bottle of fine French champagne lay buried up to its neck in a sterling bucket filled with ice.

It was time to celebrate her project's completion. But would Clint accept her invitation? And her dare . . . ? "Well, I can always drink the whole blasted bottle if he doesn't," she whispered, walking nervously over to the freestanding oval mirror in the corner and inspecting herself once again.

Then she heard footsteps coming down the deck . . . and

recognized the soft, graceful way Clint walked. "This is it. Let the game begin," she whispered to herself as she walked to the door and opened it.

Clint stood dumbfounded, not only by Deelie, but by the space behind her. She wore a silk cloak that swathed her from her neck to the floor, revealing nothing of her lush body. But the room was unrecognizable, no longer a cramped little sitting area. Now the back three cabins had been converted into one generous room, complete with upholstered chairs, a settee and a dining table groaning with a lavish spread of food. At the opposite end, two cane-backed chairs were placed across from a smaller table. It was covered in green baize. A deck of cards served as centerpiece.

"You fixin' on having a card game, Deelie?" he asked, breathing in her rose fragrance. Lordy, she smelled good enough to eat; forget the aromas of Luellen's fine cooking!

She reached out and pulled him inside by the lapel of his jacket, closing the door behind them. "We're going to play poker. And this time you won't palm any cards."

"I didn't bring much cash," he said with a smirk. "You intend to win my share of the boat?"

"I'm not interested in that. What I had in mind was playing for . . . articles of clothing."

"Like that cut of cards when you stripped me buck-arse naked?" he asked.

"Not quite. We'll both gamble using our garments as currency," she replied, allowing the rusty red silk cloak to fall open just enough so he could catch a glimpse of the delights beneath it. Then she closed it again. If she hadn't seen the way his Adam's apple bobbed in his throat and his eyes widened, she might not have had the courage to proceed. "Showdown poker. Seven cards dealt up for each of us," she added in the coolest voice she could muster.

"Last man—or woman—still wearin' anything wins?" he asked, his mouth gone dry. Suddenly he was dead sober in spite of what he'd drunk earlier in the evening. Damn, Horace had warned him she'd stop at nothing! When she nodded, fingering the drawstrings to her cloak, he nearly choked. "Once one of us wins, then what?"

"I haven't finished laying out the house rules." She moistened her lips before continuing. "If I win, you stay in partnership with me on the *Nymph*. If you win . . . it's your choice. You can bow out and I'll buy your share. Or . . . you can stay and live like this." She took his hand in hers and walked over to the table, gesturing to the food and iced bucket of champagne. "First we feast."

"First?" he croaked.

"Then . . ." she murmured, opening the door at the back of the room to reveal a bedroom almost as large as the living quarters—with a huge bed front and center. A few candles flickered enticingly from side tables and a second bottle of champagne, also chilling in an ice bucket, sat within easy reach. "My offer's pretty obvious. Do you have any more questions?"

"Do we have to eat Luellen's food first?" he asked, knowing what her offer really entailed.

A teasing grin moved from her eyes to her lips. "We'll do things in any order you wish . . . if you win."

He knew her game—and it wasn't cards or a sybaritic delight just for tonight. It was spending the rest of their lives on this boat as husband and wife. Clint felt a sudden urge to give in to the inevitable. "You're just plannin' to get me naked again," he said with an arrogant grin of his own.

"I've always liked what I saw when you were." She could not believe how brazen she'd become. How brazen he'd made her, as her eyes swept from his thick straw-colored hair slowly down to his polished black boots, pausing to admire every inch of his long, tall body on the way.

"Hell, Deelie, let's play poker."

They took their seats and she picked up the deck. "Cut the cards to see who deals first," she said, all business now.

She shuffled, then shoved the deck to him for a cut. He drew a king of hearts. "Kinda appropriate," he said, watching as she took her turn. She drew a queen of diamonds. "Must be your lucky card."

"Your deal." She leaned back so the heavy silk draped the soft curves beneath, pleased when the cards nearly exploded in his hands as he shuffled. But he quickly recovered and they got down to the business at hand. By the end of the deal, he had won with two pair, kings and deuces. Delilah had only a single pair of sevens. "Where should I begin?" she asked herself.

She raised a slippered foot, turning the slender ankle enticingly while her fingers toyed with the tie to her cloak. He considered, rubbing his jaw as he eyed the ankle, then moved higher to her throat. "The cloak?"

"Why not?" She pulled the bow and it slithered loose, allowing the heavy silk to pool around her chair. Beneath it, a rusty red peignoir made of some kind of translucent lacy material revealed several layers yet to be stripped away while enticing his eyes to look through the outer robe to the low-cut chemise and slim skirt beneath it. The color caught the reddish highlights in her rich chestnut hair, burnishing it to living flames dancing in the soft lantern light.

Delilah was delighted to have lost the first deal. This would really upset his concentration. She could see him move uncomfortably, his lower body in obvious distress. Perhaps it would help if he lost his breeches . . . She won the second hand on the last of her seven face-up cards, a four to complete an eight-high straight. Since there was no way to get to his ever-tightening pants without first removing his boots, she suggested, "A boot?"

"So I can limp up the cobblestones barefoot?" he asked in a mocking drawl, but he raised his leg.

"We'll see. Let me be your valet?" she asked in a husky voice, and swished provocatively over to his side of the table. She straddled his outstretched leg and tugged off the boot, tossing it in a corner. She knew she was giving him an irresistible view of her derrière and couldn't resist wriggling it just the tiniest little bit.

The cards fell good and ill, back and forth between them as the candles burned lower. But one thing was growing, increasingly clear: In spite of her outer calm, Delilah was losing at a slightly swifter rate than Clint. "Are you dealing yourself face cards?" she asked breathlessly as he peeled down her second stocking and tossed it over his shoulder. It floated to the pile where its mate and both rust silk slippers lay.

He raised his hands. "No jacket sleeves left. Shirt's too tight. Where in hell would I be hidin' cards? In my armpits?" He'd lost his jacket and other boot earlier.

She had worn a ruby necklace, earrings and a bracelet, all bargaining chips to prolong the game . . . and the torture. But the gems winked from the discarded clothing in the corner. So did Clint's gold cigar case.

The next round of cards gave him a pair of jacks, her an ace high with nothing else. She appeared to consider, then slid off the robe, revealing the ripe curves of her breasts and the way the lace skirt hugged her hips. "Thirsty?" she asked when he swallowed hard.

"Double-dealin' witch," he murmured as she rose and poured two crystal flutes with icy champagne, then handed one to him. "A very good year," she said consideringly.

As he took a swallow, a thought suddenly occurred to him. "Horace know about this?"

Delilah gave a low, throaty chuckle and shook her head. "You needn't fear he'll burst into the room with his rifle and a preacher," she said. "Now, deal."

This time he lost and removed one stocking. He lost again and removed the other. Delilah pouted. "When are you going to take off that shirt?"

"I was only bein' considerate. That would ruin your concentration."

"Vain man," she huffed, and dealt.

He grinned when his full house beat out her flush, but his heart pounded as she slowly unfastened the long row of buttons on her slinky lace skirt and wriggled out of it. She grinned when his face registered disappointment that she still wore silk pantelettes beneath. *An entire damned dress shop!*

His shirt came next.

But he'd been right. Her concentration was in tatters as she watched him unbutton it and slide it off his broad shoulders. She was glad he hadn't worn shirt studs and cufflinks, else they would've been playing until daybreak. Delilah had more pressing plans. It was pure pleasure to see the bronzed muscles of his chest ripple sinuously when he threw the shirt onto the growing pile.

"Time to get serious, Deelie," he said in a husky dare, staring at the cleavage of her lace chemise. Now they each had two articles of clothing left to remove.

Who would win . . . or would they both? With a cunning smile, she began laying out the cards in two rows once again. His winning streak picked up again. He won the hand and waited to see whether she would remove the chemise or the pantelettes. Clint had never been so intent on the outcome of a hand of cards in his life. The tension in the room made the candles flicker even though there was no breeze stirring on the river.

When she began to untie the drawstring holding the neckline secure, his breath caught. The seductress allowed the lace to drop from one breast, cling to the other. The warm air caressed her nipple, and it hardened to match the ache in his pants. He wanted to sweep the cards from the table and carry her off to bed, but somehow that seemed wrong. No, this was her game and he needed to allow her to play it out.

The second breast peeked over the chemise as the lace dropped to her waist. "Take it off," he said hoarsely, then watched as she stood and pulled it up over her head, thrusting forward those glorious breasts so that he was dying to cup them in his hands. "A perfect pair," he whispered, taking the cards in clumsy hands and somehow managing to shuffle them before he dealt again . . . and lost.

"Unlike me, you appear to have no choice about what to

remove next," she said with glee in her voice. He had early on relinquished his belt. Pants and underwear were all he had left.

He muttered an expletive as he stood up, revealing his all-too-obvious condition to her while he struggled to unbutton his fly, no easy feat considering how rock hard his erection was. She stood up and moved over to him, reaching down to deftly slip the buttons from their fastenings.

Her fingers brushed against the probing length of his shaft, and she could tell he was exerting extreme willpower not to stop the game and take her right there on the carpet. That both pleased her and made her wary. "Now, doesn't that feel better?" she cooed.

Clint shucked the breeches without comment as she returned to her seat.

Delilah picked up the cards while he sat down, clad only in black silk underdrawers. When he growled at her, she began to lay out the last set of cards, taking her time, her breasts jiggling as she dealt.

All he could look at were those magnificent breasts with their hard pink nipples, palm-sized breasts that stood up without the assistance of corset stays. He found it incredibly difficult to pay attention to the cards as she began laying out the final hand.

After six cards, he had four clubs, seven high, while she had four spades, ace high. If she got another spade, she would have an ace-high flush. There was no way he could beat that even if he filled his flush, but he had an ace of hearts and a king of clubs. His two high cards would take the game if she didn't get her flush.

Delilah moistened her lip and shifted in the chair, pausing before laying out the final two cards. She could feel his eyes burning her sensitive breasts, feel the perspiration trickle between them as she studied his scarred yet sensuously handsome face. He did not get another club. Then she dealt herself a three of hearts.

Clint leaned back in his chair. "I win, Deelie." His eyes devoured her slim body, admiring the pale, milky breasts and the golden, sun-kissed skin above them. He did not have to ask her to remove the lacy drawers. She slipped the tie and very slowly began to roll them over the curves of her hips, pausing when she reached the burnished curls at the juncture of her thighs.

He could see the thin sheen of perspiration glistening on her body and knew he was hotter yet. "By heaven, I'll lick every damp, lovely inch of you," he said in a low growl.

"Well, then . . ." She lowered the pantelettes and kicked them away, then stood before him completely naked. Her heart was pounding and her mouth was dry with fear. He could accept her invitation to make love, then leave her afterward, more alone than she had ever been in her life. Although she knew he understood the commitment she wanted, she had not made it a part of this night's wager, insisting only that he continue their business partnership if she won. And she had lost . . . he could do exactly as he chose.

"You win me, Clint . . . if you want me," she said simply.

"I've wanted you since the day I met you, woman," he said, sweeping her into his arms and striding to the bedroom. He tossed her slender body onto the large, soft mattress, then stood back and slid his underdrawers off, watching in hungry pleasure as she reached for his erection and took it in her hand. Fists clenched at his sides, he let her slide her warm, soft fingers around, up and down until he could stand it no more.

"Enough!" he growled, pressing his knee on the bed while he pried her eager hands away from their toy. He gently pushed her back against the pile of pillows at the head of the bed and lay beside her, caressing her breasts, cupping one, suckling the other until she moaned and dug her nails into his shoulders.

Her hands moved up, seizing fistfuls of his coarse, straight hair and pulling him up for a searing kiss that deepened as he slanted his mouth over hers at various angles, letting his tongue rim her lips, demand entry, then plunder. She returned the thrust with her tongue, twining it with his, clamping her thighs around his narrow hips. The stars and all the planets seemed to whirl around her as she held him fast and felt their hearts beat as one.

He desired her with a blinding passion . . . but was that passion enough to hold him? Delilah did not know, but for right now it was enough. More than enough. She felt the crisp abrasion of his chest hair when he slid down her body, licking and kissing her throat, tracing dancing patterns along her collarbone and in the vale between her breasts, then swirling the tip of his tongue inside her naval. She arched as he laved her concave belly and moved inexorably lower toward the dark curls below.

He tasted the creamy moisture, sweet and rich as an elegant dessert, and knew her fierce desire, knew how to slake it . . . and to reawaken it again and again.

When his mouth brushed her, she cried out, begging him for more. He obliged, using his lips and tongue to bring her to a shattering climax that left her limp and spent for a moment, while he kissed the sensitive insides of her thighs and moved down to the backs of her knees. He knelt on the bed, lifting one leg at a time to apply the magical restorative, bringing her hunger back to a keening peak when he nuzzled the arches of her feet, first one, then the other.

Her toes curled with pleasure.

But when he moved back to her center, she pressed her hands against his shoulders, stopping him, murmuring, "Now it's my turn." She pushed him flat on his back and knelt beside him, taking in the sight of his big, hard body. She began by kissing every scar, the angry slash that sheared his left eyebrow, the narrow white line below his right eye. Ever so slowly, she paused to lick and tease the ridges of healed flesh on his chest, nuzzling both small brown nipples until he growled.

"You're not the only one who wants to taste," she whispered, breathing on his chest hair, moving lower to the long, deadly scar curving around his side. It could have ended his life. In time, perhaps, he might tell her where he had received it . . . but not now. His legs were corded with sinewy muscles and she kissed each scar on them, allowing the tips of her breasts to brush one thigh while she touched the other with her mouth. When she moved up his right leg, her hair brushed his groin and he bucked, emitting an oath as his hands seized it, pulling pins free so that it spilled over him.

But when she held his pulsing shaft in her hand and pressed her tongue to the head, he grew very still. "Deelie, you're killin' me," he whispered.

"A good way to go, is it not?" Her voice was low, rich, confident as she licked a pearly drop from him.

He let her tongue dance up and down the steely length of his staff, pressing his palms against the mattress to keep from grabbing her. Let her have her way for a moment longer . . . only a moment. He could withstand the intensity of the pleasure no more than that! When she took him in her mouth, the heat sent a lightning bolt searing through him and he reached down, pulling her up and under his body, spreading her legs with his knee.

"Now, my love, now," she whispered, raising her head to kiss him while he plunged deep inside scalding, wet satin, and seated himself to the hilt. They exchanged kisses, tasting of each other, adding to the building excitement. She wriggled her hips but still he did not move.

"Slowly, love, slowly," he crooned, beginning to stroke as she wrapped her legs around his hips and followed his pace.

It was leisurely and it was glorious, drenching them both in sensuous feelings of oneness. Where did he end and she begin . . . or she end and he begin? She looked up at his sweat-sheened face and her eyes locked with his. Brushing back the thick lock of hair hanging across his forehead, she pressed her mouth against his throat and whispered very low, "I love you, Clint," not expecting any words in return, yet still hoping.

He said nothing. His mind, all his senses, were reeling with emotions he had never felt before in his life. This was so utterly different from what he had known with any other woman, even his wife. . . . That life was over and he could let go of it now. This one was only beginning. The certainty filled him as surely as her sweet heat surrounded him.

While the tempo of their lovemaking intensified, he knew that Deelie had won. He allowed her to rush to the crest, then followed her over the tumbling abyss into ecstasy. Delilah felt him swell and spill himself deep inside her as her own body shuddered with passion. The weight of his body pressed her into the mattress as they struggled for breath. His face was hidden by her tangled hair.

Over labored pants, she thought she heard him murmur, "I love you, too."

But she could not be certain. Perhaps he had not heard her declaration of love. But she would have to work up courage enough to finish tonight what had begun between them so many months ago. A soft, sad smile curved her lips as she held him closely and said, "This all began with a poker game . . . and now it's come full cycle."

"Mmm," he murmured, nuzzling her neck, planting a kiss on her shoulder, ready to resume making love again.

"No, Clint," she said softly, firmly, sliding from beneath him and sitting up. "There's something we have to discuss." He watched as she raised the dripping bottle of champagne from the bedside ice bucket. "Will you do the honors?" she asked, offering him the bottle and a linen napkin.

He took the bottle and opened it quite expertly, pouring into two glasses, which she provided from the small table beside the bed. He leaned back against the pillows and pulled her to his side, raising his glass for a toast. "Shall we drink to next spring's run up the Missourah?"

She clinked her glass against his and took a sip. "It's Missouri," she corrected, watching him swallow. "But that isn't exactly what I wanted to discuss."

He looked at her over the rim of his glass. "No?" he prompted, taking another swallow.

"You're not going to make this easy for me, are you?"

"Only seems fair, Deelie, considerin' you haven't exactly

been easy on me since the day we met," he said with a glint of amusement in his eyes.

"All right," she said, tossing back the rest of her glass and placing it forcefully on the table. "Will you marry me, Clint Daniels?"

He could see she was holding her breath. Ever so slowly, he drained his glass, then tossed it on the thick carpet beside the bed. "Yes, I do believe I will, Mrs. Raymond . . . even though you did cheat."

Delilah was flummoxed. Should she yelp with joy or pummel him? Instead, she squeaked, "Cheat? What do you mean, cheat! I never cheat. I'm too good—I don't have to."

"How could a man concentrate on the cards with these beauties dancin' in front of him?" he asked, cupping one breast, then the other. "I love you, Deelie. I reckon it took some grit for you to make me understand that. I'm sorry I've been too wrapped up in my own guilt to see the plain truth. We're too damn good together ever to let this go . . . and I don't just mean in bed. You're strong and smart, the best partner I could ever have. 'Course, you're also a mite stubborn and devious—"

She placed her fingers over his mouth, grinning and giggling like a schoolgirl. "Yes, I am devious. I wanted you to be watching my breasts when I dealt that final hand. You see, darling, I did cheat. I palmed a six of clubs and dealt myself that three of hearts so I'd lose. I wanted the choice about us to be up to you. It still is. Just because you won the game . . . and tonight . . . well, it doesn't mean you have to accept my proposal of marriage."

"I call that proposal and raise you a couple of babies," he said, pulling her into his arms.

"Only two? I call those two and raise you another two," she said as he enfolded her in his arms, and they sank back against the pillows once more.

Late that night they sat in their undergarments, feeding each other bits of chicken, deviled eggs and other delicacies from

Luellen's kitchen as they talked about the shadows in their pasts before moving on to the bright promise of the future.

"Jacques Dubois told me about your aunt. It must have been horrible losing every woman you loved," she said softly.

"I've never loved any woman the way I love you, Deelie. I've finished my mourning for Teal. She was a fine woman and I loved her, but we were young and that way of life was endin' for the Ehanktonwon even then. I'll always regret what I did after that, but you've put the ghosts to rest. Just promise you'll never leave me."

"Never." She placed her finger in the cleft of his chin and felt the abrasion of whiskers. "I never imagined there could be a man like you for me. Poor Lawrence was a boy who would never have let me be anything but a child if he'd lived. At first it made me horribly guilty, but now I realize that I would've outgrown him even if life hadn't pushed me in the direction it did. I hated being outside 'respectable society,' being a gambler, but gambling brought me to you."

"And got you the *Nymph*," he reminded her with a grin. "You told me you wanted to take on high-falutin' passengers. Have you finished fixing up the cabins so we can charge more for fancy accommodations?"

She returned his grin and popped a bite of chicken in his mouth. "I wanted *us* to have the fancy accommodations. The hell with the passengers. Let them travel steerage!"